B'RIT HADASHA

ALL THINGS MADE NEW

ANA WATERS

For Joyce.
God's not done with either of our stories.

"For your Maker is your husband—the Lord Almighty is His name—the Holy One of Israel is your Redeemer; He is called the God of all the earth."

— ISAIAH 54:5 NIV

TRIGGER WARNING

This novel portrays acts of domestic violence, including scenes of emotional, physical, and psychological abuse (with references to sexual trauma). While this is depicted with zero salacious intent, it may be triggering or difficult to read. The goal is to illustrate a path to healing and wholeness while realistically showing the survivor's difficult road to freedom. For readers who have not survived this type of abuse themselves, my hope is they will better understand and empathize with the plight of victims struggling to be heard and believed.

PROLOGUE

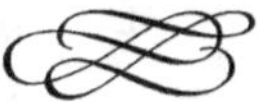

Eighteen Months Earlier

"I LOVE YOU," HE PLEADED. "DOESN'T THAT MEAN anything to you?"

I struggled against the vomit rising in my throat.

"Lauren, I'm serious!" my husband cried, his eyes welling with tears. "I've really been talking to God and reading the Bible. He would want us to believe He can heal our marriage. We just need to let go of all the anger and bitterness."

My eyes narrowed at the hyper-spiritual word salad. "We" always meant *me*. Six years ago, I thought I had married a godly, trustworthy man. Nathan Adam Fein had presented himself as a Jewish believer in *Yeshua* who heroically struggled against his "ongoing issues."

His betrayal told a different story.

Sick of the lies, I said, "You expect me to turn a blind eye the same way our whole congregation did. You're not the only one who talks to God, and you're definitely not the final authority on what He would want. God's given me plenty of Bible verses about what He thinks about *your* behavior."

My husband's tears evaporated with the look of shock on his face. Recovering easily, he said, "I know you'll just believe whatever you want to anyway."

"That's right, I will," I said, trying to instill some steel in my tone. "I'm allowed to have feelings you don't approve of."

"How about you show some submissiveness?" he demanded. "I think God has some choice words to say about *that*."

"How about loving your wife?" I shot back, unconsciously rubbing my arms. The lingering bruises spoke of Nathan's most recent bout of temper. Softening my tone, I added, "You were supposed to get better after Ari and I moved back into the house, but things have just gotten worse."

His eyes narrowed into reptilian slits. "You never give me credit for anything. It's always your way or nothing at all."

I schooled my anger and frustration into a neutral expression. My misery was Nathan's fuel, and we both knew it.

"I'm done with this conversation," I said coolly.

He glared at me. "Coward."

Rather than reacting to his taunt, I felt the Holy Spirit calming me. Resolution stiffened my shoulders. "I can't live like this anymore. It's not healthy for you, for me, or for our son."

"So, you just let your little friend, Charlotte Williams, do all the thinking for you, right? You should hear what her husband has to say about her! Rick told me she would fill your head with her feminist garbage." When his baiting didn't receive the response he wanted, my husband pushed harder. "Charlotte is nothing but a bad influence who thinks everyone should ignore their marriage vows just like she did. And for what? To try to steal every penny Rick makes. Is that really what you want to become, Lauren? A money grubbing pig?"

"I'm sure Charlotte's ex-husband has plenty to say about me," I clipped. "You're always in a good mood after you come home from those bash-your-wife lunches."

He smirked. "It's not bashing if it's true."

I pressed my lips together. The obscene hypocrisy of Nathan's slander was a bitter pill. Finally unloading my secret weapon, I said, "Jessica Ballinger agrees with me."

Nathan's smile fell as his face went white. "You talked to her?"

"Yes, I met her for coffee."

"You don't drink coffee."

"I ordered tea."

"How could you betray me like that?" he gasped, clutching at his imaginary heart.

"Talking to your ex-fiancée about your porn addiction wasn't betrayal, Nathan. Having you lie to me about Jessica so that I would feel sorry for you and marry you was betrayal. Having your parents cover your porn issues and then blame *me* for it was betrayal. Getting our synagogue to believe you're the victim of some vengeful, unforgiving wife was betrayal." I felt the sting of tears but pressed onward. "Standing there, lying to my face and pretending you finally learned to love me when the truth is that you love *using* me is the real betrayal. All of the bruises you've put on me and our son, promising us you'll change but then hurting us again—*that's* betrayal."

"I do love you!" he cried, switching to the adoring, broken husband persona.

"I'm done, Nathan."

Dropping the facade as easily as he'd picked it up, my husband wagged an accusing finger in my face. "Jessica poisoned you against me! How could you believe her lies instead of your own husband?"

"And what do you call Rick Williams texting you last Mother's Day and blaming his divorce on me? You didn't question a single word that jerk had to say about me."

"He's not a jerk!"

"Rick calls me 'the false prophet' because I share posts about spiritual abuse on social media. Meanwhile, you both still attend *Beth Shalom* with that two-faced hypocrite in the pulpit. Who knows how many other sins have been covered up in that place?"

"No congregation is perfect," Nathan said dismissively. "You just don't like that people took my side instead of yours. Rabbi Lebow is a good man."

Exasperated, my own temper flared. "Oh, please! We both know the false prophet is actually Rabbi Lebow. He covered up what you did at the synagogue and got everyone to feel sorry for you too. All of the 'prophetic words' he gives from the *bima* are about how wonderful Beth Shalom is. Letting anybody know the truth about what you did would tarnish his precious image."

"It's not my fault my wife refuses to forgive me," Nathan said with a sniff of self-pity. "Rabbi Lebow just understands how much damage your bitterness has caused to our marriage."

"You downloaded underage porn on the synagogue computers!" I screamed. "The police raided the synagogue!"

"And I told you I had nothing to do with that!" he yelled back. "I had no idea those girls were underage. As you will recall, the police dropped all charges against me. I'm innocent."

"So, that suddenly makes your filth okay?" I asked incredulously. "Because the teenager *looks* eighteen?"

Nathan seamed his lips, apparently not wanting to dignify that with another lame denial.

"No matter what age you thought anybody was, that still doesn't excuse the photos I found on your phone. *You* are responsible for that, Nathan Fein! There's nothing 'innocent' about the smut you've brought into our home."

"Yeah, and thanks for teaming up with my brother against me. So much for family loyalty. Thanks to you, Matty won't talk to any of us."

"Matty got tired of covering for your addiction after seeing how you and your parents treat me."

He looked affronted. "What do you mean how I treat you? You have no clue what it means to be a Biblical wife. You need to obey God instead of following every word Charlotte spews."

I had grown accustomed to Nathan's insults about my intelligence. I could brush those off easily. Disparaging my relationship with God was another story. "The Bible doesn't command husbands to trample their families under their feet. Your version of a 'Biblical wife' means enabling you to be a monster to me and our son."

"You leave Ari out of this," Nathan growled. "He's going to grow up to be gay if you don't stop treating him like a mama's boy."

"He's *three*, you idiot!"

I clapped my hands over my mouth, shocked how easily the words flew out. Nathan looked stunned. I usually kept my feelings hidden no matter how much he provoked me. I shifted my body as anger glowed in his dark eyes.

I anticipated Nathan's usual bellowing about my "rebellion" and "Jezebel spirit." Instead, his slow, cold smile caught me off guard. His smirk transformed into a backhanded slap across my face, and the blow sent me crumbling to the carpet. His volcanic fury exploded in rivers of insults and profanity. I withdrew inside of myself, praying and mentally shielding myself from the surreal nightmare.

Nathan yanked me by my already bruised arms and screamed in my face. "Do you hear me, Lauren? You will never disrespect me like that again!"

I flinched, expecting another blow. Instead, he shoved me away. The momentum caused my head to bang against the floor. From the next room, I could hear my son screaming.

"Look what you've done!" he roared, turning his gaze toward Ari's bedroom.

"No!!!" My shout reverberated inside of my throbbing skull. "Leave him alone, Nathan!"

Ignoring me, the snake slithered to the baby's room, ready to unleash his undeserved anger on an even less deserving target.

I pulled myself to my feet and staggered as the room spun around me. Leaning against the wall, I stumbled down the hallway to prevent any further horrors Nathan might inflict upon our child.

When I arrived at the doorway, I saw Nathan holding Ari in his arms. He cuddled and calmed the baby as if nothing was wrong. The rapid switch in Nathan's mood made my knees buckle.

"What were you expecting?" he sneered, his voice dripping with icy daggers. "I love my son." He looked me up and down, his eyes flickering over the knot I could already feel forming on the side of my head. "I would never do anything to harm *him*."

I clenched my jaw. The bruises I had photographed on our three year old told a different story. The day before, I had finally called the Department of Child and Family Services when I realized my husband's anger was no longer reserved for just me. I inwardly cringed, knowing I was unleashing a new hell for me and Ari once Nathan found out.

As if reading my thoughts, he said, "If you start this war, Lauren, you'll live to regret it."

CHAPTER 1

Present Day

"ARE YOU SURE THIS IS A GOOD IDEA?" I GLANCED around the room of familiar faces and fought against the pull of steel blue eyes I needed to ignore.

"Lauren," Rebecca Margolin said, "half the people in our Bible study have worked at Culver, and three of us have also worked in the marketing department. Carly, Poppy, and I will help however we can to help get you acclimated."

Rebecca's husband, Ted, smiled at me encouragingly. "As Culver Incorporated's top east coast producer and newly appointed Executive Vice President," he said with false bravado, "I think I can pull a few strings with Bonnie in HR."

I glanced at Carly Trautweig who'd most recently vacated the graphic design position to become a fulltime mom. She cradled her sleeping son, Shai, while her husband, Joe, paced the room bouncing his twin sister, Ilana.

"I don't know," I said, "I mean, I know the mall is a dead

end job, but I haven't worked in an office in so long. I don't have that much experience with graphic design."

"I didn't when I started either," Poppy Levine chimed in, "but I've been at Culver for almost four years. You're young and smart, and I'm sure you'll pick things up much quicker than I did. Rebecca took a chance when she told Bonnie to hire me, and I'm happy to help anyone else in my shoes. I know you can do this. The job is also half administrative."

I felt the concern of the stormy gaze resting on me, and Aaron Davis's eyes may as well have been his hands. Blushing, I glanced at my bare ring finger. I knew what Aaron wanted from me, but I had never wanted the same thing. Maybe in another life, at another time, I could let my heart consider a different path. Now, however, was not the time.

The rest of the Margolin Bible study group took turns offering their support, including members of my former congregation, Beth Shalom. I looked at Poppy's husband, Jared, and his pitying smile provided validation for all that I had endured. Jared was on the synagogue leadership team when my life had publicly fallen apart. It was my husband's betrayal that had opened Jared's eyes to what Beth Shalom looked like beneath their whitewashed exterior. Other than the owner of the steel eyes begging me to glance their way, nobody knew my story better than Jared Levine.

Eight years earlier, I had fallen in love with a mirage and woken up next to a monster on my honeymoon. I'd spent the remainder of my twenties trying to save a marriage doomed to fail. At nearly thirty-one years old, I felt like a hollowed out version of the naive college grad who'd descended into hades with Nathan Fein. A temporary protective order had only been good for thirty days, and Nathan had been incident-free since then. I thought if I allowed him some visitation with Ari, Nathan might realize I just wanted to peaceably end our marriage. Instead, he kept our divorce proceedings crawling at a glacial pace.

The matriarch of our Bible study and Ted's mother, Rose Margolin, studied me. "I think we may be overwhelming Lauren with our enthusiasm. I know my son and daughter have made a terrific spread, so why don't we dig in?"

Grateful, I shot Rose a smile, and she winked at me. The group disbanded from the sofas and folding chairs to huddle around the dining room table. A collective gasp went up at the charcuterie boards covered in soft cheeses, cut fruit, crackers, and veggies.

"They always have the most gorgeous set up," my friend Abigail Goldstein murmured as she held her newest son, Levi. She turned to her husband. "Babe, I feel bad we can't do this when we host Bible study."

Kyle Goldstein gave his wife an encouraging smile and kissed her temple. "Ted and Rebecca live for this kind of stuff. Nobody's judging you, sweetheart."

I slipped an arm around my friend for a quick hug. "Abs, your spinach and artichoke dip should be in a magazine."

"I agree. It's legendary," Aaron Davis added over my shoulder.

I felt the weight of his blue eyes before I turned to face them.

"Hey," I said.

"You were so quiet tonight, Aaron," Mrs. Goldstein said with a bright smile. "Everything okay?"

"Fine," he replied.

Kyle cleared his throat. "Babe, it looks like they've got smoked salmon. Why don't you get some? I have to go rescue

Natalie Levine from watching Isaac and all of the Margolin kids."

"God bless that girl," Abigail said with a laugh. "How she handles our hyper little man plus everyone else is a miracle." Turning to Aaron and me, she said, "You'll have to excuse me. I've waited nine months to eat raw fish again."

Kyle smiled down at his second son cradled in his wife's arms. "Mommy's cravings didn't end after she had you, did they?"

I smiled at the happy couple, and they turned to join the rest of our Bible study filling their plates with upscale Margolin snacks.

Aaron chuckled under his breath and then took a step closer to me. "How are you doing? Any change?"

I finally looked into his gray-blue eyes, seeing my old friend from high school rather than the scruff faced, grown man who wanted what I couldn't give him. Being three years younger than me, I'd always thought of Aaron as a younger brother. Two years ago, however, Aaron ensured I'd never view him as a kid again. Unfortunately, no matter how objectively handsome he was, I just didn't reciprocate his feelings. I had hoped he'd find a girlfriend during the last few years and move on, but he'd insisted on remaining a steadfast friend during my divorce. I knew I had come to rely on Aaron more than was healthy for either one of us.

I shook my head free from musings better left alone. "Nathan just ignores everything my attorney sends. It's his usual game of pretending the problem doesn't exist so it goes away. Unfortunately for me and Ari, we live in a no-default state."

"Which means what?" he asked.

"It means Nathan can drag out this divorce for years if he wants to."

"Years?" Aaron choked. "Hasn't it been long enough?"

The stranglehold Nathan Fein kept on my life felt even tighter with one foot out of the marriage and the other still legally bound to it. I swallowed a lump of self-pity and said, "My attorney told me that no matter how uncooperative Nathan is, the judge won't just sign off on a divorce since we have a child involved. Marianne said he'd basically have to be in prison for that to happen."

"What about the underage pornography and all of his abuse? Anybody in their right mind can see Nathan is dangerous to you and your son. Can't your attorney do something to get things moving?"

"She's mentioned getting a *guardian ad litem* to help my case, but I thought the substantiated abuse from Family Services would be enough to make Nathan back off. Marianne is pushing for the guardian, and she says it's our best option. The problem is that it's thousands more in a new retainer for the GAL and then more lawyer fees for Marianne on top of that."

"A GAL?" he asked.

"It's just the abbreviation for the guardian."

He nodded. "Okay, but why is it so expensive?"

"With cases of contested custody, either Nathan and I agree on a GAL to hire, or the judge winds up appointing a guardian to represent the best interests of the child anyway. Since Nathan is fighting me for primary custody of Ari, we're going to need a guardian no matter what. At least this way, I have some say in who it will be."

Aaron frowned. "When you say 'guardian,' it sounds like you're talking about foster care. How can the courts just take Ari away like that? You're a good mother!"

I smiled at the passion in his tone. "It's not that kind of a guardian. It's just the legal term. I promise, nobody is taking Ari away. Children can't testify in court, so the GAL will do that on Ari's behalf."

"So, they're going to interview a preschooler?" he asked with raised eyebrows.

"No, the GAL will watch the forensic interview Family Services ordered after the abuse charges against Nathan last year. The guardian isn't on my side or Nathan's, but they will interview us and get my version and Nathan's. Marianne said that based on Nathan's abuse, this is the best way to ensure I get primary physical custody and maybe even supervised visitation when Nathan has Ari. Unfortunately, there's no getting around the GAL or the expense. Marianne has also hinted that Nathan may not agree to go to mediation unless we get one. The GAL investigation delays the divorce, and there's the off chance they might even decide Nathan should get more visitation time or rights."

Aaron pushed a hand over his buzzed haircut. "Lauren, I hate that you have to go through all of this. It should be obvious to anyone with two brain cells that he's an unfit parent. Why are you the one spending all of your savings just to be free?"

"Because the system is broken," I said sadly. "Because the people who need help are at the mercy of the people legally trained to provide it. They know they can charge an arm and a leg and get away with it."

Aaron shook his head. "You deserve so much better than this."

I fought the temptation to reach out and take Aaron's hand. I wanted comfort, but I knew how Aaron would interpret the gesture. My fingers balled into a fist, and I looked away.

He exhaled a heavy sigh. "I wish there was something I could do."

"You're already doing it, believe me."

His eyes recaptured mine. "I don't feel like I've done anything, Laur. I feel helpless, and I hate it. I want to pound that slimewad into the dirt. It's the least he deserves for what he's done to you and Ari."

I took a much needed step backward. "I can't do this anymore."

His eyes widened in alarm. "Do what? The divorce?"

"This," I said, gesturing between the two of us. "It's not right."

"We've been friends since we were kids. There's nothing wrong with that."

"We haven't been 'just friends' since the night everyone found out what Nathan did at Beth Shalom. I appreciate all of your help, but I see how you look at me. I feel like I'm leading you on by being your friend."

Aaron's eyes flickered, clearly remembering his frantic, late night knock on my parents' front door and everything that transpired after. My lips quivered at the memory, and they drew the attention of that steel blue gaze just as they had that night.

Hating myself for having to hurt my friend, I said, "Aaron, we need distance. Our friendship is confusing for me, and I feel like it gives you false hope. You also know Nathan will twist it into something it isn't."

"You're *allowed* to have friends," he argued. "You've been alone with Ari in that apartment for over a year, and even though you're meeting Nathan at the police station to handle visitation, I just don't trust him. You need to feel safe, and you need to have support."

"I also need to focus on getting a better job and figuring out how I'm going to keep paying my lawyer plus the GAL. You know I love hanging out with you, but I can't risk losing my son. Some days, I think I can handle being 'just friends,' but then you look at me like you are right now, and I just..." my voice trailed off as my eyes pleaded with him to understand.

Shelving his own desire, the fire in his eyes retreated into anger on my behalf. "Family services substantiated abuse allegations against Nathan, didn't they? Why isn't that enough for the judge or even the police? How can Nathan fight for primary custody when he doesn't have a leg to stand on?"

I sighed. "Nathan can posture and do whatever he wants until we actually get in front of a judge. DCFS exists within this space between family and criminal law. They don't have the power to legally kick Nathan out of a home he owns. They also can't make a determination about custody or tell law enforcement to arrest him."

"But they can threaten to take your son away from you," Aaron said bitterly. "They can strong-arm you into leaving your home with your child because Nathan refuses to move out. Sounds like they have the power to threaten and manipulate *you* because it's easier than doing their jobs and protecting both of you from Nathan. How is that fair to you or Ari?"

"It isn't," I said, "but their point of view is that they're doing what's best for my child."

"By threatening to take him away from his mother?" he demanded.

"No, by forcing me to decide if protecting my son from his father is more important than the financial comfort of staying in a house with Nathan and risking abuse."

"In a house that you *also* legally own," Aaron growled. "Like I said, they punish *you* for Nathan's crimes because the cowards know you're vulnerable and easier to push. They put the burden on you because it made it easier for themselves."

"You're right," I said, retracing the events with a new perspective. "They pretended to be sympathetic, but it was really just about closing the case as fast as possible." Bitterness filled my mouth at how trusting and naive I'd been. The abject terror of secretly moving in with my parents was only worsened by Nathan's rage that followed. I shuddered.

"Laur, you okay?" Aaron reached out a hand to my shoulder, and I didn't brush off his comfort. "Stay with me."

I met his eyes. "How could I have been so stupid?"

"You weren't," he said gruffly. "They're a government agency looking out for themselves. If there's any bright side here, at least you're not sharing a roof with the demon anymore. I rest easier knowing he has no idea where you live."

I patted his hand and then stepped back. "I needed that, thank you. The sadistic mind games are bad enough when we do the visitation exchange. I don't think I would survive living under the same roof as him waiting for the divorce to be over."

"I don't understand why Nathan is still fighting you. He put bruises on you and Ari. How could he think any judge would rule in his favor?"

"Because even with the substantiated abuse, it's a worthless piece of paper right now. The DCFS report helps my case, but it's not legally binding. That's why Marianne thinks we should get a GAL. The judge follows their recommendation ninety percent of the time, and having their backing plus the report from family services will strengthen my case in civil court."

Aaron exhaled a low whistle. "It's just so much money for you. Why isn't the protective order enough?"

"Because after the first one expired, Nathan was incident free."

"That's only because he doesn't have daily access to you anymore. Do they need him to livestream the abuse in order to get a conviction?" he snapped.

"It feels that way. For now, at least, we meet at the precinct for drop off, and Nathan doesn't know where we live. Carly's lease still has her name on it, and it's on the opposite side of town. I was just following my lawyer's advice."

Aaron frowned. "Well, I hope for your sake that she's right. You told me that Marianne got good reviews online, but every time you talk about her, you sound confused or frustrated with something."

"Divorces are expensive. At least that's what Marianne keeps telling me."

"Didn't you say Charlotte got divorced from Rick for less than $5,000? Your attorney has already billed you almost $7,500. All she's done so far is file the paperwork and bill you for answering emails."

I pushed down the sense of dread that Aaron was completely right. Half the time, I was playing monkey in the middle with Marianne's paralegal or feeling like things were explained to me only after I had to ask. Based on their bimonthly billing statements, each email to Marianne Abbey cost me anywhere from $20 to $350 to answer.

Breaking through my troubled thoughts, Aaron said, "When do you find out about child support?"

"We are so far away from that. We could try to negotiate at mediation after the GAL's investigation is done. If that doesn't work, we'll go to court for a hearing and take our chances with the judge. In the meantime, Nathan won't agree to any dollar amount because he doesn't have to yet, and his lawyer is being paid to do what he wants—no matter how reprehensible it is.

Nathan wants me to run out of energy and money fighting him."

Aaron raked a hand over his dark blonde hair. "This is all so insane."

"I know. My parents offered to help pay for the GAL, but that still doesn't solve the issue with Marianne. I didn't tell you this yet, but now she's saying she can't work on my case anymore because I don't have any money left in my retainer."

Aaron looked appalled. "She's already wiped out every drop of savings you have, and she doesn't seem to care."

"Divorce is—" I cut myself off, realizing I sounded as brain-washed as I did while attending Beth Shalom. "Oh, Aaron," I said softly. "Oh, no." My shoulders shook with tears. "I've known something's been wrong with Marianne for a long time. Why didn't I listen to my gut? I'm going to be in divorce hell for the rest of my life!"

Uncaring of the countless sets of eyes watching our every move, my old friend pulled me in for a hug. I gladly accepted his comfort and indulged in a few sobs. I'd been crying on his shoulder since we were teens. I never realized Aaron Davis had been in love with me the entire time. Not until it was too late.

CHAPTER 2

AFTER PAYING THE COLLEGE BABYSITTER WHO LIVED in the apartment upstairs, I flopped onto my sofa courtesy of Carly Trautweig. I scrolled on Instantpics, chuckling at memes and liking photos and video clips of a few celebrities I followed. A message from Charlotte popped up on my phone.

Hey girl, she wrote, *how'd it go with the new sitter tonight?*

Pretty well, I think. She said she took Ari to the playground, and he went down easy for bedtime. Thx for checking in.

What about blue eyes?

I snickered at Charlotte's preferred nickname for Aaron. *Same.*

How much longer before you're legally free from the psycho? I want to see that gorgeous "just friend" of yours lay a big fat smooch on you!

I cackled loudly and then clamped a hand on my mouth. I heard Ari stir in his bedroom, and I held my breath until I knew he'd fallen back asleep. Texting Charlotte, I said, *I almost woke up Ari. Thanks for that.* I added some angry emojis followed by laughing ones. *Aaron is definitely JUST a friend. Knock it off.*

Girl, if I was ten years younger I'd be hitting that up myself.

I had to grin at Charlotte's uproarious sense of humor. One of the things I loved about the woman was how she'd say something as outrageous as possible just to make people laugh. Rick had always hated Charlotte's humor and made her feel self conscious about it. The reality was Rick didn't want his ex-wife upstaging him with her wit, charm, and personality since he possessed none of those things.

You and your younger men, I wrote.

Charlotte's response was to send me a .gif of a diapered baby shaking his behind for the camera. I saw ellipses showing her typing, and I could hear Charlotte's saucy tone as I read her response. *Listen, I was married to a porn addicted, selfish slug whose one redeeming quality was being fertile. Thank God, or I doubt my girls would even be here. Withholding sex was one of many ways the pig lived to torture me.*

Surprised, I said, *Are you sleeping with your bf now?*

Girl, please! she wrote back. *He's not my boyfriend, and it's only been a few weeks. Just because I've been a shiny red sports car sitting neglected in the garage doesn't mean I'm giving out test drives!*

I laughed. *You are too much, my friend.*

Look, she replied, *I haven't suddenly turned my back on Jesus just to get laid, ok? All I'm saying is that when the time comes, it might just take a younger man to keep up with me once I get a ring on my finger.*

I blushed, knowing my friend meant every single word.

When I didn't respond immediately, Charlotte wrote, *Did I scandalize you, youngin?*

Sometimes I can't tell if you're joking or not, I wrote back.

Charlotte sent back a series of angel emojis followed by a winking face.

I laughed again. *Text you in the morning. Have a job interview in the AM.*

Good for you! Who's watching the baby?

Rebecca Margolin.

Ah, Charlotte said, *and you're going to start working at Culver, fall in love, and write a book just like every other person who's worked in that marketing department, right?*

I snickered. *Could be worse.*

What happened after Poppy got a sneak peek at Carly's book? You told me things got pretty tense because they disagree about how things happened. Is the drama still going on, or is everybody making nice now?

I've read Carly's manuscript too, and I can see both sides. Talk to them in real life if you want to, Charlotte. They both changed details to protect their families.

You just want me to come to your Bible study. I know what you're doing, Little Miss Innocent. I told you, I am done with organized religion. Not after what I went through at Beth Shalom and then with Tina.

I shuddered, knowing the agony Charlotte had been put through by her former best friend. Tina Fournier was a Beth Shalom member who pretended to be a soft landing ground for Charlotte to escape during her divorce from Rick. Instead, Charlotte was texting me about increasingly bizarre behavior once she and the girls moved into Tina's basement. All Tina wanted to talk about was Tina it seemed. Otherwise, she was taking potshots at Charlotte's mothering or constantly reminding Charlotte of all the generosity she'd shown her.

Things came to a head when Tina exposed and infected Charlotte and her girls with Covid-19 in 2020. A week later, Tina unceremoniously evicted them because Charlotte dared to be upset about it. Tina, meanwhile, went around telling people she was the victim of Charlotte's lack of appreciation. Frantic, Charlotte had forwarded me the text messages between herself and Tina wondering how things had gotten so far out of hand. As much as I had hoped the former best friends could reconcile, I couldn't get past the vitriol in Tina's messages. She insulted and demeaned Charlotte while simultaneously demanding gratitude. She praised herself as the only thing keeping Charlotte and the girls off the street and away from Rick. In Tina's twisted version, Charlotte had abandoned Tina in her "hour of need" by not jumping to meet Tina's ridiculous demands while Charlotte lay bedridden with the virus. Any time my friend advocated for her own health, Tina went ballistic. I was shocked to see the level of callousness toward Charlotte's suffering on top of the divorce and caring for two pre-teen girls.

I shook off the horror of Tina's words, once again feeling the sucker punch as if they had been sent directly to me instead of Charlotte. With regards to my own messy divorce, Tina took it upon herself to send me a Bible devotional against holding grudges. I politely thanked her and then deleted it. Once I saw the text messages to Charlotte, I debated blocking her entirely off my social media accounts. The final straw was Tina fawning all over Nathan's FaceSpace page with Bible verses about suffering for the Lord and withstanding undeserved criticism. At that point, the block button became a necessity.

Turning my attention back to Charlotte's text messages, my own heart hurt thinking of all my friend had endured. *I just want you to know that the Margolins aren't like any of the people at synagogue. They don't just talk big about "mishpocha" and all of the nonsense they fed us at Beth Shalom. They really do treat each other like family.*

Charlotte was quick to fire back. *Yeah, but Jared Levine is still there, and he was all buddy buddy with my ex, your ex, Rabbi Lebow, and that entire cabal of morally bankrupt frauds.*

I was tempted to clap back at Charlotte to tell me her *real* feelings, but I knew that beyond the snark, my friend had been deeply wounded by our old congregation.

Instead, I wrote, *Unlike everybody else, Jared really did change. You met Poppy at my birthday dinner.*

She was also still mooning over her almost ex-boyfriend for a while, so forgive me if my opinion of her isn't quite as high as yours.

I raised an eyebrow at the change in Charlotte's tone.

After a lengthy pause, Charlotte wrote, *Anyways, time for both of us to get to bed. Ttyl.*

I sent back a thumbs up emoji and then tossed my phone onto the couch. I glanced over at it, both wanting and dreading a phone call from Aaron. I felt at war with myself, and I knew from experience nothing good ever came from confusion. I picked up my Uber Teen Translation Bible from my coffee table and tried to flip through the *Psalms* for some kind of guidance. Instead, I felt empty and alone.

"I know I need to lay this down," I said, glancing up toward heaven. "As much as I like Aaron as a friend, I just can't make the switch to seeing him as anything else. And now isn't the time anyway, right? I love the guy...just not like that. Even a career criminal would still be an improvement over Nathan, but it seems too easy, Lord."

My phone remained silent, but the gnawing angst in my stomach grew.

"Stop it," I finally told myself. Memories from three years earlier surfaced, and I relived the feelings of both longing and guilt over what had transpired with Aaron. I exhaled in disgust and went to bed.

After a fitful night of sleep, I was glad to awaken to the sounds of Ari playing in his toddler bed.

"Morning, buddy," I called to my little cherub.

"Mama!" he squealed, holding out his arms for me.

Gleefully, I swung my son into a tight embrace and kissed those chubby cheeks until I'd had my fill.

"I missed you last night," I said, planting a few more kisses along his forehead.

"I missed you too, Mommy." He grabbed my face with his pudgy hands and planted a loud kiss on my cheek. I laughed and snuggled him closer. After changing his overnight diaper, I got Ari dressed and then brought him into our shared bathroom to get ready.

"Hands and face, hands and face," I sang, rubbing the baby wash onto his hands.

Ari bopped along with me, giggling as he wiggled his hips from side to side.

"Gotta wash our hands and face," I sang again, doing a quick swipe of his oval face and rinsing off the suds. I toweled off my son and rubbed his hair for good measure.

"Again!" he said, liking the mess I'd made of his curls.

Smiling, I made an even poofier version of Ari's overgrown mane. His peals of laughter felt like medicine to my soul.

"Mommy has a big day today," I said, meeting his wide eyes in the mirror.

"Big day?" he repeated.

"Yep, buddy. I'm going to take you to play at Miss Rebecca's house with Tabby, Eva, and baby Max."

Ari's brown eyes lit up in the mirror. "I love baby Max! He's so cute, Mommy!"

"Yes, he is," I said. "He looks just like his daddy too."

"Do I look like my daddy?"

"No, you look a lot like Mommy." I ruffled his wheat colored curls again.

"But I'm not a girl!"

I smiled at my precocious four year old. "No, you're definitely all boy, but you do look like Mommy." I pulled my face down next to his in the mirror so he could see the side by side comparison. "See?" I said, pointing to our reflections. "You've got a nice long face, just like Mommy."

"I do?"

"Yup. And see, you've got brown eyes like Mommy, but yours are a little darker because your dad has dark eyes."

Ari's face scrunched in the mirror as he very seriously contemplated my words.

"Nose," he said, pointing to his face. "I have Mommy's nose."

I smiled. "Yep. You got the Gellar nose, buddy. Mommy has it, my mommy has it, and her mommy has it."

"Gellar nose," he said, pushing on the tip. "I like my nose, Mommy."

I dropped a kiss on the bridge of it. "You should, buddy. It's my favorite feature on your whole face."

"It is?" he asked in wonder.

I kissed it again for good measure. "Yep. When you get mad, all I can see is this tiny little nose all scrunched up, and it's the cutest thing ever. It's hard to stay mad at you, Ari, because you're just so cute!"

He grinned at me. "Yes, I'm very cute, Mommy."

I chuckled. "And see, look at those big pink lips. Those are very good kissing lips. One day, you'll get married, and you'll have a wife who will give you lots of kisses."

"Can I marry Eva?" he asked. "She's cute and funny and nice, and I like her."

I laughed. "Well, today you're just going over to play with Eva. We don't need to worry about you getting married just yet. You've got time to figure that all out."

"Did you and Daddy kiss when you were married?"

I swallowed down bitter memories and plastered a smile on

my face. "Yes, I did kiss your daddy. Husbands and wives will do that, but you don't need to kiss Eva."

"What if we get married, Mommy? Then, can I kiss her?"

I exhaled a short laugh at the thought of Ted Margolin's reaction to any little boy trying to kiss his daughters. "Let's just focus on getting you ready for your play date today, okay? We have to leave in a few minutes so I can be ready to get a new job."

"You look pretty, Mommy," Ari said. "What color is on your eyes?" He gestured for me to close my lids so he could inspect my sparkly brown eyeshadow for himself.

"I think it's called cinnamon swirl," I replied. "Miss Charlotte gave me some pretty colors she didn't need. She said she got them for free and wanted me to have them."

Satisfied with my answer, my son released my cheeks. I opened my eyes and stared back into the coppery brown pair on his perfect face. We exchanged a silent joke between us, and then my son bestowed another heart melting grin on me.

"I love you, Mommy. Stay with me and God."

Blinking back tears and keeping my mascara at bay, I took his advice to heart.

CHAPTER 3

"Good morning, I'm Bonnie," a pleasant woman in her fifties said as she extended her hand to me.

"Hi, I'm Lauren." I sat down at the conference table seat adjacent to her.

"I've been the hiring manager here at Culver for fifteen years, and to say that our marketing department has evolved over time would be quite an understatement."

"So, I've heard."

Bonnie smiled back good naturedly. "So, the entire world has heard, but obviously, you know Poppy in our department."

"I do," I said, "but I hope you'll consider me for the job because you believe I'll be the best fit, not just because I'm friends with people who work here."

Bonnie jerked her chin in surprise. If I could tell anything by the slight twinkle in her eye, my answer impressed her. "Just being candid, Lauren, your resume is pretty thin, but Poppy has been singing your praises so loudly, I can't ignore her."

"I did have some administrative experience before I became a mother," I said, "and I'm a very fast learner."

"So, what makes you think you're qualified to handle Culver's Fortune 500 clients with the small amount of experience you have? I have other applicants for this job with years of graphic design work and pretty impressive portfolios."

I swallowed down a lump in my throat and tears of humiliation.

Bonnie reached her hand out to mine across the table. "Are you okay?"

I waved her off. "I just...I guess you need to hire the person you feel will do the best job for Culver. Even though I don't have all the experience as some of the other candidates, I also know that you've hired people who didn't have a perfect background either."

Bonnie conceded the point with a small smile.

Continuing, I said, "Sometimes, it's not just about the skills but also about the personality fit. In my other job, I had some experience with the Macroplus Office Set, but I took online classes and watched videos on how to do things I needed for work. I taught myself how to make tables and convert them between the design programs. My old boss loved my attention to detail and how I made sure all of the columns and rows lined up perfectly. It may seem silly, but some people just copy and paste and can't see their font sizes are different or they need to redistribute the column width so the table looks balanced. That's the kind of pride I take in my work. I feel like anybody can learn a skill or program software, but some people really care about the job they do, and other people just show up for a paycheck."

I saw a genuine smile on the hiring manager's face. "Your references were glowing, by the way, and I don't just mean

Rebecca or Poppy. Your old boss described you the same way, and it's been almost five years since you worked with that company," she said, glancing down at my resume. "That does speak highly of you, Lauren."

I finally felt a glimmer of hope. "Thank you."

"Not that I don't already know what Poppy will say about you, but I'm going to bring her in to describe the day-to-day of what you can expect in the marketing department. We are still considering other applicants, Lauren, and all hiring decisions go through me."

"Understood," I said, meeting her eyes. "I don't expect any special favors. Culver does seem like a wonderful company, though, and I know I'd be an asset."

Another spark of approval flashed in Bonnie's eyes. "I'll have Poppy come talk to you in just a moment."

Several Culver employees walked past the glass walled conference room as I waited, and they stared at me like a new creature in the fishtank. Nervous, I offered a tiny smile and then stared at the table. A burst of noise from beyond the room caught my attention, and I spotted a matronly woman clutching a pearl necklace as she laughed at a joke with the receptionist. I had to assume this was the infamous Miss Belle.

"Ooh child!" the woman exclaimed beyond the glass walls. "Brooklyn, you are too much!"

Snickering, I wondered what it would be like to step into the actual world of Culver Incorporated beyond the pages of my friends' books. When I heard manly guffaws added to the cackling at the front desk, I figured Ted's boss and Culver's CEO, Phil Robbins, had joined the party.

"Hey!" Poppy exclaimed from the doorway. "I hope you haven't been waiting long."

I greeted her with a quick hug. "No, I'm good. Is that Phil and Miss Belle?" I asked, gesturing toward the ruckus.

Poppy grinned. "They're hard to miss, aren't they? It's one of the things none of us changed for our books. You'd know those two anywhere."

"Poppy Levine, are my ears burning?" Miss Belle called. "I *know* you ain't telling people who don't even work at Culver all of my business."

"Come on," Poppy said, "let me introduce you to the natives."

I followed her toward the front desk.

"This is Lauren," Poppy said. "She's interviewing for Carly's old position."

"Do you write books?" Phil asked me, his blue eyes holding mischief. "Apparently, that's how we know if we should hire anybody around here."

"You must be Phil," I said, warmed by his sense of humor. "I've heard and read a lot about you."

"And it's all true!" he said laughing. "Actually, Poppy and the rest of the girls were probably too kind to me. Miss Belle says I'm going senile."

"You hush your mouth, Phil Robbins, I never said nothing like that!" She swatted at his arm playfully. "But you're fixin' to drive me crazy with all of the carrying on you do."

I couldn't help but smile.

"Don't scare her before we hire her," the receptionist added, flipping silky black hair over her shoulder. "I'm Brooklyn, by the way, and I hope you do write books. I've read all the Culver ones, and they're *so* good. Do you have some hottie who's been secretly stan-ing you too? I love a good, slow burn romance!"

I blushed and looked away while Poppy coughed. "Okay, guys, I think that's enough hazing for today. If Lauren even wants to take the job at this point, it won't be because of the three of you."

Miss Belle tried to look affronted, but Phil and Brooklyn seemed proud of Poppy's remark.

"Oh, put your pearls down," Phil chided Miss Belle. "You know you cause more trouble around here than anyone."

While another argument broke out, Poppy brought me back to the conference room.

"Sorry," she said, closing the door. "I hope I didn't scare you off the job by introducing you to the gang."

I shook my head. "No, they're pretty true to life. I just hope I'm the right fit for you guys. Bonnie said my resume was thin compared to the other candidates you're considering. I will definitely work hard and do my best here, but I want you to go with the person you think will really do the best job. If that's not me, you won't hurt my feelings."

"Lauren, you do *want* this job, don't you?"

"Of course!"

Poppy smiled. "Then, quit trying to convince me I should go with someone else and let's talk about how this can work. If I don't think this is a good fit, I'm going to be honest with you. I don't want things to be weird at Bible study if they get weird at work. Been there, done that," she said, referring to a fight she'd had with Carly Trautweig.

Poppy spent the next thirty minutes describing her daily routine, and I found myself intrigued and intimidated. The balance of administrative and creative design felt like an ideal situation for me, but I also knew I'd have a huge learning curve navigating the ArtHut Design Suite. Poppy showed me some sample designs asking if there were things I would change. Feeling like it was a test, I eyed the documents critically. I pointed out some misaligned objects and typos and asked questions about changing some of the lengthier bits of copy into information graphics. Poppy's eyes held a warm glow the entire time.

Bonnie rapped on the door and exchanged a quick conversation with Poppy outside. Turning back to me, she said, "Lauren, thank you for coming in today. We'll let you know by the end of the week if we'd like to proceed with a second interview."

"Thank you for the opportunity," I said, shaking her hand.

Bonnie smiled warmly. "You're very welcome."

I picked up my folder and purse and waved past Brooklyn as I exited the glass entry doors and walked toward the elevators.

"Nice to meet you!" she called from the front desk.

I pushed the elevator button not sure if I had aced or failed my first job interview since my early twenties.

"Going down?" a male voice asked.

I nodded, still focused on the elevators.

"I'm Grant."

I glanced over, surprised the man was still talking to me. I encountered chocolate brown eyes under thick brows the same color. Immediately, I was reminded of my favorite iteration of Peter Parsons from the Spider Guy movies, and I did a double take. If Peter had grown up, grown a beard, and taken a job at Culver Incorporated, this guy would have been a dead ringer. My pesky hormones reminded me that even though my marriage was dead, I most certainly was not. I wondered if his cropped, curly hair would be anything like Ari's if he grew it out longer.

"Are you new here?" Grant asked, studying me.

"Possibly," I said. "I just had an interview."

"CID or Benefits?"

Smiling, I felt flattered he assumed I'd been interviewing for a position with the commercial insurance division or employee benefits rather than their support staff. "Marketing department," I replied.

He leaned in closer as if sharing a private joke. "Apparently, you have to be an author in order to work there. I've read all of the books too. Are you ready to tell your story to the world?"

Rising to the challenge and holding his gaze, I said, "I have enough writing material to make your head spin. Whether I ever publish it or not remains to be seen."

Half of Grant's mouth cocked into a smile. His eyes glowed with an approving gleam. "Well, I hope you get the job. It'll be nice seeing you around here. What did you say your name was?"

"I'm married," I blurted out.

His eyes zeroed in on my empty wedding finger.

"And I don't do office dating or anything like that," I added.

Grant held up his hands in innocence. "I was just saying 'hello' to a new face, that's it."

I raised two suspicious eyebrows, but Grant maintained his surprised expression. Unfortunately, the dancing butterflies in my stomach did not abate after my faux pas. Part of me wanted to crawl into the nearest hole, and part of me wanted to challenge Grant's quick denial. Instead, the elevator doors dinged open, and Ted Margolin stepped out.

"Lauren!" Ted exclaimed. "I thought I'd missed your interview. Rebecca just texted me that Ari wants to marry Eva."

"Oh," I said, embarrassed. "Yeah, he mentioned that while we were getting ready this morning."

Grant watched me closely.

"Kaplan, do you need the elevator?" Ted asked, assuming his "mighty Margolin" persona.

"Just meeting a potential new recruit," he answered. "Lauren, it was nice meeting you. I hope you get the job." He offered a salute and headed to the reception desk beyond the glass doors.

I didn't like how Grant Kaplan now knew my name or that I felt a small thrill at the sound of it on his lips. I immediately felt guilty—as if I was cheating on Aaron rather than Nathan. I sighed at the ridiculousness of that thought.

"Kaplan is new around here," Ted said quietly. "Not sure what I think about him yet. Did he make you uncomfortable? Things seemed a little tense."

The answer was yes, though not in the way he supposed.

"Lauren?" Ted prompted.

"I'm fine," I said. "It's awkward talking to any man these days. He didn't do anything wrong. Sometimes, it's hard to tell what's just friendly conversation."

"Well, from the way he was looking at you and the fact you're still blushing, it does concern me a little bit."

I met Ted's golden gaze. "It's fine. You don't need to play father figure with me."

He looked taken aback but didn't comment further. Clearing his throat, he said, "Did the interview go well?"

"I think so."

"I'm sorry for interfering. You know we all care about you."

Mollified, I smiled back. "I know. I'm sorry I snapped at you."

"Apology accepted. Go give my wife a hug when you see her, and we'll be praying God opens the doors for you to get a job—whether it's here or somewhere else."

I patted his arm. "Thanks, Ted. I appreciate it."

He nodded and then stepped through the front double doors as I got into the elevator. I had a sudden urge to text Aaron and clear my mind of chocolate brown eyes.

CHAPTER 4

"Congratulations!" Charlotte squealed, pulling me into an embrace. "I'm so glad you called me to celebrate with cheesecake!"

I smiled and took in my dear friend who glowed with happiness. "You look great, my friend. I think dating agrees with you."

Her sparkling eyes only added to her appeal. Though not beautiful by conventional standards, Charlotte's unique features were designed to catch attention. Deep, wide set eyes of the palest blue could have been overshadowed by her strong nose, but the ever present smile on her pouty lips made her impossible not to love. She was a fun, flirty enigma with enough mystery dancing in her light eyes to keep any man guessing.

I had never seen my friend blush before, but there was an extra pink flush in her cheeks as we sat down at our Parkview Diner table. "You're embarrassing me now, youngin."

"Would you stop calling me that! You're forty-two, not eighty-two."

"Feels like it some days with my back," she said, reaching toward her hips. "My sacrum keeps sliding out."

"That sounds awful."

Charlotte rolled her eyes. "Literal pain in the butt. Not unlike my ex. My chiropractor said he couldn't believe how much the nerve damage improved once Rick and I finally got divorced. He told me he'd never seen anything like it. I used to cry when Dr. Oliver adjusted me, or he'd have me contorting off the table in pain. Now, I can just lay there like it's no big deal."

"Wow," I said, "and you told me Dr. Oliver looks like the actor from *Crossbow*, right?"

Charlotte's eyes sparkled. "Yeah, he looks like the lead character, Oliver Quinn."

"Is he the guy in all the promo photos for that show?" I asked, trying to place him.

"Yep. Broody, blue eyes, facial scruff, and abs you can wash your clothes on. All Dr. Oliver's missing are some leather pants and a mask."

I cracked up laughing. "Have you told your chiropractor any of this?"

"Funny enough, Dr. Oliver says he's never seen an episode."

"No wonder you like getting adjusted," I said with a wink.

Charlotte rolled her eyes. "He's sweet and also a newlywed. Nothing happening there."

"So, tell me about this Paul guy you've been seeing. Sounds like he has potential."

Charlotte demurred, giving our server the perfect window to take our matching drink and dessert orders. I raised my eyebrows waiting for an answer.

My friend finally shrugged. "It's going okay. He's just boring."

"Boring? Well, compared to you, anybody would be."

"No," she said, tossing espresso colored tresses over her shoulder, "I mean it's clear he's into me, but I don't really know what he brings to the table. He doesn't talk about much other than his job. He always flips the questions back onto my life when I start to dig a little. It's happened too many times to be an accident."

"I thought most women want a man who's actually interested in what we have to say."

"No, it's more than that," Charlotte said as our waitress placed twin, chocolate swirl cheesecake slices in front of us. "It makes me feel uncomfortable, like I'm under a microscope. I don't know anything meaningful about the guy, but he keeps asking about my marriage with Rick or about the girls. I don't know, something about it just gives me the creeps."

I frowned. "Weird."

"Exactly," Charlotte said around a mouthful of cheesecake. "Something is just off, and if I've learned anything after the fiasco with Tina, it's to listen to my gut."

"Speaking of Tina, has she left you alone yet?"

Charlotte rolled her eyes. "Oh, she sent me another text that she found things of mine in her basement."

"But you moved out a year ago."

"Honestly, it feels like an excuse to contact me. I don't understand why, since she's made it clear she hates my guts."

I reached out a hand across the table. "I just don't get what happened, Charlotte. You guys used to be best friends."

"We were," she replied, "or at least I thought we were. It just always seems to happen with these girlfriends of mine. We bond over shared tragedy or trauma, pour out our hearts to each other, but then the relationship sours."

"Have you found any patterns?"

Charlotte twirled a glossy tendril around her finger as she

pondered my question. "You know, it's like we commiserate over the pain, but then they get a new boyfriend, best friend, job promotion, ministry position, or just something they've always wanted, and then suddenly, I'm a burden. They still want to dump all of their problems on me and expect me to jump the second they call or text but blowing *me* off is totally okay."

My ears perked up. "Wow, so it sounds like narcissistic supply."

"What's that? You're the one who became the narcissism expert."

"It's a term that means attention for the narcissist. Whether it's good or bad, the narc always needs someone to give them emotional fuel. If they don't get what they want organically, they'll create the drama themselves. After they've discarded you, they try to hoover you back in with flattery and gifts, or they might even attack you out of the blue. They feed off your reaction to their antics because it's ultimately about proving they still have power over your emotions. Narcissists always need to feel in control of others."

"That sounds exactly like Tina," Charlotte said. "Every few months she invents something else I did wrong. I feel bad ignoring her or just giving her one word answers, but I just don't have anything else to say at this point. She used to tell me I was her only real friend."

"If she's texting you, it's because she's bored, not lonely for friends. Tina has hurt so many people at Beth Shalom, and she's pushed her own kids away with her behavior. None of that is your fault or responsibility to carry."

"I'm still mad at her, but I feel sorry for her at the same time. Mostly, I just wonder where my friend went and who this witch is who replaced her overnight."

"And that just shows your heart, my friend. You're an

empath. I keep telling you that. The problem is that you've also got to work on boundaries because narcs love empathetic people. While you're busy trying to help them, they're busy bleeding you dry like they're entitled to every drop of energy you have."

Charlotte's pale blue eyes widened. "You make it sound like she was never my friend. It wasn't always like this."

I shook my head. "I know it's confusing when you have happy memories with her, but the woman abusing you on those text messages is the real Tina Fournier. The second you told her to back off because you were sick, she went off the deep end. A normal person would actually care about your health, first of all. The woman gave you Covid and then completely dismissed how sick you were because she decided *she* was sicker. She had no compassion for you or the girls, by her own admission. All that mattered to Tina was that you weren't available to jump because *she* had to discuss something with you. Meanwhile, you were too sick to even get out of bed! She kicked you out, knowing you had nowhere else to go other than back with Rick because all of you were still contagious. It was cruel, Charlotte. Tina Fournier doesn't deserve your pity. She deserves your indifference. The worst way you can injure a narcissist is by ignoring them."

Charlotte pursed her lips. "Maybe you're right. I just hate walking around wondering what went wrong. I keep thinking Tina will snap out of it and be her old self again."

"That's the empath again. You want to get into Tina's head and figure out her motivation. I'm telling you, it doesn't actually matter. No true friend, let alone someone who says they love Jesus, would ever treat you and your girls that way. Her behavior was vindictive and evil, and Tina knew exactly what she was doing. You went through hell just getting back into your old house, and then Tina went and trashed you to Rick behind your back as an added bonus."

The sparkle in Charlotte's eyes faded into pain and wariness. "Yes, and the pig was all too happy to make me stay in the guest room since he took over the master suite. Rick's lawyer almost quit when he refused to let me back in the house."

"I remember," I said, "and I have a question for you, speaking of lawyers."

"Are you finally going to dump that awful attorney of yours?"

"Awful?" I repeated, feeling myself pale. "You think she's awful too?"

"I think she's taking you for a ride, and she's no match for the shark Nathan hired. For all of the talks we've had about narcissists, how do you not see some of those tendencies in Marianne? How many times is she going to bill you for 'misunderstanding' her? What about that video call with her and the billing department? You called me in tears afterwards. You said all she did was argue with you or change the subject."

I sniffled, feeling the sting of those tears once again. "What do I do, Charlotte? Am I supposed to just start over? Where am I supposed to find the money for that?"

My friend took another bite of cheesecake then gestured for me to do the same. "Have you ever heard of a fee based attorney?"

"Fee based?" I asked.

"Yeah, I think you'd already hired Marianne when I found Sondra Joyner. She was amazing. Probably saved me at least $10,000 fighting Rick before the new wife came along and sped things along."

"How?" I asked.

Ignoring my question, Charlotte said, "Girl, please take a

bite of that dessert before I snatch it off your plate and take it home with me. You're too skinny as it is."

I shoved a piece in my mouth, but I didn't feel like eating at all. "Happy?"

"Good, now do a few more and remember that we escaped from our kids to *celebrate* tonight. You got a new job, and you should be proud of yourself. All of this talk of Tina and lawyers is just depressing."

"No, no, no," I said waving my fork at her, "I'm not letting you off the hook. Give me some hope, Charlotte. Are there actually divorce lawyers who aren't trying to make a fortune off the suffering of their clients?"

"Believe it or not, they're not all bottom feeding leeches. Sondra was an answer to prayer, and we wound up becoming friends during the divorce."

"Tell me more."

"Well, she charges the same $3,500 retainer that Marianne did up front. Then it's $500 a month after that, but she doesn't bill you for every question and email. Mediation and trial are separate fees, but you don't have to dread every communication or avoid asking questions because you know each email is going to cost you a million dollars."

"That's still a lot of money up front," I said, feeling the air leak out of my small balloon of hope.

"True," Charlotte conceded, "but look how fast Marianne blew through your $3,500 retainer anyway. She and her paralegal completely botched getting Nathan served with papers, and they billed you for all of the mistakes with the process server. You told me Marianne didn't explain anything to you up front, and it felt like she purposefully left out details so she could make you feel dumb for asking. Oh, and she billed you for that pleasure too. Keeping you scared and uninformed makes you easier to control. Also, don't think she won't bill you for every little second Nathan or his scumbag lawyer wastes her time either. That's all billable too."

Weakly, I asked, "So, Sondra didn't treat you that way?"

Charlotte shook her head emphatically. "No, Sondra was wonderful. Take the money your parents said they could offer for a GAL and see about hiring Sondra instead. You've got a much better job now, so you'll have money on top of the piddly amount Nathan pays in support for Ari. If things get really bad financially, you can always move back in with your parents after your lease is up, but I know you can make this work, Laur."

Feeling peace rather than anxiety, I exhaled a pent up breath and took a bite of cheesecake.

Charlotte grinned at me. "There's my girl! Now, tell me all about this Grant character."

I didn't have much to tell my friend other than our awkward first meeting, but the man himself made sure to stop by the marketing department office on my first day. Seeing his perfectly coiffed curls, I snickered at the thought that Grant probably put more effort into grooming than I did. My own wheat-colored hair fell in a combination of loose waves and curls, never quite sure what it wanted to be. Depending on my mood or patience for styling products, I typically just washed it and let it decide its own fate.

"Good morning, Poppy. Good morning, Lauren," Grant said, sweeping into the room.

Poppy raised an amused eyebrow. I saw the question on her lips followed by a sip from her to-go cup of *Vincenzo's* coffee.

"Grant," I said evenly, "I've just settled in here, so I'm not sure if there's anything I can do for you work wise."

Poppy chimed in, "Has anybody ever mentioned a guy named Zack Perkins to you?"

"Perkins? You mean the guy that got fired before me?"

"Mmhmm," Poppy purred. "He also got punched in the face for sexually harassing Carly and pestering her in the office."

"Hey now! I'm not sexually harassing anybody," Grant said, putting on that same wide-eyed look he performed by the elevators. "Strictly business."

"So, what brings you to the office?" Poppy asked.

From behind his back, Grant pulled a thick pile of papers covered by a blue worksheet. "RFP for Happy Monkey."

"Happy Monkey?" I squealed. "My son loves that place! Is that one of the clients here? How cool!"

Poppy looked amused while Grant seemed intrigued. Embarrassed, I sat down in my chair. Grant's chocolate brown eyes sparkled as he looked at Poppy but addressed both of us. "Happy Monkey is fishing for someone else to handle their employee benefits. They haven't been happy with their current broker for a while. Irene said that everyone around here uses the presentation from the Geneva Group RFP for their template, so I just marked that one up."

"What's an RFP?" I asked.

"Request for Proposal," Grant answered before Poppy could. "A potential client makes a list of questions they want competing brokerage firms to answer. We create a response based off of the questions and then present it to the client on why we can service their needs better than our competitors."

Poppy nodded. "I have created RFPs in every design program imaginable. It really just depends on the producer and what medium they feel most comfortable with. Corporate is trying to streamline the document templates so we don't keep reinventing the wheel, but we tailor each presentation specific to the client and their industry. We use shared folders on the network so you can reference other clients, and we also have a spot for information graphics that can be used interchangeably within the document types."

I tried to absorb all of the information, but I felt myself getting overwhelmed.

"Lauren, are you okay?" Poppy asked.

"It's just a lot to take in," I said, fighting off tears. "I'll be fine."

Grant's amused expression changed to concern. "I can come back later."

"That's probably a good idea," Poppy said. "This job isn't that complicated, Lauren, but you have to remember a ton of little things all at once. We also have branding guidelines we have to follow, so be prepared for push back from the associates."

My heart beat faster as my breathing became labored.

"Lauren?" Grant asked, studying me. "Hey, are you sure you're okay?"

"Sorry, panic attack," I said, slapping my hand on the desk. "Poppy?" I whispered, meeting her eyes.

She rushed to my side. "Carly dealt with these too. You're going to be fine. Just focus on your breathing, okay? First, let's start with five things you can see," she said, listing off the five-step grounding technique I'd known and used before.

Sometime in the ten minutes it took to calm me down, Grant Kaplan had disappeared. His work request showed up on Poppy's desk while Phil, Ted, and Poppy treated me to lunch. All I knew was that I didn't like Grant's effect on me, and I needed to see my old friend as soon as possible. If it was male attention I needed, I knew there was a much safer place to receive it.

CHAPTER 5

"So, what happened at your new job?" Aaron asked. We sat on swings at a local park while Ari played on the jungle gym. "You sounded upset in your text."

I paused as I watched my son go down a big slide for the tenth time. Turning my attention back to Aaron, I said, "I had a panic attack on my first day of work."

"What caused it?" he asked with a thunderous expression. "Is your ex bothering you?"

Sighing, I decided to just rip off the bandage. "No, there's this guy that sort of hit on me when I was interviewing for the job. He showed up in the office today, and I got flustered with learning all the insurance lingo. Then there's the design software, branding guidelines, figuring out their file system, and making sure I log my time on each project into the company-wide database."

Undeterred by my list of job requirements, Aaron's stormy eyes darkened to a deeper gray. "What do you mean this guy 'sort of' hit on you?"

"He was just being too friendly for my comfort level. I feel stupid for turning it into a big deal. You and I both know how sensitive I am right now." I didn't want to admit that my surprising attraction made things feel more intimate than they probably were. I glanced away from Aaron, feeling guilty for even entertaining thoughts about Grant.

"Don't discount your gut," Aaron warned. "You have that discernment for a reason. It doesn't make you paranoid or any other lie Nathan used to gaslight you. If something feels off, it's because it *is* off."

Thinking over my interactions with Grant Kaplan for easily the tenth time that day, I had to admit he hadn't done much more than show an interest in me personally. I frowned, mystified why I felt anything toward him at all. Was my unease from Grant's actual behavior or from my own guilty conscience? It seemed hypocritical to accuse him of any wrongdoing when I knew exactly how much Aaron admired me. I sighed heavily.

"Aaron, I'm not really sure of anything right now. The guy didn't touch me or harass me. He just made it a point to show up early in the day and use my name."

"I already don't like him."

"Well, Poppy and Ted seem to agree with you."

"Then, I rest my case," he said. "They're your friends too, and we all want what's best for you and to make sure you're safe."

"Or you guys could all be over protective."

"Or," Aaron argued, "we see something that you may not want to."

"Look, I told him I'm still married," I said, annoyed, "and that doesn't make me hanging out with you any less inappropriate either."

He sighed. "Are we going to do this again? We've been friends for fifteen years."

"And then you made it more than friends when you kissed me."

It was the first time I had spoken aloud what transpired the night I'd left Nathan. I knew Aaron didn't stop by to take advantage of me, but a moment of weakness on his part and vulnerability on mine had left us in the current state of warring emotions.

His eyes held mine. "The kiss shouldn't have happened, and I take full responsibility for that. But it *did* happen, and we're still talking about it."

"It doesn't matter, Aaron. I was married. I'm *still* married, and it was still wrong. Whatever God has for the future, I am not going to tell my son I started dating you while I was still legally married to his father."

Aaron slumped in his swing and ran a hand over his shorn hair. "I should have told you years ago how I felt. You never would have married that psycho if I had."

"I also wouldn't have my son," I said, tracking him across the playground. "If there's one good thing that's come out of this nightmare, it's Ari."

"He's a great kid," Aaron said, following my gaze.

"He's a miracle. He's the beauty out of the ashes of everything else."

The weight of Aaron's stormy eyes rested on me once again. "He's lucky to have a mom like you, Laur. You're the bravest person I know."

"Brave?" I scoffed. "I've been a complete basket case."

Aaron's jaw locked. "You're a 'complete basket case' with the courage to leave an abusive sociopath who put bruises on you and your son. You stood up to our entire congregation and all of their threats for exposing what Nathan downloaded at synagogue. You didn't back down when Rabbi Lebow kicked you out, slandered you to everyone including your parents, and tried to cover up Nathan's porn and lies. Don't tell me you're not brave, Lauren. Tell me anybody else who could have gone through all of that and *not* lose faith in God or be entitled to a meltdown or two."

"More than two," I mumbled, uncomfortable with his praise.

He rolled his eyes. "You know what I mean. You don't give yourself any credit, and that's probably because Nathan never did."

"But he always accused me of treating *him* that way," I said, my voice hardening.

"Nathan Fein is the biggest baby I've ever met. He's also a bully. I saw it at synagogue for a long time, but I didn't realize how bad it was until the porn scandal. He was a leadership kiss-up even before he got hired as the temple IT Director. Being at Rabbi's beck and call made him act even more self-important."

"I didn't know him back then," I murmured.

"You were away at college. I was still in high school."

"I'm surprised you remember."

"Nathan wasn't easy to forget. He made it a point to let you know your place in the synagogue. With anybody he thought of as beneath him or who wasn't Jewish," Aaron gestured to himself, "Nathan only acknowledged you when he needed something."

"Which is ironic considering his mother isn't Jewish," I said. "According to every traditional rabbi I know, Nathan wouldn't be considered Jewish either."

Aaron smirked. "Better not let facts get in the way or anything."

I rolled my eyes. "You know, I don't think I ever realized

how much Nathan treated me like some sort of trophy wife until after we separated. In this case, the prize was me being Jewish on both sides. One time, he referred to me as a 'thoroughbred' in front of the other elders, and I wanted to punch him. It felt so degrading."

Aaron pressed his lips together and his hand clenched tighter around the chain of his swing. "He *wishes* he deserved someone like you."

I reached out to cover Aaron's hand with my own. "I'm over it, I promise. I find it morbidly humorous more than anything else. Nathan was just like most people in that synagogue obsessed with all things Jewish."

"Maybe it's because I'm a gentile, but I will never understand why so many Messianics worship the whole 'Jewish identity' thing. They don't seem to care if you have a real relationship with God, treat others like garbage, or cover up sin. As long as you're *Jewish*, that's all that matters, right?"

I winced at the bitterness in his tone. "Aaron, you know that I'm not into all of that self-worship, don't you? I didn't marry Nathan because he was Jewish by blood. I married him because I thought he loved me."

"It really doesn't bother you that I'm not Jewish?" he asked.

I waved him off. "You know me better than that. I never wrapped my value in being Jewish or not. I just want to follow Jesus as best I can."

He grinned at me. "It's still weird hearing you say Jesus instead of *Yeshua.*"

I smiled back. "I do it a little bit out of spite, to be honest. Everyone at Beth Shalom acts like saying His name in English is some kind of a curse word. It's ridiculous."

"Agreed," Aaron said. "I don't think I realized how weird it was until I stopped going. At the same time, I didn't realize how much it had become a habit. I'm not even Jewish, but going to a regular church still feels weird. It's like I saw something I can't unsee. I know so much of what Beth Shalom taught was wrong, but I can't help feeling like there might be some truth mixed in. Is it weird for you since you're actually Jewish?"

"I don't know. My spiritual identity was wrapped in believing in Jesus first, not in being Jewish. Everyone I knew at Beth Shalom who got caught up in the Jewish identity stuff had something to prove. Nathan grew up with a Christmas tree, and his father had no interest in Judaism. When their family got involved at Beth Shalom, suddenly, the Feins were trying to outdo and out-Jew everybody. His mother got the same second-class citizen treatment you did for being a gentile. She magically changed her name from Linda to Liora, and because of her last name, nobody questions if she's Jewish anymore."

"That must have been a while ago," Aaron said.

"We were both young and in school. I found out some of this from Nathan and some from Lior—Linda back when she was pretending we had a special mother-daughter relationship."

"Was this before or after she and the rest of Beth Shalom tricked you into marrying her son?" Aaron asked. "Sounds like lying is nothing new for the Fein family."

"Both," I said tightly. "Things went downhill after I caught onto Nathan's double life. The second I stopped falling for his phony repentance and empty promises, they turned on me."

"I'm so sorry, Laur."

I shrugged and sniffled down my tears. "I just don't understand how people who claim to love God can act this way. I don't understand with all the so-called 'prophetic words' they claim they get, the Bible verses they quote, and the worship music they play that they could choose to act this way. They know the Bible says how despicable their behavior is, but they justify it by blaming someone else and playing the victim."

"You know what Rose Margolin would say, don't you?"

"Leviathan," I said. "The nasty, counterfeit spirit of God that pretends it's holy but does the work of the devil instead. The shoe definitely fits."

Aaron raised a dark blonde brow. "I think you just answered your own question."

"Doesn't it seem too easy?" I asked. "You know, just throw a demon name at the situation and call it a day?"

"No, it just takes out all of the guesswork and overanalyzing you like to do," he said, grinning at me. "Also, you're a big softie, and you always want to see the best in people."

I smiled ruefully. "I think you know me better than anyone."

The longing in Aaron's eyes transformed the color from more gray to blue. I turned away and inhaled a deep breath.

"Lauren?" he asked in a pained voice.

"Aaron, I love you like a brother, but I just don't see you that way. You're torturing yourself, and I don't understand why. I'm not worth all of this. I can't promise that when everything is over with Nathan that I'll suddenly have feelings for you. Please, you need to move on. I hate the idea of hurting you."

"I'd rather be your friend than nothing at all," he vowed.

I opened my eyes, first to locate my son, and then to gauge his sincerity. "Are you sure about that? I see the way you look at me."

"I've waited for thirteen years. I will wait for you to be free from that psychopath as long as this is something you might want too."

"Aaron, I don't know if anything will change after the divorce. It's hard to think about a new relationship while I'm still trying to get out of this one."

He nodded. "We can talk about something else if you want."

Once again struck by the disparity between my husband and my friend, my eyes clouded over. Telling Nathan that something hurt my feelings or annoyed me was like sticking a bullseye on myself. He'd go out of his way to hit the target for his own sick amusement. With Aaron, I knew he'd walk on broken glass if it meant protecting me. My mouth slid into a frown, once again wishing that things could be different for all of us.

"Mommy! Come watch me," Ari called from the top of the slide.

Eager to end my silent anguish, I hopped from the swing to get a closer look at my son.

"Ooh, that's really high," I said.

"But I'm brave," Ari replied, flashing me a grin.

"Yes, you are, honey."

Aaron came to stand beside me, silent and watchful. My heart squeezed as if crushed inside an iron fist. How I wished I'd recognized Aaron's feelings for me beneath the longing glances I'd chalked up to my own imagination. Maybe things would have been different if Nathan hadn't come along and ruined my life.

"Aaron! Aaron!" Ari called. "Can you see me?"

"Yeah, I see you, buddy," he replied. I smiled as I noted the tension missing from his handsome face. Lately, Aaron had seemed so much older and weary. At that moment, however, he simply looked like my old friend from the temple youth group.

Ari stood at the top of the slide ready to go down for the twentieth time. In slow motion, I watched him trip over his shoe and fall down the slide screaming.

"Ari!" I yelled, frantically running toward the bottom.

Too late to rescue him, my son went face first into the mulch and came up bleeding.

"Mama!" he wailed as blood ran out of his mouth.

"Ari!!!!" I scooped him up from the ground, my heart pounding in my ears.

"Mama!" he kept crying. Blood covered both of us within seconds. I saw Aaron talking to another mother who handed him something. He rushed back over to me and Ari.

"Here," he said, holding out baby wipes. "The lady over there said she's got plenty more if we need them."

"Thank you," I whispered. I managed to hold back my own hysterics in order to keep my son calm.

Ari continued to cry into my shoulder, now soaked with blood, saliva, and tears. Aaron led me toward a bench so we could better assess the damage.

"Buddy, can you open your mouth for me?" I asked.

Ari shook his head into my shoulder.

"You and your mom are the two strongest people I know," Aaron said as he rubbed Ari's back. "Buddy, we need to see what happened in your mouth and why it's bleeding."

"Hurts," he whimpered.

I felt my heart shatter into a million pieces. "Please, baby. Let Mommy see your mouth."

Ari shook his head.

Shocking me, Aaron began to dance around like a gorilla. He pounded his chest, made ridiculous monkey noises, and soon, Ari was sniffling and giggling into my shoulder.

"Me. Open mouth. Super big," Aaron said, widening his mouth as large as possible. "Ari do too. Ari be big gorilla like Aaron."

Tentatively, Ari opened his mouth.

I saw shock in Aaron's eyes before he hid it again. "Ari is good gorilla," Aaron said, followed by more grunts.

"I'm a good gorilla," Ari repeated, giggling.

"Time to clean up the messy gorilla," Aaron said, handing Ari some wipes and then the package to me.

While my son busied himself with his hands, I leaned in toward Aaron and asked, "How bad is it?"

"You know that old kid's song about all I want for Christmas?" he asked. "Not the Maria Curry version, but the really old one that says I want a hippopotamus too?"

"Yeah," I said warily.

"Well, now you know what Ari can ask Santa to get him this year."

CHAPTER 6

"So, you decided to come back," Poppy teased. "We didn't scare you off after your first day at Culver?"

"My son knocked out his two front teeth on the playground last night. If I can handle that, I think I can deal with the crew here at the office."

"Oh no!" she said, her hand flying to her heart. "How bad was it?"

"Blood everywhere. We got home looking like we survived prom night with Steven Kline's *Corey*."

Poppy winced. "Oh, I hate that movie, and I'm so sorry, sweetie. That sounds awful."

I sighed and flopped into my chair. "Also, the kid is only four and a half, so he's going to be smiling with a big window for another three years according to his pediatrician."

"Can I get you a coffee from Vincenzo's? My treat. Sounds like you could use one."

I pulled a box of chai teabags from my desk drawer. "I think I'll stick with this."

"Not a coffee drinker?" she asked.

I shook my head. "I was always told coffee is an acquired taste. Fortunately or unfortunately, I never acquired it."

"Carly used to be the same way."

I smiled, remembering that tidbit both from her manuscript and conversations during Bible study. "I like the smell, just not the taste. I'm not a fan of bitter food anyway. Hate cranberries, don't like dark chocolate, and grapefruit is the devil."

Poppy's eyes widened in shock and amusement. "Okay, so make sure to give milk chocolate and sugar water for the newbie. Got it."

I laughed. "I'm not *that* bad, I'm just not into bitter flavors. One of my good friends, Charlotte, loves to drink sparkling water. I tried it once and nearly spit it out. I don't know how she drinks that stuff."

Poppy chuckled. "To each their own, I guess. Can I see the tea you've got? I've only ever heard of chai lattes. To be honest, I've never been much of a tea drinker."

"Sure," I said, handing her the box. "I love this stuff. The first time I ever had it was at a gas station in Israel with my cousin."

"Really?" Poppy asked, her eyes twinkling. "I've always wanted to go to Israel. What was it like?"

"Amazing," I said, happy to think of a time pre-Nathan. "My grandmother took me before she passed. I had family I'd never met before, and I hit it off with my cousin, Yoni. We fought like brother and sister, which was fun, and he was definitely handy to have around at the airport."

"Why's that?"

"Well, security is pretty tight coming in and out of Israel. When I flew over, they must have grilled me with ten different questions making sure I was who I said I was. Mentioning my *bat mitzvah* definitely helped. On the way back, Yoni dropped me off at the airport and just rattled off in Hebrew at both security checkpoints. They let me through like I was the queen of England."

"Wow," Poppy murmured. "Sounds like it helps to have connections over there. Jared has mentioned making *aliyah* off and on, but things have been so crazy since the world went on lockdown. He hasn't talked about moving to Israel in a while. I know it was a big thing at the Messianic synagogue."

I gave Poppy a tight smile. "Yeah, making aliyah was like getting into heaven at Beth Shalom. All of the Messianics I knew acted like Israelis were these demigods and emigrating to Israel was like gaining sainthood. I can't tell you how many national and regional Messianic conferences I attended where they brought the Israelis on stage just to applaud them for gracing us with their presence. I don't think it's much different than the well-intentioned, pro-Israel Christians who act the same way about Jewish people in general."

Poppy rolled her eyes. "Jared used to eat up all of that nonsense back when he was at Beth Shalom. I hated listening to him talk about 'the importance of maintaining a Jewish identity' when his behavior was still as horrible as it was before he left us."

I frowned, remembering details of Poppy's book combined with the persona Jared Levine had maintained as my synagogue elder.

"It's all in the past now," she said, noting my expression. "The man you see at Bible study is the man he is at home."

"Glad to hear," I said. "Rabbi Lebow loved to praise the leadership team from the *bima*. I never realized how much he was gaslighting the audience into believing the hype until I watched a few of the online services during quarantine."

"Why would you watch them at all?" Poppy asked. "You know what monsters those people are, Lauren. You barely survived it. Why would you want to cause any trauma triggers?"

I shrugged. "Morbid curiosity, I guess. It's been so long, and I knew they'd never let me back in the doors of that place. I wanted to see if anything had changed. Probably more denial and hoping that God had gotten ahold of some of them. I've heard rumors of so much turnover there, and I wanted to see who had stayed."

Poppy smiled at me sympathetically. "How was it?"

"Like I'd never even left. The usual group of cronies was there, of course, and they've just plugged new faces into the same old machine."

"Wow."

"The scariest part was seeing Rabbi Lebow pander to an empty room the same way he did to a packed house every week."

"Really?" she asked, surprised. "How does that even work?"

"During his sermons or the announcements, Rabbi likes to name drop and point to people in the pews. Because of all of the social distancing laws, they could only have ten people in the building during the pre-recorded sermons. So, he's still pointing and throwing out names like he always did, only it looks idiotic because everyone knows the room is empty."

"Does anybody realize the emperor has no clothes?" she asked with a raised eyebrow. "Jared wouldn't watch any of the online videos. He said it made him nauseous."

"It took me a while to stomach the sound of Rabbi Lebow's voice when I first started. It was funny seeing him on mute because his mannerisms are so exaggerated and ridiculous. He mugs and points at the camera like a used car salesman."

Poppy chuckled. "Based on Jared's description of him, that

sounds pretty accurate. He said Rabbi Lebow enjoys the sound of his own voice."

"He also laughs at his own jokes. It was cringey back when there was an audience who gave him pity laughs. Watching him do it with an empty room showed me how Beth Shalom is the same rehearsed performance week in and out. Then, there's all of the brainwashing that happens throughout the service."

"Brainwashing?" she repeated. "I heard that accusation from the old rabbi at my Reform synagogue. I always thought it was just scare tactics to keep anybody from looking into the New Testament or Christianity for themselves."

"I don't mean brainwashing about Jesus," I clarified. "The main focus of Beth Shalom will always be Beth Shalom. They tell you how great everything is at the synagogue. The leader recites the same shtick about their *beautiful* music and *timeless* liturgy and Rabbi's *powerful* sermons. Every word of praise out of their mouth is completely scripted no matter who is leading the service."

"Scripted? What do you mean?"

"All of the flowery adjectives are literally written on the papers a service leader reads as he goes through the liturgy. The older members have some more polish, so it almost sounds genuine when they're praising the congregation. The newer ones read it off the paper like robots. It's the exact same words, week in and out. Every aspect of the service or a synagogue event has some hyperbolic description to go with it. Rabbi Lebow isn't all that creative either, so he just recycles the same few words for everything. If there was a drinking game every time you heard the word *exciting* to describe an event at Beth Shalom, you'd be passed out on the floor halfway through the service."

Her mouth fell open. "Wow, it sounds like you really studied this, Lauren. Did it do you any good? Do you feel like you have closure now?"

I sighed. "Not really, to be honest. I mean, I'm glad I can see Beth Shalom for the self-promoting, theater production it is, but I don't have more peace knowing what I always suspected. Mostly, I just want to know why God hasn't shut the place down yet. It's also frustrating that people I know and love can't see through the sham."

"I guess they just see what they want to," Poppy said, mulling over my words. "Maybe it's a comfort for them to hear the same things at home with the synagogue being closed. A lot of the members at our Reform temple attend services because of their familiarity with the liturgy. It might not be a Messianic thing but just a Jewish thing in general."

"Well, Rabbi Lebow likes his liturgy too. He also loves parading the two Israeli men in the synagogue when they do any of the chanting. Since they're native Hebrew speakers, it makes the liturgy sound more authentic to visitors. Before the Israelis joined the synagogue, the Hebrew was getting butchered, even by the Jewish-born members of the congregation."

"How did you realize that?" Poppy asked. "I thought you grew up going to the Messianic synagogue."

"I had a Reform bat mitzvah. We used to attend traditional services pretty regularly before my parents got saved. I can still chant the liturgy based on how I learned it in Hebrew school. None of the guys at Beth Shalom ever could." Suddenly struck with a terrible revelation, my shoulders jerked back. Wow," I murmured.

"What?"

"Every time one of the Israelis led liturgy, Rabbi Lebow cracked the same tired joke about them not pronouncing the Hebrew correctly. I just realized he was projecting."

"Projecting? How?" she asked.

"Well, obviously, the Israelis can speak and read Hebrew," I said. "That's why they're brought on stage like living Bible characters. Rabbi Lebow fakes the Hebrew he knows and uses this super cringe, fake Israeli accent. You will never catch him reading from the actual Torah because he doesn't know how."

Poppy's dark eyes widened into huge circles. "Are you kidding me? The *rabbi* doesn't read Hebrew? How is that possible?"

"It's sort of an open secret at Beth Shalom. Rabbi Lebow came out of the Jesus movement in the 1970s. Almost none of the messianic rabbis his age has any formal Jewish training, but since they were Jewish believers in Jesus, they decided to call themselves *rabbis* instead of pastors. There's this weird obsession with placating the traditional Jewish community and wanting to be accepted as Jews rather than 'Christians.' They act like it's the lowest insult if they're ever called one."

"Probably because they were rejected by their parents for believing in Jesus," Poppy surmised. "It makes sense. Jared would go ballistic when I called him a Christian."

"Based on everything I saw, fighting for their identity and 'not assimilating' turned into identity worship. Like I said, I grew up Reform, and then my parents got saved when I was ten. I had my bat mitzvah at Temple Beth Ami in Hillcrest because Beth Shalom didn't have a bar mitzvah program at that point. Honestly, I'm glad I did. The kids who came after me at the Messianic synagogue all faked their Torah readings."

"What do you mean they faked it?" she asked. "Not that we

would have had Natalie's bat mitzvah at Beth Shalom anyway, but what would have been different?"

"Poppy, those kids weren't reading from the Torah. Yes, they took the Torah scroll out of the ark and did all the pomp and circumstance of marching it around the congregation. The cantor would give some spiel about how special the Torah is and go over all of the ornamentation on it. Then, they'd slap a nasty piece of paper with transliterated Hebrew on top of the scroll. The kid would pick up the pointer and then pretend they were reading the Hebrew off the actual scroll instead of English phonetics."

Poppy was irate. "But that's *the Torah*! How could they disrespect it like that! What about smudging the actual scroll? Lauren, I can't even comprehend that. I mean, how can you go on about Jewish identity and then do something so blatantly disgusting and dishonest? To me, that's Judaism 101, and I was never that religious. That's like slapping a fashion doll on a crucifix and calling it Jesus."

"Good analogy," I said dryly.

"Did anybody know that the kids weren't really reading Hebrew? Surely the parents had to know, right?"

"The families all played along with the charade. I only found out when the bar mitzvah director passed away and a friend of my parents took over the program. He was outraged just like you, and he said he would personally make sure the kids knew how to read Hebrew and never disrespect the Torah like that again."

"Well, thank goodness for that at least," Poppy said. "Does the guy still go to Beth Shalom? Would Jared know him?"

"Derek left the synagogue when my parents told him the truth about Nathan. He's a sweet guy. I keep telling my friend

Charlotte to give it a shot since they're both single now, but she doesn't trust anyone from Beth Shalom other than me."

Poppy looked intrigued. "Didn't I meet Charlotte at your birthday dinner? You've mentioned her a few times."

"She knows Jared from his leadership days, and she's pretty leery of the Margolins' Bible study because of it. She was hurt by people at the synagogue, including her ex best friend."

Poppy frowned. "Jared's not that person anymore. Charlotte could read it in my book if she wanted to.

"She did," I said quietly. "She also heard about Carly's book draft from me."

My brand new coworker exhaled a weary sigh. "What a mess. I know why Carly wrote what she did, but it's been hard."

"You guys worked it out, right?"

"We've agreed to disagree on some details. In the end, it doesn't matter. Carly's happy with Joe, and I'm happy for both of them. Jared and I worked through what we needed to, and our marriage is stronger because of it. Carly's version was a lot of humble pie for me, especially seeing her take on things. I know it's part of her story, and I can't begrudge her that even though it's a less than flattering picture. Leah Halpern had plenty to say about my book after I published it, so I'd be the pot calling the kettle black."

I studied Poppy, noting a prominent white streak amidst her dark brown curls.

She caught my gaze and grinned. "You like the wisdom high-light? I think it's my permanent reminder of God knocking me upside the head."

I laughed. "I just thought it looked cool."

She rolled her eyes. "That's because you're still a baby with your natural hair color. I keep threatening Jared that I'm going to just go platinum blonde."

I grinned. "What did he have to say to that?"

"He told me if blondes really do have more fun, then he was all on board."

I cracked up laughing. "Maybe it's a good thing you and Charlotte aren't friends. You guys would get in so much trouble together."

"I hope I get to know her one day."

I had a feeling the two of them would set the world on fire.

CHAPTER 7

I PULLED MY CAR INTO THE POLICE PRECINCT parking lot specifically designated for child custody exchange. Because of Nathan's track record of abuse, my lawyer had negotiated two Saturday visits a month from 9 am until 5 pm. It was my sole opportunity for free time that didn't require a babysitter or dodging Nathan's spies around my parents' house. I hated being around Nathan and the hatred glittering in his eyes, but even worse was having to hand my son into his keeping for any length of time. Nathan had enough sense to avoid further physical abuse with Ari and potential jail time, but subtle jabs at me were commonplace. Ari was too little to understand what his father meant with his passive aggressive barbs, but he was not too young to ask me what Daddy meant when he said, "Mommy needs to start listening to God."

The familiar knot in my stomach tightened as I checked the time on my dashboard clock.

"9:15," I murmured. "He loves making me wait."

"Mommy, are you okay?" Ari asked from his booster seat in the back.

"Daddy's just running behind," I said, forcing a smile on my face.

My son frowned. "Why is Daddy always late?"

I inhaled a deep breath, not sure how I should answer. Nathan had been crying wolf about me "alienating" him from Ari. Of course, his abuse, chronic lateness, and overbearing correction of our son couldn't possibly be the culprit for Ari's distance from him. Walking the tightrope of validating my son's feelings without adding any fuel to Nathan's imaginary fire felt like canvassing a minefield...blindfolded. I never knew what Ari would repeat or what Nathan would twist into an accusatory text message. What I knew for certain, however, was that Nathan would project all of his toxic behavior onto me and then paint himself the victim of the sadistic games he played.

"I'm not sure, buddy," I finally said.

Ari exhaled his own sigh. "I'm bored."

"I'm sorry, sweetie. Do you want me to put a new movie on my phone?"

"No, I just want Daddy to be here."

With my own day planned to read, relax, and do nothing, I actually agreed with my son.

At 9:25, I began texting Nathan. At 9:35, I received a text stating that he had stopped off to get a special treat and would be fifteen minutes later than his text. At 9:55, Nathan finally pulled into the parking lot sipping on a gourmet coffee from Charred Cups.

Breezily, Nathan got out of his car as if nothing was amiss. I didn't expect an apology, nor did I receive one. Instead, I noted the actual time and emailed myself the details to use for custody documentation.

"Hey, pal, are you ready to go?" Nathan asked Ari.

I averted my eyes so he wouldn't see me roll them at his syrupy tone.

"Mommy said you got me a surprise. Can I see it?" Ari asked.

"Oh, uh..." Nathan faltered. "I'm not sure why Mommy told you that, Ari, but she made a mistake. Sometimes she gets confused. I know she didn't mean to get your hopes up, pal."

I glanced sharply at Nathan, sickened and stunned at how easily he set the trap. Clearly, the *special treat* had been for himself, but he wrote the message to be intentionally misleading.

"No mistake at all," I said coolly. "Sweetie, I'll make sure to have something for you when you get back. Why don't you go have a good time with Daddy, and I'll see you at five, okay?"

Ari looked up at me with big brown eyes. "But I want to stay with you, Mommy."

I inwardly sighed, desperately wanting the same thing but also knowing I needed the emotional break from motherhood to simply breathe.

"What happened to his teeth?" Nathan demanded. "Why didn't you tell me about this, Lauren?"

"I did tell you," I snapped, feeling the familiar anger well up. "It was in the same text where I asked you when you plan to deposit money for child support again. How many times do you plan to 'forget' we need money for clothes? Obviously, you didn't bother to read my message."

"And obviously, you like to discuss grown up issues in front of our four year old in order to turn me into the villain. It's bad enough he asks for you the entire time he's with me."

Knowing our conversation was recorded on police surveillance helped calm my growing anger. It took a mountain of self control to keep my emotions well hidden. Nathan's go-to tactic of *reactive abuse* had certainly served him well with the Beth Shalom faithful. Before I'd emotionally cut myself off from the relationship, Nathan had twisted my frustration at his betrayal and framed it as "abuse" toward himself. He played the role of clueless victim trying to make our marriage work and painted me as the unforgiving shrew. The part he deliberately omitted was how many times he'd poked and provoked me before he'd finally gotten me to break. My *reaction* was always the problem, not Nathan's intentionally horrible behavior.

Calmly, I replied. "You asked a question. I answered it."

Nathan mocked me with his facial expression. His concern for Ari witnessing a "grown up" conversation only extended one way. It was a silencing tactic, and one I'd learned to disregard.

"Daddy, stop being mean to Mommy!" Ari frowned with all of his pre-school might.

Nathan flustered in outrage. "I see you're poisoning our son with your lies."

Though my insides quaked with adrenaline and old trauma triggers, the year plus separation had also allowed me time to heal from being under constant, daily assault. I ignored Nathan's landmine insinuation and side stepped it instead.

Focusing on my son, I rubbed a comforting circle on Ari's back. "Mommy will be back at five to pick you up. Then, we're gonna have dinner with Grandma and Grandpa."

"Dinner with who?" Nathan asked.

"I wasn't talking to you."

"He's still my son."

"And it's still none of your business. Butt out."

"He's my son. I have a right to know," he insisted.

I turned my back on Nathan completely. "Okay, buddy, give

Mommy a hug and a kiss." I bent down to enjoy those cherub cheeks. "I love you, Ari. Be a good boy, okay?"

He nodded dutifully. "I love you, Mommy. Stay with me and God."

Tears smarted my eyes as I caught Nathan smirking. I knew exactly what he wanted to say and the condescending tone he'd use. Thrusting the thought aside, I stood to my full height. Ari still clung to me, and I grudgingly walked closer to Nathan. He took the opportunity to brush against me to grab ahold of Ari's arm, and I jumped back.

"What are you afraid I'm going to do?" he taunted. His dark eyes held malicious glee.

I silently prayed for God's protection over my son as I stared back and didn't flinch. "Make sure you're back by five. Last time, you were thirty minutes late."

Nathan's petty victory ended quickly at the reminder of yet another "failure." The accusation was already forming on his face.

"Of course, we'll be on time," he scoffed. He secured Ari and began leading him to the backseat of his sedan. "Unlike some people, I honor the commitments I make."

I nearly laughed out loud at his hypocrisy, but I thought better of it. Pointing out Nathan's coffee cup, let alone seven years of porn addiction and abuse, would be an exercise in futility. Instead, I imagined the lavender bath salts awaiting me in my tiny tub.

"Bye, buddy," I called, waving to my son.

Ari looked dubiously from his father to me. I could no longer hear them as Nathan got in the driver's seat, but I recognized the overly peppy mannerisms through the car window. Ari loved "fun daddy," and Nathan could turn it off and on at will. I heaved a sigh and walked back to my own car.

"Please protect him, Lord," I prayed aloud. "Please, let my baby have a good time."

I didn't feel any better after my prayer and decided to take a drive to Parkview instead of dropping directly into the tub. I'd been so busy learning the ropes at Culver that I hadn't made time to explore the area. Weekend traffic still kept things busy around the two malls near the Culver high rise, but it was no comparison to weekday rush hour. I took advantage of my free parking pass in the deck to traipse around the uptown area.

Walking past the main entry to my office high rise, I headed directly into the bustling intersection connecting Culver with the rest of uptown Parkview. As I turned the corner, the display window of a high end thrift store caught my eye. It had been a bridal boutique just a few weeks earlier, and I stopped to admire some antique candlesticks and a tea set.

"Shopping for relics?" a familiar voice asked.

I whirled around to see Grant Kaplan dressed in jeans, a chunky sweater, and a beanie. He looked much younger than he did in his office suits, and I struggled with my unwanted and involuntary flush of attraction toward him.

"Hi," he said, offering a cheeky smile.

I gave a quick wave and then used the window display to look anywhere other than his chocolate brown eyes. "Poppy said she found some really cute *chachkas* in there."

"Chachkas?" Grant repeated. "Are you Jewish, or has Poppy been teaching you Yiddish during your down time in the marketing department?"

A genuine smile formed on my lips as I glanced back at him. "My grandmother's house looked like a museum with all of her knick knacks, so it's a word I grew up hearing. My mom rolled her eyes about 'Bubbe and her chachkas' all the time."

"Ah," he said with a wider grin. "So, you're MOT?"

"Member of the Tribe?" I asked. "Yes, I am. And Kaplan is a pretty dead giveaway too."

"It wasn't the nose?" he teased.

I shook my head and laughed. "Your nose is perfectly fine."

"So is yours."

As we smiled at one another, the silence stretched and so did our prolonged eye contact. No matter what his own feelings were, something about Grant Kaplan felt dangerous to me. My initial gut instinct was not unfounded even if I didn't know why. I took a step backward.

"Anyway, it was nice seeing you," I said breezily.

"Lauren, wait." He reached out a hand toward me.

I retreated further.

Grant frowned. "I don't understand why I seem to make you so uncomfortable. Please, tell me what I'm doing wrong so I can stop."

"You're not," I said, stumbling for words. "I just...it's me."

"I like you," he finally said. "I liked you from the first time I saw you. That doesn't mean I'm interested in something more than friendship."

"You're not?" I blurted out.

"I have a girlfriend," he said, his posture relaxing. "She just took our dog to the groomer up the road." He pointed two blocks away from where we stood. "We're supposed to meet at The Soaring Scone in five minutes for brunch."

"Well, then why did you...?" my voice trailed off. I fought back tears. "I don't understand."

He smiled gently. "Do you have a lot of male friends?"

"A few. One really good one, I guess."

"Well, word of advice," Grant said, lowering his voice and taking a step closer, "not every man who talks to you is trying to get in your pants, and sometimes 'interest' in you, is exactly that. *Interest.* Your eyes tell a story before you even speak. It's hard not to be fascinated by that."

Embarrassed, my cheeks flushed.

On cue, an attractive blonde joined Grant's side and looped her arm through his. She was taller and fuller figured than me, and she left me feeling completely inadequate by comparison. I exhaled a soft chuckle at my own silly thoughts. Clearly, I'd been projecting my own feelings and completely misreading Grant's displays of *interest.*

"I'm Lauren," I said, extending my hand to her. "I work at Culver."

The split second wariness in her gaze melted as her blue eyes traveled between me and Grant. "Hayley," she replied, shaking my hand. "Nice to meet you."

"Lauren works in the marketing department," Grant said as he slid his arm around his girlfriend's waist. "I guess you're already done with Lucy."

"She's our cockapoo beagle," Hayley said to me. "Cutest dog ever."

I smiled back. "I'm sure. Grant said you guys are on your way to go eat, so don't let me keep you. I was just window shopping."

"Hope you find some cute chachkas," Grant said with a wink. "Something to make your bubbe proud."

I turned my focus to his girlfriend. "Hayley, it was really nice to meet you."

"You too," she said, but with significantly less enthusiasm than a moment earlier.

She tightened her grip on Grant's arm, and I took an additional step toward the antique shop. After a tiny wave, I avoided Grant's eyes and feigned interest in a wooden dollhouse just inside the front window.

I waited for them to leave before I heaved a sigh of relief.

I began the trek back to the parking garage, my sudden interest in exploring Parkview all but forgotten. At that moment, I wanted nothing more than to go back home and stick to my original plan of a bubble bath and maybe re-read Poppy's book, *Tikkun Olam*. She'd recently given me some tidbits she'd excluded from her memoirs, and I wanted to compare the two versions.

In the meantime, I walked and scrolled on my phone to check for updates on Instantpics. Only half paying attention to my surroundings, I bumped right into Grant Kaplan for a second time that morning.

"Oof! Sorry!" I exclaimed as my cell phone clattered against the pavement. I froze as I recognized his beanie covered head bent over to grab my phone.

Grant swiped it from the ground moments before another passerby nearly stomped on it. His chocolate brown eyes seemed just as surprised to meet mine when he stood up. "Hi," he said. "Didn't think I'd be seeing you again until Monday."

My overly analytical brain wanted to create a million different meanings of his words other than the obvious. I found my voice and managed to eke out, "Hi."

After an awkward beat with Grant staring into my eyes, he cleared his throat. He ran a hand over his beanie as he broke eye contact. "Hayley thought she dropped Lucy's leash over here, but I didn't see it."

My gaze darted toward the entrance of Chick-A-Yum next to the antique shop. "Is that it over there?"

The tension on Grant's face melted into a smile. "As pink as it can be," he said.

I walked the few feet over to the bench and returned with the leash in hand.

Grant held out my phone as a peace offering. "Care to swap?"

"Thanks," I grinned. "I hate how much of my life is tied up in that thing, but I need it. Obviously, your fur baby needs her leash too."

"It's a necessary evil," he said with a wink.

When Grant's fingers brushed mine handing me the phone, an electrical current passed between us. It didn't make sense, I didn't like it, and when I looked at Grant, I saw the shock in his eyes too. *Interest* I could buy as an excuse, but there was also an awareness I wasn't too naive or broken to miss.

I made sure our hands didn't touch when I handed Grant the leash. Determined to squash any attraction under two tons of reality, I said, "Your girlfriend is lovely. I hope you two enjoy your brunch and the rest of your day."

Grant's smile no longer reached his eyes. "Thanks, you too."

I pushed my cheeks into a forced smile, sidestepped Grant, and walked as quickly as I could back to my car. I caught Grant in my periphery as he entered The Soaring Scone Eatery while I continued past the restaurant toward the parking deck elevators. He rubbed his beard in agitation as the door closed behind him.

As soon as I was safely ensconced within the closed elevator, I looked up and said, "God, what in the world is going on?"

CHAPTER 8

"Charlotte," I groaned into my phone, "what's wrong with me?" I kept my phone on speaker as I submerged deeper into my tub full of bubbles.

"There's nothing wrong with you," her cheery voice blasted into the bathroom. "You're waking up. You've been a poor, deprived wife living with an emotional vampire who nearly sucked out your entire soul. This is all perfectly normal."

"Normal? I'm legally married to Nathan, one of my best friends is in love with me, and suddenly, I'm three timing it with some dude from work who already has his own girlfriend. I don't think the Karducci sister reality show is even this ridiculous."

"No, those Karducci girls are much worse," she deadpanned. "Although, I think Nathan's mother could give Mama Karducci a run for her money."

I swatted a poof of bubbles. "I'm being serious, Charlotte. I'm such a mess!"

"Well, I wasn't joking," she retorted. "First of all, get it out of your head that you're cheating, okay? Your marriage is dead and has been for a while. The only thing that's left is signing paperwork."

"That still doesn't make any of this okay. I feel guilty as heck."

"I'm not telling you to go sleep with anyone," Charlotte said matter-of-factly, "or even date. But you've kept all of these romantic, goo-goo feelings under lock and key for a long time. You feel like it's 'cheating' because you've noticed there are other men on the planet who are attractive. You're allowed to notice things, Lauren."

"What about lusting with the eyes? Didn't Jesus call that adultery?"

"Look, the reality is that you *are* still legally married to Nathan. You can't go more than half in with Aaron or even Spider-Guy-work-hottie because you're *not* the type to cheat or just have a fling. Being attracted to someone or having an emotional connection is not the same thing as acting on those feelings. Yeah, you're being *tempted,* but don't equate that with actually doing the deed."

I refused to let myself off the hook so easily. "Well, aren't we supposed to take our thoughts captive?"

"Lauren," she said with strained patience, "are you sitting at home fantasizing about your Peter Parsons lookalike coworker?"

"Of course not! I hate that I feel anything at all."

"Well, there you go," she said, and I could imagine how she would have extended her french-tip, manicured hands while making her point.

"There *what* goes?" I asked.

"It's hormones, babe. It's an attraction. It happens. Grant's taken. You're legally taken, and you've also got Blue Eyes who's been gaga in love with you for centuries."

"But what does it *mean*?" I whined.

"It means you're *alive*. That's it. It means you're going to have to watch how much alone time you spend at the office with Grant since you guys are chemically into each other. 'Interested' in you as a person is one thing. The second that pheromones get involved, everything changes."

"Well, what do I do? I can't just flip a switch and turn off biology. Aaron would probably do cartwheels if I could."

"Laur, if you were in a wonderful marriage, this Grant guy probably wouldn't be a blip on the radar. Heck, if you were free and dating Aaron, you probably wouldn't pay this guy much attention either. Yeah sure, you might think your coworker is attractive, but that's as far as it would go. The problem is that you've been in the exact opposite of a loving relationship, and for whatever reason, you can't take Aaron out of the friend zone."

"I'm listening," I said. "Keep going."

Charlotte inhaled and then continued. "Rick was a negligent, selfish creep, but he never went out of his way to torment me the way Nathan does to you. Anything short of abuse is going to feel like gold—even if it's just a dog turd instead of a grenade. Unfortunately, you still wind up with a handful of poop. The problem is, you don't have any other past boyfriends for comparison, and you're also not in a position to start dating and find out. Aaron is stuck in the same friend zone that Grant is—even with the history you two have. At this point, they're both technically a possibility, but that's all it can be for right now."

Frustrated, I said, "Well, then what the heck can I do, Charlotte? This feels impossible!"

"It means you either find out some things that are very unattractive about Grant Kaplan to combat the hormones, or you use the same self control you used today. You're attracted to an adult male. Yay, you're still alive," she quipped, "but it doesn't have to 'mean' anything more than that. You're not even thirty-one yet, kiddo, and you were denied any kind of a healthy sex life. It's normal to be curious, have urges, and to be attracted to grown men of the opposite sex."

"So, I didn't fail? I'm not some two-timing skank who's lusting after every man she meets?"

"No!" Charlotte exclaimed. "Girl, if this was a test, you aced it!"

"Then, why do I feel so awful?"

Her tone softened. "Kiddo, you've been made to feel ashamed of your emotions and God given desires for so long. No matter what that lying pig has done, you are still an honorable woman who committed to her wedding vows despite everything Nathan's done. You don't need to repent for being a human or even for being tempted with Grant. You didn't act on it. As far as I know, you're not writing poems in your diary about chocolate brown eyes or running your fingers through his hair. You're also not prancing around Aaron in cute little outfits trying to tempt him or use him to feel better about yourself."

I laughed and sniffled away tears. "You always know what to say to make me feel better."

"That's what friends are for."

"Thank you," I whispered.

"No sweat. Enjoy your time off and go binge watch something to take your mind off all of this testosterone, okay?"

"Okay."

Changing the subject, Charlotte said, "Ooh, before I forget, I've got a virtual coffee date with this new guy I met on Love-JewSchmooze.com. It happened last minute, but the girls are with Rick this weekend, so I figured, why not?"

That piqued my interest. "Tell me more!"

"Well, he says he used to be Messianic, but now he considers himself just Jewish."

"Oh," I said, my enthusiasm dropping considerably.

"He says he still believes in Jesus, but he was burned pretty badly."

"Did he go to Beth Shalom?" I asked.

"I didn't get that far," Charlotte said. "I mean, it's not like it's the only Messianic synagogue around here, but I'd rather not talk about it anyway. He's cool though. He's forty-five, has two adult children, and I'm not sure what the deal is with their mother. It hasn't come up yet."

"What made you agree to coffee so soon, even if it's just drinking a cup into a camera? Don't you usually vet these guys to see if they pass the one week, 'hot and heavy' test?"

Charlotte chuckled. "Yeah, most of them quit messaging me after a week, or even a few days once they find out I won't put out. It's plenty of flirty texts and getting to know you banter until they realize there's only so far that they'll 'get to know' me."

"That's horrible!" I gasped.

"Meh, it's how people are these days. Doesn't mean I like it, but just because you initially find someone attractive doesn't mean you'll have enough in common once you get past the fun, surface stuff. When I first started online dating, it seemed like every scrap of attention meant stars and roses and happily ever after. I would start imagining how the girls and I would fit into whatever living situation the guy had."

"When did you become such a romantic?" I teased.

"I didn't," she said. "I just wasn't used to positive male attention. At first, I think it was just filling the void that Rick left. I wanted to prove that I'm not dead or damaged goods.

That part felt good. But after enough bozos and their bottle rocket interest, I learned to take it slower and just enjoy things for what they were instead of fantasizing about what they could be."

Taking her words to heart, I said, "I don't want to invent a future with Aaron just because he's always been there, and I know he has feelings for me. It feels too easy, you know? Sometimes, I wonder about it, but how do I know it's not just because of the convenience or the fact he seems like the complete opposite of Nathan?"

"Kiddo, I don't think you're going to know until you're fully free to find out. What I do know, however, is that stewing about it day after day isn't helping you. It's adding stress you don't need."

"I know," I said morosely. "I mean, I absolutely love the guy. We've been friends for so long. I guess it's easy to want to fall in love with someone who already loves me."

"Go easy on yourself, Lauren. Breathe. Enjoy your time off today and make sure you take time just for you. It's not selfish to rest and ignore your to-do list. I gotta go, but I know you're going to get through this."

I took Charlotte's advice and did exactly that. After the incident with Ari on the playground, I knew I was getting into dangerous territory by imagining a new happy family with Aaron. He was almost *too perfect*, and it killed me not knowing if I'd ever muster the feelings I knew he deserved.

After binge watching my favorite comfort tv show from the mid '90s, I pulled back into the precinct parking lot at five. I knew Nathan would find some way to keep me waiting, but at least I could use my own punctuality as proof of solid parenting. As expected, I received a text at 5:10 that he and Ari would be at the precinct in ten minutes. I automatically made it twenty and read an eBook on my phone app. Knowing Poppy's past struggles with medieval bodice rippers, I didn't want to disclose my secret penchant for zippy romcoms. I avoided the super steamy ones, but there was something to be said for escaping into a world where the heroine was some plucky extrovert, usually clumsy and a bit neurotic, and who was basically the total opposite of me.

Lost in my latest novel, I saw Nathan's car pull up, but my foggy brain remained within the confines of my novel. His knock on my car window nearly gave me a heart attack.

"Good book?" Nathan smirked, reading over my shoulder.

I turned off my phone and hid my scowl as best I could. I knew Nathan didn't actually care what I was doing. He was simply being nosey because he felt he had a right to know my every move. I rolled down my window. "It's fine, thanks."

"Hi, Mommy!" Ari called from just beyond his father. He wore a paper hat from the Parkview Diner where Charlotte and I indulged during our cheesecake get-togethers.

I beamed at my son, and he returned my grin. I resisted the urge to open the driver's side door into Nathan's abdomen even though he wasn't supposed to stand so close to my vehicle.

I twisted to open the passenger door behind me. "Hop in the car, buddy. We've gotta get you home for a bath."

"Daddy can help you," Nathan crooned, stepping in front of our son.

"I can do it," Ari said, trying to push his father. Nathan transformed into an immovable wall, and Ari quickly grew frustrated. "I can do it myself, Daddy. Get out of the way!"

"No, son!" Nathan barked. "You need to show Daddy respect. You don't just shove me. You need to ask me nicely to move."

"Daddy, stop!" Ari wailed.

"You need to say, 'Please, Daddy, may I open the door?' and *then* Daddy will move," he said primly.

Ari's cries of protest intensified, but Nathan wouldn't budge physically or otherwise.

This time, I did fling my door open. Not enough to clip my son's father, but enough to get his attention.

"Move," I said coolly. "You had your time. You were late. The visitation time is over. Let Ari get into the car and stop aggravating him."

"Aggravating him?" he scoffed. "You're the one teaching my son it's okay to defy his father and his God given authority."

Done with the shenanigans and with Nathan, I blocked him from the back door and opened it for Ari. My son gladly climbed into the car.

"That wasn't necessary," Nathan said with a sniff of indignation. "I was going to let Ari open it once he could speak to me respectfully."

"Who do you think you're fooling? There are police cameras everywhere. You deliberately got in Ari's way."

"What do you mean I deliberately got in his way?" he said, his eyes wide in faux innocence and effrontery.

I refused to be baited into a pointless argument. I simply stared at him with pursed lips, hoping he'd leave.

Repeating my words again, Nathan said, "I didn't *deliberately* get in his way. Ari was getting violent and pushing me. I was simply trying to teach him how to use good manners. Obviously, it's another area where you're failing as a parent."

"Whatever."

I tried to sidestep Nathan back into the driver's seat, but he blocked me.

"Get out of my way," I grit.

"You need to lose that nasty attitude when you talk to me.

Clearly, our son is learning all of this horrible behavior from your poor example. Apologize, Lauren. Now."

Ignoring his ridiculous command, I said, "You need to get out of my way, or I will scream and let a police officer move you for me."

His eyes narrowed. "Are you finally admitting that you've manipulated the police and government agencies against me?"

"No," I said, inching closer so I could get into my car, "I'm telling you that your actions have consequences, and bullying me in front of the police station will not go well for you."

As if by divine orchestration, several officers exited through the glass doors of the precinct behind us. Immediately noting the tension between us, a female officer called, "Is everything okay over there?"

Nathan's eyes welled with instant tears. "I just want a few more moments with my son. Why does the system always punish loving fathers?"

The officer glanced over at me.

Not missing a beat, I said, "He was supposed to be here twenty-five minutes ago but showed up late. I'm trying to leave now, and he won't let me."

"Sir, you heard her. If your visitation time is over, you need to leave."

"Your lawyer is going to hear about this," Nathan hissed, ditching the waterworks.

"The part about you being late again, or the part where you tried to prevent me from getting into my own car?"

He pursed his lips. "The part where you denied me the right to parent my son by alienating me and empowering Ari to rebel against me."

By sheer supernatural strength, I kept my calm. I glanced at the set of officers who seemed closer than they had moments earlier. Nathan saw them too and made an elaborate show of saying goodbye to Ari by switching back to his "fun daddy" persona. After wasting another three minutes trying to coax a smile from our son, the officers were now within a few feet of us.

"Sir, you need to leave now," the female officer repeated. "You've said your goodbyes."

Nathan's eyes flashed hatred as he stalked back to his car. I knew his revenge would be both swift and vicious. I took a calming breath and then forced myself to smile for my son. Ari spent the whole ride informing me of all the fun things they'd done that day, and I ground my teeth wishing that I'd made a son with anyone other than Nathan Adam Fein.

CHAPTER 9

THE FOLLOWING DAY AT WORK, MY HANDS SHOOK AS I finished the kiss of death email from my attorney, Marianne Abbey. Slipping through my trembling fingers, my cell phone clanged against my desk like a gunshot.

"No," I said. "No, no, no, no."

The sound of squeaky loafers and jangling keys preceded the arrival of the mighty Margolin to my office space of just over three weeks.

"Lauren?" Ted asked. "Are you okay?"

The look on my face must have said it all because he rushed into the room. "What happened? Is it Nathan? What has the cretin done this time?"

I shook my head as I began to shudder. I knew right then if I didn't leave the office, the silent sobs would rip out of me in uncontrollable wails.

"Come on," Ted said. He ushered me toward an empty office away from the cubicles. "Lauren, you stay here as long as you need, and be sure to text Rebecca, Poppy, or whomever when you're ready." He handed me my cell phone. "Do you want me to stay?"

My breathing labored into dry heaves, and I rushed past Ted to throw up in the women's bathroom. When my legs would no longer support me, I sobbed and gasped for air as I sunk to the bathroom floor. I snatched some toilet paper to wipe my mouth.

"Oh God," I moaned. "Why? Why!" I screamed.

Timidly, I heard another voice ask, "Are you okay, child?"

I hastily flushed the toilet and scrambled to my feet. "Who's there?" I croaked.

"Miss Belle," Culver's mama hen replied.

Not knowing where else to turn, I opened the stall door.

Miss Belle's eyes widened. "Baby, you look white as death. Come over here and sit down away from those nasty toilets." She gestured toward a cushioned settee opposite the bathroom sinks.

Obediently, I sat while she grabbed a container of hand sanitizer and a wet paper towel. She held them out for me, and I got to the business of cleaning my hands and my face. When she tenderly stroked my shoulder, I let loose silent tears.

"It's okay, baby," she soothed, "you just get it all out, ya hear? Ain't nobody else in this bathroom but you, me, and Jesus. He sees you, honey. You're not alone. Not now or ever."

I nodded as I continued to sob, my heart rent in two.

The entry door to the bathroom suddenly flung open, and the sound of sensible work flats skidded against the tile floor.

"Lauren," Poppy said breathlessly, "are you alright? Ted just flagged me down in the hallway. What's going on?"

I held up my phone and handed it to her. Marianne's email was left open on the screen.

I didn't have to look up to know Poppy's reaction. The sharp intake of breath followed by half uttered curse words spoke loudly enough.

"Unreal," she finally said. "That is so unbelievably cruel and disgusting. That woman is evil and so is Nathan's attorney for wasting *her* time and *your* money."

"She took all of it," I choked. "Marianne took every penny. I have nothing."

"You have a job," Poppy said, crouching down on the opposite side of Miss Belle. "You are not penniless or friendless, and we are all here for you. You are *not* alone! Nathan is not going to win, and let's hope this is the trash taking itself out. Jared and I both know a few divorce attorneys, and Carly's father has a few hundred on speed dial."

"But how?" I moaned. "How could Marianne abandon me like this? She knows what I've been through. She knows what Nathan is."

"All you are to that woman is a paycheck," Poppy said. "You've mentioned how the only thing Marianne Abbey seemed to care about was your money. She just proved that. I also think it might be worth it to contact the billing office of her firm and go over those invoices they sent."

"They'll just tell me it's justified billing," I said, blowing my nose. "I tried once already. I got steamrolled by Marianne. She insisted on being there for a video call, and then she argued against everything I said. I got off the call and cried to Aaron about it. She and the billing department rep played good cop bad cop."

"Did the rep seem sympathetic on the phone?" Poppy asked. "Do you think the good cop shtick was just a routine?"

"I could tell it wasn't the first time they'd run a client over like that. The two of them just kept listing off price after price for all of the legal services they said I'd need. Neither one of them cared that I had to wipe out the savings account we set up for Ari. All they wanted to know was how much *more* money I had in my bank accounts."

"Disgusting!" Miss Belle hissed.

I continued, "Marianne argued against every point that I made or acted like none of my grievances were her fault. The billing rep tried to cover for her too. She pretended Marianne would *want* to help me, but the billing department would be the one tying her hands if I didn't give them more money."

Poppy blew a raspberry. "What a load of manure! It definitely sounds like they have a pre-set routine for manipulating dissatisfied clients. Which firm did you say she was with?"

"Witherspoon & Thorne."

Poppy's eyes lit up. "Jared used that firm when we were going through our divorce. He took a closer look at his invoices and saw where he had been double billed by his attorney and the paralegal even though the firm states in writing they won't do that to their clients. When we were negotiating to get both of our attorneys paid off, Jared did some digging online and found out that W&T has a reputation for padding their time. He found complaints from clients and even former employees about how much pressure they receive to rack up their 'billable hours' from management."

"Really?" I asked.

"Yeah. Jared and I went over the invoices and sent a fourteen page .pdf disputing the charges and citing emails from the attorney or the paralegal with conflicting legal advice. W&T gave him back four hundred dollars like it was a king's ransom, but it was better than nothing."

"That's still a lot of money for me," I said, feeling my first glimmer of hope that morning.

"It's worth a shot," Miss Belle added.

I sniffled back the rest of my tears. "What am I going to do about a new attorney, Poppy? We're still in the middle of proceedings, and I can't fight this on my own. Nathan's lawyer is a shark, and his parents are paying for everything. I don't have the money to fight back even if my parents completely finance the GAL for me."

"Don't you worry about that," Miss Belle said. "My Mama and I will be glad to help."

Stunned, I turned to face her. "Are you serious? You don't even know me."

"Baby, yes I do!" She cupped my face in her palms. "I've been reading all about you since Rebecca published her book six years ago. I know what kind of no good scoundrel you married."

"It's too much money," I objected. "How would I ever pay you back?"

"You don't, child. You accept a gift from a sister in Christ and then praise our mighty God for providing for you. The Bible says not to withhold good from people when it's in your power to give it. My mama and I would have been sitting on our last stimulus check not sure why God had blessed us again."

"Miss Belle, I can't."

"You can and you will," she said in an unmovable tone. "You find yourself a good attorney, and then you tell me where I can send the money. This is a blessing for me to help you and your son."

Although the tears flowed again, this time it was relief rather than abject terror. Miss Belle excused herself to call her mother and her bank, and Poppy sat next to me on the bench.

"How is this possible?" I asked, looking at her through my tears. "I went from hopeless to hopeful so fast. Nathan stopped his support payments again, and he's not answering any of my texts."

"Isn't everything court ordered at this point?" she asked. "It's not legal to withhold money from you and Ari, and Nathan's already skating the line with the stalking by proxy."

"Marianne had mentioned an emergency hearing, but that got put on the backburner once Nathan's attorney signed off on the GAL we suggested. I know Nathan is trying to bleed my resources dry so that I can't fight him anymore. He's been sitting on our proposed temporary agreement for over a year so I can't nail him in writing for not supporting us. It's so unfair, Poppy. He should have been arrested for what he did at Beth Shalom. That filth he downloaded, not just at synagogue, but at home…"

"I don't even want to imagine," she said.

"You couldn't possibly," I replied, "and trust me, you don't want to know."

"How did he get away with it when the police investigated everything?"

"His record was clean, and Nathan played clueless like he always does when he's in trouble. He also gave quite a show about how he'd betrayed God with his 'weakness' and had lost his wife and son because of it."

"The same wife and son he put bruises on?" she asked pointedly.

"That didn't happen until after the arrest. He had been physical with me a few times, but nothing that left marks. I came back to the house after Nathan fooled me with his phony repentance act."

"I'm so sorry," Poppy said, wrapping her arm around my shoulders. "That is so much for one person to endure, especially someone as young as you are."

I thought back to those horrible weeks of anguish after I'd fled our home to stay with my parents following the police raid at Beth Shalom. Ari was still in diapers, and at that point, I hadn't realized Nathan's depravity was a calculated, willful choice. At the moment, I just needed the comfort of my parents.

"How long has this been going on?" my mother had asked me over shared mugs of tea at her kitchen table.

"What do you mean?"

"You know exactly what I mean, Lauren. Nathan says everything Rebecca Margolin wrote in her book is a bunch of slander, and I'll admit that I used to believe him. What's the truth? How long has he really been struggling with this?"

I didn't want to think about *Tabula Rasa* or how perfectly Rebecca had described Beth Shalom and its IT Director. Reading about my husband from the perspective of his ex-fiancée, Jessica, had also troubled me greatly. One of them was lying about why that relationship failed, and I no longer believed it was Jessica Goldstein's fault.

"Nathan always referred to his porn addiction as an 'ongoing issue,' but he made it sound like it was something he would conquer with God's help."

"Which clearly wasn't the case," my mother said through tight lips. She set her mug down. "I can't even drink this right now."

"That's not even the worst of it," I mumbled.

"There's more?" she gaped. She reached across the table to take my hand. "Baby, what else haven't you told your father and me?"

"They all knew, Mom."

"Who's *they*?"

"Rabbi Lebow, Liora, Matty, and the entire Beth Shalom leadership team. They all knew about it. They told me I could help save Nathan if I would just stick by him and keep praying."

"Help *save* him?" my mother choked. "Since when is it your

job to save anyone? It's not a wife's job to save her husband from his own choices. It's the husband's job to repent of his sin and get his heart right with God. I've heard Harvey Lebow preach that message a million times. Why is Nathan's addiction your responsibility to fix instead of Nathan's problem to deal with?"

A knock on the front door followed by my buzzing cell phone interrupted me before I could respond.

"It better not be that lowlife," my mother growled.

I picked up my phone. "It's Aaron. He says he's outside."

My mother glanced over to the clock on her wall oven. "It's nearly midnight. What's he doing here now?"

"He says he wanted to check on me. He texted me earlier, but I never got a chance to reply." I held up the phone so she could see for herself.

My mother's hazel eyes scanned the message before they rested on me. "It's up to you, honey. I know the two of you have been friends since you were kids, but you're not up for company right now. You need rest. Aaron, of all people, should understand that."

"No, I want to talk to him. Nobody else from temple will answer my messages."

"That's strange," she murmured.

"I thought so too. You don't think Rabbi Lebow would have told them not to respond, do you? You told me about the sermon he gave last week about gossip—except we both know it was really about damage control and making sure people don't find out what Nathan did. It would be naive to pretend it was anything else."

My mother's grim expression turned cold. "I don't know what to think anymore, Lauren. Harvey called for a leadership meeting two weeks ago, but he excluded your father and me.

Then, he gave that horrible sermon the next Shabbat. Your father and I have felt blindsided by all of this *chazarai*."

I had to agree with my mother's choice of Yiddish, feeling that "reprehensible trash" was an apt description for all that had transpired. Mulling over her other words, I frowned. "What do you mean Rabbi Lebow excluded you and Dad from a leadership meeting? Why would he do that? You guys have been *shammashim* for years, plus, it was your son-in-law who was caught downloading pornography. Shouldn't everyone have been comforting you guys instead of just Liora and Mark?"

"Or you," my mother said pointedly.

"I know," I said, biting my lip, "and I can't help but feel like they're blaming me for all of it."

My mother's expression soured further. "As far as being in leadership, I assure you, that the title of 'shammashim' is mostly in name only. Your father and I aren't responsible for all that much—despite what Harvey likes to tell everyone from the pulpit. We've never been part of that inner circle like the Feins or that new guy, Jared Levine. Speaking of Jared, he didn't seem to care for Harvey's sermon either. He left in the middle of it like he was going to be sick, and then we didn't see him at Shabbat services this week."

I waved off my mother's last comment as I barely knew the man. "I just don't get it, Mom. We've been a part of Beth Shalom for so long. I thought Rabbi liked me."

"I don't get it either, honey, but I don't have a good feeling about any of this."

My phone buzzed again, and I replied to Aaron before I thought better of it.

"Is he still here?" my mother asked.

"Yeah. He said he just wanted to make sure I was okay."

"Why don't you go out on the porch so you can have some

privacy? Your dad is such a light sleeper anyway. Talk to Aaron, and you and I can talk again in the morning." She stood up from the table, kissed my forehead, then padded her way toward the stairs.

When I opened the front door and saw the concern on Aaron's face, I fell into his arms and wept.

CHAPTER 10

AT SOME POINT DURING MY HYSTERICS, AARON LED me to my parents' front porch swing. I continued to cry against his chest as he held me.

He didn't say much, not that Aaron Davis was much of a talker anyway. As he sat in silence, I poured out everything. The lonely nights. Nathan's excuses for being on the computer at all hours. Countless weeks in a row of begging for my husband's time, attention, or even joining me in bed. Not that I was always disappointed given some of his baser appetites. I left that part out for Aaron. When I mentioned the neglect in our love life, my friend finally spoke up.

"Are you serious?" he growled.

"Am I serious about what?" I picked up my head from Aaron's chest almost in a daze. Confused by the expression on his face, I frowned.

"He made you beg for sex?" he asked incredulously.

Embarrassed by how much I had revealed, I tried to brush off his concern. "I didn't say I *begged* for it."

I had never seen Aaron look so fearsome or angry. "You just told me Nathan kept 'forgetting' to come to bed. Did you mean to go to sleep, or did you mean something else?"

Blushing, I looked down. "Both."

"Unbelievable," he muttered.

"I mean, he wasn't *always* like that. Sometimes it was okay. Nathan said my nagging all the time made him avoid me."

"More like your husband was too busy looking at kids in their underwear to give any attention to his grown adult wife," he spat. "None of that was your fault, Lauren. None of it."

"Aaron, it wasn't—" I caught myself, not wanting to argue or provide further details of our dysfunctional love life. "Nathan does have a hard time taking responsibility for things, but I know he feels guilty about his addiction. Maybe it was the guilt that made him avoid me. Nathan does eventually apologize, though, and he always thanks me for showing him grace."

"I thought the idea of repentance was to turn away from your sin—not keep repeating it."

I frowned. "It's an addiction. I don't think it's that simple."

"How can you defend this?" he demanded.

"I'm not defending anything! It's disgusting! I hate it. It makes me feel cheap and degraded, especially knowing that I *wanted* him in my bed, but he was too busy fondling his precious laptop...and himself."

At that last painful admission, I began to weep again.

Aaron's defensive posture slumped. "Laur, I'm sorry."

I waved him off. "I know you're right. It just hurts. Rabbi and everyone else in leadership act like Nathan's addiction is somehow my fault. They have no idea that it was the husband— not the wife—withholding sex, and I'm too embarrassed to tell anyone. Aaron, you're the only person who knows, and I'm begging you, please don't say anything."

He looked aggrieved. "Lauren, it doesn't matter whether you were withholding sex or not. There is *no* excuse for the garbage that Nathan downloaded. It was underage girls! How could anybody at Beth Shalom think that it's okay or your fault? It's obvious that Nathan is the one with the problem."

I shrugged, not wanting to think about the implications.

My friend was not done. "Rabbi keeps Nathan at synagogue at all hours of the day and night. Has he or any of the other leaders bothered looking in a mirror? Maybe if your husband was able to spend a decent amount of time with his wife, he wouldn't need to look at that trash. Is anyone at Beth Shalom planning to take responsibility for *their* part since they'll blame anybody for Nathan's porn addiction except for *Nathan*?"

I shook my head.

Aaron sighed wearily. "Is he going to jail?"

"I don't know," I said, looking down at my clasped hands. "The police seem to believe Nathan's story that he didn't know the girls were underage."

"Not that it changes what kind of a husband he's been to you. He shouldn't have been looking at porn no matter how old the girls were."

I looked into Aaron's stormy eyes that seemed more gray than blue.

"Do you believe him?" he asked.

"I don't know," I finally whispered. "I don't know what to believe anymore. I want to believe my husband is telling the truth. I vowed to love him for better or worse, but I just don't know how much more of Nathan's 'worse' I can take."

"Has any part of your marriage been *better*? You were so excited when you guys got engaged, but something's been off since you came back from your honeymoon. I didn't see you really smile until you found out you were pregnant with Ari."

My mouth opened and shut at that revelation.

Aaron continued, "You look happy when you're with your son, but you don't look that way when Nathan is around. Your body language changes completely."

Stunned, my hands fluttered in my lap. "I didn't realize you were paying that much attention to me."

"You're one of my best friends, Laur. It's my job to notice things, and I feel like there's more. Have things always been this bad?"

I wanted to look away from Aaron's probing eyes, but I was also tired of hiding Nathan Fein's dirty secrets.

"How long?" he asked again.

I sniffled back fresh tears. "The beginning," I whispered.

Aaron's eyes widened first in shock, then anger. "That was four years ago."

"I know."

"And it was never good? You suffered this long without telling anyone for *four years*?"

"Aaron!" I gasped. "It sounds awful when you put it like that."

"How else should I put it? This is a horror movie. You never deserved any of this. I thought you were in love with Nathan."

"I thought I was too," I said. "I've been trying to make it work since our honeymoon. Nathan acts so affectionate and loving at synagogue, and I kept thinking maybe it would change at home too."

His eyes flashed. "Yeah, he definitely likes being all over you when other people can see. Especially me."

"You?" I asked, searching his face. "What do you mean?"

"Lauren," he choked.

My brows knit in confusion. "Nathan thought you were possessive of me, but he didn't like any guys showing me attention. Actually, I kind of liked it because it felt like he was being a protective husband." I frowned as I began to recount instances of Nathan's supposed *protectiveness*.

Aaron noticed the change in my expression. "What?" he asked. "What's wrong?"

"Maybe I was wrong about Nathan."

"Wrong, how?"

"He didn't protect me at all, now that I think about it. I can't tell you how many times he would ghost me, and I'd have to go look for him. I told Nathan I felt ignored, but he accused me of not allowing him to have a social life. One time, he told me to get friends of my own and stop being so needy."

My friend sucked in a sharp breath, and I glanced up at him.

"You okay?" I asked.

He gave a tight lipped nod, but those stormy gray eyes flashed anger.

I shifted at the intensity of Aaron's gaze but pressed forward. "It confused me for a while because I was doing exactly what Nathan told me to. I found people to talk to while I was stuck waiting for him to finish making the rounds. I talked to plenty of women too, but Nathan got really bent out of shape if it was ever a man—even if the guy was married or just an old friend like you."

"Why?" he asked coldly, "because it would show what he deliberately withheld from his own wife?"

"Aaron," I drawled, "what are you saying?"

The man of few words communicated with eyes that had shifted from a cold gray to a warm blue. With a sinking feeling, I realized I had seen that look on my friend's face countless times over the course of our friendship. Denial set in as I refused to believe what sat before me. I offered a tentative smile hoping to ease the growing tension.

A frustrated growl tore from his throat. "I love you, Lauren."

My shoulders slumped in relief. "I know. I love you too, Aaron. We've been friends for a long time." I clapped a platonic hand to his arm.

"No, I mean, I *love* you," he said. "Not love like a friend. *Love,* like what your husband should be doing but isn't."

"Since when?" I gaped.

"Since always."

"Aaron, I don't...why are you telling me this now?"

"Because I can't take it anymore. I tried to be happy for you because I thought you were happy with Nathan. But you're not happy. You never were, and it's killing me."

His hand came up to brush the tangled mess of hair from my face, and my heart melted. I couldn't remember the last time Nathan had touched me at all, let alone with tenderness. When Aaron's hand didn't leave the side of my face, my mind screamed at me to flee. My starving heart, however, gobbled up every morsel like a feast. As much as I knew I should turn away, jump off the swing, and run inside, I couldn't. I didn't want to. The heady rush of male attention flooded my senses. How long had I been deprived of basic human contact let alone the desire I saw in Aaron's eyes?

The sound of my gasp lingered in the air as my friend of thirteen years made his intentions known. For a moment I gave in, reveling in the feel of passion rather than soulless duty. Nathan had never kissed me like that, and I now knew how it felt to be cherished, loved, and wanted while wrapped in a man's arms.

I also realized that no matter Nathan's sins against me, God would never bless what Aaron and I were doing.

I broke away from the kiss and stood on trembling legs away from the porch swing.

Aaron reached out a hand toward me. "Lauren."

"Don't," I said, my voice breaking. "I have to go."

"Lauren," he pleaded. "I'm sorry. That shouldn't have happened."

My eyes welled with tears. "Why?" I said, my voice cracking. "Why did you have to do that to me?"

"Lauren, I—"

I cut him off. "How do I ever tell Nathan what I've done?"

Aaron stood up to his full height, towering over me. "You didn't do *anything*, do you hear me? This was my fault, not yours. I knew what I was doing. You didn't do anything wrong, Lauren. This is *my* fault," he repeated.

I shook my head. "I should have left. I should have left as soon as I saw how you were looking at me. I shouldn't have let you kiss me, and I know I shouldn't have kissed you back."

Aaron took a step closer to me. "Don't blame yourself."

I jerked away, knowing I didn't have the willpower to withstand another gesture of comfort. "Why now?" I asked through tears. "What am I supposed to do? Everyone expects me to try to work this out with Nathan. How can I do that now?"

His expression darkened. "What do you mean?"

"Well, I mean, the Bible says believers shouldn't get divorced unless there's adultery."

"What do you think looking at porn is?" he spat.

"That's not the same."

"You don't think so? Didn't Yeshua say that if you lust after a woman with your eyes that it's the same as adultery?"

"Yeah, but—"

"And what about how Nathan has treated you the entire marriage? The Bible says husbands and wives shouldn't withhold sex from one another unless it's by mutual agreement and for prayer. How about all of the other cruel things that he's done to you?"

I faltered, knowing my confessions had barely scratched the surface. "Aaron, I—"

"And before you give me that song and dance about unsaved wives sanctifying their husbands, Nathan says he *is* saved. He knows he's living a double life. He's a liar and hypocrite, not an unbeliever."

"What about all things being possible with God?" I asked. "I'm supposed to believe that for my marriage, aren't I? And after what just happened, how can you judge Nathan for adultery when you kissed another man's wife?"

Aaron's mouth flattened as pain flickered in his eyes. "Is this what you want, Lauren? Do you want to stay married to him?"

"I don't know what I want," I said, my lips still tingling, "but I made vows in front of God for better or for worse."

Aaron's jaw rose in the air as he visibly swallowed what may have been the bitterest pill possible. "What if it doesn't get better? Ever?"

"I have to try, don't I?"

Without another word, my old friend turned on his heel and left. Once I heard his car drive away, I slumped back down on the porch swing and sobbed.

CHAPTER 11

"You're back!" Nathan exclaimed, grappling me into a bear hug a month later.

My hands stayed at my sides, not sure how to process the conflicting emotions within me.

"Lauren?" He pulled back to cup my face. "What's wrong?"

"What's wrong?" I repeated, sure I'd misheard him.

"Oh," he said, his joyous expression falling. "You're still upset about the *incident*."

I closed my eyes and inhaled a tremulous breath.

"I thought I'd lost my family forever," he said, his voice thick with emotion. "I thought I'd lost you and Ari." He broke off into a high pitched sob.

Moved by the sound of remorse, I peered into my husband's dark gaze. "How could you do it?" I whispered. "How could you hide it for so long and then lie to me?"

My husband turned away and ran a hand through thinning hair as his hysteria vanished as quickly as it had begun. "It's an ongoing issue, Lauren. You know that."

I frowned at the familiar words. "And how do you plan to fix it?"

"Fix it?"

"Yes, fix it. As in stop looking at porn. As in stop avoiding me in bed. As in stop pretending that what the police found at the synagogue is the only time you've looked at stuff like that."

"You don't sound very forgiving," he grumbled.

I pushed aside Aaron's words and memories of a kiss I'd nearly convinced myself was a dream. As much as I wanted to confess my own indiscretion and the hours I'd spent tearfully repenting to the Lord, I heeded the inner voice telling me to carefully guard this secret. While Nathan was quick to demand my forgiveness, he'd never been quick to extend it. I also knew he'd never liked Aaron or our friendship.

"Where's Ari?" Nathan asked, breaking through my troubled thoughts.

"With my parents. I wanted to meet with you alone first."

"I'll do anything to keep our family together." He looked at me with earnest eyes. "Please, just tell me I haven't lost you for good."

"You need help, Nathan. Professional help."

His expression pinched. "I can do all things in Messiah Yeshua who strengthens me," he quoted from *Philippians*.

"But you haven't been," I said gently. "Your 'ongoing issue' has been going on since before we got married. You need professional counseling."

"That's all secular garbage. I don't want a bunch of new age nonsense telling me to find the power within."

"Nathan, men struggle with pornography whether they're believers in Yeshua or not. Just because the support a counselor might provide would be 'secular' doesn't mean that it's automatically garbage. Plenty of men have successfully gotten help."

He rolled his eyes dismissively.

"Look," I said, my patience waning, "you've already read a bunch of books from Christian authors about struggling with pornography. Obviously, none of that worked. It can't hurt to try something else."

"I don't understand why God just won't deliver me. Doesn't He want me to be free? My mom says everyone is praying for my healing, but I don't see any changes."

The petulance of his tone shocked me.

"What?" he asked, searching my face.

"Are you blaming God for why you still look at porn?"

He looked initially affronted before his expression turned sheepish. "Well, He hates it, right? Why won't He help me?"

I took a step backward. "I don't think it works like that. You have to make changes too. I don't think God just snaps His fingers and then, poof, all of our struggles are gone. We're supposed to work out our salvation with fear and trembling, right?"

"Rick Williams says he got instantly delivered of it," he argued. "I'm sure your pal, Charlotte, has told you all about it."

I didn't like the acid in his tone at the mention of my friend, but I kept those thoughts to myself. "Actually, I wasn't aware Rick looked at pornography at all. Charlotte's never mentioned it."

Nathan paled.

"Regardless of the accusations from you or from Rick," I continued, "Charlotte and I do not spend our days trashing the two of you. Whatever Rick's private struggles might be, they've never come up."

"Uh, well, just, forget I said anything," he mumbled.

I raised my eyebrows. "Nathan, do you want this marriage to work or not?"

"Of course I do!"

"Well, then it's going to take *work*. If I wanted to lose fifty pounds, I wouldn't ask God to just suck it off of me. I'd ask him for the strength to eat less and exercise. Why do you think finally defeating this 'ongoing issue' is going to be any different?"

"Well, what work are *you* planning to do?" he countered. "Not every problem in this marriage is my fault."

I gaped at his audacity. "Are you serious right now? You're going to make this about *me* when I just had to deal with the police raiding our home and our synagogue? I had to stay with my parents because I couldn't deal with all of the gossip and people feeling sorry for you."

"You didn't 'have' to stay with them," he argued. "You could have stayed by my side and supported me."

I struggled against frustration with his childish antics. "The fact I'm even standing here instead of sending you divorce papers should speak volumes."

Nathan's lips pursed. "I'm just saying that, yes, I made a mistake, but it's not like you haven't made mistakes too. You can't just blame everything on me."

"I am not blaming you for everything," I said, my voice rising, "but you're going to have to start taking responsibility for *something*. I can't make this marriage work all by myself. I've already tried. And failed."

As if coming back to his senses, my husband spent the next few hours pouring his heart out. He confessed how his addiction had begun and how the guilt caused him to hide in shame. He wept about his own lack of confidence and how saving himself for marriage made him question his ability to be a good lover. He avoided any talk of our honeymoon and the horrible fight we'd had, and I didn't have the emotional energy to revisit that nightmare. He finally confessed he was afraid of me and my reactions to him.

"My reactions?" I asked. "You told me I hurt your feelings when I tried making suggestions in bed. You asked me not to say anything, and I haven't."

He nodded tearfully. "But that's just it. You don't give me any praise either. I know we had some struggles before Ari was born, but that's in the past. It's hard to know if I'm doing a good job when you're so quiet."

"We have a baby," I said, skirting around the real reason for my silence. "I can't exactly scream from the rafters. I'm not some chick in a…" my voice caught, realizing what I was about to say. Nathan's expression darkened. Cautiously, I asked, "You know that none of the stuff in pornography is real, don't you? People don't actually make love like that."

"How would you know?" he said. "You won't even try."

"We have tried," I said in a choked voice. "It feels perverted, and even Rabbi Lebow said he didn't think it was the best idea to improve our love life." It was, in fact, one of the few instances of Rabbi Lebow not giving Nathan carte blanche approval for all of his marital complaints. He'd been unable to hide his look of disgust before softening his reprimand of Nathan in marriage counseling. My husband had broken down in anguish, and the rest of the session had been spent calming him down.

"Would you try now?" Nathan asked. The hope in his voice along with the knowledge of his private desires caused me to physically recoil.

"I still have to work on trusting you," I said, looking into his eyes. "I told you I forgive you, but there's so much that's wrong with our marriage." Nathan's response when I refused to comply with his porn-inspired demands always resulted in him being extra critical of me and withholding any kind of affection.

"Don't you think that trying some new things in bed might help? All men have these desires, Lauren. It's not just me. Pornography wouldn't exist if there weren't men who wanted to do those things. No offense, but you're kind of being a baby about it."

Appalled, I said, "There's also a market for people who want to have sex with animals or children! Just because it's out on the internet doesn't mean that it's okay or normal. How can you tell me that secular counseling wouldn't be beneficial to our marriage, but imitating porn in our sex life would be? That makes absolutely no sense."

"Well, I'd be less curious about what else is out there if you'd be willing to be more adventurous. There's nothing wrong with it when you're married. Rabbi Lebow has a lot of wise counsel, but he's a little naive when it comes to stuff like this."

"Nathan!" I gasped.

"What?"

"Are you seriously trying to blame your porn addiction on me?"

"I never said that!"

"It sure sounds like it," I said, twisting my body away from him.

He tried to place his hands on my shoulders, but I backed further away.

"Look, I'm trying to be honest with you," he said. "I hated lying to you about the porn, but I didn't know what else to do. It says that husbands and wives aren't supposed to deny each other sex."

"I didn't deny you!" I fumed. "I had to beg you to come to bed."

"You denied me what I wanted."

"That is not the same thing," I spat, rising up in disgust. "You are *not* going to blame your addiction on me! You said you've been looking at porn since you were eleven years old. You were thirty-three when we got married. Watching all of that trash for so long has warped your mind. What makes you think any of it is normal?"

My husband crossed the room to face me, and his eyes bored into mine. "How do you know that it isn't?"

Overwhelmed and confused, my own defenses began to crumble at the constant onslaught to my arguments. I tried to consider Nathan's perspective, but when I recalled the instances where I'd indulged his darker fantasies, I remembered the sinking, slimy sensation of everything being all wrong. I also didn't like the current gleam in his eyes as he watched me internally struggle.

The words flew out of my mouth before I thought better of them. "Why are you smirking? None of this is funny."

His jaw fell open, but he recovered quickly. "I'm not smirking, Lauren. Why would you even think that? Do you think I enjoy upsetting you? That's so messed up!"

At that moment, that's exactly what it felt like, but the idea seemed too crazy to believe. I ran a hand through my hair and sat down wearily on the edge of the bed. Nathan and I had been at this conversation for nearly five hours, and it felt like round after round of the same thing. I was emotionally and physically exhausted. For a man intelligent enough to hold down a six-figure salary, I couldn't fathom why he acted so utterly clueless.

I exhaled a heavy sigh. "Can't you see that everything you want me to do is tainted by how you learned about it? You avoided me to watch that stuff on your computer. Why would I *want* to do anything that's just a reminder of how it kept you away from me all those nights?"

Nathan's eyes welled with tears to match mine. "I guess I never thought of it that way."

Wondering if maybe I was finally getting through to my husband, I looked up and met his gaze as he stood over me. "That stuff is fantasy. It's not real. I don't see how God is going to bless our sex life if it's based on the filth you see on the internet."

Nathan's lips pinched together, but he didn't break eye contact with me. "You may be right about that," he conceded.

At my own breaking point, I began to cry. "Honestly, I don't know when I'll feel safe enough to have sex with you again. I don't want you thinking about porn or wishing I was doing other things that I just don't think are right." I shuddered at the memories, still feeling dirty. "You're so stuck on the things you want, but it doesn't seem like you care that it bothers me. My feelings matter too."

"What if we just start here?" my husband asked, his voice turning husky. His hands cupped my face again, and he looked at me with the same tenderness he did before we were married.

Deep down, I knew my husband wouldn't change one iota. He was still the man who discarded me on our honeymoon because "everything's holy when you're married," even when I told him it wasn't. As he showered me with kisses that seemed to have more tenderness than the robotic efforts of the previous four years, I didn't need the passion of a few seconds with Aaron Davis to know the difference. Everything about Nathan Fein was for show or came with an ulterior motive. In that moment, however, I allowed my own wishful thinking to override the truth I didn't want to face.

Unfortunately, that same denial emboldened Nathan and his bullying tactics against me.

Two months after our reconciliation, my husband hit me hard enough to leave physical evidence of his anger. Back then, I'd made excuses for the bruises and cuts—it was my poor diet, my lack of iron, or my inability to keep my mouth shut that had finally made him snap. I apologized to Nathan for not being better aware of his bad moods and the stress of the police investigation. The first time he bruised our son, I told myself it would never happen again as Nathan tearfully begged me not to call Child Protective Services.

The second, third, and fourth times that Nathan bruised my face, Charlotte didn't mince words with me about it, but I blew off her concerns about my physical safety. She had just filed for divorce from Rick, and I accused her of wanting me to follow her lead. To her credit, Charlotte remained my friend.

The last time Nathan ever laid hands on me was the day after he'd "accidentally" bruised our son again, and I could no longer make excuses for what was happening. Instead of Nathan seeing the error of his ways, he'd gotten worse.

I had to rest in God's promises that no matter how long or how ugly this divorce would be, His plans for my life did not include subjecting myself or my son to a lifetime of cruelty. As for the commentary and judgment from the outside world, my survival took precedence over their smug, self-righteous opinions.

CHAPTER 12

"Lauren?" Poppy asked, snapping me out of my thoughts. "Lauren?"

I shook my head from the agonizing memories as I realized we were back in our office. The momentary crisis of Marianne Abbey had been solved, and I'd already reached out to Charlotte's attorney, Sondra Joyner, to vet her as a potential replacement. "Sorry," I said. "I didn't realize I'd zoned out."

"Did you finish the changes for Grant?" she asked. "He just sent me an email about his presentation. I told him I handed you the revisions because the mighty Margolin slapped another RFP on my desk."

"Oh," I said, clicking around on my computer. "Yeah, I made the changes, but I wanted to print and double proof everything before I gave it back to him."

She smiled at me. "It's going to be okay, sweetie. Why don't you go to lunch, and I'll finish up? It's already been a long day for you. I'll get your proof from the copier."

"But you just said you had to work on Ted's RFP," I said, confused.

She waved me off. "I'll let you know if you forgot a comma, but you worry too much. You've proven to be very good at your job, Miss Thang."

I chuckled softly. "This is when I can tell the generation gap between the two of us."

Poppy rolled her eyes. "Please, don't remind me how ancient I am. It's still crazy that my baby is only a few years older than your son."

"So, I shouldn't ask about Natalie babysitting for Ari anytime soon? After all, your oldest just got her license."

"Ugh, stahhhhp!" Poppy said, mimicking her teenage daughter perfectly. "I don't need any reminders that Natalie can't wait to grow up. Now, go enjoy some sunshine before it gets any colder outside."

I smiled back and then clocked myself as "at lunch" on the online, company phone directory. Armed with my e-reader and a homemade lunch, I sat at a table under the covered walkway separating the Culver high rise from the parking deck. I munched on my waldorf salad while wrapping up a semi-steamy romcom from a new author I'd found. Skipping over a few pages, I tried to get back to the humor and plot of the story with the characters' clothes still on their bodies.

"Hey," I heard Grant say. I recognized his voice before I even looked up.

Startled, I snapped the cover closed on my e-reader. "Poppy's got your revisions," I blurted out. The imprinted images of what I'd just read combined with Grant's presence made for a heady combination of imagining myself as the heroine and Mr. Kaplan as my amorous, billionaire boss.

"You okay?" Both eyebrows raised over his chocolate brown eyes that held a touch of amusement. "You seem a little jumpy."

"Fine." I forced a smile on my face. "Like I said, Poppy's got your revisions, so I'll see you later."

He studied me. "You're doing it again."

"Doing what?"

"Nevermind," he said with a rueful shake of the head. "I'll see you back in the office."

"Grant," I called after him.

He turned around.

"I'm sorry. It's not you, I promise."

He gave me a tight smile as his eyes drifted to my e-reader. "Good book?"

I blushed. "Yeah. I was a little embarrassed you caught me reading it."

"You mean it's not the Bible?" he teased. "Doesn't everybody in the marketing department read that on their lunch break?"

"How would you know about all that?" I asked. "Did you read all of the Culver marketing department memoirs too?"

He grinned. "Hayley did, so I did by default. She's obsessed. She calls them the *Parkview Chronicles*. After we ran into you on Saturday, she asked me if I thought you'd be publishing your own story."

The tension left my shoulders as Grant easily brought his girlfriend into the conversation. Visions of Grant and I tangled in a similar scenario as my book heroine faded from my mind.

"Lauren?" he asked. "Are you still with me?"

"Sorry," I said. "Sometimes, it's hard to switch from one reality to another. When an author knows what they're doing, I just get completely lost in the story. It takes a minute for me to snap back."

"Ah," he said, lifting his chin as his smile grew. "I take it this is a good author."

"She's definitely got a way with words and witty dialogue."

"So, why are you blushing?" he asked, amused. "What kind of novels are you reading?"

"Romance," I said quickly, "but not the super spicy kind. I'm not trying to read word porn." That last word hitched in my throat. Although Nathan would call me a hypocrite, I enjoyed the *romance* in my novels, not the explicit bedroom scenes.

"Word porn," Grant said with a laugh. "That's one way to look at it. Hayley likes to read all of the costume drama, bodice rippers. If she ever leaves me, it'll be for some British guy who dresses like Mr. Dancy."

"What do you know about Mr. Dancy?" I asked with a surprised smirk.

Grant laughed. "Are you kidding? Do you know how many times I've had to watch *Prideful Prejudice*? The *long* version? Hayley says she's been in love with Callum Frost since her British Lit class in high school."

"I think the whole world has been in love with Callum Frost since that movie. He was so good as Mr. Dancy, two other authors became gazillionaires writing novels just based on his performance."

"Ah yes, *Gidget Holmes's Diary*," Grant said with a playful eyeroll. "Another favorite of Hayley's."

I finally grinned back. "Sounds like you've seen that movie a few times too."

"Hayley and I have been together for almost three years, so yeah, maybe one or two hundred times."

"Are you guys going to get married?"

His eyes widened as they locked with mine. "What?"

I cringed and looked away. "Sorry, none of my business."

"You're fine," he said, "you just reminded me of my mother for a second there."

"Let me guess. She's probably bugging you for grand-children."

Grant gestured to the chair across from me, silently asking if he could join me. I nodded, and he smiled as he sat. "Good guess, by the way. It took her a while to warm up to Hayley, but they get along pretty well now. At this point, I don't think my mother would care if I married a dairy cow just as long as she got some grandchildren."

I couldn't hide my mischievous grin. "Moo!"

We both laughed, and I realized I liked the sparkle in Grant's chocolate brown eyes. I also liked knowing I'd been the one to put it there. The fact he was unavailable made him feel "safe." At least that's what I told myself as a surge of attraction and connection kept my eyes locked with his. He looked away first.

He cleared his throat. "So, do you think you'll write? Can I tell my girlfriend to expect another addition to the *Parkview Chronicles*? I heard rumors Carly Trautweig might be publishing, and Hayley has re-read the other three books I don't know how many times."

Letting my inner thoughts run aloud, I said, "I don't know if I'll actually publish. Poppy's book had more details than Rebecca's, and so far, my ex hasn't gone after either of them for defamation of character. Then again, this would be me telling our story instead of someone else's second hand version of it."

Grant raised an eyebrow.

I noticed his confused expression, but my own thoughts swept me away as I mused over the possibilities. "I mean, I could still publish under a pseudonym to protect my son, I guess, but anyone from our old synagogue could probably figure out who it is. I wouldn't be writing to publicly tar and feather Nathan, but they'd all assume that anyway."

"Lauren?"

My eyes snapped to Grant's face, and the bottom fell out of my stomach. Of course, now he would know exactly who I was beyond the new hire in the marketing department. I'd just outed myself as that "poor girl" married to Nathan Fein chronicled in Rebecca's, Taylor's, and Poppy's published memoirs.

Grant rubbed his beard before speaking, and I recognized it as a sign of agitation. "It's obvious you've been through a lot," he began, "but I never would have guessed." His eyes shifted toward the table. "I'm so sorry."

"Sorry for what?"

Grant still didn't meet my eyes as he continued to stare at the table top. "I mean, if your story is close to what was put in Rebecca's book and also Poppy's, then my heart legitimately hurts for you. Hayley always wondered what happened to your character."

I exhaled a bitter laugh. "I'm not a fictional character, and neither of them were exaggerating about what Nathan has done. There's a lot more they don't know, to be honest. You mentioned the rumors about Carly publishing her memoirs—and it's true—but I made her promise to wait."

"Why does she need to wait?"

Thinking of Aaron and what I'd read in her draft, my cheeks heated. "My story ties into Carly's, and she even quoted my request asking her to hold off on printing. I have to wait until my divorce is final so Nathan can't use it against me. Carly had me beta read the manuscript to make sure I was okay with everything she'd included."

He finally ventured a gaze at me. "You seem a lot more peaceful than I would be in your shoes. You said your marriage was worse than what was published in the other books, and I can't even imagine the kind of pain you're in. I'm sorry I asked about writing your own book. I can see how thoughtless that was."

I swallowed down the lump of emotion in my throat. "Grant, you don't need to apologize. You had no idea. I know Poppy's story was all about God saving her marriage, but my story is different. It is what it is."

"Do you wish it wasn't?" Catching himself, he added, "You don't have to answer that."

"You didn't offend me. I've already heard all of the sermons from my old rabbi how 'divorce shouldn't even be a word in your vocabulary.' I used to believe that too. Unfortunately, when you're married to someone who thinks deliberately hurting you is a game, there's no amount of loving them, praying and fasting for them, or even sacrificing your own happiness that's going to make them change."

Grant's deep set eyes grew even larger on his face. Impulsively, he reached his hand across the table and squeezed mine. I gave a light squeeze back before withdrawing my hand to wipe the tears from my face.

"Thank you," I whispered.

"For what?"

"For caring," I sniffled. "For not lecturing me or giving me some stupid speech about how you hope we can work things out."

"Look, I don't know you that well, but I can tell you're a good person. My dad is a clinical narcissist, and I saw first-hand what it did to my mother. She's not perfect by a mile, but my mom suffered so much because of him. I also know that she protected me and my brothers from a lot more. You're brave to get away from your ex, and if you do decide to write, I think your story will give courage to a lot of other women."

His last statement brought on a cascade of tears, and I sobbed in my chair. I was surprised when I felt Grant's hand on my back. He knelt beside me, and I finally glanced over to see him watching me with concern on his face.

"There's hope on the other side," he said, his eyes holding mine. "I promise. My mother is living proof. My stepdad is a good guy, and he loves the heck out of my mom."

I smiled down at him. "I know. It's just a constant battle in my head. There are days when it feels like it's always going to be this endless misery of never being free from my ex."

Grant's hand stilled on my back. The air began to feel thick between us, and when my eyes inadvertently darted to his mouth, he stood up.

"I should get back to the office," he said.

I nodded. "Sorry for the outburst. Probably the last thing you needed, right? Weepy female coworker oversharing her problems." I exhaled a sigh and went in search of a napkin to blow my nose.

"Don't apologize, Lauren. It's obvious you're going through a lot. I just don't think I'm the best person to talk to about it."

I balled up my used napkin and then dropped my e-reader into my purse. "Yeah, you have your own stuff to deal with. I didn't mean to dump all of that on you."

"Well, yeah, but that's not what I meant."

Something in Grant's tone caught my attention. He rubbed the back of his neck and fumbled for words.

"You okay?" I asked.

"You said Poppy had my revisions, right?"

"Yeah," I drawled. "Are you sure you're okay?"

"Fine," he said, his voice sounding choked. "Look, I don't

want you to feel bad for talking with me. I promise I won't be sharing any of your information, including with Hayley."

I stood up and took a step toward him, but Grant took a step backward. "What's wrong?" I asked. "Usually, I'm the one who's skittish and overthinking everything, but now, you're...oh," I said, cutting myself off. It became painfully apparent my secret crush on Grant was not so secret anymore. I took my own step backward this time.

"I have a girlfriend," he said, "and you still have a husband. Obviously, nothing is going on, but you know how everyone at Culver loves to gossip."

"Right," I said, doing my best to hide the disappointment I knew I had no right to feel.

Grant pressed his lips together and nodded. "So, I'll see you back in the office?"

I couldn't help but meet his eyes one more time, wondering if I was crazy for thinking I saw more in Grant's behavior than what his words led me to believe. Despite Charlotte's advice to keep my thought life clean, lonely late nights had resulted in imagined conversations leading to imagined kisses and more. It was a horrible torture, and one that made interacting with real life Grant rather than the fantasy version harder to manage. As long as we were simply coworkers, I could justify my behavior as a harmless indulgence that had no chance of becoming reality. Seeing a connection beyond acquaintanceship felt like a fire that would burn more than just my overactive imagination.

"See you around," I said with a forced smile.

Grant's brow furrowed, but I wasn't given much time to over analyze what he was thinking. He turned and walked back to our office high rise, and I exhaled a shaky breath once he departed. For my own safety, I knew Poppy needed to handle any of his requests for the marketing department.

CHAPTER 13

"I DIDN'T KNOW WHO ELSE TO TALK TO ABOUT THIS," I said a week later, absently swirling a finger on the to-go cup lid of my tea. The warmth of the container felt good on my ice cold hands. I cast a glance at my coffee date seated in the brown leather chair next to me.

Taylor Horner eyed me over the rim of her own cup as she took a quick drink. We sat in a secluded corner of Vincenzo's Cafe, both of us sipping on something other than coffee. Even though Taylor was seven or eight years older than me, she still looked to be in her late twenties. Her hair was styled in a cute pixie cut, and she used winged eyeliner to emphasize her large, greenish brown eyes. She didn't wear much makeup beyond that, and she still retained her Florida tan after her recent move back to Parkview with her husband and family.

"Your text sounded pretty serious," she said. "I remember when I sent a similar 911 message to Rebecca. Of course, mine had to do with a dating crisis."

I didn't know how to respond, so I sipped on my tea.

Taylor exhaled a soft chuckle. "It can't be as bad as a pre-Abigail, Kyle Goldstein, can it?"

"Oh no, it's definitely worse," I said with a self deprecating laugh. "My friend, Charlotte Williams, says that everything I'm feeling is pretty normal, but that doesn't make it any easier. Also, I'm not 100% sure I believe her when she says that it's okay to feel this way."

"Does she go to the Margolins' Bible study? I don't think I've met her."

"And you probably won't," I said. "Jared Levine knows Charlotte from Beth Shalom, but she says she's done with organized religion."

"Does she still believe in Jesus?"

I nodded emphatically. "Totally. She was just hurt really badly by Beth Shalom and the people there."

"You were too," Taylor said, gesturing toward me, "but you still go to Bible study."

"To be fair to Charlotte, everyone at the Margolins' group knows what a slime Nathan is. That's been common knowledge for a long time—even before everybody started publishing their books. The group has several former members of Beth Shalom. Abigail and another friend of mine got the Bible study to help me move to a safer location last year. Charlotte didn't have any of that. She was on her own with her two daughters. Her mother lives locally, but she has a lot of health issues."

"Oh," Taylor said. "That's too bad. Does Charlotte still need help? Maybe we could talk to Rebecca or Poppy."

I shook my head. "No, Charlotte's got things pretty settled now. To be honest, I don't think she trusts a lot of people, even on a good day. She wound up with the house after her divorce, but he got all of their friends. With the market the way that it is, she'll probably sell soon and downsize."

Taylor winced. "Yeah, I know what that's like. Is that why you wanted to meet with me? Do you feel like you can't talk to Charlotte about your situation?"

I shook my head. "No, like I said, Charlotte already knows the whole story. She's usually the first person I talk to about anything. My parents are supportive, but they still have too many ties to people at Beth Shalom. Sometimes, I think it's safer for me and for them if they don't know everything going on in my life. No chance of something accidentally slipping out."

"I'm sorry," Taylor said. "Our situations aren't identical, but there are some pretty obvious similarities." She reached over to take my hand into hers and gave it a gentle squeeze. "I'm glad you texted me. I will try to help you however I can."

I smiled back at her. "That means so much to me, thank you."

"No problem." She grinned as she picked up her cup for another sip of Vincenzo's organic green tea. "I can't speak to the coffee in this place, but whatever honey and tea leaves they're using are absolutely divine."

"Niccolo is a magician," I said, glancing over at Vincenzo's owner as he fluttered behind the coffee bar like a whirling dervish. "I'm always telling Charlotte to come down here and talk him up. Niccolo's such a shameless flirt anyway. He could probably get that barstool to blush with his Italian accent."

Taylor laughed. "So, I guess Charlotte is single and ready to mingle?"

I grinned widely and thought of my friend's comment about being a sporty red car in the garage. "Charlotte is just naturally charming with personality for days. Her ex is the total opposite. Charlotte calls him a wet noodle, and I know he resented her for outshining him. Half the time, I don't think Charlotte realizes she's flirting because she's this tsunami of charm ready to break through and captivate you at any moment. Watching her in action should come with popcorn because it's a full-on show."

Taylor chuckled at my description but raised her eyebrows. "Are we going to talk about Charlotte the whole time, or are you ready to tell me why I'm here?"

I gulped. "I felt like I needed to explain a little so you can understand where I'm coming from. Charlotte is playing the dating field at the moment, and she's not in the same position I am."

"And what position is that?"

I blushed.

Taylor took another sip of her tea before replying. "Okay, so there's definitely a man involved. Is it that young guy at Bible study? I met him last week. He's like what, twenty-five, right? I caught him staring at you a few times."

"Twenty-eight," I said quickly, "and no, it's not Aaron."

Taylor watched me closely. "Okay," she drawled, "but it's obviously a man who isn't your husband...well, future ex-husband."

"Correct," I said. "He works at Culver."

"Oh," she said with a knowing smile. "Since he works at Culver, you can't talk to Rebecca because then she'd talk to Ted. And you can't talk to Poppy because...well, you all work together, and it would definitely get weird."

"Pretty much."

"Well, who is this guy?"

"He's new at the office. The only friends of mine who know him are the ones at work. Also, the situation is a little more complicated than me still being legally married to Nathan."

Taylor surprised me with a full grin. "Okay, well now the 911 text makes sense. This is bringing back memories, except it was brunch at Soaring Scone with me and Rebecca."

"If that's the case, then I guess I shouldn't even bother," I said with a playful sigh. "I'll wind up with Aaron at the end of the day—the same way you did with Ian. Grant will just be a blip for the memoirs I might have the guts to publish one day."

"Grant?" she asked. "Is this the man in question?"

I nodded.

"So, what's the deal with you and him?"

"We met the day I interviewed at Culver. I was waiting to catch the elevators downstairs, and he introduced himself. We've run into each other a couple of times outside of the office too. I told him that I was married, but he insisted he wasn't interested like *that*."

"What do you mean? How else would he be interested?"

"He said my eyes tell a story, and it's hard not to be fascinated." I blushed as I recalled his words and the sincerity in those chocolate brown eyes as he said them. "We had an awkward moment the other day, and he made it pretty clear that he wants to avoid any gossip. He does seem to care about me and my divorce situation, but I think it's because it reminds him of what his mother went through with his dad."

Taylor pursed her lips. "Home boy is definitely *interested*-interested whether he wants to admit it or not. You basically just said the same thing."

"What? Why?"

Taylor smiled. "Men are pretty simple creatures compared to us. At least the non personality disordered ones anyway. If a man's not physically attracted to you, he's not going to spend that much time sniffing around. He'll be friendly, but he won't go out of his way to be attentive or seek you out. He's definitely not going to talk to you about his mother or wax poetic about the story in your eyes."

"I don't think I'd call it sniffing, Taylor. Besides, the person struggling is me, not him."

She raised an eyebrow and leveled me with a potent stare. "Then, why are we sitting in a gourmet Italian cafe when neither of us can tolerate coffee? Lauren, you're the one who's got to go back to the office and deal with this Grant guy, so let's get down to brass tacks. Where's the confusion?"

"Because he's also in a relationship."

"He's married?" she gasped.

I shook my head. "No, but he may as well be. Grant lives with his girlfriend. I've actually met her. She's nice. She's also big, blonde, and beautiful. Like a '40s style pin up model. I shouldn't be in any kind of a competition with her, but I'm also not blind. The way Grant looks at me sometimes...I just, I wonder if he's uncomfortable because *I'm* uncomfortable or maybe there's something more. Honestly, it feels so conceited and ridiculous. The problem is that I can't stop thinking about him. I keep praying for God to take it away from me, but I don't know if this is an attack from the enemy or if God wants me to pray for him. To be honest, I don't really understand what's going on with me right now."

"Can I ask a blunt question?"

I nodded.

"So, Grant's got this voluptuous, blonde bombshell girl-friend, right?"

"Right."

"And you're still married to Nathan?"

"Right."

"Does he know that?" Taylor asked.

I nodded again.

"Okay, well it's obvious that you've got some kind of feelings, or at minimum, a crush or we wouldn't be sitting here."

I conceded her point with an embarrassed shrug and then picked up my cup of tea to hide behind it. Drinking the now lukewarm liquid felt more comfortable than swallowing the uncomfortable truth of my situation.

Taylor took her own sip before asking her next loaded question. "So, if Grant's already got a girlfriend, and he's theoretically just as unavailable as you are, why is this an emergency? If you want me to reassure you that the attraction is all in your head, I can't. I absolutely think this is mutual. I also think you like Grant a lot more than you're letting on."

I gulped down another mouthful of tepid tea.

Taylor continued, "I get the feeling you don't actually *want* to be wrong about what you're perceiving on his end either. The issue isn't that you've caught feelings for this guy, it's that you want him to catch feelings for you too and it looks like he has. Does that sum it up?"

"Yes!" I said with an overly dramatic smack to the forehead.

Taylor looked thoughtful for a moment. "Okay, so which part of this involves your friend, Charlotte? Is she suggesting you go for it with Grant?"

My eyes grew wide. "No, not at all! Charlotte has commended my self control around him and keeps telling me to keep clear or start finding some flaws with him."

"Well, have you found any?"

"Other than wishing he'd grow his curly hair out a little more, not really."

Taylor playfully rolled her eyes. "That's not a flaw. My ex was bald."

"My son has a head full of curls, so I guess that's why I'm

partial to them. Your husband also has some amazing hair, by the way."

Mrs. Horner smiled, and her eyes sparkled. "Ian's so overdue for a haircut, it's not even funny. Kate, his sister, said she's coming over with scissors and clippers this weekend to take care of it."

"Must be handy having a sister-in-law for a hairdresser," I said, "and I'm sure she's glad to have her brother and the boys back in town."

"My niece, Fiona, has already offered to babysit. Ian's parents were more helpful when the boys were babies, but they're pretty involved with their condo HOA and seniors' organizations down in East Palm. They were sad when we told them Ian had to transfer back to Hillcrest, but they're really loving life in Florida. At least we know we have a nice place to visit when we make it down there again."

"You've still got your Florida glow," I said, gesturing at her tanned skin.

Taylor watched me with an amused smirk on her face. "You're still not off the hook, by the way, but good job getting me distracted talking about my husband."

"Can I be even more honest?" I asked.

She winked at me. "I would hope for nothing less."

"In my head, I can tell you all the reasons why any sort of relationship or flirtation with Grant is doomed from the start. Aside from the Nathan issue, there's the fact that Grant is not a believer, he's been living with his girlfriend for years, so they're basically married, and oh yeah, we work together too. I think maybe I'm just entertaining all of these romantic thoughts because this is a 'safe' way to handle loneliness."

"Safe how? It sounds pretty dangerous to me."

"Well, *safe* in the sense that nothing is ever going to happen.

It's a comforting distraction from the hell of this divorce from Nathan. Aaron, on the other hand, is a legitimately safe person. He's been one of my closest friends for forever, he loves me, and I already know where we align spiritually and theologically."

"So, what's the problem?" she asked.

"I just don't have those feelings for him, and he knows it. I feel bad for Aaron because he says he just wants to be my friend if he can't be anything else, but I feel like any time I spend with him gives him false hope for the future. I want better than that for him. I wish I could be what he wants me to be, but I can't. That's what makes this Grant situation even more frustrating. It doesn't make any logical sense for me to be attracted to him instead of Aaron."

"Not to mention the fact you're still legally married and in a contested custody divorce with your ex."

"Exactly," I said. "I wish I could make all of these feelings go away, but I can't. It's just constant frustration about wanting it and not being able to do anything about it."

The door to Vincenzo's opened, and something caught Taylor's gaze behind me.

"You okay?" I asked.

"What does Grant look like?" she said behind a strained smile.

I frowned. "He looks like the actor who plays Peter Parsons in the Spider Guy movies. Not the new ones, but the ones from the 2010s. Tall, curly brown hair, nice beard, well fitted suits. Why?"

"Because he's here, he just saw you, and he's headed right toward us."

CHAPTER 14

"Lauren," Grant called as he approached, "I've been looking for you."

Taylor's eyes widened. "We're in the middle of Lauren's lunch break right now. Can it wait until after she gets back to the office?"

I smiled at her protectiveness, but after one glance at Grant, I knew something was off. Turning my entire body to face him, I asked, "What's going on?"

"Some guy was at the office demanding to see you. He won't take 'no' for an answer."

"Well, call security!" Taylor snapped. "Lauren's ex shouldn't be allowed anywhere near her! She's already had to get a restraining order."

Grant glanced between me and Taylor for a beat. "This guy says he's your rabbi, but he's already been escorted out of the building. There's some concern he might be lurking outside."

I blanched. "What?"

"Do we need to call the police?" Taylor asked. "Lauren, what does your paperwork state about friends of Nathan harassing you?"

"That they're not allowed to," I said, my hands shaking, "but the courts are so backed up because of Covid that getting an emergency hearing is next to impossible. Nathan's been skating by on a lot of technicalities because he knows he can. Sondra told me they're only taking criminal cases right now."

"I'm here to help," Grant said. "Margolin is holding down the office, but he's also got meetings all afternoon. Poppy said you were here with a friend, and she asked me to come find you."

"She did?" Taylor and I gasped in unison.

Grant nodded. "Poppy said she'd cause a scene with the rabbi and didn't want it to look bad for you in your divorce."

"Thank you," I said to Grant. "Can you sneak me back into the building?"

"Absolutely! I'd also like to walk you to your car after work too."

Taylor glanced sharply at him. "And you don't think *that* looks bad?"

"Why would it?" he asked with narrowed eyes. "Lauren and I aren't dating, and I have a girlfriend."

"So, I've heard."

Grant's gaze lasered over to me, and my cheeks warmed. Taylor slunk in her seat and hid behind her own cup of tea.

"Lauren?" Grant asked. "What's going on?"

I shook my head and willed the tears in my eyes to dry and go away. "Why can't they all just leave me alone?"

Recovered from her blunder, Taylor stood to put her arms around me. I had a feeling Grant would have embraced me just as easily as my new friend had, but I was relieved Taylor beat him to it. The last thing I needed was a repeat of Aaron Davis on the front porch.

"You *will* get through this," Taylor said close to my ear. "It took me over a year to get rid of Mitch, but I did. It took three years to heal, but I did that too. You can do this, Lauren. This is not going to be your forever. You *will* get past this divorce and have the life you deserve." She leaned back and held me by the shoulders. "Don't give up, and don't let that monster win. He wants you to feel defeated and hopeless. I promise that you are neither. You are *more* than a conqueror in Christ Jesus, do you hear me? The Bible says no weapon formed against you will prosper, and every tongue that rises in accusation will be silenced. You are a mighty woman of God and a *warrior,* or Nathan and his minions wouldn't be trying so hard to destroy you. Fight for yourself and for your son."

Strengthened by her words, I met her gaze through wet lashes. "Thank you."

Taylor pulled me in for another hug and then gathered her purse. "I'm going to text my husband and ask him to pray for you, if that's all right."

"Totally," I said dabbing under my eyes and at the likely mascara mess underneath them. "I'm sure Ted and Poppy have messaged everyone else at Bible study already."

"What about your friend?" she asked, referring to my not so secret, Bible study admirer. "Are you going to tell Aaron yourself or wait for Ted to do it?"

I caught Grant in my periphery watching me closely.

"I've got it, thanks," I murmured.

Taylor collected her empty cup of tea and mine. "I'll text you later. I'm going to ask Ian to hang with the boys one night so you and I can have some actual girl time. Sound good?"

I smiled at her. "Thank you, Taylor."

Her petite hand squeezed mine, and she took her leave, side-stepping Grant as he studied her in fascination.

"Is that the *Parkview Chronicles* Taylor?" he asked as I stood from my seat.

"The one and only."

"She's tinier than you are," he said, surprised.

"What is that supposed to mean?"

Grant shook his head. "Absolutely nothing. Stupid comment. Are you ready to go?"

I eyed him curiously as I gathered my cross body purse and slung it over my midsection. "Ready as I'll ever be."

"I'd offer my arm, but—"

"Stop," I said, cutting him off. "We're coworkers, and we might even be friends one day. We don't have to make it weird."

A glint of humor finally appeared in his eyes. "Thanks for that."

"I can't control what my ex is going to say or do. If I walked in there with Poppy, my ex would accuse me of being a home-wrecking lesbian. It's fine, Grant."

He exhaled a small chuckle. "I'm sure Poppy's husband would have a thing or two to say about that."

I giggled. "No doubt."

He smiled down at me, and my grin widened.

"Thanks for coming down here to help me," I said. "I appreciate it."

"Seriously though, do you need my arm?" He extended it back toward me. "No weirdness, I promise."

I waved him off. "No, I'm good. If I have to deal with that old fraud, I'm going to do it on my own terms. That man put me and my son through hell covering for my ex. If Rabbi Lebow wants a fight, he'll get one."

"I like this side of you."

"Thanks, I think I do too."

"Where have you been hiding this version of Lauren?" He winked at me as he opened the door to Vincenzo's.

I stepped through, and he followed behind me. "I save the fire breathing for when I have to play Mama Bear, but I have definitely been working on my roar."

"That's quite a collection of animals you just listed. I'm trying to imagine a roaring, fire-breathing Mama Bear. Lions and dragons and bears, oh my!"

I laughed.

Grant's eyes sparkled as they met mine. "You're going to get through this, I promise."

Feeling a supernatural calm wash over me, I knew that God would do exactly that. "Thank you, Grant."

He winked at me, and we marched toward the Culver high rise heading to battle. With my senses on high alert, I scanned the area for signs of my grizzled, former rabbi. I had a nagging feeling in the pit of my stomach, but nothing seemed amiss in the covered walkway separating the parking deck and the revolving glass entryway to our building.

I pulled away from Grant and continued my search. I frowned, both dreading and eagerly anticipating my confrontation with Rabbi Lebow.

"Do you see him?" Grant asked.

I shook my head. "No, and it's creeping me out. I feel like I'm being watched, but I can't see anyone."

He turned to survey the glass walled restaurants behind us. "I don't see anyone inside of Soaring Scone or Let it Fro-Yo."

"It's probably for the best. It'll be hard enough to concentrate on Ted's latest RFP knowing Rabbi Lebow's still lurking around here."

Grant looked down at me, searching my eyes. "You okay?"

I nodded. "Yeah. Thanks for coming as my extra muscle."

He smiled. "Well, it's been a while since I've worked out, but I do what I can to maintain this tip top physique."

I smirked and rolled my eyes. "I'm sure Hayley appreciates the effort."

His smile faltered. "I'm sure she does."

I glanced away and then over my surroundings but found nothing amiss. With a resigned sigh, I said, "I want to go back to the office. I'm not going to stand out here waiting for that charlatan—or whoever else—to jump out of the bushes and scare me."

We turned to face our office high rise just as Rabbi Lebow rounded the corner. I knew the second he spotted me because his posture grew rigid and he beelined toward us.

"I see him too," Grant said under his breath. "What do you want to do?"

"Get your phone out. Now," I said, steadying the trembling in my knees. They didn't shake from fear but from adrenaline. "I want everything documented."

He whipped the device from his pocket within seconds. "Done."

"Mrs. Fein," Rabbi Lebow sneered, looking me over with palpable disdain.

"Cut the baloney," I clipped. "You know you're not supposed to be here. My coworker is filming all of this right now, so just know that whatever gaslighting and games you and Nathan have planned will be used against both of you in court."

Grant waved from behind his phone. "Say, 'cheese'!"

"I had hoped we could discuss this privately," Rabbi Lebow said with a peevish tone.

"You mean you didn't want any witnesses to your psychological and emotional abuse," I countered. "What you did to hide

Nathan's sin was reprehensible. What you've covered up to protect your ministry empire at the expense of me and my son is something you will have to answer to Jesus for doing."

"*Jesus*," Rabbi Lebow scoffed. "Without Nathan's good influence, I doubt your son will even grow up knowing he's Jewish. What a waste! Does your little Bible study even have a name other than 'former Jews who hate Beth Shalom'?"

I felt the steam emanating off my camera man, but I reached out a hand to hold him off. "Spare me the Jewish identity shtick. The real issue is the sin you deliberately hide at Beth Shalom. You care more about your image than your integrity."

Rabbi Lebow puffed his chest. "I'm not the one who should be worried about answering to God for my actions, Mrs. Fein. The Lord hates divorce."

"He hates *abuse* a whole lot more," I spat, "and what He really hates is misusing His Name in order to manipulate and control others. When was the last time you read *Ezekiel 34* about judgment for the wicked shepherds abusing the sheep in their care?"

Unmoved, Rabbi Lebow said, "I've been your spiritual authority for nearly twenty years, young lady. Your mother would be ashamed of how disrespectful you're behaving."

"There's a huge difference between spiritual authority and acting like a controlling *macher*," I shot back, "and you most certainly are not Yeshua or His stand in."

Rabbi Lebow's face reddened as he spoke through clenched teeth. "Go back home to your husband, and work this out. Nathan is devastated by what you've done to him. You should be on your hands and knees begging for his forgiveness."

"Did Nathan send you down here to do his dirty work, or are you on some self-appointed mission to keep me from airing your dirty, synagogue secrets?"

His eyes narrowed in hatred, but I wasn't finished.

"I also don't appreciate you coming down here trying to intimidate me. You and Nathan are going to have to accept the fact you no longer get to control and bully me. That 'spiritual authority' card doesn't work anymore."

Rabbi Lebow cursed at me, reiterating his insane demand with even more venom. His hands fisted and rose at his sides.

From next to me, Grant growled, "You better watch your next words real carefully, old man, and keep those hands to yourself. This camera is still rolling. I'd be more than happy to help Lauren get a restraining order on your miserable hide. Videos like this tend to go viral."

Rabbi Lebow's self control finally broke as he swore at both of us and then charged at me. Grant shoved his phone into my hands as he pushed Rabbi Lebow backward and ducked a punch probably meant for *my* face rather than his own.

Building security swarmed in immediately, and I silently thanked God that I'd texted Poppy before we'd left Vincenzo's. She had alerted security to watch for potential trouble outside the building, and they arrived just in time.

Leonard, everyone's favorite evening security guard, blockaded Grant and me while police officers dragged my old leader away.

We gave official statements, and one of the officers watched the video recorded on Grant's phone before handing him a business card with information on where to upload the footage. I texted my attorney, Sondra, to let her know what happened and asked about filing a new TPO against Nathan.

I don't know, she wrote back, *we'd have to prove that Nathan put the rabbi up to harassing you. I believe you, Lauren, but unless you've got some kind of documented communication between the two of them or the rabbi admitting it on camera, it's circumstantial. I wish I had better news for you.*

I sighed. Texting back angrily, I wrote, *Will Nathan EVER be held accountable for his behavior? Why are his minions allowed to do this to me????*

They're not! Sondra responded immediately. *We could look into some kind of a restraining order against the rabbi, but nothing that would really impact your divorce, unfortunately. Nathan has the rabbi listed as a credible witness to your so-called, 'mental illness,' so he just shot himself in the foot on that one, at least.*

I frowned. *Not the answer I was hoping for, but I guess it's better than nothing.*

"You okay?" Grant asked, rejoining me as the officers headed back to their squad cars. "You were incredible, by the way."

I pushed my mouth into a tight smile. "I wasn't scared, just angry. The adrenaline is starting to wear off, though. I feel light headed."

This time, Grant didn't ask before offering his arm. He tucked me into his side and walked me back to the office. "I'll get you some lunch once I know you're safe inside."

I looked up at him as we stepped into an awaiting elevator in the lobby. "You don't have to do that. Poppy and Ted will want to take care of me, but as you saw, I'm more than capable of taking care of myself."

His expressive brown eyes met and held mine. "Is your ex like that?"

"Like what?"

"The way you handled the rabbi and stared him down like he was a cockroach. It wasn't your first time dealing with phys-ical violence, was it?"

I pulled my arm away from his. "You and I are not 'friends' yet, and I don't want to talk about it."

"Sorry, I'm just concerned, not trying to be nosey."

I swallowed down the lump of tears threatening to spill over. "It's okay. I just didn't expect or need this all to happen today."

"Lauren, I…" he cut himself off as if searching for the right words. "I'm a little confused by something that happened at Vincenzo's. Why did your friend act so hostile? Did you tell her something about me?"

My heart fluttered, knowing exactly where the conversation was headed.

I met his eyes and silently begged him not to ask the next question. Grant's eyebrows raised in shock, then lowered in studied concentration of my face. My mind replayed his fierce protectiveness outside, now mingling with new thoughts I had no business entertaining. Inch by inch, our faces drew nearer.

When my lips involuntarily parted, I realized my secret was no longer secret.

Grant ripped his gaze from mine, expelling a harsh gust of air. As an act of mercy, the elevator doors dinged open. I allowed the escaping whoosh of tension to carry me along with it and hurried to a side entry door. Another look back would likely transform me into a pillar of salt.

My attraction had developed far beyond a simple crush.

CHAPTER 15

"Lauren! You should have called me!" Aaron grumbled in the Goldstein's dining room the following Sunday at Bible study.

"Were you going to drive an hour to be there? I had it handled."

"With that Grant guy?" he spat.

"Is that what this is really about? That I was in danger, or that it was someone else who rescued me? And besides, nobody rescued me at all. I held my own just fine."

"Yeah, until Rabbi Lebow lost his mind and tried to assault you!"

"Lower your voice!" I hissed, feeling the pitying eyes of everyone else upon us. Ted and Poppy had disseminated information about Rabbi Lebow's appearance at the office, but nothing much beyond that. I waited a few days before texting Aaron, wanting to calm down and process the incident. Grant kept his distance at the office, but I found two gift cards on my desk, one for Vincenzo's and one for Soaring Scone. The dollar amount for both establishments was more than what I spent on weekly groceries for Ari and me. I hadn't spoken to Grant directly about it, but I knew we were due for an uncomfortable conversation.

Aaron's stormy eyes forced my thoughts away from my enigmatic coworker. "You should have told me," he said again, "and you've been blowing me off all week."

I wanted to deny it, but I couldn't. I wanted to deny that I was glad Grant was with me instead of Aaron. I wanted to deny that I felt safer with him because no matter my infatuation, Grant proved he wouldn't prey upon years of neglect and pent up hormones. My real issue was the generous displays of concern wreaking havoc with my imagination.

"Something's different," Aaron said, still watching me. "This isn't like you."

"Well, what did you expect? To see me falling apart at the seams?"

His mouth dropped open, and his face paled.

"Wow," I said. "Thanks for the vote of confidence."

Aaron's scowl matched mine. "I've already told you that you're one of the bravest women I know."

"That's also because you think you're in love with me."

"I don't *think* anything," he growled. "I know."

I held out a palm. "Just stop! I don't feel that way about you, and I don't know if I ever will."

His face crumbled.

"I'm sorry, Aaron. You know I don't want to hurt you, but I don't want you holding onto false hope that anything will ever happen between us."

"Is it because of Nathan or because of Grant?" he asked through clenched teeth.

"Neither," I replied, willing to walk on the waves of those

stormy eyes. "I wish I could feel for you what you do for me, but I just don't."

"What about that night?" Lowering his voice, he added, "On your parents front porch?"

"What about it? It was a moment of weakness, and it shouldn't have happened."

"You kissed me back."

"It was wrong," I said with conviction. "It will never be 'right,' no matter how much you want it to be. I regret it ever happening."

"Because of the guilt?"

I sighed. "It's more than that. I love you like a brother, but I can't tell you what I know you want to hear. I feel like I'm leading you on by texting you and keeping such a close friend- ship. It's not healthy. I don't want to see you torturing yourself waiting for me to have feelings I may never reciprocate."

"Never?" he breathed.

"Look, anything is possible, but I've just never seen you that way. You're a handsome, smart, wonderful guy, and you deserve so much more than waiting for me to be free from Señor Psychopath. I've caught Chelsea making eyes at you a few times at Bible study. She's cute." I cast a quick glance to the blonde, twenty-five year old chatting with Abigail Goldstein. She and Aaron would have the most adorable, golden haired cherubs if they ever got together.

"She's not you. I haven't spent the last twelve years in love with *Chelsea*," he glowered, saying her name loud enough for a few heads to turn.

I turned toward the Goldstein boys' playroom located off the foyer. "Come on. We need some privacy."

Aaron followed behind me in stoic silence.

I closed the french doors before I tried to reason with my old friend again. "Look, I can't tell you to turn your feelings off, but there's no way our current situation is good for you. As your friend, I absolutely want you to be happy, but I need you to accept the fact it may not happen with *me*. Sondra told me it could be another twelve to eighteen months before we ever get this to a judge, especially since we've got a guardian ad litem involved. Our meeting with the GAL is set for next month, and I have no idea how long the investigation will take. We both know Nathan doesn't want to let go of the only means he has to control me. You deserve to have a life of your own instead of pining away because I'm unavailable."

Aaron stepped toward me with sad eyes. He reached a hand to my arm, and I didn't pull away.

"I'm sorry," I whispered. "I really am."

"I just don't know how to think about a future that doesn't involve you in it."

"What about when I was married to Nathan?" I asked. "Even before the porn scandal? That was three and a half years that you could have tried to find someone else."

"But I didn't want anybody else."

"And if Nathan and I had been happy? What would you have done? What if we weren't happy, but I had chosen to stick it out with him anyway? Would you spend forever waiting for me? Aaron, as your friend, I love you, but that's no way for you to live. I want you to be happy, and I want you to start working toward a future where you can be happy with or without me."

At the defeated slump of his shoulders, I slid my arms around his waist. He held me tightly and rested his head on top of mine.

"I'm sorry," I whispered. "I wish I could."

He held me for another tenuous moment before releasing me. "So, I didn't do anything wrong?"

I shook my head, mirroring the sheen in his eyes with my own. "You deserve to be ridiculously and blissfully happy. I want to dance at your wedding and celebrate that what you have will be real and lasting. Your marriage will be the complete opposite of what I had with Nathan because *you* are the complete opposite of the psycho I married."

"But you want that *for* me, not *with* me," he said sadly.

"God may strike me with lightning and open my eyes to something I can't see right now, but you can't make me responsible for your happiness...or your misery. Aaron, you've got a purpose that's so much bigger than waiting for me to love you the way you deserve. I think you've just been doing it for so long that the idea of change seems scary."

He shook his head emphatically. "Don't put words in my mouth or try to psychoanalyze me, Lauren. And don't minimize my feelings either. This isn't puppy love or some kid crush. I know how I feel about you. God does too."

I sighed wearily and held his gaze for a long minute. "I wish I could give you what you want. The truth is even if I could, the timing would be all wrong. We both know that. You've been jealous about Grant, but I'm telling you the same thing I'd be telling him too."

Aaron took a step backward and pressed his lips together. "Okay, Lauren. It's enough. I'm gonna need some space. I want you to know that I'm not ignoring you or even mad at you. I just need time."

"I understand. I'm sor—"

He cut me off. "Don't apologize again. I can't take it. I'll see you around."

I watched his lanky frame turn and exit the dual french doors with the weight of the world on his shoulders. I fought the urge to cry, wondering if I'd just made a colossal mistake.

A soft knock came on the open door frame moments later.

I looked up to see Taylor Horner holding a plate of snacks. "You didn't get a chance to eat anything, so I grabbed a few things before Abigail put the food away."

"Thanks," I murmured, taking the plate. "To be honest, I don't really feel like eating."

"I guess things didn't go so well with Aaron," she ventured.

I flopped onto a giant, navy bean bag chair. "Ugh, Taylor, it was awful."

"What happened?"

I sniffled back tears. "Other than breaking Aaron's heart?"

"Ah," she said, smiling sadly. "Rebecca and I have both been there. Funny enough, with the owner of this house."

I exhaled a soft chuckle. "It's hard to think of Kyle as anything other than Abigail's husband. I forgot that you and he dated."

Taylor smirked. "Barely, and it's all water under the bridge. He's married to the woman he's supposed to be with, and obviously, Ian and I were meant to be. My poor husband had the patience of a saint waiting for me."

"Did I make a mistake?" I asked, my eyes welling up again. "What if Aaron is another Ian, and I just blew it?"

She shook her head. "Sweetie, your story is your own. You can find similarities in my story, Rebecca's, Poppy's, or even Carly's—if she ever gets around to publishing—but I hope nobody is looking at them as a blueprint for how God will work in their own life. All of us want to give inspiration to other women with what we've survived, but every story is different. God didn't choose to save my marriage to Mitch. He didn't save Joe's marriage before he met Carly either. Your story will be the one God wants to give you, not a carbon copy of mine."

I exhaled a weary breath. "I know you're right."

"If you don't mind me asking, how are things with Grant?"

I looked down at my hands to hide my blush. "They're fine."

After a long pause, I glanced up to see Taylor didn't buy a word of it.

"Are you rejecting Aaron because you have feelings for Grant?"

I shook my head. "No, I'm honestly not even sure what I feel for Grant. It might just be a chemical addiction to all of those 'what if?' hormones. I've struggled with Aaron's crush on me long before Grant ever came into the picture—and Grant isn't really even *in* the picture. He just happens to be someone I work with."

"Who dropped $400 worth of gift cards on your desk," she deadpanned.

"Who is going to have $400 worth of gift cards returned on his desk tomorrow morning," I amended. "I can't accept it."

"Good," Taylor said with a tight smile. "The two of you are dancing across a very fine line."

"The two of us?"

She nodded. "Yeah, girl. It takes two to tango. No matter how 'unavailable' either of you are, you both keep pushing the boundary a little farther each time."

"Why do you think that is?"

She shrugged. "Curiosity? Pheromones? You said you guys connected that one day at lunch when he shared about his mother. It sounds like there's been an attraction since day one. The fact you both know you shouldn't act on it is what makes it feel so exciting and dangerous. It's the thrill of the temptation. Logically, you both know the right thing to do. The tension is what keeps you coming back to each other, but I don't think it's any healthier than doing that same dance with Aaron."

"You're right," I said quietly. "I think you're completely right."

Taylor wrapped her tiny arm around my shoulders. "You have been deprived of every good and loving thing a man should provide for his wife. I know. I've lived it too. It feels wonderful when someone you find physically attractive suddenly gives you that attention and validation—when there's a man protecting you instead of betraying you."

I nodded.

She continued, "The problem isn't what Nathan will accuse you of doing or even questions of right or wrong. This is God showing you areas of your heart that need to heal, Lauren. He wants to be all of those things you've been missing. He wants to show you how *He* will pursue you, cherish you, protect you, love you, and call you His own. He wants to be your husband first and foremost."

I blinked back tears. "Wow."

She pulled me into a motherly hug. "Whatever is meant to happen with Aaron will happen in God's timing. Whatever is meant to happen with Grant will happen because God orchestrates the details, not either one of you. Worrying about it, fantasizing about it, or agonizing over it gives you the false sense of being in control, but it's creating unnecessary anxiety. Stop striving, stop spinning, and let God handle it. Girl, you need rest right now. If you can enjoy the gift cards without any guilt, then do it. If not, give them away. Rather than finding an excuse to go talk to Grant and twirl another tango over forbidden fruit, focus on getting that need met by God first. I promise, He'll take care of the rest."

CHAPTER 16

WHEN I ARRIVED HOME FROM BIBLE STUDY, I MULLED over my feelings for both Grant and Aaron. More than anything, I wanted to avoid a repeat of how I'd been duped into a relationship with Nathan Fein. Nine years earlier, I'd just gotten back from a youth retreat during my senior year of college when I noticed Nathan Fein watching me from across the fellowship hall at synagogue.

Over the years, I'd seen Nathan helping out Rabbi Lebow with AV and computer issues, but Nathan was more than a decade older than me. Like the light fixtures, stained glass windows, or burgundy carpet of the synagogue, Nathan was just *there*. I knew he'd gotten engaged to some Jewish girl the year before, but I'd heard that she'd cheated on him and broken his heart. Nathan was considered "the catch" of the synagogue, and his mother, Liora, made it her life's mission to find her baby boy a wife. The senior Feins had been just as much a staple of Beth Shalom for me growing up, but after a brief move to Virginia before Nathan got engaged, his parents came right back to Hill-crest to help mend his broken heart.

My own mother waved me over as she stood in the down-stairs kitchen of Beth Shalom, serving apple juice and coffee from behind a breakfast bar. As was custom after Friday evening and Saturday morning services, Beth Shalom held an *oneg*, or small get together, featuring beverages, bagels, and cream cheese.

"Hey, Mom," I said and snagged a cup of juice from the counter. I looked into the empty space behind her. "Do you need any help? I thought you weren't on oneg this quarter."

"God bless you!" she sighed, her shoulders slumping in relief. "Both of the ladies on the schedule tonight no showed, and Rabbi asked me if I could pinch hit. If you can check and make sure we have enough cream cheese and napkins on the tables, that would be wonderful."

After a quick survey of inventory, I rushed into the kitchen to grab additional cream cheese packets from a large cardboard box in the fridge. I placed packets on each of the three picnic tables that formed a u-shape in the center of the room. Once I'd finished that task, I set about straightening a pile of napkins and gathering dirty, plastic knives strewn about.

"Thanks," Nathan said, suddenly standing next to me. "Bagels and cream cheese are a match made in heaven. You've made my bagel dreams come true."

"Oh," I said, stunned that Beth Shalom's most eligible bach-elor was even talking to me. "Well, enjoy your bagel. Shabbat Shalom."

The plastic knives clattered in my hands as I scooped them up. I felt Nathan's dark eyes on me, but I didn't dare look up to confirm it. I inched past him to dump the dirty napkins and debris into a nearby trash can.

I didn't realize he had trailed behind me until I turned around and knocked into him. I startled as I backed into the garbage can and nearly tumbled over my own feet.

Nathan chuckled as he held onto my arm to steady me. "You okay? I didn't mean to scare you."

"Fine," I said, blushing. "Sorry about that. I didn't see you there."

"Accidents happen," he smiled. "It's Lauren, right?"

"Yeah," I said, unable to hide the surprise in my voice. "Obviously, I know who you are."

Nathan's dark eyes sparkled. "I guess I'm kind of an institution around here. Comes with being so old," he said with a wink.

"Old?"

"Well, older than you, anyway. What are you? Eighteen?"

"Twenty-one," I replied.

"Even better," he said, his smile widening.

"Is there, um, something I can help you with? My mom is about to clean up the coffee, and I told her I'd help with oneg."

He gave me a sidelong look and lowered his voice. "No offense to the Beth Shalom coffee, but I prefer Charred Cups. Would you like to join me once you're done?"

"Join you?"

"Yeah. Like a date," he said with a note of teasing. He nudged my arm, and I jerked away. Nathan's eyes bored into mine, and I felt pinned between his gaze and the trash can pressed against the backs of my legs. With a chuckle, he added, "I won't bite."

"Oh, I didn't think that," I murmured.

"Do you like coffee?"

"I prefer tea."

"Too pure for coffee, huh?"

I gaped, sure I'd misheard him.

His expression turned sheepish. "Don't mind me. Just an old-man joke."

We stood in awkward silence, and Nathan watched me as if waiting for me to say something. I looked past him, sure my mother would be wondering why I'd disappeared.

"So, I'll see you at Charred Cups in half an hour?" he asked, drawing my attention back to him.

I gestured toward the fellowship hall behind him, knowing he'd be fully aware of the remaining work for Friday night clean up and subsequent set up for the following morning. "I don't think I'll be ready by then, sorry. It's just me and mom tonight doing oneg. Whoever is on the schedule didn't make it."

He rolled his eyes. "I don't understand why it's so hard for people to volunteer. We're supposed to be serving God, not idolizing our jobs or our families above Him."

"Idolizing our families?" I asked.

Nathan scoffed. "Oh, you know, those nonfat, vanilla latte soccer moms who think sports and ballet come before being in God's house. Then, there's all the men who won't usher because they're too busy working. Rabbi Lebow always says that if you're not making plans to be serving God, you're not making the right plans. If these guys are so determined to *work*, there's always plenty they can be doing around the synagogue."

I nodded impassively as I recalled that well-worn phrase from our rabbi. Something in the way Rabbi Lebow chided the members to volunteer came across as though not serving at Beth Shalom meant you weren't serving *God*. While he would never come right out and say so, the insinuation was clear. He emphasized how God was pleased with cheerful givers and those who 'served in His house.'

Meanwhile, I struggled with guilt over my coursework at

school and not being able to volunteer with the children's program like I had during my first two years of college. The temple's education director still called me regularly to see if I could squeeze in a shift or two, but my mother finally put the kibosh on that with Rabbi Lebow.

At the time, I was upset with my mother's meddling and felt like I was sinning against God. I quoted the same rabbi maxim Nathan had, but my mother reminded me that God loved me just for being His daughter—not because of how hard I worked on His behalf. She assured me that I was not displeasing God because I had real world priorities outside of the congregation. By contrast, people like Nathan and his parents seemed to dedicate their entire lives to Beth Shalom and were publicly praised by Rabbi Lebow as examples to follow.

Nathan glanced at his phone to check the time. "So, Lauren, can you meet me at Charred Cups by eleven?"

I wasn't sure whether to be impressed or unnerved by Nathan's persistence, but a small part of my ego enjoyed the attention from someone so well respected in the synagogue. Before I could answer, Aaron Davis sidled up next to me and pulled me into a hug.

"There you are!" he said, tucking me into his side. "I didn't know you were back home yet for break, Laur. Everyone's going out to the Parkview Diner."

Nathan's chest puffed out as he looked down his nose at Aaron. "Lauren already has plans. I'm sure you kids will have plenty of fun without her."

"Lauren?" Aaron said, turning to me. "You always come with us on Friday nights when you're home from school."

"That's true," I said with an apologetic smile to Nathan. Feeling guilty, I added, "You could always join us if you want."

Aaron looked from me to Nathan with questions in his

stormy eyes. "I don't know if Nathan really wants to hang out with us *kids*, but yeah man, if you want to come with us, there's always room for one more."

Nathan eyed Aaron and I more closely. "Are the two of you dating? I mean, he's practically all over you, Lauren. Is this why you won't give me an answer about going out for coffee?"

Aaron looked like I'd just betrayed him, and Nathan's jealousy could not have been more apparent. Confused, I took a step away from Aaron and also retreated from Beth Shalom's biggest catch.

"You know what," I said, "I'm actually pretty tired. I think I'm going to help my mom clean and then just go home. Aaron, thanks for the invite, but I'll see you tomorrow night at the College and Career pizza party."

"Great, so I'll see you tomorrow night," Nathan said with a smile.

"Aren't you a little old for that?" Aaron snapped.

Nathan looked Aaron up and down before dismissing him and addressing me directly. "I'm sure Rabbi Lebow can make an exception for a few of us old timers since the rest of the Beth Shalom's singles are practically in their eighties. Lauren, I look forward to seeing you there." He touched my arm again before walking away.

"Laur, what the heck?" Aaron said, pulling me aside.

"Excuse me?" I hissed. "Why were you acting like that?"

"Like what?"

"Like a jealous boyfriend! You're one of my best friends, but you were flat out rude to Nathan."

"Didn't you see the way he ignored me just now? He acted like I was nothing."

"I saw it," I admitted, "but you also called him old."

"That's because he *is* old. He's gotta be thirty-three or thirty-four, at least."

"So what?" I rolled my eyes and barreled past my old friend to take my frustration out on lingering table trash from the oneg. Aaron followed and collected garbage from a neighboring table. When we met together at the third table, Aaron blocked me from moving toward the garbage can.

"Look, it's already weird that we have thirty-year-olds hanging out with us at College and Career activities, and Nathan's even older."

"Okay," I said, meeting his eyes. "It *is* weird when the old members show up even though they're married with kids now. What makes Nathan any worse?"

"I just don't like the guy."

"Well, Rabbi seems to trust him," I said. "Why don't you?"

"It's not just him," Aaron said, "it's their whole family. Whatever happened with his older brother, Matty? He used to come here with his wife, and now it's like he doesn't exist. Most people think Nathan is an only child."

"His brother got divorced," I whispered. "Liora told my mom about it. His ex didn't like Beth Shalom and said she wanted to go to a church."

"Did they get divorced over *that*?" Aaron asked incredulously.

I shrugged as I side stepped Aaron to toss away my trash. He followed me again, mirroring my clean up and set up actions as we put on plastic table cloths and fresh plates, napkins, and knives for the following morning. My mother nodded her appreciation at the two of us while she wrangled the industrial-sized coffee maker.

"Seriously," Aaron said as we finished with the third table, "what gives with the older brother anyway? Your parents are on leadership with the Feins, right?"

I lowered my voice and glanced around, not sure if Nathan or his parents might still be lingering per their usual custom. "I got the impression Liora didn't like Matty's wife very much, but I've never really asked. I've overheard Liora telling my mom that Matty's ex didn't understand the *messianic vision,* and she was trying to force Matty to become a Christian."

"But he *is* a Christian. All of us are. We believe in Jesus."

I rolled my eyes. "You know what I mean. *Gentile* Christian. The Feins are one of the most Jewish families I know. Can you imagine Liora with a Christmas tree?"

Aaron chuckled. "Not with the three inch Star of David she wears around her neck."

I laughed, thinking about the gaudy diamonds Liora donned like a superhero crest. "Yeah, it's definitely 'extra,' but you know how the Feins are. I don't agree with how they talk down about Christians, but they're just really into their Jewish identity and not wanting to assimilate."

"Laur, have you ever noticed how they treat gentiles in our congregation? Like just now? Nathan acted like I didn't exist."

"I think that's because he was trying to ask me out, and you made it look like we're a couple. Jealousy doesn't look good on anybody," I said with a pointed look. "Why do you care anyway? I thought you'd be happy for me. You're always telling me God's got the perfect guy waiting for me."

Aaron's eyes flashed with an emotion I didn't care to identify. "Laur, I absolutely believe that. You know I do. But Nathan is way too old for you!"

Aaron's anger only fueled mine. "No, he's not! Yeah, I mean he's in his thirties, but it's not like he's old enough to be my dad or something. Nathan's already self-conscious about it, and you basically just rubbed it in."

"Why are you defending him? I didn't even know you liked Nathan Fein."

"I don't. I mean, I've never really noticed him like a *guy* before."

Aaron frowned. "You mean that he never noticed *you*."

"What's the difference?"

"Did you agree to go out with him?"

"What do you care, and what's the big deal?"

Aaron pressed his lips into a line, and I scowled in frustration. I wanted to ask what had him so irritated, but he gave me a curt nod and walked away. I didn't realize Nahan had been watching our exchange until I caught him staring from the corner once Aaron retreated back to our group of friends.

After everyone left for the Parkview Diner, Nathan rejoined my side and apologized for not being around to clean up. He chatted with me and my mother until one of the ushers needed to lock down the synagogue for the evening.

Between Nathan's persistence, furtive glances, and the encouraging winks from my mother, I agreed to a coffee date that night and skipped the College and Career event for another date the following day.

Aaron texted me late Saturday and asked where I was, but it was too late to tell him I was on my way to an eight-year journey into hell with Nathan Fein.

CHAPTER 17

"When are you going to divorce him?" Charlotte Williams demanded seven years later.

I shielded my phone into my chest, fearing my husband would overhear my friend's outburst. I huddled farther into the corner of my master closet and scanned my darkened surroundings. Nathan had said he would be downstairs working late, and I lied and said I'd be going to bed early. I knew Nathan wouldn't come upstairs before one or two, but I'd been walking on eggshells with him more than usual. With my husband working from home, it was the only time I knew he wasn't eavesdropping on my phone calls or sneaking glances over my shoulder to see who I was texting.

Even as I spoke in feather light tones with my best friend, I feared the hanging clothes above me wouldn't completely muffle the sound. "I can't."

"What do you mean you can't?"

"Ssh!" I hissed. "He'll hear you!"

"Lauren, this is no way to live. You're hiding in a closet

scared to death your husband will find you on the phone with me. This is ridiculous."

"Well, it's not like he outright forbade me to talk to you, Charlotte. Nathan's just over-sensitive about his privacy."

"When are you going to stop making excuses for him? Your husband called me a bad influence and said that talking to me about your marriage emasculates him. We both know this is really about Nathan not wanting anyone to know what he's like at home instead of his picture perfect image at synagogue."

"Charlotte—"

"And the one *you* put on social media," she added.

My pretty little lies shriveled under the searing light of reality. Charlotte continued to chip at my protective armor of denial.

"Lauren, your husband also says you need to be talking to a therapist about your marriage problems and not to anybody else. That's not normal. It's controlling. And it's not like Nathan even follows his own advice. I've seen the texts between him and Rick badmouthing you. Nathan would have an aneurysm if the situation was reversed."

"You told me," I said, feeling my husband's betrayal like a fresh punch to the gut. "I just don't understand why he would lie about me when he knows how hard I've tried to make him happy."

"Because Nathan needs to blame anybody other than himself for why your marriage is horrible and you're so miserable. He also failed to tell Rick how he puts bruises on you and Ari—or that he likes causing you pain in the bedroom too. It's no wonder why you don't want your husband touching you."

"Charlotte!" I gasped. "That's not exactly how it happened. The porn scandal at Beth Shalom has really made things hard for us."

"The porn scandal has nothing to do with it. You didn't even know how messed up your sex life was until you told me what's been going on. You said you've had to hide the pain for years because Nathan will complain that you're hurting his feelings if you say anything. Can't you see how wrong that is? He thinks his precious little feelings are more important than causing you bodily harm."

"I know," I whispered.

Charlotte softened her tone. "Sweetie, you need to hear it from someone who loves you. Your husband is deliberately harming you and your son, and he has no intention of stopping."

"I don't think the sex part is on purpose, Charlotte. I mean, Nathan and I were virgins when we got married, and—"

"And what?" she interrupted. "The pig certainly doesn't act like a virgin! You said he's been watching porn since he was in middle school, so it's not like he doesn't know how sex works. Even without it, he could still ask a marriage counselor for sex advice, read a freaking book, or care more about his wife's feelings than just pleasuring himself."

I sniffled back tears. I hated myself for how long I'd let Nathan convince me his depravity was normal and my reaction was the real issue. I hated myself for marrying a man who convinced me I could "help" him with his issues and inspire him to do better. I hated myself for believing that Nathan's crumbs of affection or occasional good deeds were the *real* Nathan, but his typical, sullen behavior was because I'd always done something wrong. I hated myself for sitting on a closet floor still wondering if my husband's abuse, neglect, and contempt were really as bad as it seemed.

Charlotte sighed. "I know this is hard. I could lie to you and tell you to keep praying for Nathan or just 'trust God,' but this isn't a problem with your faith. You're not responsible for Nathan's choice to harm you in or out of the bedroom. Your husband knows what he's doing. This is abuse!"

"Not if you ask his mother," I muttered.

Charlotte gave an unladylike snort. "If Nathan asked Liora to take care of his sexual needs, she'd probably do it. That twisted relationship would make Oedipus blush."

"Charlotte!"

"Give me a break," she huffed. "The woman gave you lingerie at your wedding shower after you told everybody a million times you didn't want to open that kind of stuff at synagogue. It's not like she even got you the good kind. It was cheap polyester garbage from K-World. Who the heck wants to wear a zebra thong from their husband's mother? It was completely inappropriate."

I rolled my eyes and permitted myself a tiny groan. "The worst part was when she acted like it was some big joke with Nathan's dad. She didn't care how humiliated I was with her *little surprise*. Bruce didn't think it was so funny when Liora told him the black lace set she got me was the same lingerie *she* has —and then began describing it for him."

Charlotte audibly gagged. "Are you serious?! What is wrong with these people? I was only half kidding when I said Liora would take care of Nathan's libido issues."

"I don't know," I said, running my hand over my tangled, unwashed hair. "How is any of this real? How is this my life? Charlotte, I did everything right. I saved myself for marriage, we didn't kiss until our wedding day, and, and..."

"And you got conned by a snake and his team of sycophants," she finished. "Liora's performance at the women's breakfast when you left Nathan was award-worthy. The way she carried on about her son's crumbling marriage and your lack of forgiveness had everyone in tears. Well, except for me and your mom. Liora shot us dirty looks the entire time."

"Shot you dirty looks? My mom didn't mention that, just that Liora was being dramatic. Was it really that bad?"

"Yeah, it was *that* bad and probably worse, to be honest. I didn't want to say anything at the time because I knew you were already dealing with so much."

"It's okay," I said. "I had a feeling Liora was running her mouth at temple. Her clique of Karens still give me the side eye every time I go."

"No doubt," Charlotte replied. "They do whatever Queen Bee commands. I only wish I'd gotten the spectacle on my phone. One second Liora's crying for her innocent little baby. Two seconds later, she's raging at how you're a poor excuse for a believer for leaving Nathan when he needed his wife the most. Your mom and I left when Tina told everyone to gather around Liora and pray against all of the spiritual attacks on the Fein family. Tina means well, but I had to talk to her about it later. She said she thought she was just helping, but it's obvious she got all of her information from Liora."

My stomach knotted at the convoluted storytelling where my mother-in-law made me guilty of everything her son had done to me. The betrayal of being subjected to Nathan's abuse only to have his mother disguise it with hyper-spiritual theatrics had me clawing at my hair.

My voice trembled with adrenaline. "So, all of this behavior is only reprehensible to Liora Fein if she can accuse *me* of committing the crime, right?"

"Apparently," Charlotte deadpanned. "It also gets that drama queen attention for herself and sympathy for Nathan. She's the star of the show and also a victim—her two favorite roles in life. I knew something was off with her the first time we met."

Liora's ongoing slander had also mobilized an army of Beth Shalom flying monkeys to attack or shun me while I was emotionally bleeding out from Nathan's betrayal. The behavior of my congregation had blindsided me, and Nathan feigned complete ignorance about it. His response to my anguish was tepid at best, and now I understood why.

He agreed with them.

Liora's minions blamed me for Nathan's imaginary injuries while further adding to my actual wounds.

"Laur? You still there?" Charlotte asked.

"How do I get out?" I whispered. "How do I ever get out of this nightmare?"

"This is the biggest step you'll ever take, my friend. You know that I know."

I shook my head, already regretting my words. "What kind of a legacy am I giving my son by getting divorced? I can't do this, Charlotte. There has to be another solution."

"The legacy you're giving your son is one where he learns that his mother doesn't deserve to be abused and disrespected. You're also teaching your son how he should be treating any female in his life. Do you really want him following Nathan's example?"

My vision blurred from tears. "I just...I don't know how I can ever escape. It's impossible. Nathan controls everything."

"And that needs to change," Charlotte said. "One of the first ways I got my independence was going back to work after being home with the girls for thirteen years. I had my own money, my own bank account, and Rick didn't have access to any of that information until I had to submit it for discovery in our divorce. I'd already been saving for a year before I filed. Rick thought I was bored being a housewife and 'spending all his money' anyway. I think God just blinded him so I could eventually get out."

"How are things going with the divorce?" I asked, wanting to get the focus off myself. "How's life over at Tina's? Did you guys patch things up after the fight you had?"

Charlotte sighed. "I think so, but our friendship feels different. Tina says it's just growing pains since we only moved in a month ago, but she drops everything when her boyfriend calls or he wants to go out. I see less of her now than when I was still living with Rick."

"You're not jealous, are you?"

Charlotte blew a raspberry. "Not at all! I just remember all of the girls' nights Tina promised me before we moved in. Instead, it's either excuses and broken plans or she's only available when I've already got something going on. She's my best friend, but I've just been really irritated with her lately. She bought herself a second car and keeps bragging about it like I'm supposed to be impressed."

"You mentioned that. Why does she think you care?"

"No clue, but she won't shut up about how she paid $75,000 *cash*. I work an entire year to make half that much money, so it seems like a waste to me. I'm not a car person, so maybe that's why, but she's in love with all of the bells and whistles. She knows Rick isn't giving me a dime of support either, so I don't get why she keeps rubbing her money in my face."

"Yeah, that's definitely strange," I said. "It's not any secret Tina has money, but it's pretty insensitive considering your current situation." I thought of the one holiday party Tina had invited me and Nathan to attend. Her house was enormous, certainly more than she needed since her children were grown.

"I know you guys had no problem fitting into Tina's basement, but it sounds like you may not fit into her lifestyle."

Charlotte grunted. "I guess. Tina has been living high from the life insurance and investment accounts David left her. She'll never have to work a day in her life again, but I'm just annoyed with her behavior—not her money. Anyways, at least I can go to work. Do you have any ideas of what you could do?"

"Nathan complains that I don't have a job, but every time I suggest getting one, he only wants me to work when Ari is in school. Pre-school is just four hours a day, not including the time for drop off and pick up. I told Nathan that for me to legitimately work, Ari would have to go into the aftercare program or switch to a regular daycare. Suddenly, Nathan says it's too much for Ari. A week or two goes by, and then it's the same argument all over again. It's like Nathan doesn't even know what he wants, but no matter what I choose, I can never get it right."

Charlotte tsked. "You know that Nathan will change his story just to contradict you, right? If you say 'zig,' he'll say 'zag.'"

"True," I murmured. "He complained when I would eat dinner with Ari and not wait for him. I told him that he never kept a set work schedule and Ari couldn't wait until seven to eat. I asked Nathan to text me when he was on his way home, but he said I was trying to control him. I finally just gave up, but it was the same cycle all over again. Since he's been working from home, he still won't tell me when he's starting or stopping his work day. He just shows up when I tell Ari to eat because he can hear me in the house. He also leaves his dirty cups and dishes everywhere and asks why it's such a big deal for me to clean it up. You should have seen the look on his face when I asked why he thinks it's no big deal for *me* to do it, but it's a monumental task when he has to do it for himself."

I could feel Charlotte's eye roll through the phone before I heard the disgust in her tone. "Your husband is only happy when he's miserable. He also can't take responsibility for anything, as you've told me time and again."

"Yes," I breathed, seeing the situation with a new pair of eyes. "It's always somebody else's fault, or he accuses me of overreacting. And I've told him so many times that he exaggerates the good things he does, but he minimizes the bad."

"And those good things are the bare minimum," Charlotte added. "Nathan acts like he deserves a trophy for wiping his own behind."

I chuckled. "If Nathan sent his mother a filthy wad of toilet paper, Liora would fawn all over him and thank him for thinking of her *in such an intimate moment*," I said, mocking the flowery prose she used in her cards to Nathan. "Did I ever tell you about the time Liora sent Nathan a thank you note for sending *her* a thank you note?"

Charlotte laughed. "I know you're not kidding, but it sounds too ridiculous to be true."

"Oh, it's all true," I said. "You're completely right about the emotional Oedipus relationship. Liora has zero regard for Bruce, but she treats Nathan like he walks on water. She also treats Matty like he's nothing but a screw up. Do you know he's the only one in that twisted family who took my side with the porn scandal?"

"Well, Matty spent long enough covering for his baby brother, so it's the least he could do," Charlotte said. "I didn't need to read about it in Rebecca Margolin's book to know how much Matty and that entire family whitewashed Nathan's addiction. The Fein family has been lying for that pig for thirty years. And don't put Matty Fein on some pedestal just because he's not quite as reprehensible as the rest of that messed up family."

"I know, Charlotte. I see how critical and overbearing Bruce and Liora are, and I wonder if that's why Nathan is the way he is. I know he has a lot of pain from his upbringing."

"Nathan is also a grown adult. His choices are his own. *Nathan* lied and covered up his porn problem before you got married. *Nathan* lied and covered up the garbage he downloaded at temple. You can't trust a single word out of his mouth. The actual *ongoing issue* is the fact he's an abusive pig who gets off on hurting anybody weaker than him—including his two-year-old son."

"So, you're saying I'm weak?"

"No!" Charlotte exclaimed. "Laur, you're one of the strongest women I know! You're surviving a hell that most women can't possibly imagine, and most men think is just made up for Lifeline movies. When you got married, Nathan convinced you that he could get cured with your help. When that didn't work, he had to convince you that it was your fault he couldn't stop. He has done everything possible to drive you crazy. Like, literally *crazy*. You told me he wakes you up in the middle of the night by turning all the lights on, or he sets his alarm at five am and then lets it go off every ten minutes for another hour and a half. None of that is normal—it's sadistic."

"Lauren!" Nathan bellowed from inside the master bedroom. "Where are you?"

"I have to go!" I whispered frantically, fumbling with my phone.

The closet door flung open, and the overhead, fluorescent light had me burrowing further into the corner.

Nathan exhaled in disgust before muttering curses about

me. I sat stunned, disbelieving my ears as my husband let the evil words fly. He'd shamed me for watching movies with less profanity than his vile diatribe. He growled one last expletive as he slammed the door.

His footsteps thundered furiously down the staircase like a stampede of horses, and I knew he would check my car next to see if I was on the phone with Charlotte. I scrambled to my feet and raced to Ari's room. Relieved that Nathan's outburst hadn't woken the baby, I curled on the floor next to the crib and shut off my phone. I found a realistic position to feign sleep twenty seconds before Nathan ripped open our son's bedroom door.

"Figures," he muttered angrily.

I expected Nathan to wake me, but he rumbled back downstairs to his precious laptop.

My entire body trembled as I permitted myself a true breath of air. I turned my gaze to my son and watched the steady rise and fall of his chest. Whatever demons Liora and Bruce Fein had unleashed onto Nathan had to end before they took root with my own child. A lineage with divorce was far better than another generation of abuse.

And so began a three-year battle for my freedom.

CHAPTER 18

"I'M GLAD YOU BOTH COULD MEET WITH ME TODAY," the guardian ad litem, Carson Gentry, said. He glanced between me and Nathan. With a new outbreak of Covid cases in our area, we both were asked to wear facemasks for the meeting. Nathan and I sat across from one another at a conference table while Carson sat between us at the head. I was surprised Nathan and his attorney had agreed with our suggestion of Carson Gentry when we rejected their first option, but it felt like such a huge victory and one step closer toward ending our divorce. Hunched over in his chair, I realized Nathan intended to use his practiced, tail between the legs pose to play for sympathy like he did during our marriage counseling with Rabbi Lebow.

Speaking with a southern accent straight out of a Civil War movie, Carson began our meeting. "I asked to meet with y'all together so we only have to do this once. It saves you both time and money this way."

Nathan cocked his head as Carson was already speaking his language.

"I don't volunteer to be a guardian," the GAL continued, "I don't request it. I do this for the children. I couldn't give a rip about you," he gestured at me, "or you," he said, pointing to Nathan. "Your divorce means nothing to me other than how it affects your kid. I'm not here to take sides. I'm going to push both of you to see how you react, and I don't care whether you like me or not. You hired me because you two can't put aside your differences and agree to custody and just settle this thing. Your son is the one stuck in the middle of your mess."

With Nathan's record of abuse against both me and Ari, I didn't expect to be on the receiving end of such hostility or to have my parenting equated to the monster who had deliberately hurt us. I pushed down the panic and traumatic flashbacks of Nathan's lies being believed once again. *Settling our differences* to Nathan meant nothing other than complete surrender—and he'd still find something to complain about afterward.

"I couldn't give a flying flip about you or your money," Carson sneered, adding in some other colorful adjectives that shocked me. Nathan's gaze darted to me, equally as stunned to hear the attorney curse.

"I just had one client pay me $35,000, not including her own attorney. We don't need to do all of that, Mr. and Mrs. Fein. The two of you need to sit down and talk and do what's best for your son. He's only five years old. He doesn't need to see Mommy mad at Daddy or Daddy mad at Mommy. He needs to see two parents who love him and who can put aside their personal feelings to put *his* best interests first."

My eyes bugged out of my sockets at both the dollar amount and what felt like another accusation. I felt convicted about angry responses I'd had to Nathan and his antics after our separation, but I knew Nathan poisoned our son with passive aggressive comments regularly. I glanced across the table to see Nathan looking pained.

Surprisingly, he spoke up. "I agree, Carson. Bitterness doesn't do our son any good."

I schooled my reaction knowing that's exactly what Nathan wanted to elicit from me. In a sudden shift from his aggressive tone, Carson shuffled through the papers in a manila folder in front of him and then stared down Nathan. "So, you think it's surprising your wife would be bitter about the bruises DCFS recorded on both her and your son? Am I understanding you correctly?"

Nathan fumbled for words. Finally, he said, "I don't remember things happening that way. Lauren tends to confuse things, and she also manipulates people for sympathy. It's one of the reasons we can't work out this divorce amicably even though I've tried many, many times."

I inhaled a taut breath, my hands clenching on the sides of my chair. As I opened my mouth to set the record straight, Carson held up a palm to silence me. Lasering his focus back to Nathan, he said, "So, you don't remember how the documented bruises were placed on your wife or your child, or are you claiming someone else put them there? A TPO against you was approved by a judge, so clearly law enforcement might not be as 'confused' as you think your wife is. If it was my child who had been bruised, I would not have been as accommodating as Mrs. Fein with the current visitation set up."

I swallowed back a lump of emotion fused with adrenaline. Marianne Abbey had told me I couldn't afford the fight to keep Nathan from seeing Ari without supervision. She said allowing Nathan to see Ari alone would show a judge I was willing to work with him despite our troubled past. Nathan didn't see it that way, however, and he accused me of "cruel and abusive treatment" in our discovery paperwork. His list of witnesses to support the slander included his mother and other Beth Shalom acolytes.

When I switched counsel, Sondra Joyner advised me to wait and see the GAL's custody recommendation because it would help end our divorce stalemate. I raged back that my son was not a science experiment for the legal system, but my lack of funds prevailed over my mama bear instincts. Sondra said that because most fathers had to be cajoled into spending time with their children, even one with an abusive past like Nathan would be supported by the courts to receive more visitation time. It had become painfully clear that unless Ari's father snapped a selfie with a knife in his hand, nobody would withhold my son from him. Abuse only seemed to matter *after* the fact—of course, when it would be too late to prevent the damage.

"I just want more time with my son!" Nathan cried, his voice breaking. He sniffled back tears and reached for a box of tissues in the center of the table.

Carson cleared his throat. "While all of that's understandable, Mr. Fein, you also need to understand that your past violent behavior has consequences. The law is not here to cater to your feelings, and I'm sure Mrs. Fein has already spent enough time trying to do that."

Nathan's eyes flashed anger, glaring suspiciously from Carson to me. I thanked God that the facemask hid the tiny smile of satisfaction on my lips.

"And you," the GAL said as if reading my thoughts, "better not think you can use Nathan's past as a chance to club him in mediation or that you get a free pass for primary custody. Mr. Fein claims he's a changed man, and he has not put any further marks on you or your son. He also claims you're not mentally stable, which is something I have to take into consideration as well. Things won't go well for you, Mrs. Fein, if you're fanning any flames of animosity between Ari and his father. It helps make Mr. Fein's case against you, no matter his past behavior."

Now Nathan wore a smirk that I could feel before looking up to confirm my suspicions.

Digging at me even more, Carson said, "So, why are we here, Mrs. Fein? Trying to push Nathan for money because he lost his temper a few times?"

I choked, stunned by the coldness in his tone and insulted that he would trivialize my pain and suffering into something as disgusting as greed.

Before I could speak, Nathan chimed in. Chest puffed out, he said primly, "For the record, I didn't 'lose my temper.' Lauren just doesn't understand what it means to be a submissive wife. She does whatever her feminazi friend, Charlotte, tells her to do. No one at our synagogue believes Lauren's lies, and they will testify to that in court. These are all good, godly people who know how to discern the truth from unfounded accusations."

The lid finally snapped on my self control. "Of course, they took your side! Your mother and Rabbi Lebow covered up the underage porn you downloaded while supposedly doing IT work, and then they lied to the entire synagogue about why there was a police raid. Beth Shalom leadership doesn't want the members to find out that Rabbi's right hand man is a degenerate who beats his wife and son at home and then beats himself off looking at naked high schoolers!"

Carson Gentry stared at me with wide eyes as Nathan looked like he'd been slapped. He recovered quickly and jumped out of his seat.

"You lying, dirty—"

"That's enough!" Carson roared, surprising both Nathan and me. After exhaling an expletive, he said, "Well, it's no wonder y'all are getting divorced. Do either of you understand that the choice for your son isn't good versus evil? It's 'sucks' versus 'sucks more.' That's it. Now, both of y'all need to calm down, or we can end this meeting right now."

Nathan sat, simultaneously seething at me but also exultant in his success. He'd managed to make me look as unhinged as *he* was behind closed doors. Unlike Nathan, my posture of defeat was authentic, and my shoulders slumped.

"Mrs. Fein," Carson said more gently, "What's all this about underage porn? I didn't see any mention of it in the records."

I sniffled back tears of frustration and tried to keep my tone neutral. "My husband downloaded pornography on the computers at synagogue. The girls in the photos were minors, but Nathan said he didn't know. That's what he told the police anyway. He volunteers as the IT Director there to help offset his tithes."

"Tithes?" Caron asked.

"Beth Shalom believes you should give ten percent of your income to the synagogue."

"Well, that sounds like a Ponzi scheme if I've ever heard one," Carson quipped. Nathan made a high-pitched, strangled sound in his throat, and Carson chuckled to himself. "I'm guessing Mr. Fein disagrees."

I didn't take the bait and join the banter. It felt like a trap, and I still had egg on my face from my outburst. Ignoring Carson's comment, I said, "I found some of the same pornography at home and confronted Nathan about it. He cried and told me he was ashamed of himself. Nathan calls porn his 'ongoing issue,' and he struggled with it before our marriage— and obviously afterward."

"Porn isn't illegal, you know," Carson said.

I swallowed another bitter pill of truth. "Yes, I'm aware, but pornography of minors *is* illegal, and that's what got the police involved the first time. Nathan will tell you that he was exonerated because he was unaware the girls in the photos and videos were underage, but it was a scandal at our synagogue, and everyone blamed *me* for it."

Nathan was about to jump in again, but Carson held up a hand to silence him. "How did they blame you, Mrs. Fein?"

Tears flowed freely as the wound opened again.

"They called us in for a leadership meeting with Nathan's parents, the rabbi, and some others. My parents are also leaders, but they weren't asked to attend." I shot a pointed look across the table at Nathan. "I ran away to my parents' house after the scandal became public knowledge, and the leaders told me I had abandoned my husband. We had already met a couple of times with Rabbi Lebow about Nathan's porn addiction, and he told everyone at the meeting that Nathan suffered from my cold attitude toward him and my unwillingness to submit to my husband. Everything was all about Nathan," I said, fighting back tears. "Nobody cared about me at all."

Carson's gruff exterior looked infinitely more sympathetic. "I imagine that was very difficult for you. Is that when you began divorce proceedings?"

I shook my head. "No, I went back home and tried to salvage our marriage. I told Nathan I would work with him, but he had to actually make an effort to work. Instead, Nathan's abuse got worse. He became violent toward me and my son."

"But it was just a few times, right?"

"A few times?" I said, struggling for control. "No, sir. It wasn't a *few* times. Abuse was daily. Verbal and emotional abuse were a constant, even before the scandal. Physical abuse became a regular thing after Ari and I moved back into the house. I never knew what kind of mood Nathan would be in, and it got to the point where I couldn't make excuses for the bruises on me or my son."

"Is that true?" Carson asked, turning his attention to Nathan. "Did you abuse your wife and son daily?"

Tears filled Nathan's eyes. "No, sir, I would never do anything to harm Ari. Or Lauren," he tacked on after a delay. "It's just that she's got all these crazy ideas about 'the patriarchy,' and anything other than agreeing with whatever Lauren wants means that I'm abusing her. She also insults me to her friends and calls me lazy and selfish."

Carson raised silver eyebrows at Nathan's claim. "Are you saying that you've never said a negative word about your wife to any of your own friends or family?"

"Never!" Nathan vowed, lying through his forked tongue.

"Is that true, Mrs. Fein?" Carson asked, his voice dripping in disbelief as he turned back to me.

I shook my head. "Nathan blames a lot of our marriage problems on my friend, Charlotte. What he won't tell you is that he's been getting together with Charlotte's ex-husband for years to badmouth me. Rick blames me for his divorce from Charlotte the same way Nathan blames Charlotte for supposedly brainwashing me. I've also seen some of the text messages between the two of them. Charlotte sent me screen shots before she and Rick separated. Calling Nathan lazy or selfish is nothing compared to the things Nathan says about me."

"But *did* you call Mr. Fein those words?" Carson asked me.

I nodded. "In moments of frustration, yes I did."

"But Mr. Fein, you claim you've never had an unkind word to say about Mrs. Fein?" he asked, turning back to Nathan.

"Maybe one or two times," Nathan grudgingly admitted.

Carson's expression remained neutral as he faced me again. "Mrs. Fein, weren't you afraid of getting more bruises by mouthing off like that? If your husband was as abusive as you claim, I'm surprised you would call him names. Why didn't you leave with your son sooner?"

Nathan hid a smirk before Carson could see it.

Glaring at Nathan, I said, "Because my husband and our rabbi kept saying Nathan's abuse was my fault. And honestly, I wanted to believe it was something I could fix instead of Nathan choosing to treat me and our son like that. I didn't call him names when the physical violence escalated. I was too scared. Yes, my friend Charlotte told me that my marriage wasn't normal or healthy, especially when I had to hide the fact she and I were talking. Nathan would get furious if he thought I was texting her."

Carson slid his gaze back to Nathan. "And this is the 'feminazi' friend, right?"

"Yes, she poisoned Lauren against me, as you can see," he said with an indignant sniff.

Carson looked at Nathan with strained patience. "And you don't think any of your own behavior contributed to the problems in your marriage? Underage porn? Hitting your wife and son? Disparaging your wife to the husband of the friend who is supposedly a bad influence?"

"I never hit them!" Nathan shouted. His gaze darted to Carson and then lowered his voice. "Lauren will do anything to cover up how she treated me during our marriage. She could have put those bruises on Ari herself. It wouldn't be the first thing she's lied about."

My hands slapped down on the table, ready to reach across it and give Nathan Fein as good as he ever gave to me.

"Look at her!" Nathan said, gesturing at me. "I had to deal with her temper all the time."

I wanted to scream in frustration at how easily Nathan still played me like a fiddle. Tears burned my eyes as bile burned my throat. "I apologize," I murmured, choking on the words.

Carson nodded, his eyes unreadable. "Well, based on what I've seen, it's obvious what's best for both of you and your son is to end this divorce as quickly as possible. I want you both to speak with your attorneys and prepare any documentation, recordings, and witnesses you feel will help with my decision. These need to be impartial people who have nothing to gain. Your family doesn't count. I'm talking about school teachers, babysitters, and doctors who know the both of you. Once you have that information ready, have your attorney send it over to me, and then I'll schedule an appointment to speak with you individually."

I took in the information, already feeling like a complete failure. Nathan jotted notes on a legal pad in front of him.

"Mrs. Fein, this isn't going to be about you finally getting your freedom," Carson said, looking at me, "or about you controlling your ex with money," he added, looking at Nathan. "The parent I recommend for primary physical custody will be the one who can best communicate with the other spouse about the children and put their personal differences aside. I also want you both to sign up for the Wizard Family app."

"Wizard?" Nathan repeated, choking on the word. I knew anything remotely sounding like *witchcraft* would raise his hyper religious hackles.

"Yeah, wizard," Carson said. "It's a messaging app that allows the courts and your lawyers to view all communication between the two of you. That way, we can make sure there aren't any issues with doctored text messages or screenshots."

"Is that really necessary?" Nathan asked, paling.

"For someone who claims he's being falsely accused of abuse, I would think you'd be all in favor of it," Carson said pointedly.

Nathan pulled at his mask and readjusted it. "But why is it called *wizard*?"

Carson released an exasperated breath. "The heck if I know, son. I didn't make the dang thing! But if you expect me to believe anything you're alleging about Mrs. Fein, you better make sure you've got that in her own words, especially because I hear you're very handy on the computer."

I caught the implication in the guardian's words, wondering if all hope wasn't completely lost.

"The amount of time I spend on your case is completely up to y'all," Carson continued. "The best thing you can do for your son is sit down, talk, and settle all of this. The longer this divorce drags on, the worse it is for your son."

"I just think it's a travesty the law doesn't care about destroying families," Nathan said with his martyr voice. "It's probably why our society is so broken."

Not sparing him a glance, Carson said, "I've always found that the best place to look when broken things need to get fixed is in a mirror."

CHAPTER 19

Following the meeting with the GAL, I clung to Ari more than usual, scared that it may be my last chance to enjoy the amount of time we shared. Sondra assured me Carson was just doing his job, and we worked on pulling the list of school teachers and doctors to see if they would attest to my primary role in handling Ari's appointments and meetings. Nobody wanted to get in the middle of our divorce, and it felt like pulling teeth trying to convince them that I was just looking for factual information, not custody recommendations.

As I dropped off Ari at his pre-school on Monday morning, I held him extra tight.

"Mommy!" he fussed. "No more hugs and kisses!"

I chuckled as I snuck one more peck to his cheek. "But you're so delicious!"

Ari feigned a pout to cover the smile tickling at the edges of his mouth.

"Please?" I begged, fluttering my lashes.

"Okay, Mommy, but just *one* more," he said sternly.

I glanced over to the daycare worker who held back a laugh. "You're doing great, Mama."

As promised, I bestowed my son with a lone kiss before ruffling his curls. I watched him take the hand of his teacher, Miss Brittany, and called, "See you after work, buddy."

Ari nodded and then scampered to his classroom, practically dragging his college-aged teacher behind him. I chuckled to myself and then began my commute to Parkview and the Culver Incorporated high rise. Traffic was lighter than usual, and I walked to Vincenzo's for an early morning treat.

After purchasing a chai latte, I sat in the same set of chairs I'd shared with Taylor Horner two weeks earlier. I waved hello to Joe Trautweig, Kyle Goldstein, and the mighty Margolin as they stopped in for their morning caffeine rush. I couldn't help but smile at those three unlikely heroes and everything God had done in their lives.

"Mind if I join you?" a female voice asked from just beside me. "It's been a while since we've caught up."

I blanched at the sight of Jessica Ballinger, the ex-fiancée of my soon-to-be ex-husband. Our meeting nearly two years ago had cemented my decision to divorce Nathan rather than wistfully hope for the *courage* to go through with it. Jessica and I were acquaintances on social media, but given my contentious divorce, we kept communication to a minimum.

"Hi," I said, still stunned.

Jessica waved at her brother, Kyle, and he walked over with a wide smile. He kissed his sister's cheek and then smiled down at her baby bump. "No espressos for my nephew, okay?"

"You try being pregnant and not allowed to drink caffeine," she pouted, socking him in the arm. "You can ask your wife all about that."

"Oh, trust me, I had to hear about no sushi for nine months."

Jessica grinned. "Abigail is a saint for putting up with you."

"Speaking of our long-suffering spouses, what brings you to Vincenzo's this morning? Didn't feel like using the fancy coffee maker Micah got for your birthday? You'd save your husband a small fortune if I ran into you less often around here."

Jessica stuck out her tongue at her twin brother. "I just came in for some tea and then ran into an old friend." Her gaze flicked to me and then back to her brother.

I knew the exact moment Kyle remembered that Jessica and I had someone very important in common because his face paled. "Everything cool?" he asked.

"Totally," Jessica answered for me. "I saw Lauren and just wanted to say hello."

I nodded at Kyle. "I have to be at work in a few minutes anyway. Just ask Ted."

Jessica's eyes followed my words, and she gave an uneasy wave to the mighty Margolin. I knew Jessica had made her peace with Ted's wife a while ago, but he was very protective of Rebecca. It was something I both admired and envied. Ted lifted his chin in acknowledgement, but Joe gave Jessica a hearty wave and smile.

Kyle smirked. "It's quite a tangled web, isn't it?"

This time, I spoke up. "Yes, and they are connections I am very thankful to have. Please give Abigail a hug when you see her tonight and tell her I can't wait for our mom's night out."

"How about it, sis?" Kyle asked his twin. "You want to come too? I'm sure you're included in the invite for next weekend."

Jessica gave a noncommittal shrug. "I'll let you know. I'm a lot more tired now that I've got Aria too," she said, referring to her two year old daughter.

Kyle threw his arm around Jessica's shoulders and gave her a squeeze. "Well, just text me or Abigail either way. Enjoy your chit-chat," he said, gesturing toward me. "Lauren, I'll pass along your message to my wife." He gave one last smile to both of us before rejoining the guys across the room.

"So, how goes it?" Jessica asked, easing herself into a leather chair on my left. "And it's peppermint tea before you make any judgments," she said. "I've already had my one measly cup of coffee for the day."

"I'd be the last person to judge anyway. You know that."

She grimaced. "I'm sorry. I wish I could have warned you eight years ago."

"I don't think either of us knew what Nathan was truly capable of eight years ago."

Jessica glanced over my appearance and frowned. "Were you always this small?"

"And here I thought I'd put on a few pounds after I had Ari," I quipped.

She smiled back. "If you were skinnier than this, I'd be scared to see it. How is everything going with the divorce?"

I sighed. "Feels like it will never be over. Nathan is fighting me for custody, and he's done everything he can to stall things. It's not like he wants me back or even loves me. He just doesn't want the stigma of being divorced. We've already had our initial meeting with the guardian ad litem to get that process going."

Jessica nodded, apparently familiar with the term. "I have an old friend from my paralegal days who used to work in family law. She said the GAL investigation can take a while depending on how thorough they are. But with a case like yours, you don't want somebody cutting corners when it comes to the best interest of your son. Who is the guardian?"

"Ever heard of Carson Gentry?"

Jessica nodded enthusiastically. "Yeah, he's one of the good ones. Was he court appointed, or did Nathan actually agree with you on something?"

"Nathan's first choice was some lady with a reputation for selling out to the highest bidder. The online reviews were horrifying."

Jessica rolled her eyes. "Let me guess, it was Marlo Meeks, right?"

"Yes!" I exclaimed. "Oh my goodness, you know about her?"

"*Everybody* knows about her. I don't know how any judge in their right mind would go with her as a GAL, but who knows what pockets she greases? I'm glad you got Carson."

"Any advice for my one on one interview?" I asked. "He wanted to meet with both of us together, and that was a roller coaster."

"What did your lawyer say? Are you still with Marianne Abbey?"

I shook my head. "No, she fired me after she wiped out my bank accounts first."

Jessica tsked. "You know my story with Schwartz, Zendler & Hoffer, but even those guys have more integrity than anybody at the Abbey firm. More things I wish I could have told you before we finally met."

I waved her off. "God took care of it. I had some help from a friend to hire my new attorney, and thank God, she's fee based. Have you heard of Sondra Joyner?"

"Yes, and I have only heard good things about her. Sounds like you've got the right people fighting on your side. You're going to need it with Nathan."

I exhaled a heavy breath. "I hate what he did to you, Jessica, and everything that happened after. You never deserved how Nathan treated you or the lies he told everyone."

Her honey brown eyes widened. "No, hon, if anybody deserves sympathy right now, it's you! It took me a while to get there, but I got my happily ever after. I still can't believe I married someone six years younger than me, but Micah was worth the wait and has more maturity than men twice his age."

I smiled at the lovestruck look on her face. "I'm glad you're happy, Jessica. Truly."

"You deserve to be happy too," she said, patting my arm. "I know you can't date or anything yet, but after all the hell that Nathan has put you through, you deserve a win."

I blinked back tears. "Thanks. Sometimes, I wonder if there are any good men left in the world. Then, I see your brother and the guys over there with him, and I know it's not impossible."

"Don't you have a guy friend?" she asked, raising an eyebrow. "I saw you two talking at my brother's Chanukah party and wondered if there was something going on."

I shook my head emphatically. "No, Aaron and I are *just* friends even though nobody seems to believe me."

"Does Nathan know about him?" Jessica asked, lowering her voice. "You know that snake will twist anything if it makes him look like a victim."

"Nathan already knows Aaron, but he'd never consider him as any kind of a threat. Honestly, Nathan has such a high opinion of himself—and such a low one of me—that he thinks I should fall on my knees in gratitude that he lowered himself to marry me. To any other man, I'm just as ugly and undesirable as he pretends I was." I sniffled and wiped back tears, pushing down the montage of Nathan's ridicule in our marriage bed. "Even when Nathan acted jealous of other men at synagogue, it was because I was taking attention away from *him*, not because he thought someone else wanted me. I think he just wanted me to be miserable, alone, and begging for any scrap of attention from him."

Jessica watched me as she took a long sip of her tea. "You've come a long way," she finally said.

"What do you mean?"

"When we first met, you sat with your shoulders hunched, you barely made eye contact with me, and you were just broken. You're not like that anymore."

"I'm not?" I asked, stunned. "That's how I feel."

She shook her head. "No, hon. I remember it because it reminded me of Rebecca after she left that crazy cult with Pastor Sociopath. You both looked like someone had sucked the life out of you. Having survived a relationship with Nathan Fein myself, I can only imagine how much worse he was as a husband."

"Yeah," I said softly. "Definitely worse after the wedding."

She exhaled a sigh. "That pig has hurt so many people with his lies."

"Not just his lies," I said, unable to stop the tears from falling down my face.

Jessica's mouth fell open. "Lauren, I know you're not lying, but are you saying what I think you are?"

I pulled my shoulders back and inhaled a fortifying breath. "It was more than just mind games and lies, Jessica, and it wasn't just directed at me."

"He hurt your son?" she gasped.

"Repeatedly. DCFS got involved, and they substantiated Nathan's abuse against both of us. Nathan refused to leave the house, and he assumed I didn't have the money or the guts to move out with Ari. Thank God, my parents opened their home until Ari and I could find a place of our own. I also have a dear friend, Charlotte, and Nathan hates her because she encouraged me to divorce him. She helped me pack up our things to leave when we knew Nathan would be at services for a few hours."

"Wow," Jessica breathed, digesting my story. "I definitely want to meet this friend of yours and tell her she's a rock star."

I smiled. "I'm sure she'd like that. Charlotte is one of a kind. I don't know if she'd ever go to Bible study, but maybe something non-religious."

"How did you two meet?"

"Beth Shalom," I answered. "She and her ex-husband were members there, and her ex is good friends with Nathan."

"Which tells me all I need to know about the guy," Jessica said with an eye roll. She took another sip of her tea and added, "Lauren, I meant what I said. You look nothing like how you did when we first met. The way you're carrying yourself now, making eye contact, and the way you talk about Nathan is completely different."

"Really? Is it that noticeable?"

"Absolutely! When we talked the first time, it was obvious you were terrified of him. You kept looking around the room like he was going to pop out of the corner or something."

I nodded. "That sounds about right."

"And now you sound like you're just *done* with him. I thought you might be angry or upset, but you're detached. It's impressive."

"Why?"

"Because in a way, you're already free."

The moment Jessica Ballinger spoke those words, I felt the weight of chains fall from my shoulders. Clear in my mind, I heard the words from *Nahum 1:13:*

**Now I will break their yoke from your
neck and tear your shackles away.**

I shuddered and released a soft gasp, crumbling to my knees on the floor.

"Lauren!" Jessica exclaimed.

I could not stop the wave of sobs pouring out of me. I experienced the simultaneous flood of grief and relief that my season of darkness with a merciless beast would truly come to an end. I heard male voices surrounding me, and in the periphery of my mind, I realized that the very pregnant Mrs. Ballinger had gotten help from her brother and his friends.

"Lauren," I heard the mighty Margolin say close to my ear. "Can you hear me?"

"I'm free," I murmured, my face still bent toward the ground. "I'm free."

CHAPTER 20

I RECOVERED QUICKLY, MUCH TO THE SURPRISE OF Jessica, Kyle, Ted, and Joe. They all seemed intent on checking to make sure I was *really* okay, and I assured them I'd never felt better.

The gentlemen eventually took their leave, but Jessica remained beside me.

"Wow, wow, wow," I murmured, reveling in how light I felt.

"What happened?" she asked, eyes still wide,

Beaming, I said, "What you said about me being free, Jessica. It was like these invisible chains came off, and I heard God speak a Bible verse over me."

"What do you mean, you *heard*?"

I grinned like a fool and didn't care one iota. "In my head, not out loud," I said with a laugh. "I'm not hearing voices, I promise."

Jessica smiled back. "I know you guys are pretty intense about your Jesus stuff. Rebecca always talks about 'hearing from the Lord,' but I know it happened to Joe and Carly too. Carly shared an early copy of her manuscript with me, in case you're wondering."

"Jessica, if you want, I can show you the Bible verse I'm talking about. I'm not trying to push anything, but I thought you might want to see it."

"I know you're not trying to push, but it does make me feel weird. I was never very religious, and I know you guys wish Micah and I would just fall in line with everybody else."

I pulled a face. "Your brother loves you for *you*. Periodt. And that's with an extra 't' on the end. I just thought you'd want to see the verse and how your words matched it perfectly."

Tears filled her honey brown eyes. "Did they really?"

"Are you kidding? Did you miss what just happened?"

"I thought you were having a breakdown, so maybe it's not such a good idea," she laughed. "I can't imagine God using someone like me anyway."

"Someone like you?"

Her expression sobered. "Well, the whole world knows my story. Thank God, my husband says he doesn't care."

"And you think God does?"

Jessica rolled her eyes. "I'm not an idiot."

"Look, God has used prostitutes, adulterers, murderers, lepers, inmates, and even a talking donkey. Trust me, you are *not* unworthy."

She smirked. "Well, I guess I'm only guilty of being a few of those."

"Well, I married the last one, so what are you gonna do?"

We both burst into a fit of giggles.

"Talking donkey sounds about right," Jessica said, regaining her breath and placing a hand on her belly.

I grinned. "I'm just glad I can laugh about it. It's been such a long road trying to get rid of all the anger and bitterness. I definitely haven't arrived yet."

"Which you have every right to feel," she added quickly. "Seriously, I know you'll probably give Jesus all the credit, but I have no idea how you've survived everything you have, and you're still so positive."

"One of the hardest realities I had to face was seeing the toll Nathan's abuse took on me. Even after Ari and I moved into our apartment, I'd catch myself cursing Nathan under my breath as if we still lived together. I'd be washing dishes, and it would trigger all the times he nagged me for leaving the sponge in the sink. Of course, *he* was the one who did it all the time and then 'didn't remember' or 'couldn't recall' doing it and then blamed me instead."

Jessica pursed her lips. "He did stuff like that to me too. I think it's called *gaslighting*, right? They act like you're crazy, and they deny things you *know* happened."

I nodded. "One of Nathan's many little tortures. He also likes to pretend he's stupid and forces you to explain something a hundred times to see how long it takes before you get aggravated. Then, he plays the victim when you finally lose your patience with him."

"Of course," she scoffed. "Nathan plays that victim role to a tee."

Lost in flashbacks, I continued on. "Then, there were all of the mind games. I had a certain way I loaded the dishwasher. It wasn't really a big deal, but on the rare occasion Nathan actually loaded the dishes, it looked like Ari had gotten in there. If I corrected him, Nathan told me I treated him like a child. Then, he would ask me to show him for the 900th time how to load the dishwasher as if he forgot the other 899. I realized it was all just for attention when I stopped doing any of his dishes.

Suddenly, Nathan could load the dishwasher just fine. It was stuff like that and anything else he thought would irritate me. If I ever complained, Nathan would do it ten more times out of spite."

"I can't even imagine," Jessica tsked as she placed a hand on my arm. "I have to run, but I'm glad we ran into each other today. It sounds like things are looking up for you too."

"I hope so," I said, not feeling quite as light as I had a moment earlier. "Thank you for what you said."

She smiled back. "My pleasure, hon."

Over the next few days, I wrestled with the triggering thoughts about life with Nathan and if I'd truly forgiven him. I still remembered his angry accusations of bitterness and the hatred in his eyes. From the age of ten, I'd heard nothing from the pulpit other than how carrying pain from a relationship conflict equated to unforgiveness and holding grudges. Rabbi Lebow's form of conflict resolution always whitewashed the offense and shamed the survivor if they didn't immediately "forgive" and act as though nothing had happened. Setting those old tapes aside, I prayed and asked the Lord if my lingering pain stemmed from a desire for justice or just my badly injured heart still healing from all the horrors I'd endured.

Entering my shared office the following Friday morning, I waved to Poppy as she worked through a stack of insurance proposals on her desk. I wanted to turn off the churning, conflicting thoughts still warring in my mind, but I wrestled with guilt about letting go, guilt about *not* letting go, and guilt about not knowing what to do. My earlier freedom had spiraled into confusion and condemnation.

"Morning," Grant called from our open doorway. "Everybody ready for the weekend?"

Poppy glanced at me and then back to Grant. "We're all good, thanks. What can we do for you?"

He produced a dog-eared copy of an Employee Benefits Guide. "Poppy, you look swamped. Lauren, do you have time for some changes? I promised the client I'd have a draft out to them before EOB."

"How many changes are we looking at?" I extended my hand to take the document, but when Grant's fingers grazed mine, I snatched the packet with more force than necessary. Poppy raised an eyebrow and then pretended she wasn't side eyeing our entire exchange.

"Is everything okay?" Grant asked.

"I just have a lot on my plate today. Sorry if I was a little rough with your document."

He leaned in closer. "Did you ever get a chance to use the gift cards?"

Poppy cleared her throat as she clicked away on her keyboard.

"No, not yet," I said tautly.

His happy expression faltered as he cocked his head to the side. "Are you sure you're all right? You don't seem like yourself this morning."

"How *should* I seem?"

Grant looked affronted, and Poppy took the opportunity to announce a sudden need for caffeine from the break room. She departed the office and mouthed, "You got this" over her shoulder as she left.

Crossing his arms over his chest, Grant asked, "What's going on? Obviously, something's up."

"I've been meaning to tell you this since last week, but I haven't had the chance. I can't keep the gift cards. I appreciate the gesture, but it's just too much."

"What? Why?" he asked, alarmed. "Is it your ex-husband?"

I waved him off. "No, it's you. It's us. It's too much."

"What are you talking about?"

"Really?" I asked with a self deprecating laugh.

"Really, what?" he repeated. "Lauren, I don't get where you're going with this."

I sighed, ready to put an end to the torment of *what if* and crush my "crush" into smithereens. Grant would apologize for unintentionally leading me on, reiterate his love for Hayley, and then I'd finally be free. I leveled him with a stern look I reserved for Ari's shenanigans. "Whatever your *interest* in me, the gift cards are crossing a line. I've been out of the game for a while, but I'm not stupid. Neither are you."

"Lauren, I'm with—"

"With Hayley, I know," I said, cutting him off, "but there's always this undercurrent with you, and it's more than being 'interested' as a friend. It's sending me mixed messages, and even if I wanted to, there's nothing I can do about it."

His chocolate brown eyes searched mine, and I returned his stare, finally ready to face the source of my confusing feelings.

"You've sent me some mixed messages too, you know. Like in the elevator."

I broke eye contact and feigned nonchalance as I shuffled papers on my desk. "You're taken, I'm still legally married, and that's the end of it. I'm just letting you know that your behavior is creating confusion. I don't think Hayley would appreciate it either. She's the one whose eyes you should find fascinating, not mine."

"Things with Hayley haven't been great for a while," Grant said, lowering his voice. "I want to get married and start a family. She doesn't."

"No offense, but shouldn't you guys have discussed that before you moved in together?"

"We did discuss it," he shot back. "I thought we were on the same page. Apparently, Hayley changed her mind."

"Oh," I said, meeting his eyes again. "Sorry."

He shrugged. "The writing's been on the wall for over a year. We have a good rhythm and routine, but we're basically roommates who happen to love each other. Hayley knows it too."

"Is that why you've been doing this hot and cold stuff with me? Am I just a distraction from an unhappy situation? 'Fascinating' because the status quo with Hayley got stale?"

Grant lifted an eyebrow. "I could ask you the same question."

I blushed and seamed my lips, not sure my heart could handle where the conversation was headed.

Taking a step closer, he said, "Lauren, you were my wakeup call that I want more in life than settling for what's easy or comfortable. Hearing your story and watching you stand up for yourself has been inspiring."

I began to reorganize my already organized cup of pens. "Well, I don't think I'd consider myself *inspiring,* but thanks. Even if it's not with Hayley, I hope you find what you're looking for. Everyone deserves a chance to be happy."

"That's the thing," he said, his voice growing husky, "I think I have."

My heart beat like a drum in my chest as my head whipped back to stare at him.

When Grant took another step toward me, I flattened my palm against his document on my desk to steady myself.

"Lauren, you're these incredible contradictions of bitter and sweet, empathetic and strong. You make me want to be a better person, and I don't think I've ever met anyone like that. I can't stop thinking about you. I know it's wrong. The whole situation is wrong, but it sounds like we both want the same thing despite our best efforts to deny it."

"So, I'm not just a way out or an excuse?" I whispered.

He shook his head vehemently. "I never saw you as a way out of things with Hayley. You just helped me realize that more was possible than what I thought I could ever have."

I blinked back tears as I felt the pull of mirrored longing in Grant's eyes. Temptation clamored to unleash eight years of being unloved, rejected, and abused onto a man willing to descend into sin with me.

I couldn't speak for Grant's feelings or how they'd begun, but I knew I'd set my own trap. I wanted to drown in those chocolate brown eyes as easily as I had submerged into every daydream about them.

His gaze veered toward my mouth as he closed the remaining distance between us. Poppy returned with a fresh cup of coffee at the same time. Her entry shook me back to my senses, and I startled in my chair.

"Did you guys, um, work out what you needed to?" she asked, side stepping Grant to settle into her desk.

"Almost," he replied, placing his hand on top of mine as I held onto his work request.

A jolt of electricity shot through me, and I pulled my hand away.

"We need to talk," he mouthed.

I shook my head.

"Lauren," he whispered on a ragged breath.

"I can't do this," I said quietly. "Please, just go." I reached into my purse and pulled out his pricey gift cards. I laid them on my desk rather than placing them anywhere our hands might touch again. Speaking in my regular tone of voice, I said, "I'll take a look at your revisions once I get through my leftover stack from yesterday."

"Thanks," he mumbled, swiping the cards from my desk and rushing from the office.

"Well, what the heck was that about?" Poppy asked with wide eyes. "Geez Louise, the two of you could have posed for one of my R.D. Hampton steamy historicals." She fanned herself with her hand.

I cringed. "That bad?"

"You could save money on a space heater with the fire you two are playing with."

"There's no playing, and there's no fire."

"Tell that to your boyfriend."

"He is *not* my boyfriend, Poppy. Not going to happen."

"Girl, if I had come back half a second later, you and I would be having a very different conversation right now. You were on a collision course for no good, and there's a lot you need to figure out if you decide to go down this road. The timing is still a huge problem."

"I know," I murmured. Finally admitting the truth, I said, "I just wish it wasn't."

CHAPTER 21

Prayer felt like offering lead weights following my conversation with Grant. It seemed so unfair that I'd been freed from my past only to feel weighted by my present. I didn't want to pray because I feared condemnation and shame for the lonely moments spent thinking about Grant or how strongly I wanted to act on our now-confirmed, mutual feelings. Even Charlotte would give me her loving version of the "I-told-you-so" speech, and the idea felt even more bitter knowing her divorce was over and she was free to date. I dropped off Ari at my parent's house to get some self care time over the weekend, but that quickly became brood and *what if* time. The weekend weather grew darker and more miserable, perfectly matching my mood.

When my phone buzzed with a text message late on Sunday, I assumed it was Charlotte checking up on me.

"Time to face the music," I muttered.

As I swiped my phone open, I realized the situation was even worse.

You okay, Laur? Aaron had texted me. *I know we're taking a break from the friendship, but I was praying for you this morning and had a nudge to reach out.*

Tears wet my lashes and my cheeks. "No, it's not Nathan, this time. It's me," I whispered.

Sniffling and wiping my eyes, I replied, *Everything's fine. No worries.*

Little dots showed Aaron typing and deleting before I finally received a message back. *I have some news. Can we talk?*

Surprised, I wrote back, *Sure. What's up?*

My phone rang a second later.

"Hey," I said, answering. "You all right?"

"More than all right," he said, his voice sounding lighter than I could remember.

"Aaron, what's going on?"

"You were right," he breathed.

"Right about what?"

"Me and you."

My stomach dropped. "What do you mean?"

"I've had this fantasy about us getting married for a long time, and I needed to let it go. I think I just wanted it so badly, I convinced myself it was from God. It wasn't."

"It wasn't?" I repeated, my voice wobbling.

"Laur, are you sure you're all right?"

Silent tears fell down my cheeks. "What's her name?"

"Oh," he said sheepishly, "I guess you figured it out. Her name is…are you crying?"

"It's about something else," I said, feeling the loss of our friendship even more. In that instant, I also understood why I'd never reciprocated Aaron's feelings for me.

He *was* safe.

He *was* good.

I had never been free to fall in love with Aaron Davis because the guilt would have eaten both of us alive. God didn't condone adultery, and Aaron and I would never have lived down the weight of our sin if our relationship started that way. No matter the many sermons or Bible verses about forgiveness, it would have been a black rain cloud over any romantic relationship we shared.

It also made me wonder why things didn't feel so "wrong" with Grant, but I shelved those nagging questions to focus on my friend. "Is it Chelsea?" I finally asked.

"No, not her!" Aaron said, laughing. "She's tried dating every single guy at Bible study, so I've never been interested."

"Oh," I said. "Well, who is it?"

"Do you remember Ruthie Roseman from Beth Shalom?"

"Isn't she twelve? I think I danced with you at her *bat mitzvah*."

"She was twelve when you were in college, Lauren. She's twenty-three now. We ran into each other at Charred Cups in Hillcrest. Her family left Beth Shalom during the pandemic. Her dad lost his job and couldn't tithe anymore, and she said Rabbi Lebow demoted him from cantor because it set a bad example for the congregation."

"That's awful!" I gasped. "That place is so toxic!"

"I watched a few of the sermons online and wondered why we hadn't seen Mr. Roseman cantoring. He was the one of the best guys we had. Now I know why."

"True," I said. Jon Roseman had grown up Conservative Jewish and knew Hebrew better than most of the men Rabbi Lebow put on the bima to chant the weekly liturgy. He had also become a single father when Ruthie's mom passed away from cancer not long after the bat mitzvah. Other than Nathan, Jon was considered "the catch" of Beth Shalom for the forty-plus crowd. Unfortunately for the available women, he revered his late wife so much, I didn't think he'd ever date again. Not with Ruthie and her sister, Rachel, to raise. Rachel was only seven when her mother died.

"Are you still there?" Aaron asked.

"Yeah," I replied. "I was just wondering if Mr. Roseman had ever found somebody."

"Rachel is a junior in high school this year, and Ruthie thinks her dad has been waiting for both of them to be out of school before he started dating. She said he met some lady online, but he's not talking about it much."

"Wow," I said, feeling the pain of my own situation even more. Inhaling a deep breath, I set aside my pity party to give my long suffering friend the support he deserved. "Aaron, I'm happy for you. And for Ruthie," I tacked on. "I think she's had a crush on you forever."

The irony of the situation wasn't lost on either of us.

"It's funny how God chooses to answer or not answer prayers like that, isn't it? I never would have imagined things ending up this way, but it just feels right."

"Sounds like things are already serious," I mused. "I don't have to ask if Ruthie feels the same way. You also have the bonus of knowing each other for over a decade."

"Are you sure you're okay to talk about this, Laur? You sound really down."

"You're right," I admitted, "but I'm truly happy for you, Aaron, and I've wanted you to find someone who deserves you and loves you back. I'll admit, I didn't think it would happen so soon, but I think it's good that this door closed for both of us."

"So, does that mean things are happening with you and the guy from work?"

"*Nothing* is happening on that front."

"Why not?"

"Wow," I laughed, "you get your own girl and suddenly you're happy for me and Grant?"

Aaron chuckled. "I was jealous, Lauren. That's different. You know that I want you to be happy and loved."

"Well, then can I tell you the truth?" I asked.

"Always."

"I *am* jealous of you. Not because of Ruthie, but because you have the freedom to find someone and fall in love. I feel like I'll be in divorce hell for the rest of my life."

"Is Grant not interested because you're still tied to that pig who won't let go of controlling you?"

I paused as peace flooded my senses. God's compassion toward me filled my heart with gratitude and awe. "Aaron, you were the last person I ever thought I could talk to about this, but I think you're the only person who will understand."

"Understand what?"

"How it feels to think you're in love with someone who isn't available to be loved by you. How it feels to build up everything in your mind for so long that you can't tell fantasy from reality anymore."

His jovial tone grew serious. "Laur, did something happen? Did you and Grant—?"

"No!" I exclaimed. "Nothing like that at all! He just...well, I kind of had a crush on him because it seemed 'safe.' He was with somebody, he's not a believer, and I'm still dealing with Nathan."

"Ohhhh," Aaron said, drawing out the word. "He just couldn't resist you, huh?"

I laughed and cried at the same time. "Something like that. He says I inspire him to be a better person, and it sounds like he's been planning to break up with his girlfriend for a while."

My friend whistled. "Yeah, sounds like he's got it bad, Laur."

"I still can't believe you're okay with this. Ruthie must be a miracle worker. Don't tell me you're already picking out wedding venues. Save something to do for *next* week."

He laughed. "I have peace, Laur. I never had that with us. It was always anxiety and nerves, but never peace like this. I promise, though, what I wanted more than anything was for you to be free from that psychopath."

"I know," I murmured, "and thank you for not judging me."

"I would be the last person to do that, especially after what I put you through."

"What are you talking about? You've been nothing but a friend."

He blew a raspberry. "Yeah, a friend who only stared at you all the time and pressured you for more if it looked like you might be open to it."

"Aaron!" I gasped. "Are you saying you would have slept with me if I had said yes?"

The long pause on our phone call was the confirmation I needed. Finally, he said, "My feelings for you weren't healthy. It was an obsession, and I thank God that He protected both of us from doing something we would have regretted."

Feeling like I'd been punched in the gut, I frantically pieced together the history of my relationship with Aaron Davis. It all made sense, including the pedestal I'd wrongly placed him atop of, thinking his intentions were far nobler than mine. He was just as human and just as fallible as Grant Kaplan...or me. I couldn't condemn my friend for the past any more than he could condemn me for my present misery.

"Thank you," I whispered. I repeated it again with more strength.

"For what?"

"For texting me and listening to the Lord about it. You have no idea how much God just used you to help me."

"Help you, how?"

"I've been struggling. Badly."

"Oh," he said quietly. "I get it."

"No, not even that," I rushed. "I've been struggling with condemnation. I didn't want to read a million adultery Bible verses, the heart is deceitfully wicked, or hold your thoughts captive. I know all of those things. I know that fantasizing about Grant is wrong. This whole situation is my fault."

"It takes two to tango," my friend said, jumping to my defense. "Grant was even less available than you were when you met him, Laur. Yes, you're still married on paper, but you've been trying to end the relationship for years. I know you don't need to hear all the 'equally yoked' lectures. Figure out what God is trying to change in your heart from all of this, and then leave the outcome to Him. Even if nothing happens, there's still a purpose for everything. We've seen that happen with all of our friends at Bible study, and after the misery you've been through, I refuse to believe that God doesn't have a happy ending in store for you. You deserve one!"

I scoffed as I sniffled away tears. "I'm not sure 'happily ever after' really exists for me. I've got so much baggage and a little boy who has experienced more trauma than any person ever should. I don't know if I'll ever trust myself to fall in love again."

My friend remained silent as he carefully chose his next words. "As much as I want that for you, Laur, we both know it's not time. I probably know that better than anyone. No matter how much you and Grant seem to be into each other, forcing something because you're both lonely will only fill you with regret later. This is just common sense, not a sermon on adultery."

"I know," I said, "and thank you for not giving me one."

Aaron exhaled a self-deprecating laugh. "After what I did to you on your parents' porch, I'm the last person who should be casting stones."

"Don't forget there were two of us on that porch. You may have started it, but I didn't stop right away either."

"But you did stop it, Laur. You told me it was wrong, and everything you said was true. I know the circumstances are a lot different now, but God will protect you from yourself as long as you let Him. That brain of yours loves to overthink, so just remember that God has promised you peace beyond your understanding. Anxiety is what has you twisting yourself into knots and working through nine million possibilities trying to figure it out."

"I guess you're speaking from experience," I said softly. "I don't feel like I deserve all of this kindness after everything I put you through waiting for me."

"You didn't put me through anything, and I want you to stop feeling guilty about it. You never promised me anything other than friendship. I was the one pushing you for more."

"You also pushed me to see the best in myself instead of Nathan's lies. You pushed me to believe that I deserved more than a life of abuse and neglect."

"You also deserve to be more than some guy's rebound chick or the first woman he finds who also wants to start a family right now."

Warily, I replied, "That's not jealousy, is it?"

"No," he vowed, "it's from a friend who doesn't want to see you repeat the same cycle you've been fighting so hard to get out of. You just said you don't want that either."

"Grant is nothing like Nathan."

"Give him time to prove it. See if he pressures you into a fast courtship like Nathan did. Don't start planning a future with your imagination instead of with the man Grant really is. See how he handles the boundaries you set. See how he handles himself in a crisis or how he treats anyone else he'd consider 'beneath' him—like waitstaff and admins in your office. If you start planning your happily ever after before you really know his good and bad sides, you're setting yourself up for disappointment."

"Or a repeat of Nathan," I finished for him. "Thank you, Aaron. For everything. God used you more than you know tonight."

"Hey, look, if it all works out, I promise to dance at your wedding."

"I can't wait to dance at yours," I said, and I meant it.

CHAPTER 22

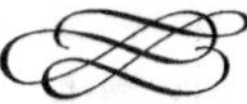

I prayed during my entire commute to work the following Monday. Not long after my phone call with Aaron, I had to own my behavior to Charlotte. She knew me well enough to know when I was avoiding her. Like Aaron, rather than speaking words of disappointment or frustration, she comforted and encouraged me as well.

"Lord, set a guard over my mouth," I whispered at my desk. I'd arrived early at work to pray over my office and soak in God's peace that had brought me to my knees just seven days earlier.

I played worship music softly on my phone and lost myself in spreadsheet edits. Formatting tables and fonts allowed me to function on autopilot while humming along.

"You're here early," Ted Margolin announced from my open office doorway. "We missed you at Bible study last night."

"Oh," I said, blushing. "Ari was with my parents, and I just wanted some 'me' time."

Ted raised an eyebrow with an amused smirk. "It wouldn't

have to do with a certain somebody who showed up last night, would it?"

My stomach dropped like a lead balloon. "What do you mean? Was Nathan there or did he send another Beth Shalom spy? I still can't believe Jackson was reporting back to them. He even helped Carly move into her apartment two years ago!"

Any hint of a smile disappeared from Ted's face. "Lauren, you know I would never make light of something like that. It's a miracle we found out Jackson was spying on our Bible study before Carly let you sublet her old apartment."

I pushed long bangs behind my ear and looked away. "You're right, sorry."

"So, you really don't know?" he asked, taking a step inside the doorway.

I jerked back at the mighty Margolin and his cryptic questioning. "What am I missing? You're usually pretty direct about things."

"Hmm," he murmured.

"What does that mean?"

He shook his head. "Nothing. It was an assumption on my part, and now I feel like the proverbial donkey for assuming something I shouldn't have."

"Margolin!" Grant called with a wide smile. "Just the person I was…oh," he said, catching my eye from the doorway. "Lauren, I didn't realize you were already here."

I glanced back and forth between the two impeccably dressed gentlemen as I tried to make sense of the situation. Fitting the missing pieces together, my eyes widened.

"Kaplan is joining me for Bible study with Kyle and Joe," Ted said, watching me closely. "He was our surprise guest last night."

I nodded, pressing my lips together and nearly biting my tongue.

"It was nice meeting your girlfriend last night too," Ted added. "I hope you both come back next week."

Feeling the air whoosh out of my lungs, I doubled over in my chair. All of my emotional torment over the weekend had been for absolutely nothing. I felt like a fool.

"Lauren!" Grant exclaimed. He rushed past Ted and kneeled by my side.

Aaron's advice suddenly felt like manna from heaven. I didn't know Grant Kaplan at all, and he was even more of an enigma than before. The details of Grant's relationship with Hayley felt as confusing as my own feelings for the man.

"Why were you there? Why was Hayley there?" I whispered, still hunched over.

"Let me explain it all later," he said. "I don't have time to do it now, and I want you to hear everything."

The mighty Margolin cleared his throat. "Everything okay? Kaplan, I think Lauren needs some space."

I dared Grant to lie to me as I searched his eyes for any hint of Nathan's demons.

"It's not what you think." He patted my hand before standing up and retreating out of the doorway. "I'll meet you guys at Vincenzo's," he called to Ted over his shoulder. "I just need to grab something off my desk."

"Lauren?" Ted asked with a fatherly look of concern. "What's going on?"

I inhaled a deep, cleansing breath. "No clue."

"You know that Kaplan has a girlfriend, right?"

"Well aware," I clipped. "I had no idea either one of them would be at Bible study, but I'm glad that God kept me from going last night. It would have been pretty awkward."

"Considering how the two of you were looking at each other just now, yeah, I'd say so."

"Don't," I said, holding a hand up. "I *know*, Ted. Believe me, I know."

He cocked his head and exhaled a sigh. "Just one more thing to pray about, I guess."

"Prayer would definitely be appreciated, and I sincerely mean that. I won't make a move without God's blessing on it, and I'm not about to do anything to jeopardize custody of my son."

"I know you wouldn't," Ted replied. "I'm sorry, Lauren. It's obvious I don't have the whole story."

"And neither do, I," I said, "but I'm looking forward to hearing about what happened yesterday. I can't imagine how or why Grant wound up at Bible study."

Ted smiled back. "He texted me late Friday asking for information, but I didn't expect him to show up. Kyle and Abigail were hosting, so it was a double surprise when Kaplan arrived with his girlfriend. After the study, Grant asked if we could meet with him today to answer some more questions."

My heart pounded in my chest, disbelieving that this insane desire of my heart might actually be from God after all. I shook my head and nearly laughed at how quickly I'd turned an office crush into happily ever after within seconds.

"You okay over there?" he asked again.

I chuckled softly. "To be honest, I'm dumbfounded more than anything. I can't wait to hear about your conversation with the guys."

Ted smiled back. "I have a feeling Kaplan will let you know one way or the other."

"Sounds like."

Adding to the commotion, Poppy nearly bumped into Ted as

she sipped on her own Vincenzo's coffee. Her cell phone sat squished between her shoulder and her ear.

"Oof! Sorry, Ted!"

"Join the twenty-first century and get a blue tooth," he teased. "You won't have to worry about near accidents in the office."

Poppy stuck her tongue out at him. "I only use that in the car, smarty pants. And don't you have another multi-million dollar client to impress?" Pausing as she listened to the person on the other end of her phone call, she said, "Yeah, it's Ted. Oh, okay. Love you too. Bye." Keeping her phone precariously perched on her shoulder, she glanced at the mighty Margolin. "My husband says hello and that I shouldn't be so mean to you."

Ted laughed. "I'll text him later. Ladies, I'll see you in about an hour."

Poppy side stepped Culver's top, east coast producer as he exited for breakfast. She plopped her bagel, coffee, and purse on her desk before turning to face me. "Is Ted actually *not* starting work at the crack of dawn? There's got to be pigs flying somewhere. Don't tell me Rebecca's pregnant again."

"Poppy, you're a whole vibe today," I grinned. "What's up?"

She leaned in and lowered her voice. "Have you seen *him* yet?"

"Are you talking about Grant showing up at Bible study yesterday? Yeah, I heard."

Her eyes brightened with excitement. "So, you've talked?"

"No, not really. Ted filled me in, and then Grant was here and gone in a flash. He said he'll tell me later."

Poppy took a sip of her coffee as she threw her purse in a desk drawer. "Girl, let me tell you what I saw yesterday. You know how men always leave out the important details."

"Important details?" I repeated. "I know about Hayley being there."

"Well, she was physically there, but definitely not in mind."

"What do you mean?"

"You could tell things were really tense between the two of them." She paused to wipe cream cheese from the side of her mouth as she munched on her bagel.

"Tense, how?"

"Well, this Hayley chick looked very uncomfortable, and she spent the whole night looking around the room. I don't know what she was looking for. Maybe an exit."

"Probably me," I surmised, stirring my own lukewarm tea.

She shrugged. "I guess we'll find out after you talk to Grant. His girlfriend didn't smile once, and she couldn't bolt out of that room fast enough. Maybe she's got a bad history with religious people, or she thought we would condemn her and Grant for living together. I think Ted and I are the only ones who know, but nobody mentioned it."

"Would it make a difference?" I asked. "Would Ted or Kyle have asked them to leave?"

Poppy took another bite before answering. "Not likely. Honestly, their situation isn't anybody's business. I spoke with Ted and Rebecca afterward, and we just want to show God's love and let them know they don't have to be perfect in order to be accepted by any of us."

I raised my eyebrows. "So, what they're doing is approved by omission?"

"No, no, no, like I said, their personal life isn't anybody's business."

"Unless you want to dissect it at work," I deadpanned.

Poppy waved me off. "Totally different. I have much less holy reasons for wanting to talk about Grant's relationship with

Hayley. We need to find out what's happening with that smolder you've got going on with Captain Curly Locks."

I rolled my eyes. "You better hope he doesn't hear you call him that. And wow, Poppy, you have totally turned this into one of your old bodice rippers. Courtly love and all that forbidden romance shtick."

"Yeah, act like I don't see you reading your Barbara Kellogg, workplace romance novels on your lunch break," she teased. "How *does* that hypocrisy taste in your tea?"

"Whatever," I scoffed. "I read those books because they're cute. I skip over the steamy parts."

She smirked. "So, you're saying there won't be any makeout sessions pressed up against the copier?"

"Poppy!!!"

"Be honest…is the smell of printer toner kind of a turn on?"

I threw a pad of sticky notes at her. "You're going to get me in trouble. And *nothing* is going on. Sounds like Grant may finally make an honest woman out of Hayley. She'll be the only person swapping spit with him at the copier. That's probably what he came here to tell me."

She shot me a side eyed look. "Grant seemed like he was getting into the Bible study and asked some good questions. Hayley looked like she wanted to be anywhere else."

"So what? Is the next logical step that Grant dumps Hayley so he and I can make out while I'm scanning documents? You know, while I'm still unhappily, yet legally married? I'm sure God would *totally* be on board with that."

She rolled her eyes at me. "Okay, so let's turn off the sarcasm font for a half second and get serious. I remember what it was like when I was searching for God and wondering if believing in Jesus and being Jewish could possibly coexist. I think Grant might be there too. No matter what happens with him and Hayley or him and you, it sounds like this is where things might be headed."

"I don't know, but I hope so," I replied. "Grant asked to meet with Ted, Joe, and Kyle today. That's why the mighty Margolin said he would be coming back later."

Poppy whistled. "That's quite a turnaround from Friday."

"Which doesn't change the fact that Grant still has a girl-friend, and she also went to Bible study last night. I know you said she looked uncomfortable, but what if God is working on both of their hearts? They've been together for so long, and it makes the most sense. Plus, as we know, I am very unavailable at the moment."

"Not for forever," she said with a saucy wink, "and stranger things have happened."

CHAPTER 23

I sighed and slumped in my chair. "This divorce sure feels like forever."

"How much longer until you're officially single?"

"Ask the slower-than-a-slug court system," I said morosely. "I think that's the worst part of this entire mess. In my heart, I'm not married to the monster anymore, but it just feels like there's no end in sight, even with the GAL now starting his investigation."

"You told me about that," Poppy said with a grimace. "This Carson guy sounds like quite a character." She finished the remains of her coffee and tossed it into her trash can. "But it's one step closer, right?"

"I guess."

She met and held my eyes. "It *will* end, Lauren."

I shrugged, blinking back tears. "I just wonder—whenever I finally get to the end of all this—if anyone would want me with all of my baggage. What if all of the quality men are already taken or just figments of my imagination?"

"What about Aaron?" Poppy asked.

"What about him?"

"Well, he's a good man who exists in real life. He's also head over heels in love with you."

"About that," I said, my voice trailing off.

"Oh girl, don't tell me you're in love with two men at once!"

I shook my head with a rueful smile. "Now, you definitely sound like R.D. Hampton. No, I'm not in love with either of them. And Aaron isn't in love with me either."

"Since when?" she gaped. "I refuse to believe that with the way he looks at you when he thinks no one is watching."

"Aaron got reacquainted with someone from Beth Shalom who's had a crush on him since she was a kid. It looks like she might be the one. He says he has peace, and I could hear it in his voice."

Poppy's hand slapped the top of her desk as she nearly fell out of her hair. "Shut up! Are you serious? What the heck happened this weekend?!"

I laughed at her outburst. "Apparently quite a bit."

Sobering, she gauged my expression. "Are you okay?"

"Fine," I said. "I talked to Aaron yesterday. I'm genuinely happy for him and Ruthie. She was always a sweet girl, and her dad was one of the few good ones at Beth Shalom."

"Ruthie what? Maybe Jared knows the family," Poppy said.

"Ruthie Roseman."

"The name sounds vaguely familiar. Do you have any other deets about her?"

"She's twenty-three now and has a younger sister graduating high school next year. She's shorter than me, brown hair, blue eyes, freckles, and one of the most genuinely kind people I've ever met. She's the type of person who pulls out the personality in others because she makes you feel safe. Aaron definitely needs that."

"Wow," Poppy murmured, "she sounds incredible. And you sound incredibly gracious about the situation."

"Gracious, how? I'm not in love with Aaron. I never was. I've been telling him to find someone else and stop waiting around for me to catch feelings."

"Yeah, but there's also the very human side of you that may not want something until it's no longer available. Or maybe the fear that it was your only shot at happily ever after."

I raised my eyebrows. "I think Aaron will be a terrific husband and father one day, but I wasn't pinning any hopes on things just falling into place for the two of us."

"You just said you didn't think there were any quality men left in the world. I didn't know if that's what you meant."

"No, not at all! Depression is a daily battle for me, and so is getting rid of Nathan's voice in my head. Would I love a stepfather for Ari? Sure. Do I want my son to see what a healthy marriage looks like so he knows how he should treat his own wife someday? Absolutely! But even if I never get remarried, date, or whatever, I could never keep Aaron dangling like an insurance policy because of my own fears and insecurities. That just sounds so selfish. It's something Nathan or his brother would do."

Poppy looked remorseful. "Sorry, I guess I was putting myself in your shoes. Looks like I still have a lot of work to do on my own."

I smiled back. "You're forgiven. I didn't take offense."

"So, what about Nathan's brother?" Poppy asked. "Nobody ever talks about that guy. Rebecca met him a hundred years ago when she was dating Ted."

"Matty is three years older than Nathan, so he's forty-five

now. He hasn't remarried since his divorce. I didn't see him that often when Nathan and I were together, and I doubt I will now."

"Did he treat you like everyone else did?"

I shook my head. "No, Matty was more guarded than the rest, but he also seemed to genuinely like me and pity me at the same time. When the porn scandal was exposed, he called out his brother for looking at that garbage and his parents for covering it up."

Poppy whistled. "I bet that went over like a lead balloon."

"Yeah, Matty is 'he who shall not be named' in the family right now. Nathan acts like he's an only child, and his parents treat him that way too."

"Probably because big brother doesn't go along with their charade," she mused.

"He's just not into the messianic stuff like the family is. Not that Nathan or his parents act all that 'Jewish' at home. His mother loves bacon cheeseburgers, only celebrates holidays at Temple with an audience, and when I asked her about it, she said, 'Why would I do all that work at home when the synagogue will just do it for free?' Of course, that didn't stop her from bashing her friends for posting pictures of their Christmas trees on FaceSpace."

"Yeesh! She sounds like a delight."

"Yes, a delight where a little goes a very long way—and it takes a while to get that taste out of your mouth."

Poppy smirked. "I'm sure salty and bitter aren't two flavors you'd like to have lingering on your tongue."

"What's worse is the stench of hypocrisy and deceit on the entire family. I hate that Ari will have to spend any time with them alone."

"Are you worried that some of their stink will rub off on him?"

"Yeah," I admitted. "He's still so little and impressionable. I have no control over what happens when he's not under my supervision, and Nathan and his mother will work overtime to undermine everything I've done to protect him."

"Just remember that you're not fighting this battle alone," she said, "and that God cares for Ari more than you could possibly imagine."

"I needed that," I whispered, wiping an unexpected tear from my eye. "Sometimes I wonder if this valley has an ending. Nathan will drag everything out until I run out of money or stamina to keep fighting him."

Poppy tsked in disgust. "I'm so sorry you're having to deal with this, Lauren. The divorce process with Jared was a nightmare, but nothing like what you're going through. Jared dragged it out because he was lazy and selfish. Eventually, it was because he wanted to see our marriage work. Nathan clearly doesn't want a divorce, but I don't think it's for the same reasons."

"That's because your husband genuinely loves you and your children. Mine doesn't. Never did. He just wants to break me into submission."

She grimaced. "Yeah, I can definitely see that. Is there any way you can get equity out of the house? Force Nathan to sell or at least cash you out of the mortgage? Your name is on the deed too, right?"

"Yes, we did cosign on the house. Nathan will have to eventually sell or give me my share, but because we're at a stalemate, I don't know when I'll ever get access to that money. The longer it takes to get to mediation—let alone before a judge— the longer he can go without any real financial support. He won't give me a dime he doesn't have to unless the courts force him. He doesn't care how any of this affects our son so long as he can find a way to punish me for leaving him."

My co-worker put a motherly arm around my shoulders and pulled me into a hug. "You deserve so much more, Lauren. I promise, there will be a beautiful life once this is over. There is no way God intended marriage to ever look like this. In the meantime, I hope you can get some attorney's fees and court costs for your trouble."

I exhaled a sarcastic chuckle. "Wouldn't that be nice? After everything Nathan has spent on his shark lawyer, it would be nice to have him reimburse me for all the money he's cut off access to because I can't afford the same type of representation. Sondra said that we can go after him for fees, but if we wind up settling, I probably won't see any of it."

Poppy sighed. "The only people who ever 'win' in a divorce are the lawyers."

"You and Jared did. You got your happily ever after. Jared repented, and it's obvious to anyone how much he adores you."

Her smile faltered. "I suffered in a horrible relationship for eighteen years and then another two years trying to divorce my husband. Things are wonderful *now*, but that's only been recently. I'm glad I wrote my book, but I also left out some other stories that would have been too embarrassing for our family to put in print. The pregnancy scare with Leah Halpern was more than enough."

"I remember," I said, recalling that heart wrenching part of Poppy and Jared's testimony. "When I first read your book, it gave me hope that Nathan might wake up and realize he was destroying our family the way that Jared finally did."

"I was warned about that happening for readers," she replied. "I even added the disclaimer in my book."

"Miss Belle and her timely advice."

"I quoted her verbatim because it was something that really stuck with me. She told me to be careful that I didn't give women false hope that just because God healed *my* marriage that it meant He would heal everybody else's marriage the same way."

"And it's something that Rabbi Lebow sells almost weekly from the bima," I said bitterly. "I know my marriage wasn't the only one ruined by Beth Shalom. I'm not sure if Rabbi Lebow is a misogynist who thinks it's a woman's duty to put up with abuse, or if he just sided with the men because they were all *machers* in the congregation with big paychecks. Whenever I saw a couple get divorced at Beth Shalom, the husband stayed, and the wife was the one who left. Makes you think, doesn't it?"

Poppy shook her head in disgust. "I was never a member of your old synagogue, but Jared told me how Rabbi Lebow and his elders didn't care about his living situation with Leah just as long as he didn't advertise it. It was basically an open secret, and no one ever took him to task for it."

"How is what we're doing in Bible study any different?" I asked. "As long as Grant and Hayley don't talk about 'living in sin' together, everybody's cool with it?"

"Apples and oranges, kiddo. Nobody is fast-tracking Grant into leadership the way Beth Shalom did with Jared. My husband has a prestigious looking job, and they assumed he had a ton of money to tithe—not knowing he was up to his eyeballs in debt with our divorce. The choice to ignore his adultery was a pragmatic one. They needed another Jew by birth to parade around on the bima. For Rabbi Lebow, it was all about the image they presented. Since Jared wasn't wearing his ring, nobody asked any questions."

"I can't say I'm surprised, but the hypocrisy of Beth Shalom is appalling. Especially with Rabbi coming down here and acting like I'm disobeying God by protecting myself and my son from Nathan's abuse."

"Just to put any fears to rest, Lauren, nobody in our group will ever tell Grant that living with Hayley is okay. Jared and I would be the last ones to condone it. At the same time, the group isn't going to *shun* Grant or Hayley and tell them they're not allowed to come because of it. That's all I meant."

I tossed my empty cup of tea into my trash can. "I'm probably just overthinking all of this anyway. Even if Grant gives his heart to the Lord at his coffee hour with the guys, it doesn't mean that he and I are supposed to be anything other than coworkers with some confusing feelings."

Poppy smiled as she chewed her last bite of bagel. "The Lord never lets anything go to waste. Even though nothing romantic was meant to happen with me and Joe, it was the fire that Jared needed to get off his behind. My book also helped bring Joe and Carly together. I can't say I'm thrilled about how she depicted me in her manuscript, but at least I know what's coming when she finally publishes it."

"I've been meaning to ask where the two of you stand with that. My friend, Charlotte, mentioned it too."

She shrugged and sighed. "I messed up. Badly. I stuck my nose in the middle of something that wasn't my business, and I hurt two people I care about in the process. Despite that, God used my monumental blunder to help strengthen their relationship. Carly and I have talked about a few of the situations she depicted, and she said she'll take another look at how she wrote it. I hope that hearing my side helped her understand where I was coming from even though I was completely wrong for how I handled myself."

"Do you know if she's made any other revisions? I saw the

last version she wrote about six months ago. I've been leery because of how she talked about me and Aaron."

Poppy's eyes lit with understanding. "Yeah, she romanticized that, didn't she? The part when Aaron helped you and Ari move in, right?"

I chuckled. "Well, I guess it's a misdirect for anyone who reads her memoirs one day. The good guy didn't get the girl."

"Plot twist!" Poppy exclaimed with a laugh. "Maybe you'll wind up with the 'bad boy' after all."

I rolled my eyes. "Yeah, sure. And we'll get married by Rabbi Peretz in front of the copier. I'm sure that'll get the books flying off the shelves."

"So, you're going to write?" she asked excitedly. "I mean, it *is* a Culver marketing department tradition."

"The more I think about this whole ordeal with Nathan, the more I think there are other women who need to hear that divorce *is* a Biblical option, and not just in cases of adultery. I refuse to believe that God designed marriage to be a lifetime prison sentence for battered spouses and children."

Poppy looked thoughtful. "That's a pretty fair description of life in a toxic marriage, and we both know there are plenty of abusive women in the world too. My marriage was nothing like what you've experienced with Nathan, but when you're financially incapacitated, belittled, ignored, and neglected daily, it feels exactly like a prison. I know my kids weren't 'happier' after we moved out of our house, but there was no way for us to even start healing from the kind of father and husband Jared used to be until we had our own place."

I sighed. "So much of the healing for your family happened after Jared really repented and made amends with them. That's not the case with Nathan, and I don't know if he'll ever turn from his behavior. How does my son heal from having a narcissist for a father who uses the Bible to club him into submission?"

"I have no easy answers, my friend. My story didn't work out that way. That's going to be something you figure out for yourself. And when you do, make sure you add it to your book. There are plenty of other women *and* men who would like to know the answer to that question."

CHAPTER 24

I SAT AT A SMALL TABLE IN TORNADO ALLEY READING my latest Barbara Kellogg novel and trying to escape real life. I didn't want to think about commercial insurance, what happened with Grant and the guys earlier that morning, or my never-ending divorce. I giggled at the flirty banter between the radio deejay heroine and her hunky coworker, Brick.

"I bet they *do* start making out by the copier," I murmured. Reading a little further along, I laughed out loud. "Okay fine, the vending machines."

"Lauren!" Grant called with a wide smile. "I went right into a meeting after I got back to the office, and I missed you before you left for lunch."

"Well, here I am," I said, hoping for a nonchalant tone.

He smiled. "There you are, and I want to explain what happened after we talked on Friday. It feels like so much, and I'm not sure where to begin."

As he pulled out a chair to join me, I quickly said, "Would

Hayley be okay with whatever you're about to say? Once it's said, it can't be unsaid."

Grant sat down and rubbed his beard. "I texted Haley this morning about my meeting with the guys, and she told me she's moving out. At this point, I don't think she'd have a problem with the discussion you and I need to have."

"You broke up?"

"Looks like," he said with a downturn of the mouth. "She said she'll be out of the house and out of my life by Sunday."

"Wow," I said, shaking my head in self pity. "I follow every rule in the Bible, save myself for marriage, think I'm 'equally yoked' with a godly, Jewish man, and I'm teetering on financial ruin just to be free. You live in sin with your girlfriend for years, and then poof, everything's resolved. Where's the justice in that?"

"I, uh, really don't know what to say to that. I don't have any control over your circumstances or mine."

I waved him off and snapped my e-reader shut. "Sorry, I'm just frustrated with God. Frustrated with my life. I hate the feeling of being helpless and being hopeless, and right now, it feels like both."

His expression turned sympathetic. "I feel like anything I try to say right now will sound hollow. I'm not sure how to comfort you."

"Nobody's asking you to. I'm just feeling sorry for myself. You don't need to stay for my pity party."

He hesitated before speaking again. "I thought you might be interested to hear what happened this weekend, but it doesn't seem like now is really a good time."

"I definitely want to hear it," I said, meeting his gaze. "You don't know this, but a dear friend of mine just got reconnected with a girl from our old synagogue. She's had a crush on him for years, and he finally woke up and noticed her. While I'm happy for both of them, it just sucks watching everyone else get their happy ending while I'm wondering if I'll ever have my own."

Grant raised an eyebrow. "Was this a guy friend you were interested in?"

I shook my head. "Other way around. He thought he was in love with me."

"Hmm," he murmured.

"Aaron was always just a friend," I added. "I love him like a brother, and I want him to be happy. I'm just struggling to muster joy for anybody else. I never thought of myself as a bitter person, but it's something my ex loves to accuse me of."

Grant watched me closely. "So, you're wondering if his accusations are true because you're having a tough time dealing with things, right? And if what he said is actually true, then how many other things was he right about?"

My eyes widened. "Wow, yes. How did you know?"

He offered a sad smile. "You're not the only person getting out of a difficult relationship, remember? The pain is still real even if I don't have all the legal bills to show for it."

Seeing my own insensitivity, I shuddered. "Grant, I'm so sorry! I don't know why I assumed things would be so easy for you."

He pressed his lips together. "Yeah, there have definitely been some assumptions made, but I won't hold it against you. Hayley and I were together for almost four years. I thought we wanted the same thing when we moved in together. This wasn't exactly the future I had planned for my life either."

I reached over to touch his hand across the table. "I've been so busy wallowing that I didn't even consider how hard this would be for you. Please, forgive me."

He sighed, pulling his hand away to rub the back of his neck. "Sunday night really opened my eyes. Hayley has never been religious, but she told me I lost my mind after I said I wanted to go to Bible study. When I told her it was hosted by Margolin, she assumed I was going there to see you."

"Me? Why?"

Grant's color heightened, and I felt a blush steal across my own cheeks.

"Your name has come up," he said quietly.

"Well, yeah," I said. "You told me the gift cards were Hayley's idea."

"Not just the gift cards," Grant said. "I didn't realize how much I'd been talking about you until Hayley pointed it out. She wasn't happy about that either. She found the gift cards sitting on the front seat of my car Saturday morning and asked what happened. When I told her why you wouldn't accept them, she accused me of having feelings for you."

I breathed out the next question. "What did you tell her?"

"The truth."

"Which is what?"

He held my eyes. "That I've never met anyone like you, and I want to understand more about how you love Jesus and are proud to be Jewish at the same time. That yes, there's an attraction, and no, it's not one-sided."

"Oh."

"Hayley asked me flat out if I had cheated. Obviously, I told her no and that you're still married. She asked why that wasn't a good enough reason to leave you alone since she and I basically *are* married."

I could easily imagine Hayley's pain, and I winced on her behalf. "What did you say?"

"I reminded her that *we're* not married, and that it had been her choice not mine. I told her that she was the one I wanted to start a family with when we moved in together, but she's the one who changed her mind about kids. She asked if this was about me having genuine feelings for you or just wanting a warm body to fill a role."

I sat with bated breath waiting to hear the rest of the story.

Grant continued on. "I told her that getting married now would be a disaster for us. She said that we've grown apart, and I didn't disagree with her. She also asked if you were the reason we hadn't been together in a while."

"Together?" I repeated before understanding his meaning. "Oh," I said, blushing. "Grant, you don't need to share all that."

"No, I do," he said, captivating me with those expressive, chocolate brown eyes, "because after I ran into you that morning in Parkview, something changed. Hayley felt it too."

"That was the day you told me you were only interested as a friend. I thought I was going crazy thinking there was something more. Were you lying?"

"To myself," he said, his hand running down his beard again. "I couldn't see it then. Hayley did. She saw you walking to the parking deck and me walking back to The Soaring Scone. I told her nothing was going on, because at the time, nothing was."

"So, what changed? I'm still just as unavailable now as I was then."

"I got to know you more," he said. "We fought off your rabbi together. You told me about your past, and I opened up about my mom. I don't know, I guess we just connected. And then there was that day in your office before Poppy showed up." His gaze drifted toward my mouth, and I perfectly understood his meaning.

I averted my eyes.

"Lauren, if I had kissed you that day, would you have kissed me back?"

I fumbled with the hem of my shirt, knowing my eyes would reveal the truth before the words ever passed my lips. Keeping my head bent, I replied softly, "It doesn't matter."

"I think it does."

"It doesn't change anything, Grant."

"Why, because you're afraid to admit you have feelings for me too?"

My gaze returned to him sharply. "No, because it would still be inappropriate, and not just because we're coworkers. I can't stand the fact I'm still legally married, but that doesn't change what kissing you would be. I won't make that mistake again."

Grant's eyes widened. "What do you mean *again?*"

"Nothing, forget I said anything."

"Did you cheat on your ex?" he asked. "Is that why you're so guarded around me?"

"No, Nathan's the only man I've ever been with."

"Well, then what did you mean when you said *again?*"

"What does it matter?"

"As ridiculous as this sounds given our respective situations, I guess I don't want to hear that you've got feelings for some other guy."

"Yeah, that is pretty ridiculous. And hypocritical."

"You're still not answering my question."

"And I don't owe you an answer," I shot back. "Look, I'm sorry I minimized your break up with Hayley, but I think it's better for me to get back to the office. I don't think this conversation can go anywhere good right now."

I stood up quickly and gathered my purse. Grant rose and grabbed my arm before I could flee back into the building.

"You're running," he said, his face close to my neck.

Twisting to look up at him, the potency of my lips being inches from his sent a rush of adrenaline followed by shaking limbs in its aftermath. I took a step away. "That's because we're supposed to *flee* temptation, not run headlong into its arms."

His thumb moved back and forth on my forearm. "Lauren," he whispered.

"No," I said firmly. "Not now and not like this." I yanked my arm away. "Don't you dare tell me that anyone at Bible study last night or this morning would be okay with what you're doing right now. Was all of that a con to get me to drop my guard?"

"Lauren, I think I'm in—"

"Don't you dare say it!" I growled, cutting him off. "I've already had one psycho pretend he loved me so he could manipulate me."

"I'm not your ex," Grant said, offended.

"Then stop acting like him! I'm hurting and I'm vulnerable, and it's not like you don't know that. If you have all of these supposed feelings for me, then wait for me. Love is *patient* and it's kind. It doesn't seek its own. It doesn't delight in sin, but it delights in the truth. I think you might be infatuated with me or maybe even just the idea of me. I will not go down this road with you right now, and you need to be free from Hayley and I need to be free from Nathan."

"And what happens after that?" he asked.

"Considering I feel like I'll be in legal purgatory the rest of my foreseeable future, I have no idea, but I will not be some balm for you to heal from Hayley any more than I want you to be a band aid for the Nathan sized hole in my heart."

"Are you still in love with your ex?" he asked, surprised.

I exhaled a mirthless laugh. "The man I thought I loved never existed. He was a mirage hiding a monster."

"Do you think every man is just like him?" Grant searched my eyes. "We're not all lying dirtbags. I'm far from perfect, Lauren, but I would never hurt you like that."

"You're not in a position to prove him wrong. I need to learn to trust myself and my own heart before I even entertain the idea of trusting someone else. I need time to process all the lies I still have to purge from him and his family. I need time to grieve the future I thought I had and accept the reality of my situation. Frankly, so do you. Look, if you really see something happening between the two of us, you need to heal. You need to give me time to not just get legally divorced, but to heal from the trauma of the entire relationship. More than any of that, I won't get into another relationship with any man unless I know he is genuinely committed to Jesus. I got fooled once, and I've spent the last decade trying to claw my way out of hell. I won't do that to me or my son ever again."

Grant's eyes narrowed as his mouth thinned. "I see."

Taking a step away from him, I said, "Whatever faith walk you decide to take, I want it to be because this is something you want for yourself. Don't fake it for my sake because I'll see right through it. I promise that if you go after God with all of your heart, you'll find He's keeping my heart safe with Him too."

CHAPTER 25

I picked up Ari from daycare with a lot weighing on my mind. I both hated and lauded myself for holding my boundary firm with Grant. The months of fantasies and tortured emotions beckoned me to dip my toes in that tempting pool of mutual admiration. Stronger though, was the conviction of the Holy Spirit that I would regret that decision more than any kiss shared with Aaron Davis. I hadn't been in love with my friend when he'd kissed me, but my feelings for Grant were far from platonic. I knew that a single kiss was not where things would stop.

Facing my own fears and anxiety, I attended Bible study the following Sunday night, but I asked my parents to watch Ari. On the off chance Grant decided to make another appearance, I did not want him meeting my son. It was not an introduction I was ready or willing to make.

"Lauren!" Rebecca called as I entered her foyer. "It's been too long!" She walked over to pull me into a warm embrace. "I'm so glad you made it tonight."

I took in her beautiful home, noting the magazine worthy spread on her dining room table set up buffet style.

"I thought it was supposed to just be light snacks," I said.

Rebecca blushed. "It is, but Ted and I both love to cook, and my husband enjoys entertaining even more than I do."

I smiled back. "No worries. I always know I'm going to eat well when you and Ted host."

"Lauren," Ted called, entering the room and wrapping an arm around his wife, "I'm so glad you could make it. We missed you last week."

I smiled knowingly at the mighty Margolin. "I think God had me where I needed to be."

"You and a few other people," he retorted with a golden twinkle in his eyes, "and speaking of, there are two gentlemen in the other room getting acquainted with one another. Thankfully, no fisticuffs have been involved."

"Ted," Rebecca warned.

Her husband chuckled and kissed the top of her head. "I'm going to go check on our cheese tray. I can't remember if I sliced the double cream gouda or not."

Rebecca rolled her eyes playfully. "Yes, honey, go do that. I'm *sure* that's why you were leaving."

It was nice to see this lighter side of Culver's top, east coast producer, especially when he stuck out his tongue at his wife and wiggled his eyebrows at her.

Rebecca chuckled. "Oh my goodness, that man is ridiculous sometimes."

I watched the Margolins, wondering if my own future could ever hold happiness like that. Between reading Rebecca's memoirs and talking to her myself, I knew the horrors she'd survived with her family and her old church. I didn't feel right equating the corruption of Beth Shalom with the felony crimes

Rebecca had witnessed at Sycamore Bible Church, but given that my husband indulged in underage porn on synagogue grounds—unwittingly or not—I wondered if the Messianic Jewish skeletons weren't all that different from the non-denominational ones hiding in SBC's proverbial closet.

"Grant is here." Rebecca said. She drew me closer and whispered into my ear, "And so is Aaron. I think he figured out who Grant is pretty quickly. Do you need us to run interference?"

I looked into her dark brown eyes, grateful for the motherly concern. "Not to be repeated to anyone but your husband, but Aaron has a girlfriend now."

Rebecca's eyes widened as she gasped. "Since when? How did he go from being borderline obsessed with you to having somebody else in two weeks? That really surprises me about him. I hope that poor girl knows she's nothing but a rebound. Is that who showed up with him tonight?"

"Stop," I said, placing a hand on her arm. "It's not what you think at all. Aaron and I talked last weekend. He knows the girl from Beth Shalom. We both do. We all go back at least twelve years. Ruthie's not the rebound. She's the real deal. I was the counterfeit, not the other way around."

"Counterfeit?" Rebecca repeated. "How is that even possible?"

"Because Aaron convinced himself that God wanted us to be together. His love for me as a friend is real, but his feelings got confused over time. Me being unavailable made it easy to pine after me and pretend he was waiting on God."

Rebecca raised a skeptical eyebrow. "How did he turn off years of feelings so quickly?"

"Because I told him about a month ago that I would never reciprocate those feelings and he needed to move on. It happened at the Goldsteins' house after I had that confrontation with Rabbi Lebow. Aaron was mad that Grant wound up protecting me, and I was honest with how I felt about it."

"Wow," she murmured. "That must have been an incredibly difficult conversation, but I'm proud of you two for being adult enough to have it. Was this Ruthie girl just waiting in the wings the whole time?"

I chuckled. "In a manner of speaking, I guess. She'd had a crush on Aaron for a long time, but she's younger than us. Aaron and I both remembered her as a kid. He said he ran into her at Charred Cups, and suddenly Ruthie Roseman was all grown up."

"Ah," Rebecca said with a knowing smile. "Sounds like God's perfect timing."

I nodded and smiled back. "Yeah, and I'm truly happy for him. His feelings for me weren't healthy for either of us."

"So, what about Grant?" Rebecca asked. "He came with a girlfriend last week, but he's solo this time."

I shrugged. "Not my problem right now. I didn't come here to start any man drama, and if it becomes a distraction for me or anybody else, I can leave."

"Whoa, whoa, whoa," she said holding up her hands, "I'm just gathering information. I don't mean to make it sound like the guys are about to get into a brawl over you."

"Nothing is happening with Grant and me."

"That's not what Ted said."

I grimaced. "Probably not what he saw either, but nothing can happen right now. I'm still stuck with Nathan, and Grant isn't a believer—even though it sounds like he's searching for God. If he wants a relationship with Jesus, it needs to be because he wants that for himself, not because he's trying to get into my pants."

"Now, tell me what you *really* think," she deadpanned.

I waved off her friendly banter. "I don't have time for games and fantasies and 'what ifs' anymore. They made me miserable and confused."

Rebecca looked at me with admiration. "I hope this doesn't come off as condescending, but you have come a really long way since you first started attending Bible study. I know you have a lot of healing left and dragons to slay, but the peace and confidence you have is impressive. I don't know how I would handle being in a situation like yours."

"You've handled a lot worse," I said, scoffing at her praise. "I'm not a hero. Most days, I feel like I barely scrape across the finish line."

"Which just shows how strong you are, my friend. You could have given up, lashed out, or started an affair with Aaron or Grant to cope with the pain. You didn't do any of those things."

"I've flirted with the idea more than I should have," I said, feeling the weight of guilt and repressed desire.

"But you *didn't*." She leveled me with her soulful eyes. "Yes, you may have stumbled and dwelled on thoughts you shouldn't have, but you didn't *act* on them. You didn't download illegal porn and then try to blame somebody else for your 'ongoing issues.' Sounds like you're taking on more responsibility than you should be. Intentions and actions aren't the same thing, and having Satan tempt you with the desires of your heart when you're weak and hurting doesn't mean that you screwed up. The devil doesn't fight fair, and he loves to bludgeon our thoughts with condemnation when he's the one putting temptation in our path to begin with. Trust me, gaslighting started in the pit of hell, and Satan is the ultimate narcissist."

"Wow," I said, digesting her words.

"I've got so many narcissists on my resume that you learn to see the same patterns. I could also quote *Ephesians 6* about our battle not being against flesh and blood but against evil spirits, but you already know what it says."

"True," I said. "And when you're fighting those never ending battles, it's easy to forget there's greater spiritual forces at work."

"Which is why *1 John 4:4* is a Scripture verse I pray over Ted, me, and the kids daily," she replied. "I know that Nathan and his bulldog attorney feels like fighting Goliath with unlimited financial resources, but remember that God in you is greater than whatever demons are fueling Nathan and his parents."

"It's so hard to believe it's demonic when they're praying to Jesus just like I am."

Rebecca scoffed. "If they're anything like my parents or Pastor Sociopath, their prayers are more like entitled demands and twisted Bible verses commanding God to comply with their wishes. They're fond of those 'God, we know Your Word says,' prayers followed by the vending machine approach of 'we *know* that You'll blah blah blah if we just xyz.' It's all pious sounding, hot air—manipulation and witchcraft in Christian coating."

My jaw dropped, recounting so many of Nathan's prayers sounding exactly like what Rebecca described. I remembered the confusion of hearing my husband quote Bible verses in prayer when it felt like he ignored so many that applied to his own toxic behavior.

Reading my thoughts, Rebecca said, "Satan also quotes Scripture."

"And frequently from the pulpit," I added bitterly. "I lived that too."

"Not every pulpit has a wolf residing in it. Probably seems silly for me to add that caveat given that Ted and I started our own home group, but neither one of us believe that every church or synagogue is evil."

"No, and I don't either," I said, "but I have so many flash-backs and triggers from Beth Shalom that I don't know if I'd ever attend a regular service again."

"Give it time," Mrs. Margolin said sympathetically. "I know what it feels like to have an entire congregation poisoned against you and attack you for standing up for what's right. After I left SBC, Pastor Sociopath unleashed his flying monkeys to harass me on social media and discredit me if I ever spoke up about what I witnessed."

"Rabbi Lebow, Nathan, and his mother have done that to me for the last three years with the members of Beth Shalom. Everything wrong in my marriage was my fault. They flat out lied and covered up his addictions and abuse."

Rebecca pulled me into a hug as my tears fought their way to the surface. The shock and betrayal were still fresh.

"You grew up in that place, and they turned on you," she said against my hair. "Instead of confronting Nathan's sin, they attacked your reaction to it. People devoured the lies and ignored your integrity. Liora Fein isn't in denial about what her son is."

"Are you sure about that?" I grit. "She acts like Nathan walks on water."

"She's not stupid or blind, Lauren, and she's well aware that she's lying to everyone. It's the need to cover her *own* reputation that's motivating her. My parents did the same thing with my siblings."

"Thank you," I whispered, fiercely hugging her. "You have no idea how much I needed to hear that."

Rebecca leaned back and held my shoulders. "*None* of this was your fault. You were tricked and manipulated into a hasty marriage by a master con artist. Jessica wishes she could have warned you, but she wasn't in the greatest place after she saw how quickly Nathan moved on and found another girl."

"She told me," I said. "Getting in touch with her and hearing her version of their engagement was the scariest thing I've ever done, but I had to know the truth."

Rebecca smiled sadly. "I hate that any of this has happened to you, but I hope you can see God's hand in it. Eight years ago, Nathan suggested I talk to Ted about everything that happened at SBC. Jessica may not have made that phone call to the office if not for Nathan. I don't know what it would have taken for Ted to confess his feelings or vice versa. Kyle was going to come to Jessica's condo, regardless, and our lives might all look very different than they do now."

I frowned. "That doesn't exactly make me feel better. I get that Nathan helped you, Kyle, and even Jessica to find happiness, but I'm the one who had to suffer in marriage to him."

"Oh, Lauren, I'm so sorry! I didn't mean for any of that to sound like I'm thankful for *your* suffering. I'm also not going to tell you to look at the bright side or 'you wouldn't have your son, so be thankful' spiel."

"Thank you," I said around a lump of emotion. "I wasn't sure if that's what you were saying, and I've heard enough of that garbage to make me vomit."

Rebecca shook her head vehemently. "No, not at all! I just meant to say that God sees the whole picture while we only see in part. I know that His purpose isn't to allow you to experience heartache and then only give blessings to others. That's the lie Satan wants you to believe. God isn't cruel, my friend. Satan is. His lies are vicious and meant to cut the legs out from under us. God is the one who restores what Satan has stolen, redeems what Satan has tried to break, and brings recompense to those who have suffered. You know my story and the hell I survived to get to where I am today."

"I do," I said, pushing away thoughts of self pity threatening to drown me. "It's easy to forget all that when I see how happy you are now."

"Exactly," Mrs. Margolin said with a knowing smile. "God has brought so much joy and blessings in my life that it's easy to forget what it took to get here. My past is what prepared me for Ted. His past is what prepared him for me. Trust that God doesn't let anything go to waste, Lauren. Your purpose on this planet is bigger than your love life or even motherhood. Your testimony of overcoming your demons will be the ministry God uses for every other person stuck in the same situation. Your story will be one of hope for others, and it will be your lifelong reminder of God's faithfulness even under the most unimaginable circumstances."

CHAPTER 26

Comforted by Rebecca's words, I had nearly forgotten that my future and my past were standing in conversation amidst all of the other Bible study attendees. Eyes of both stormy blue and chocolate brown turned toward me as I stepped in the room. Averting my own gaze, I planted myself as far into the corner as possible.

"Hey," a female voice said, approaching.

Stunned, I looked up at Ruthie Roseman. "Hi," I murmured. "H-how are you?"

Ruthie smiled back. "Never been better. I haven't seen you in so long, Lauren. You look exactly the same!"

I bit back the self-deprecating remark I wanted to make and tried to graciously accept her compliment. "You're all grown up," I said, painfully stating the obvious.

The charming minx had the decency to blush behind her freckled cheeks, and she looked like everything I no longer felt.

Hopeful.

Innocent.

Pure.

Maybe this was what Aaron Davis fell in love with all those years ago—the naive, undefiled version of me who hadn't been emotionally mutilated by Nathan Fein. Swallowing back tears, I mustered a smile I didn't feel. Aaron sidled up next to Ruthie and bestowed her with a beaming look of adoration I was certain I'd never seen in all of his years of pining after me.

"Glad to see you here, Lauren," Aaron said, granting me a genuine smile, though nothing like the stunning look he'd just given Ruthie. If I had ever seen *that* smile on Aaron's face, I probably would have promised him a future with fifteen children. I felt sick to my stomach at my own blindness.

"You okay?" he asked.

I forced the corners of my mouth to extend further. "Just tired."

Aaron raised a dark blonde brow. "I met your friend," he said. "Seems like a nice guy."

I glanced over at Grant and saw he had been watching the entire exchange. Looking back at Aaron, I wondered if I had made the stupidest decision in the history of stupid decisions besides marrying Nathan.

"Excuse me," I said, covering my mouth with my hand. I bolted past my old friend and the future mother of his fifteen children.

Panting, I searched for the nearest bathroom to empty my stomach. I closed the door just in time to confine my sickness to the toilet bowl.

"Lauren?" Rebecca called from just outside. "Are you okay?"

"No," I croaked.

From beyond my misery in the small, guest bathroom, I

heard hushed voices outside the door. I turned in horror as Grant stepped inside.

"You...you shouldn't be here," I said before retching.

Instead, Grant approached with a handful of baby wipes. "Rebecca thought you could use these once your stomach settles down."

"Why are you here?"

"I saw your face when you were talking to Aaron and his girlfriend. This is my fault."

I waved him off while my stomach unleashed another round of fury. As my agony continued, Grant scooped my hair into his hand. His fingers brushed my temples as he captured stray, limp strands still clinging to my forehead. When the next wave of nausea finished, Grant used the baby wipe to clean my face. I wanted to weep at the display of tenderness, painfully reminded of all the times Nathan laid hands on me and then claimed he felt too guilty to deal with the aftermath of his behavior.

"Can you manage any deep breaths?" Grant asked, snapping me back to the present.

Tilting my head, I met his gaze and let my eyes ask the question of the hour.

"I couldn't leave you all by yourself," he said. "You've suffered so much."

I exhaled a bitter laugh.

"Please," he said, "let me help you."

"You've done enough."

He winced. "I know."

I didn't respond, first gauging my stomach to see if I would humiliate myself any further. When I felt certain the worst was over, I gently pulled my hair from his grasp, flushed the toilet, and slid past him to wash my hands. I splashed some cold water on my face and then rinsed out my mouth.

When I turned back around, I didn't realize Grant had stepped into the small space behind me. With the counter pressed against my back, we stood inches away from one another.

His hand cupped the side of my face before tucking dampened hair behind my ear.

"Why?" I whispered.

I could feel his heartbeat, and it seemed as though it leapt from his chest into mine. His chocolate brown gaze communicated reassurance along with his words. "I wanted to take care of you," he said softly.

I nudged my face away from his palm and turned my body away. "It's too soon, and it shouldn't be happening now."

"So, I can't help a friend?"

"You're not supposed to look at me like that, Grant. I'm not supposed to feel this way. It should have been Aaron."

"But it's not. You told me you weren't in love with him."

The shame and regret I'd felt in seeing Aaron with Ruthie released its death grip from my mind. I took my first real breath of air since I'd seen them together. "I wasn't. I mean, I'm not."

"Well, then why are you in here tossing your cookies? You told me you wished him well and were happy for him. What changed?"

"It's just..." I paused as I stared in Grant's eyes, feeling a pull I'd only ever read about in my romance novels. I'd never experienced anything like this with Nathan, even when I was still trying to convince myself I was in love with him. When Aaron Davis kissed me on my parents' front porch, I still didn't burn with such an intense longing. Grant's gaze darted to my lips, and I blurted out, "I just threw up. Please, don't kiss me!"

He chuckled and managed a small step backward despite the cramped space we shared. "I'm not going to kiss you, Lauren."

"The way you look at me—"

"Is the way Aaron looks at Ruthie," he said matter-of-factly.

"It's too soon," I repeated again lamely. "I need to heal. *You* need to heal."

"Which is also true, but it doesn't change how I feel."

I inched away, sliding against the bathroom counter and finding more space by pushing the toilet lid down and sitting on top of it. I dropped my head into my palms and willed my heart to beat inside of my own chest instead of sharing one pulse with Grant Kaplan.

"Lauren, I'm not ignoring everything you said to me on Monday. I've tried to give you space at work and not push the issue. Hayley moved out this morning, and it was emotional for both of us. She took Lucy with her, and it's the first time I've been on my own in five years. Despite all that," he continued, "it doesn't change the fact that I want to be here with you. In this bathroom. Taking care of you."

"But why?" I asked again. "Why do you want to take care of *me*?"

"I can't explain how it happened," he said, holding my eyes. "I don't want to see you hurting or in pain. I don't want to see you suffering or thinking that you have to handle everything on your own."

Immediately reminded of my conversation with Rebecca, I blinked back tears. "But why *me*, Grant? Why not Hayley? Did your feelings for her suddenly switch off? How do I know you won't suddenly switch them off for me too?"

He sighed and then paused to collect his thoughts. "Because it's not what Hayley wants, and I can't force her into wanting the same things I do. I will always love her as a person, but we fell out of love with each other a while ago."

"You can't make a relationship succeed or fail just by being *in love*. You have to fight for it. It takes two people to make it work. Unfortunately, it only takes one to destroy it."

Grant crouched on the floor beside me. "Trust me, I learned that lesson too."

"Are you blaming Hayley for why your relationship got stale? Would you be here with me right now if she had wanted to get married and start a family with you?"

"No, I think we both got complacent. I assumed she would eventually change her mind, and she thought I had let go of wanting a family."

Venturing a look into his eyes, I said, "I guess what I'm asking is if you would still want me if things with Hayley had worked out differently."

"I could ask you the same thing, Lauren. I doubt we would be having this conversation if your ex was anything he pretended to be. It is what it is. I've talked to some of the guys about how they knew they were with the right person when they met their wives. They all talked about God's timing."

"Do you believe in any of that?" I scanned his face for any hint of a lie or discomfort. "Did you come to Bible study because you actually want to be here or because you thought you would see me?"

"I came because I wanted to be here," he replied with ease. "It's the same thing I told Hayley, and none of that was a lie. I have never heard anyone talk about God the way you guys do. Definitely not at synagogue and not even at the church events I've attended. You guys talk about God like He's real and you know Him. It's not some abstract concept like what I grew up with at synagogue."

Shame slumped my shoulders. "I don't feel like I talk about

God at all. I just whine about my ex-husband or how slow divorce proceedings are going. Here I am lusting after you while I'm still married. I couldn't be any worse of an example."

"Lusting after me?" Grant repeated with a soft smile. "I didn't realize I was so irresistible. I'll have to add it to my resume."

I pushed at his shoulder, and he toppled onto his behind. "Thanks," he said with a grin, "My ego needed a little deflating."

I stuck my tongue out at him. "You're welcome."

Grant grinned at me, and I smiled back. "Nice to see you again," he said, "and you're not the horrible example you think you are. I told you that you inspire me, and that wasn't a line. I meant what I said. The strength you have is amazing. The kindness you show to others when you could just as easily shut down or be bitter takes my breath away. You may not think you see Jesus in that, Lauren, but I do."

"You do?"

"I do," he said. "Give yourself more credit. I've dated other Jewish girls. None of them compares to you."

I blushed. "Thanks."

"You're welcome."

"So, now what?" I asked. "You've officially seen me at my worst."

"I'm not going anywhere. Not unless you want me to."

"Grant, I don't know what I want."

"I think you do." He met and held my gaze. "It's just not time yet."

"So, are we 'just friends' with some kind of an understanding? That doesn't even work in movies, let alone real life. Besides that, I told you that my ex is a sociopath. He'll twist and manipulate our friendship into something awful."

"I've already met your old rabbi, so I'm sure your ex has heard a few things about me."

"True," I conceded, "and Nathan will concoct any story he wants to fit his narrative."

"But as you keep reminding me, I am just getting out of a relationship."

"And I'm *still* trying to get out of mine."

"And then there's the Jesus thing," he added. "Probably a bigger deal to you than the psycho ex-husband."

"Yes, there's still the Jesus thing."

Grant stood up and then held out his hand for me. "I'm open to learning, which is why I'm here. Are you ready to return to the land of the living?"

I nodded but didn't take his hand. Closing my eyes, I felt peace despite the uncertainty. I stood up and offered a tiny smile. "Thank you."

"Oh!" Grant exclaimed, breaking eye contact and fumbling in his pockets, "I thought you could use this." He held out a peppermint candy.

Electricity crackled as his fingers brushed over my palm. He released the mint and dropped his own hand into a balled fist at his side. I took a step backward and looked away. Mr. Kaplan took that as his cue to open the bathroom door and shut off the fan.

"After you," he said, watching me with an inscrutable expression.

A wall of concerned gazes met us as I opened the door.

"Everything okay?" Ted Margolin asked. His gaze darted between the two of us. I turned toward Aaron's stormy blue stare and noticed he'd awaited my exit without Ruthie beside him. He inclined his head, silently asking the same question as Ted.

"Everything's...fine," I said, my voice coming out even.

I glanced back at Grant who offered a quick look of approval. Like Moses parting the Red Sea, I walked through the line of my gaping friends and ignored the tidal wave of unasked questions I wasn't ready to answer.

CHAPTER 27

I DID MY BEST TO IGNORE GRANT THE REST OF BIBLE study, slipping out like a coward. Needing to pick up my son from my parents' house served as an easy excuse, and I knew I had to flee. I feared what might happen if left alone with Grant under the stars—even in the Margolins' driveway with dozens of eyes clocking our every move. Reality was resembling far too many months of fantasy.

I took some comfort knowing that delaying the inevitable conversation with Grant meant I wouldn't have to do it with Aaron Davis watching it unfold. Despite the novel-worthy looks of adoration he'd bestowed on Ruthie, that smile did not return after my bathroom encounter with Grant. I snuck a few glances at the new object of Aaron's affection, and I noticed unease and confusion on Ruthie's face. Once the group disbanded to enjoy the Margolin buffet, I crept out the front door. I ignored my cell phone and myriad text messages flashing for my attention after I'd made my escape.

"Hey," my mom said warmly, as she met me in her kitchen.

"Ari's watching a movie with your father." Her voice faltered as she took in my expression. "Are you okay? You look pale."

"Not really." I wrestled against emotion threatening to crest above the surface. "It's just been a long night."

Her amber eyes took on a look of concern as well as wariness. "Can you stay for a minute and talk about it?

I shook my head. "I just really want to get Ari and go home."

"Lauren," she said, her gaze boring into me, "what aren't you telling me?"

"I just have a lot going on. Now that we have mediation coming up, Nathan has switched from harassing me to ignoring me."

She studied me before her eyes narrowed in suspicion. "Is it Aaron? I thought you said he has a girlfriend now."

I shook my head. "No, it's not Aaron, and I don't want to talk about it. Can you just get Ari, please?"

The sharpness of my tone had the effect of a slap, and my mother was never good at hiding her true feelings. "That's not quite the 'thank you' I was expecting."

"Sorry, Mom. Like I said, it's been a long night."

"George," she called to my father, "Lauren's here to get Ari."

Seconds later, I heard my son's excited squeal. He barreled into the kitchen and ran straight into my arms. I scooped him up and clung to him like the only anchor holding me steady in a sea of confusion.

"Hi, baby," I murmured into his neck. "Did you have a good time with Grandma and Grandpa?"

"How come I couldn't go with you?" he pouted into my shoulder. "I missed you, and I wanted to see Eva."

I smiled at the thought of Ari's future wife, something he'd been emphatic about since his last playdate with the Margolin children.

"Mommy?" Ari picked his head up and studied me. "You look sad."

I tried to summon a believable smile. "Mommy's just tired, honey. Are you ready to go?"

He nodded, and I let him drop back to the ground. "I need to give Grandpa a hug," he announced before scurrying back to the family room.

"You don't have to tell me anything if you don't want to," my mother began, "but at least just tell me that you and Ari aren't in any danger."

"We're not in danger. I just have a lot going on at work and with the divorce."

"Oh, are you having trouble at the office? I thought you said things were going well. Didn't your CEO give you a big compliment at your staff meeting?"

"He did," I said, smiling at the memory of the most recent birthday and work anniversary gathering at Culver. "Phil is a character."

"So, not just in the novels, huh?"

"Did you finally get around to reading them? You said the Parkview books were just a bunch of gossip against Beth Shalom."

My mother blushed. "I may have changed my mind about a few things. I know things aren't perfect in your life, honey, but you seem so much happier since you started attending those Bible studies. You haven't come home spouting any weird theology yet, and I've definitely gotten a hard look at how things are run at the congregation."

"And yet you're still members," I said, unable to keep the bitterness from my tone. "After everything they did to me *and* your grandson, how can you still go there?"

"Where else could we go?" she replied with irritation. "We

don't feel comfortable in a church, and we would have to hide our faith in a synagogue. They love to call themselves 'all-inclusive' until you tell them you believe Yeshua is the Messiah. Your father and I have been told we can't be Jewish and believe in Jesus from both sides. There's literally no place for us to worship and be ourselves other than Beth Shalom."

"Mom, you're turning a blind eye to their corruption and abuse because they say *Yeshua HaMashiach* instead of 'Jesus Christ.' That doesn't make you noble for staying. It means you're prioritizing your identity over your integrity."

"That's not true! You don't know what it was like trying to find a house of worship for our family, Lauren. We both know *the church* has fused pagan traditions with their own man-made holidays. Plus, their theology is based on blatantly antisemitic doctrine. Hitler wrote his book off the teachings of Martin Luther. He called Jews vermin who don't deserve to live."

"You're right, Mom," I conceded, "and all of those Messianic Judaism talking points have been drilled into my head since childhood. It still doesn't change what Beth Shalom is."

"Lauren, you can't just ignore church history."

"What about modern *messianic* history? What about what happened to me three years ago? You're deliberately ignoring that."

"It's not the same," she argued. "No, Beth Shalom isn't a perfect congregation, but God also told us not to worship idols or follow the pagan practices of the world. Keeping Torah is a beautiful blessing and part of who we are as Jews."

"Yeshua said that two most important commands are loving God and loving our neighbor. How can Beth Shalom be keeping Torah when they only 'love thy neighbor' who is tithing and maintaining the corporate image? Anybody else is treated like an enemy. Haven't you ever noticed that people who leave are never spoken of again unless it's to spread some gossip about why they left? And conveniently, it's never Beth Shalom's fault even though you claim the synagogue's not perfect. How can you be *not perfect* but take zero responsibility for why so many people come and go? It's a revolving door, and you know it."

My mother opened her mouth to argue but froze.

I seized my opening of her defenses. "Yeshua said that how you treat the 'least of these' is how you've treated Him. I have been shunned by an entire congregation because I refused to cover my husband's sin. They punished me for protecting myself and my child rather than protecting Beth Shalom. Don't you see how twisted that is? Rabbi Lebow knew what was really going on, and he deliberately enlisted his minions to hurt us even more. Do you think celebrating Passover instead of Easter erases all of that sadistic cruelty in God's eyes?"

"I never thought of it that way," she said quietly.

"Mom, the pride and self-righteousness of 'maintaining your Jewish identity' has become an idol beyond reason. Rabbi Lebow smugly puts down megachurches and Christian traditions, but he ignores the blatant sin in his own leadership team. Then, he gaslights people in the pews as having a critical or complaining spirit for noticing. The sickness of the Beth Shalom cult mindset is that you longtime members make ridiculous excuses for all of it because you genuinely believe that 'not being Jewish' is the greatest sin someone can commit. It's insane."

"But we're not called to assimilate," she said weakly, tears in her eyes.

"Nobody is asking you to give up who you are, Mom, but that's how Rabbi Lebow keeps you hooked into that place. It's all *trauma bonding*."

"Trauma bonding?"

"Yes! Rabbi Lebow gives you the hot-cold treatment. First, he tickles your ears and praises you for attending a messianic congregation. He makes you feel special and better than all those poor, unenlightened *Christians* who don't worship on Shabbat. Then, he shames and berates members who don't tithe or volunteer. He condemns people who prioritize their job or their kids above being at synagogue. He acts like not centering your life around the Beth Shalom activity calendar is idolatry, but the truth is that he's asking everyone to make an idol out of Beth Shalom. It's the same psychological abuse Nathan did to me. He builds you up in one breath, devalues you in the next, and it leaves everyone in the pews with a false sense of indebtedness."

"What do you mean?"

"Rabbi Lebow wants you to believe there isn't anything better out there. You make excuses to justify why you can't or won't leave, all while he just pounds the same message of how you're privileged to be sitting in his pews—and you *owe* him for that privilege. He dresses it up in Scripture to make it sound like God is the one displeased with you instead of Rabbi Lebow's accounting books. It's blasphemy, and you've been walking with the Lord long enough to know better."

"That's enough!" she shouted, holding up a hand. "I know why you have strong feelings about Beth Shalom, but it's clouding your judgment."

"My judgment has never been clearer. It's your own need to believe you're special and better than gentile Christians that's keeping you from admitting the truth. If everything that's been done to me had happened in a church, you would have no problem condemning the place in a heartbeat. It's because it happened in your precious Messianic synagogue that it's a different set of standards."

"That's not true!"

"Oh really? So, when the scandals at Sycamore Bible Church and First United of Hillcrest were all over the news, you weren't yelling at the TV and denouncing both of those pastors as hypocrites and liars? And if Nathan had been caught looking at underage porn at a Baptist church, or beating me and Ari in a Lutheran church, are you going to tell me you wouldn't be condemning either of those congregations? Mom, the truth is that you love your identity more than anything else."

"Stop saying that!" she said, angry tears in her eyes.

My voice broke. "I also think you love your Jewish identity more than me. You chose that synagogue over me."

"It's not the same," she pleaded. "Lauren, you know that I love you."

I shook my head. "I'm done. I can't do this anymore."

"What is that supposed to mean?"

"It means I'm taking a break from you and Dad for a while."

"After everything we've done for you and our grandson?" she demanded.

"No," I said, yanking my purse over my shoulder. "It's because of everything you *haven't* done. You know the truth, but you're choosing your own comfort instead of standing up for what's right."

I didn't give my mother a chance to respond as I quickly gathered Ari from the family room and got in the car. My body shook with holy anger and adrenaline, and I forced myself to stop replaying the conversation in my mind.

"Mommy, you look angry," Ari said from the backseat. "Did I do something to make you mad?"

"No, honey, I just have a lot on my mind tonight." I forced a smile on my face. "You didn't do anything wrong at all, and I am very happy to see you."

"Why were you talking so mean to Grandma?"

"Mean?" I repeated.

"Yeah, you were saying mean things to her, and she was crying. Why did you do that?"

I swallowed down a lump of emotion. "Were you listening, honey?"

Ari nodded, and I caught his reflection in my rearview mirror. "Grandpa was watching too. He looked mad, and then he looked sad."

"Oh," I replied, figuring my dad would circle the wagons with my mom. "Did he say anything to you?"

"He said I need to listen to you and that he has to talk to Grandma."

I jerked back in surprise. "Really?"

Ari gave a noncommittal grunt, and I knew that was all the information I would be squeezing out of my preschooler.

We drove the rest of the way home in silence, and after I got Ari to bed, I sat on my couch shell shocked from the entire evening. Finally gathering the courage to check my text messages, I was surprised to find none from Aaron. Instead, Rebecca, Taylor, and Poppy had sent messages checking up on me, and I skimmed them quickly before switching over to stream a movie on my phone and unwind. A sharp banging on my front door startled me out of my senses, and I fumbled with my phone and nearly dropped it.

"Lauren!" Nathan bellowed from just outside. "I know you're in there. We need to talk, and I'm not leaving until you open this door. You're not going to hide from me anymore."

CHAPTER 28

Frantic, I sent a group text to Aaron, Ted, and anybody at our Bible study group I thought could get to my apartment quickly. The next was a phone call to 911.

"Yes, I need to order a pizza, please," I said loud enough for Nathan to hear.

"Ma'am," the dispatcher began tersely, "this is 911. We can trace your phone number."

I gave a fake laugh and hoped it sounded genuine. "Yes, I know it's pretty late to be ordering a pizza, but I'm really hungry, and if you guys could hurry on the delivery, I'll add an extra big tip."

"Lauren!" Nathan growled, "let me in, or I'll break the door down." He followed his demand with angry profanity.

Before I could say anything else, I heard the dispatcher in the background speaking in code over the radio. Returning back to our phone call, she said, "Ma'am, do you have any fear for your immediate safety?"

"Yes, I would like to add some pepperoni. What a great idea," I replied. "I've ordered it before if you check my account."

"Pepperoni?" Nathan barked. "So, you're eating pork now? You're a traitor to God and to your own people. Open the door!"

"I see," the dispatcher murmured, loudly clicking on her keyboard. "Is there anyone else in the house with you?"

"No, we won't need breadsticks. It's just an order for me and my son."

"What's going on?" Nathan yelled. "Why are you giving so much personal information over the phone? It's just a pizza! Get off the phone, Lauren."

"Do you know the man yelling in the background?" the dispatcher asked. "I'm pulling up your phone records, and I see that your name is Lauren Fein. Is that correct?"

"Yes, I'm very familiar with your rewards program." I said. "And the last name is spelled F-E-I-N. Do you need me to repeat my address?"

The dispatcher read off the location of my shared house with Nathan, and I corrected it to Carly's apartment.

"Get off the phone!" Nathan growled. He pounded hard on the front door, and it was a miracle he didn't wake up Ari.

"What? I can't hear you," I said, pretending I was still trying to order food. "This phone connection is really bad, but we really do need to order that pizza."

"I understand," the dispatcher said. "You're doing great. It looks like you filed charges against your husband for assault and battery two years ago, and he pled *nolo*. Is that who's at the door now? Can you get to a safe place in your apartment?"

"Yes, my order should be pretty similar to what we got last time, but it's definitely pepperoni on this one. We've had pizza delivered before, but never with olives too. That's something new for us."

"Got it," she replied, clicking away on a keyboard and then murmuring something else over a dispatch radio. "Hang with me as long as you can, Ms. Fein. Officers are on their way."

"Lauren," Nathan said, changing his tone from raving monster to pleading husband, "I just want to talk to you. I want to see my son. Open the door. You know that I love you. I even forgave you for all the times you cheated on me and then stole our son away." He added that last part loudly. He followed with a fake howl of pain that sounded shockingly girlish. I realized the performance was for whoever he thought was listening on the other end of my phone call. "Please, you have to stop all the drinking and drugs. You're just hurting our family with your self destructive behavior."

"Ma'am, is the front door locked?" the dispatcher asked.

"Yes, I'm still here," I said. "Do you mind repeating my order back to me one more time? I just want to make sure you got everything."

"Please," Nathan whined louder, his voice sounding as if his face was pressed against the door. I physically recoiled and took several large steps back. "All I've ever tried to do is love you, but you just keep hurting me and Ari. I've seen the bruises you've put on our son. You're not well. You need professional help!"

"How long did you say it would be before the pizza could get here?" I asked the dispatcher. My voice trembled, and I feared Nathan would discover my ruse.

"Less than five minutes, ma'am. Try to stay on the line. You said it's just you and your son in the house, correct?"

"Yes, so we won't need any extra breadsticks, like I said."

"Are you still ordering?" Nathan asked incredulously. When I didn't answer, he roared, "Lauren! Answer me right now!" He pounded on the door, rattling my framed pictures on the inside wall.

The dispatcher also heard Nathan's display of temper. "Ms. Fein, are you okay? Do you know if Mr. Fein has any firearms or weapons on him? Is the front door secure?"

"I'm scared," I whispered. "He will break down the door if you guys don't get here. He'll kill me. He's threatened to do it before."

Nathan continued his shouting until I heard the scuffle of feet outside and muffled grunting. I heard and felt someone getting slammed against the outside wall of my apartment. Terrified, I jumped back as the impact reverberated through the room and sent one of my frames crashing down. The sound of a landed punch outside accompanied the strains of glass shattering on the floor inside the apartment.

"Stay away from her!" Jared Levine barked. "You're not going to hurt Lauren or Ari anymore, you psychopath!"

"Is there someone else outside?" the dispatcher asked me.

"Yes, a friend," I said quietly.

"Do you still believe you are in danger, Ms. Fein?"

"I...I don't know. My friend is here, and I can hear them fighting outside, but I can't see anything. I won't open the door."

"No, please don't do that. Just stay on the line with me."

"Get your hands off me!" Nathan seethed at Jared. "Why are you at Lauren's house anyway? Are you the pizza delivery man?" Turning his rage back on me, Nathan sneered, "Is this another one of your boyfriends, you filthy, lying whore!"

Before he could utter another evil word, the sound of squeaking sneakers and further fisticuffs echoed in the concrete walkway. Jared's response came out like a feral growl. "Get out of here, Nathan!"

His defense of me felt like vindication for every member of Beth Shalom who'd shunned me for leaving my abusive husband. Police sirens wailed in the distance and grew louder by the second. I heard another punch followed by the sound of Nathan's thunderous cadence down the stairs. Rather than his former stampede leading the angry charge against me, a squeak of terror escaped from him as he tried to run away.

"Thank God," I whispered. "They're here," I said to the dispatcher. "The police are here."

"Yes, I've got confirmation on my end. Please, stay on the line, Ms. Fein, until we can ensure that you're safe."

A tentative knock rapped on my front door. "Lauren," Jared called, "a couple of squad cars pulled up, and they just grabbed Nathan. He's arguing with the police officers, and it looks like he's cooking his own goose. I'm sure someone will be up here in a minute to talk to you."

"Is Poppy with you?"

"Yes, she's waiting in the car, and she's got 911 on the line."

"Good, I do too."

"Ma'am," the dispatcher said, "the officers have confirmed they are at your location and have control of your husband. Do you feel safe hanging up the phone?"

"Yes, thank you," I whispered. Tears stung my eyes as the shock and adrenaline slowly dissipated. I inhaled a deep breath as my limbs began to tremble.

"Ms. Fein, you did a great job staying calm. I hope things start looking up for you. I'm hanging up now, but what you did tonight was incredibly brave." For the first time, her voice sounded human rather than robotic.

"Thank you," I said, and ended the call. I took another look through my peep hole, seeing a distorted view of Jared. "Are you sure he's gone?"

Jared turned and looked behind him into the parking lot. "Yeah, they've got Nathan in cuffs against the car. Do you want to stay inside with Ari, or can Poppy and I come in and check on you until the police leave? Natalie is taking care of her brother and sister, so we can be here as long as you need us."

Hands shaking, I turned my deadbolt and opened the door.

I gaped at Jared as I took in a split lip with blood at the corner of his mouth. Checking for any other injuries, I noted the polo collar of his shirt had been pulled severely, and there was also blood on his fist.

"Wh-what happened?" I asked, my eyes wide.

"Nathan landed the first punch. I got the last one and a few others." He grinned at that remark and then winced as it widened the cut on his lip. "Ow! Sorry, can I come in?"

"Jared!" Poppy called, flying up the stairs. She threw her arms around him, and he staggered to catch her. "Thank God, you're okay. I recorded everything on my phone. Oh honey, I was so scared when he hit you. He looked like a monster!"

"You did worse to me at that gas station," Jared said into her hair. "Thank God, Nathan stayed away from the nose."

Poppy pulled back from her husband with a Mama Bear scowl on her face. "Don't you dare joke about anything that happened tonight! I was mad at you the night I decked you, but there's no telling what Nathan could have done."

"You're right, I'm sorry," Jared said, rubbing his hands up and down her arms, "but the one you need to be worried about is Lauren."

Turning her attention away from her husband, Poppy yanked me into her own motherly hug. "You poor thing! It's such a miracle you and Ari got away from that demon. Did you call 911 too?"

I nodded through the tears flooding my vision. With Nathan

finally in police custody, I felt safe to cry. I sobbed quietly into Poppy's shoulder.

The police officers came upstairs to take my statement at the same time Ari toddled out of his bedroom from all the commotion.

"Mommy?" he asked, his curls disarrayed from his pillow. "What happened? Why are Mr. Jared and Miss Poppy here? Why are policemen here? Why are you crying?"

My legs gave out, and I sank to the floor. Horrified at the thought of what Nathan could have done to my son that night, I let out a blood curdling scream. The room went dead silent before Ari's face crumpled and he echoed his own wail. He ran past two officers and into my arms. Jared gave his statement and showed the officers the text messages I'd sent while I wept with my son. Poppy also handed over her phone to show them the video she'd taken of Nathan and Jared fighting.

Images and memories flooded my mind over the past decade of torment from Nathan Fein. Ari's cries matched mine until I began to hyperventilate. Paramedics pushed past the Levines to check on me, and Ari screamed when they tried to separate us.

"My son!" I shrieked, reaching out a hand for him.

"Ma'am, you need to calm down," the paramedics said.

"No!" I clawed them away from me as they attempted to get an oxygen mask on my face. "My son! Give me my son!"

Ari flung himself back in my arms, and I held on for dear life.

"Ma'am," one of the police officers said, "you have to calm down so we can get your son to calm down. I promise, we'll be out of here as soon as we can get a statement from you. Do you intend to press charges?"

"Yes!" I said emphatically, meeting the officer's eyes over the top of Ari's head. "We had a TPO against his father before we moved out, and I want to get a new one immediately. I have no idea how Nathan found out where we live, but we're not safe here anymore. If you check his record, he already has assault and battery charges from 2021 against me and my son, but he didn't serve any jail time because it was his first conviction. He pleaded *nolo contendere* to reduce his sentence."

"Are you divorced?"

"Legally separated, and I've been trying to get divorced for two years. He's been fighting me for custody and forced us to get a guardian ad litem before he'll go to mediation. Just one more delay to keep me from divorcing him. We can't go to court until we've at least shown we've tried to negotiate some kind of settlement."

The officer grimaced. "I hate that any of this has happened to you or your son, but I can't imagine any GAL handing over custody to your ex after what we dealt with outside."

"What do you mean?"

The officer glanced at Ari. "Can your son go with one of your friends to another room? I don't think he needs to hear the rest of this."

"Ari?" I asked, checking on his curly head nestled into the crook of my neck.

"He's asleep," Poppy whispered. "Do you want me to take him to his room?"

I shook my head. "No, he'll just wake up again. It's fine. What happened to Nathan?"

"Mr. Fein got belligerent and threatened one of our officers. Everything's recorded on dashcam. I'm glad you're going through with pressing charges because they would be filed anyway after what happened tonight."

"Is he going to jail?" I asked.

"For tonight, yes. He'll have to go before a judge to have bail set, and unless the judge feels he's a menace, he'll be released until he stands trial. Unfortunately, they let too many of these guys back out on the streets."

"So, he could come back again," I murmured, my body already shaking at the thought.

"Do you have an attorney?" the officer asked.

"Yes."

"Good. Get on the phone with them first thing tomorrow and file the TPO. God forbid your ex comes back, he will get locked back up without a chance of release. You have plenty of evidence about what happened tonight, especially thanks to your friends," he said, glancing at Poppy and Jared. "You should be able to turn that temporary order into a permanent one."

"What about charges for felony assault against law enforcement?" Poppy asked. "Shouldn't that be enough to keep that psycho behind bars even without the stalking and harassment to Lauren and her son? Did he just threaten you guys, or did he actually take a swing at somebody?"

The detective raised an eyebrow. "Do you watch a lot of cop shows or something?"

Jared answered for Poppy with an amused smirk. "She relaxes at night listening to murder podcasts."

The officer smiled and laughed to himself before answering. "My girlfriend does too."

"What about the charges?" I asked.

"I can't comment on any charges the department might file against your ex, but since you're also pressing criminal charges, it looks like you'll have a pretty strong case in family court."

I frowned. "Well, Nathan got loud outside, but he didn't actually threaten me."

"That's still disorderly conduct," the officer said, "and dispatch confirmed they heard him on the recording of your phone call. Given the history between the two of you and that he isn't supposed to know where you live, stalking and harassment charges should also hold up. You've survived the worst of it. Mr. Fein won't be allowed anywhere near you anymore."

"You did it," Poppy said, settling on the floor to wrap an arm around me. "Lauren, you did it. You're going to be free."

"I don't feel free," I muttered. I hugged my sleeping son tighter against me.

The detective glanced at us sympathetically. "Like I said, get on the phone with your attorney ASAP, and just know that he can't come here again tonight or any time in the future. I would suggest installing a camera outside of your door so that you can record any other suspicious visitors."

"Jared and I will pick one up for you," Poppy said immediately.

"He's going to come back, I know it!" Panic rattled my body as I tried to anchor myself against Ari.

"I don't know if I have much of a case against Nathan myself, but I'll do whatever I can," Jared added. "It's the least I can do after what Beth Shalom put you through."

"He'll press charges against you, Jared," I said, meeting him with wide eyes. "Oh gosh, he'll go after your family to punish you for helping me!"

"Why do you think I let him throw the first punch?" he asked, winking at me.

"And I recorded everything," Poppy added. "I got it all. Nathan can lie all he wants, but the evidence won't."

CHAPTER 29

Everyone at Bible study knew some version of Sunday's night's events by early Monday morning. Aaron called me and apologized profusely for not being there to protect me, and I reassured him that God had me covered. Reading between the lines, something had happened with Ruthie after Bible study. I didn't pry, and Aaron said he would check on me after work. Sondra Joyner responded to my midnight text at seven the next morning and told me she'd have the TPO filed as soon as court opened at nine.

I knew I owed Grant a long conversation, but after Nathan's attempted assault, my focus shifted to the right man—my son. I hid my trauma behind a well-practiced smile, reassuring Ari that Mommy had a bad nightmare. When he asked why Poppy, Jared, and the Danbury police were there, I said that Mommy had gotten scared, but everyone came to help and protect us. Satisfied with my answer, he didn't press for more information, and I redirected his focus to anything other than Mommy's hyperactive startle reflex.

I had already called out of work, but Poppy texted me to check in on me.

How are you doing? she asked.

Numb, mostly. Just dropped off Ari at school.

Are you sure that's safe?

Nathan's in jail, and the school already knows he's not allowed to be anywhere near him. They have safety cameras everywhere. There won't be a bond hearing for at least another day or two, so this is the safest place for Ari right now. None of the Beth Shalom minions can touch my son there either.

I watched ellipses showing Poppy typing and deleting. *Grant just walked in. He's definitely looking for you. What do you want me to tell him?*

I pondered that question. He was not included in my panicked group text because I had deliberately made it a point to avoid getting his phone number. I sighed.

Is the mighty Margolin in the office yet? I asked.

Poppy sent back an eye rolling emoji. *Obvi.*

I managed a smile at her sarcasm. *Tell Grant to talk to Ted. Try not to make it sound more dramatic than it is.*

MORE dramatic? You're kidding, right? I'm just glad Jared's still got all his teeth.

Is he ok? I asked, grimacing. *I'm so sorry, Poppy.*

Girl, you are NOT apologizing for last night, ok??? Every time I think about Jared's busted lip, I think about what that psycho would have done to you or your son. I can't imagine all the horrible things that pig has already done to you.

No, I typed slowly, *no you can't.*

My phone went dark for a few minutes and then a new message popped up. *Grant is on his way to talk to Ted,* Poppy typed. *He knew something was wrong before I even said anything. I don't know what happened when the two of you were in the bathroom yesterday, but

I'm 99.9% sure he's going to beg Ted for your number when he finds out what Nathan did.

I sighed. *The only thing that happened in the bathroom was me throwing up. No copier kissing,* I added, trying to add some lightness to our heavy conversation.

If you were barfing, I should hope not. Gross!

I chuckled.

Have you talked to your parents yet? she asked next.

No. Not sure I want to.

Why not? They've got some messed up priorities, but I know they love you and your son. I think they'd want to help.

Honestly, I'm still mad at my mother, and you just summed up why. I can't handle her outrage over Nathan being a sociopath but then her willful amnesia toward the congregation that enabled him to abuse me. I'm struggling with enough of my own cognitive dissonance.

Understood, she wrote back. *I think Grant is on his way back here, and if he catches me on the phone with you, I won't have a very good excuse to NOT give him your number.*

I know I need to deal with that, and I will.

No worries. Take some time for YOU today and do what you can to get your mind off of everything. You need a break, sweetie.

I'll try.

Crud, he's here, and I think he knows I'm texting you. TTYL.

I chuckled and sent up a prayer of thanks that Poppy was there to run interference. Knowing my coworker, she'd text me a full play-by-play later.

With Ari safe at school and the day off of work, I wasn't sure what to do. I didn't want to be in my apartment alone. I just wanted to disappear.

I bought a ticket to the latest superhero movie to escape reality, but every punch landed felt like one of Nathan's blows. I got up and left after twenty minutes.

I sat in my car in the theater parking lot and finally broke down sobbing. My mind turned over every aspect of my relationship with Nathan. I'd been so consumed with surviving the divorce that I'd been unable to process the horrors of our relationship from the very beginning. I ruminated on the uncomfortable first meeting at Beth Shalom and all the red flags I ignored. Traveling beyond our rushed courtship and ceremony in the Beth Shalom gymnasium, I dared to revisit our disastrous honeymoon. Memories resurfaced of our five-day cruise with me huddled in the bathroom after Nathan had humiliated and used me.

"You're too skinny," he had said to me after a failed attempt at lovemaking. "It's hard to get excited when you look like a boy."

I jerked away from him and scooted to the far edge of the bed. "You knew what I looked like when you married me! You always said I was beautiful and that you didn't know why I would be with someone like you. You acted like I was too good for you."

"Yeah, I did say that," he mumbled.

"So, what's really going on? I mean, I've heard that nerves can cause problems like this." I cast a quick glance at the source of our mutual discomfort, and Nathan crossed his legs.

"It's just...I'm not used to women coming onto me," he said lamely. "You know I don't have a lot of experience. This is still pretty new for me."

I stared at him in disbelief. "You're the first man I've ever kissed, let alone slept with, but I don't have any problems wanting to be intimate. This is how God designed sex for marriage. My beloved is mine and his desire is for me," I quoted from *Song of Solomon*.

He lifted his nose in the air. "You'd have to be a man to understand."

"Understand what? The whole time we were courting, you told me we shouldn't kiss until our wedding day because you didn't want to stir up any lust. You said it was because of your ex-fiancée."

"Yes, all of that was because of Jessica," he said as if he'd just come up with the idea himself. "She was always trying to get me into bed. Now, she's sleeping with a married guy at her office and living in sin. Shows what kind of a person *she* is." His expression darkened further. "Why would you even bring her up on our honeymoon?"

"Because I don't understand what's going on. You've always told me Jessica pressured you for sex, so obviously, you *are* used to women coming on to you. Except I'm your wife, and God wants to bless this part of our relationship. There's no sin in this." Setting aside my own pride, I turned toward him, but he twisted further away and refused to make eye contact.

"What's wrong, Nathan? What's actually going on?

"I've told you about my 'ongoing issue,' but I need to confess something."

"Confess something? What are you talking about? You said it's been almost six months since you've looked at any of that stuff."

"While you were in the shower this morning, I messed up."

My stomach dropped. "What do you mean you *messed up*?"

He stood up from the bed, his back to me as he faced the wall. "I looked at porn."

"On our honeymoon?" I gasped, my eyes filling with tears. "How could you?"

"I know, I'm a horrible monster!" He turned around, his face mirroring my stricken expression. "I'm a disgrace to God and to my family. Your life would be so much better without me!" He let out a pitiful moan as tears filled his eyes. "I'm so weak."

I sat frozen in place, horrified by his disclosure.

"Please!" he begged. "Help me, Lauren! I want to get better."

"But why did you say those things about my body? Why did you act like it was my fault instead of what you chose to look at this morning?"

"Well, I mean, you do kind of look like a boy—if I'm being honest—but you have so much inner beauty. That's always been the most attractive thing about you."

I released a heavy breath, glancing at my sparse bosom covered in lace I'd painstakingly purchased for our honeymoon. I'd spent hours in the department store dressing room marveling that I was finally going to enjoy the fruits of marriage. Disillusioned and heartbroken, I turned away from my husband of forty-eight hours. "God, what have I done?" I whispered.

Our wedding night had been awkward and painful since both of us were virgins, but I had assumed it would get better. Something felt terribly off, and I couldn't shake the feeling of dread. Worse yet, I knew I couldn't recover my innocence after giving it away to a man I didn't recognize as the one I thought I'd married.

"Lauren, I'm so sorry!" Nathan rushed around his side of the bed to fall on his knees before me. He reached for my waist, but I pulled away from him.

"Don't... don't touch me," I said, my voice shaking.

"You're the only one who can help me," he sobbed. "Please, don't leave me."

"But you did this on our *honeymoon.*"

"Ugh, God why!" he wailed at the ceiling. "Why won't you

just deliver me? Why do you hate me? Now, my wife hates me too!" He pounded a fist to the floor and then began to beat himself in the chest.

"Nathan, stop!" I shouted. "I don't hate you." I reached for his hands to end his self-flagellating, and he nearly hit me in the face. We both froze. I held his dark gaze hoping to calm him down. "You know I don't hate you. I'm just hurt."

"And it's all my fault! Forgive me," he said, his eyes taking on a crazed, desperate look. "Please, Lauren, you have to forgive me. I want to get help. You're the only one who can help me. Please!"

I nodded and motioned for him to join me on the bed. I held Nathan's hands and tried to pray with him, but he said he felt too ashamed to talk to God. I said I understood, and we spent the next four hours discussing Nathan's issues and how he thought our marriage would be the secret to finally delivering him from the demon of lust. It felt like unending circles, Nathan often repeating himself, and me finally cutting him off and telling him that I'd already heard that part. Glaring daggers at me, he insisted he had to *start from the beginning* because I'd interrupted him, and he couldn't remember his train of thought. The end result was Nathan reciting the same few sentences but never actually getting to the point. With my mental and emotional capacity depleted, he finally initiated sex. At first, his gestures were tender and loving, but his behavior grew increasingly controlling.

"Nathan, stop, you're hurting me!" I cried.

Instead, he commanded me to hold still, something he would order time and again. I eventually learned to close my eyes, disassociate, and beg God to end our intimacy quickly. I remembered Nathan's shock after Ari had been born and I told him sex didn't hurt like it used to. A quick look of disappointment appeared on his face, and it was the first time I wondered if my husband actually enjoyed causing me pain.

After that emotional encounter on our honeymoon, Nathan looked sated lying in the bed, but I disappeared into the bathroom to weep. I knew God designed sex to be both holy and pleasurable for both spouses, but I felt defiled.

That feeling never went away.

CHAPTER 30

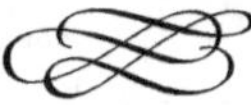

DESPITE THE LACK OF PASSION IN OUR MARRIAGE BED, I realized Nathan didn't always withhold kindness. Within the four walls of Beth Shalom, Nathan's mercurial disposition melted into charm and wide smiles for the members there. It seemed like a switch got flipped once we stepped inside the double doors of the synagogue. During services, Nathan raised his hands for worship, sometimes got on his knees or went to the altar for prayer, and I would beg God to let *this time* be the moment my husband's heart truly changed.

Unfortunately, his "breakthroughs" only lasted until we got back home.

I addressed the issue repeatedly with my husband, and he'd keep me up til the wee hours of the morning wanting to "discuss" his struggles. The discussions were circular arguments that generally went nowhere. Every instance I mentioned of his conflicting behavior was met with abject cluelessness or being told how I'd misunderstood the situation. Half the time, I was defending myself against what Nathan called my "reactions" to his behavior or peevish accusations of me trying to control or manipulate him.

As my stamina crumbled and I insisted I needed sleep, Nathan would finally admit he could improve in some areas. Even that added more time to the conversation with Nathan wanting me to list detailed, specific tasks for him to do. When I got frustrated that he couldn't figure anything out after hours of me already explaining it, he used that as proof of his baseless assertions against me. He said his reason for *not* wanting to change was because of my anger. Irritated but completely exhausted, it was easier to apologize, throw him a bone about my "reaction," and then try to get a few hours of rest.

By the next morning, however, Nathan claimed he couldn't remember saying things I repeated back verbatim. Often, he disavowed all knowledge of the conversation entirely. Instead, he regurgitated his arguments and excuses from the night before as if we hadn't spent half the night already dissecting it. If I displayed any irritation with his antics, Nathan alternated between whiny man-child who was *simply asking* for my help or raging, spiritual hypocrite.

We cycled like this for nearly two years—me wearing myself ragged trying to help my husband see his issues, Nathan denying the issues, Nathan denying he had previously admitted to the issues, or Nathan making excuses why he couldn't do anything to change the issues. No matter how many rounds we went, nothing ever stuck.

At that point, I emotionally checked out of the relationship for my own sanity. I adapted to the loveless state of things and reconciled myself to living as roommates rather than husband and wife. As time went on and Nathan's usually irritating behavior produced lukewarm responses from me, he suddenly remembered every word from conversations he claimed he'd forgotten. Promises were made of renewed efforts toward our marriage, but he still saved most of his displays of affection for synagogue.

He liked to put his arm around me during Shabbat services and stroke my palm in smooth, slow circles. He especially loved placing his *tallit* over both of us during the Aaronic Benediction, a prayer chanted from *Numbers 6:24* and designed to be a family blessing. Nathan's prayer shawl draped over us was meant to symbolize God's covering upon our marriage and Nathan's role as spiritual head of the household. I would hug his middle during the prayer and imagine the added weight of the tallit as God's promises of healing for us.

Those precious moments at synagogue gave me a glimmer of hope because I finally had concrete proof my husband could provide the displays of intimacy I craved. I just didn't understand why the behavior never traveled back home.

"I don't know why it's different," he mumbled when I finally asked him about it.

"What do you mean, you don't know? You love me, don't you?"

My husband avoided my gaze as he sat on our sofa. Facing him on the adjoining love seat, I placed my cell phone face down. I had just sent a quick text to Aaron asking for prayer and courage but not specifying why.

"Nathan?" I prodded. "What's going on?"

"I, um, need to confess something."

I sighed wearily. "What, you *messed up* again?"

He shook his head. "No, it's worse."

"Worse? What do you mean?"

"Look, I know things have been kind of off since we got married."

"Yeah," I drawled. "You told me it was your porn addiction."

"There's um, more."

"More? Did…did you cheat on me?" I whispered.

He paused for what felt like dramatic effect. Watching him and still awaiting a response, I thought I saw a satisfied gleam in his eye.

"Nathan, what's going on?"

He pursed his lips and refused to respond.

"Did you cheat on me?" I asked again, this time my voice infused with anger. "I guess maybe you *are* used to women coming onto you," I added bitterly.

He did not look pleased to have his honeymoon excuse thrown back in his face. Instead, his upper lip curled in disgust as he rolled his eyes. "Don't be ridiculous. Of course, I'm not cheating on you."

"Then what is it?" I demanded. "Why are you acting like this? You told me you needed to confess something, but you're just sitting there with this smirk on your face."

He confirmed my accusation by startling and then quickly hiding behind a mask of offense. "I wasn't smirking."

"Yes, you were! I just saw you!"

Ignoring me, he exhaled a weary sigh. "The truth is, I don't love you."

"You *what*?" I gasped.

"I mean, I love you like a friend, but I'm not *in love* with you. That's why our marriage isn't so great. It makes it hard for me to show you affection because I don't actually feel it."

My entire body trembled at the injustice of all I'd done to salvage a marriage that already brought so little joy. "How… how is that possible?"

"Well, to be honest, I kind of looked at our relationship as an arranged marriage."

"An arranged marriage?" I repeated in shock. "What are you talking about?"

"Remember in *Fiddlers on Roofs* when the parents sing that song about how their marriage was arranged, but they grew to love each other over the years? That's what I thought our marriage would be like. My mom was actually the one who pointed you out to me. She thought it would be a good idea since she knows your parents from leadership."

"But you…you told me you were in love with me when you proposed. You said you couldn't wait to marry me!" My voice sounded increasingly shrill and hysterical. "Was everything just a lie? What about the last three years? How could you do this to me?"

There was another pause as Nathan opened his mouth to speak but then froze. I watched him mentally retract the words he looked like he was about to say. Instead, his face contorted from one of irritation to one of anguish.

"I ruined your life!" he wailed. "After Jessica cheated on me and dumped me, I was scared to love anyone again. But then I saw you, Lauren, and you're messianic, and you're cute, and we believe the same things, so I thought this would be the perfect marriage."

My eyes and mouth widened further in shock. "How could you?" I breathed.

"That's the real reason I looked at porn on our honeymoon. I just wasn't that attracted to you. I sort of lied."

I jumped to my feet. "There's no 'sort of' about it! And then what you do to me in the bedroom," my voice trailed off.

His anguish shifted into indignation. "What do you mean, *what I do to you?* I haven't heard a single complaint from you."

"Yes, you have!" I shouted. "You said it makes you feel like a failure when I tell you I'm in pain. You know that it hurts when we're together. It always does."

"I can't help it that you're so small." He looked me up and down, flicking his hand dismissively. "You'll probably need a c-section if you ever get pregnant."

"What?" I hissed. "You're blaming that on me too?"

"Well, it's obvious you don't like sex. Not like how I do anyway."

I gaped at him, horrified. "You told me you avoid sex with me because you feel guilty about watching porn, but then you still ask me to copy the filth you watch. Most of the time, I feel like I'm begging you to come to bed anyway just so that you *stop* looking at it. You told Rabbi Lebow that I don't initiate sex with you, but I do! I can show you the text messages where I ask you to come to bed, and you always have an excuse. I have to beg you for weeks and weeks, and then you'll eventually confess that you 'messed up' again."

"Yeah so maybe you do ask for sex, Lauren, but I know your heart isn't really in it. You just lie there waiting for everything to be over."

"You told me not to move! You said that's what you wanted."

"Well, it's not what I want."

"Well, what *do* you want?" I spat. "It changes every five seconds, and I can't keep up anymore."

His eyes flashed angrily. "I want a wife who understands what Biblical submission means. This disrespectful attitude you have isn't pleasing to the Lord."

"And I want a husband who knows how to Biblically love his wife," I shot back. "You touch yourself and your laptop more than you ever touch me. Maybe you should have an arranged marriage with your computer instead."

"Don't you dare speak to me like that!" he roared, jumping to his feet. "You need to show me respect." He puffed out his chest as he used all four inches of his height advantage over me.

"And you need to show me love!" I held his angry gaze but slid backward a step.

"I do love you, Lauren. I just told you I did."

Nearly apoplectic, I screamed, "What are you talking about?! You just told me you faked our entire relationship and tricked me into marrying you. *That's* what you just told me!"

There was an awkward pause following my outburst. Nathan stared blankly at me, his eyes devoid of any emotion.

"Why are you yelling?" he finally asked, his tone flat. "Obviously, *I'm* calm, but you're completely out of control." Mimicking my defensive stance, he backed away as if fearing for his own safety. "Maybe we should talk when you can get a hold of yourself. I've never seen you like this."

I shook my head, fighting off tears of frustration at both his behavior and his ridiculous insinuations. Of course, I had every right to be upset! He had been yelling just as loudly moments earlier. As he continued to watch me, I faltered.

Had I overreacted? I had never been so angry in my life, but did my chauvinistic—and occasionally, downright misogynistic —husband actually perceive me as a threat?

For a split second, I wondered if I had imagined his earlier confession or misunderstood something. Just as quickly, the tidal wave of reality crashed over me and nearly choked off my air supply. My chest tightened, and I stumbled away from Nathan, trapped in a surreal nightmare where my husband couldn't remember what came out of his mouth ten minutes prior.

"I can't do this anymore," I whispered, my voice cracking. "This...this is insane."

Nathan's face went white. "What do you mean?"

"This. This *marriage*. I just...I can't. I'm miserable, and clearly, so are you." I tried to wipe the tears from my eyes, but I'd unleashed my deepest secret. The geyser of grief and disillusionment had been aching for release.

My husband matched my tears, his sobs suddenly louder than mine, his shaking shoulders bigger than mine, and his facial expression more anguished than mine.

Emulating the same behavior from our honeymoon, Nathan fell on his knees before me. He quoted verbatim words I had previously told him I wanted to hear, but his parroted declarations felt mechanical rather than sincere. When I didn't immediately capitulate, Nathan upped the melodramatic cries of self pity. By the end of his hysterics, I was comforting *him* and talking him out of suicidal threats.

Foolishly, I gave Nathan another chance.

And too many others.

Ari was conceived two months later, and the following seven months of pregnancy was the best treatment I'd ever received from my husband. Anything I needed, Nathan fetched me for me as if I was a delicate pearl. I finally felt cherished and loved. Nathan loved to talk to the baby in my belly, and when he found out we were having a boy, he made sure to brag about me to others whenever I was around.

His family happily presided over Ari's *bris* ceremony, and our baby dedication at Beth Shalom felt like a dream come true. My husband finally loved me, I had a child in my arms, and I could tell Aaron to stop worrying about me.

The first time Nathan struck me, Ari was six months old. I'd noticed my husband's extreme jealousy and near spitefulness in leaving messes around the house for me to clean. Anything that I asked him to pick up, he seemed to double down and do ten times worse. When the baby cried at night, he rolled his eyes and said, "Here we go again," but he never offered to help with nighttime feedings or diaper changes.

That fateful night, Nathan peevishly added, "Ari always comes first. Just let him cry himself to sleep. He needs to learn to self-soothe anyway. You can't keep shoving a breast in his mouth. I don't know how you make enough milk with those tiny things."

I schooled my expression, knowing Nathan had been more volatile than usual. He'd recently broken several of my belongings in fits of temper. "The pediatrician says Ari is in the ninetieth percentile for his height and weight. My breasts are doing just fine."

"Not that you let me get anywhere near them," he pouted.

"You've never been interested."

"I am now. I thought you'd be happy about that."

"Okay," I drawled, "well, that is new information. I can't do much about it right now since the baby is crying, but we can talk about it later."

"We can talk about it *now*," he demanded.

Ari's squalling picked up on the baby monitor. "Nathan, I need to get him back to bed."

"You need to satisfy your husband in bed!"

"Enough," I yelled. "It's not a competition."

The slap across my face cracked like a bolt of lightning in the room.

"I'm, I'm sorry," Nathan stammered.

Scrambling away from him, I rushed to the baby's room while the left side of my face throbbed. I scooped Ari from his crib, slightly vindicated when I discovered a full diaper and a hungry baby. I nursed my son and burped him on my shoulder. I knew he was asleep, but I let him lie there as I cried silently and eventually dozed off in the rocking chair with him.

Nathan didn't say a word about the incident the following morning, but his standard, sullen demeanor transformed into a cheery disposition. I later learned this was just part of the abuse cycle. Back then, Nathan acted more helpful, doing dishes, picking up clothes, and wanting to change diapers at night.

After three weeks and agonized prayers, I thought maybe he'd turned over a new leaf. The moment I finally relaxed and thought I was dealing with a reformed husband, Nathan reverted back to his old behavior.

I survived in our toxic marriage another year before Nathan's underage porn scandal was discovered at Beth Shalom. Knowing better, I still went back to him and hoped it was the reality check Nathan needed to finally get his life together.

Instead, he just got worse.

I knew that if I didn't escape a marriage that already meant death to my soul and spirit, Nathan would eventually kill my body too.

CHAPTER 31

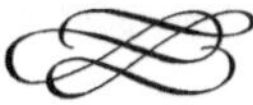

My cell phone rang and displayed Grant's name, returning me back to my present host of problems.

I froze, not sure I could handle the upcoming conversation we needed to have. I let the phone go to voicemail and assumed he'd leave a message. Instead, my phone rang again.

"Hi," I mumbled, picking it up on the third ring.

"Lauren, thank God! How are you? Are you okay? Poppy told me what happened and showed me a picture of Jared's face. I can't imagine what you went through being married to that monster."

"No, I don't think anybody could." Anxiety from remembered trauma kept my heart racing, and I inhaled a few more breaths to steady myself.

"Lauren?" he asked. "Are you okay?"

I fought through the wobble in my voice. "Honestly, no. But I'm here."

"Do you think we could meet after work?"

"No, I'll have my son with me."

"What about lunch?"

"Why?" I asked.

"Why, what?"

"Why do you want to meet with me? I can't deal with the 'we need to talk' conversation right now. I should be mad that you got my number from somebody else, but under the circumstances, I guess I can understand."

"Lauren, that's not why I want to see you. I care about you. Jared Levine saved you and your son from a nightmare I can't even begin to imagine." Pausing, he added, "I already know where we stand with everything else."

"Well, you're talking to me now," I offered. "What else do you need?"

"Maybe it's selfish of me, but I want to see your face."

"You saw it yesterday."

He exhaled a weary sigh. "Okay, let's cut the small talk. I know you're *not* okay. You survived last night, but that doesn't mean you don't need help. I want to see you for my own peace of mind, but—"

"But what?" I demanded. "What do you want from me?"

"But this isn't about me," he said, combatting my irritation with empathy. "What can I do to make this easier for you?"

Stunned, I sat in silence.

"Lauren? You still there?"

"Yeah," I murmured. "I've just never heard anybody put it that way."

"Anybody? Not even your old friend who couldn't keep his eyes off you after we came out of the bathroom last night?"

I shook off the implication of Grant's words. "No, I mean Aaron was always there if I needed him, but I also knew he wanted more. Isn't that what you want too? You comfort me, and maybe I'll finally crack and then you move in for the kill?" Bitterness seeped in along with a montage of Nathan's betrayal.

Reading my thoughts, Grant said, "I'm not him."

"How do I know? How will I ever know until it's too late and I'm trapped again?"

He paused before replying. "You said you didn't want to have this conversation now, and I don't think it's the right time either. I'm not here to trap you, tempt you, or do anything other than make sure that you're okay."

"I don't know what you want me to say, Grant. I'm not okay. I'm terrified and dealing with flashbacks and triggers from the entire relationship. I don't even know where to begin trying to process all of it. It's just so many layers of compounded trauma."

After a long moment of silence, I wondered if he'd finally taken the hint and realized I was too damaged for anyone—especially someone coming out of his own complicated relationship. I wasn't a damsel in distress for Grant to rescue. I was a domestic abuse survivor struggling to recover some semblance of the woman I was before my ex-husband obliterated my trust in men or people in general.

He finally spoke up. "I'm sorry."

Bracing myself for rejection, I asked, "Sorry for what?"

"Sorry for everything you've been through. Sorry I can't fix it. Sorry I can't wave a magic wand and make all of the pain go away."

"Well, I'm sure you...wait, *what*?"

He chuckled softly. "Not the response you expected?"

I shook my head even though I knew he couldn't see me. "No," I murmured.

"I'm not going anywhere. I'm not scared of your pain. My heart breaks for you and your son. All I want to do is help."

I didn't bother wiping the tears coursing down my cheeks. I wasn't sure I could stop them even if I wanted to.

"Lauren, are you still there?"

"I'm here," I whispered.

Livening up his tone, Grant asked, "What's your favorite restaurant? Soaring Scone?"

"The Parkview Diner."

"Awesome, what do you usually order?"

"Why? Are you trying to get me to meet you there? Look, I already told you—"

"Take your son out to dinner tonight and know that it'll be covered by a friend. Take the night off, enjoy being at your favorite place, and I'll see you whenever you're ready to come back to the office."

Somehow, Grant had managed to surprise me yet again. "Really? That's it? That's all you want from me?"

"If I can bring you a little joy after everything that happened last night, then you've given me what I want."

"Are you sure?"

I could hear the smile in his tone. "Yes, I'm sure."

My shoulders shook. I eked out a "thank you" before hanging up and bursting into anguished wails. The pain and rejection of my marriage lanced like a boil, spilling from the depths of my soul.

The years of wasted effort.

The abuse I believed was my fault.

The sadistic mind games accompanied by evil smirks.

The thought of sharing a son with the vilest man on the planet and how I had ever been foolish enough to believe he could *learn* to love me.

I wanted to be numb, and more than anything, I just wanted a moment of peace. I tried reciting *Matthew 11:28-31* and other

Bible verses, but my burdens felt too heavy to lift. Instead, God met me in the valley of my despair and reminded me of when I'd flown in an airplane during a thunderstorm. We had soared above the rain clouds and chaos below, gliding through nothing but blue skies at 30,000 feet. The angry rumbles and jagged lightning could no longer touch me. Desperately, that's where I wanted to be. Free from the unending grief of wounds that wouldn't heal.

I had always taken so much comfort during the worship part of the Beth Shalom services, but every song was tainted by the congregation where I had learned them. Instead, I harkened back to my own bat mitzvah at Temple Beth Ami. My parents had gotten saved before my Reform Jewish ceremony, but I had been the one to insist on having the service there. Thinking back to prayers I'd chanted from the *siddur,* my heart longed to go straight to the source and the heart of everything it meant to be a Jew.

Chanting within my own car, I cried out, *"Sh'ma Yisrael Adonai Eloheinu Adonai Echad. Baruch shem k'vod malchuto l'olam va'ed."* I spoke the English translation aloud, "Hear, O Israel! The Lord is our God, the Lord alone. Blessed is the Name of His glorious kingdom, forever and ever."

The comforting blanket of God's peace quieted my frayed nerves. Exhaling, I released my anxious thoughts on a slow breath. I didn't need a corrupt rabbi or a synagogue of his blind followers to validate my "Jewish identity." With every fiber of my being, I knew exactly who I was and to Whom I belonged. My fatigued faith strengthened with the reminder that the same God who delivered my ancestors from slavery in Egypt and myself from slavery to a narcissistic husband would bring me all the way through the wilderness.

I looked out to the blue skies beyond my car window. "I

want to be free! God, please! I don't want to be a traumatized mess for Ari. Please, bring justice and expose every lie and secret that's been kept in the dark." Reflecting on the phone call I'd just had with Grant, I added, "Please forgive me for stirring up love before it's time to arise. If this isn't your will for my life, please take him away. He's hurting. I'm hurting. How do I know any of this is real?"

As much as I would counsel myself or anyone in my shoes to "handle one thing at a time," I knew the attraction between me and Grant weighed just as heavily on me as Nathan's tortures. How could I be free to love again or even be loved with all of the unhealed trauma I'd been too busy or distracted by the divorce to deal with? Grant claimed he wasn't intimidated by my pain, but how would I ever know for sure?

The poem of *Ecclesiastes 3* echoed in my mind, and I opened the Bible app on my cell phone to read the words:

There is a time for everything,
and a season for every activity under the heavens:
a time to be born and a time to die,
a time to plant and a time to uproot,
a time to kill and a time to heal,
a time to tear down and a time to build,
a time to weep and a time to laugh,
a time to mourn and a time to dance,
a time to scatter stones and a time to gather them,
a time to embrace and a time to refrain from embracing,
a time to search and a time to give up,
a time to keep and a time to throw away,
a time to tear and a time to mend,
a time to be silent and a time to speak,
a time to love and a time to hate,

a time for war and a time for peace.

"Breathe," I commanded myself. I inhaled and exhaled again, reminded of the S.T.O.P. method of anxiety management I'd read about online. I stopped my mind from pinging from one anxious thought about Grant to another. I focused on my breath and grounding myself in the present. I tried to objectively look at the situation and reminded myself that Grant wasn't asking me to sign over the rest of my life. It was my own anxiety and need to know the future that created the racing thoughts. I had been at the non-existent mercy of a tyrant for so long, I realized I was desperately trying to control any and every aspect of my life to avoid being blindsided again. I needed to examine Grant's behavior without the filter of my own fears or wrongly attributing Nathan's character to his.

I coached myself aloud through the mindfulness exercise. "Nathan would have pressured you to meet with him, just like he pushed you to go out for coffee the first night he hit on you. Grant gave you space. Nathan wanted coffee and belittled you for not liking it. Grant asked you what you wanted to eat and didn't complain that you said something other than what he suggested.

"Nathan would have put a guilt trip on you for not thinking of *his* feelings when you told him 'no.' Grant didn't use his concern for you as an excuse to ignore what you said you needed. Nathan would have told you to 'submit' to him and that disagreeing with him meant that you were disobeying God. Grant isn't your husband, but he's never talked to or treated you like some flying monkey required to obey him."

I inhaled another swell of air, clearing my lungs and my mind from the traumatic memories. I knew I wasn't out of the woods yet, but I did feel significantly lighter as I continued to talk to God the rest of the afternoon and lay my concerns before Him.

I picked up Ari early from school, and I took him to his favorite indoor play arena to run around and have fun. Poppy checked in once she'd clocked out for the day, and I didn't have to lie when I told her I was doing better. I noticed that Aaron was curiously quiet, but after Grant's comment about him staring at us during Bible study, I left that stone unturned.

After an hour of jumping around, I drove Ari to the Parkview Diner. The hostess eyed me up and down as she handed me a plastic gift card courtesy of Grant Kaplan's generosity.

"Is there a problem?" I asked.

"Sorry." She blushed and pushed a turquoise tendril of hair behind her ear. "The guy who bought the gift card today said it was for the most incredible woman he's ever met."

My jaw went slack. I glanced down at Ari, but he was enraptured by the glass display case of desserts. I permitted myself a shallow breath of relief.

"You usually come in here with your friend, right?" the hostess asked, regaining my attention. "You guys always order the same dessert."

I nodded. "Yes, that's me."

She gave a shy smile. "I had no idea I'd already met 'the most incredible woman in the world.' I can't imagine anyone ever saying that about me."

"You and me both."

She looked surprised. "So, you two aren't...?" her voice trailed off.

I shook my head vehemently. "Just friends."

"Not for long, I hope."

I chuckled despite myself. "There's a time for everything," I replied, thinking of the Bible verses I'd read earlier. "Just not right now." I glanced quickly at my son, hoping she'd take the hint and drop the subject.

She nodded and gathered up two of the diner's huge menus. She handed them to our server and whispered something. Based on the expression on the older woman's face, I could hazard a guess at the topic of their hushed conversation. She confirmed my suspicions when she gave me the once over just like her turquoise-haired cohort.

"Follow me, sweetie," she said, gesturing to a nearby table.

Ari and I sat down, and then I held up the gift card. "Hey, can you explain something? I don't see a dollar amount anywhere on here."

She grinned though her faded lipstick. "That's because there isn't one, sweetie. It's a tab. You come here as often as you want, and your um, *friend,* will take care of the bill."

"Oh," I murmured. "I had no idea."

"My Mommy has lots of friends," Ari chimed in. "When are we going to see Mr. Aaron again?"

I smiled weakly. "Not sure right now, buddy."

"Ma'am, do you know what you want?" she asked, turning her attention to me.

I hesitated, feeling like her question carried more weight than deciding between my usual Greek omelet or a ham-free, Cobb salad.

"How about I bring you drinks and some bread, and then you can take some time to look things over? My name is Erica, if you need anything."

"That would be great," I said. "Strawberry lemonade for my son, and just water and lemon for me."

"You sure you don't want something else, sweetie? Maybe a glass of wine?"

I shook my head. "No, I'm a lightweight. I still have to drive us home."

"Okay, well I'll be back with your drinks, and you make sure you take *all* the time you need." This time, I did not mistake the double meaning of her words. "Enjoy every second with Little Man. You have plenty of time to figure out everything else."

CHAPTER 32

ARI LOOKED BAFFLED BY OUR GROWN UP
conversation, but when Erica flashed him a grin, he responded
with his best gap-toothed smile. She burst out laughing and
then set off for the kitchen.

"I like her," Ari said. "She's nice."

I smiled back at him. "Yes, Miss Erica is very nice."

"What's a tab, Mommy?"

"A tab?"

"Yeah. Miss Erica said a friend gave you a tab."

"Oh," I blushed. "That just means that one of Mommy's
friends is paying for our dinner and dessert."

"Which friend? Is it Mr. Aaron?"

I shook my head. "No, sweetie. It's not Mr. Aaron."

"Well, who is it?"

"Just a friend from work."

"Oh, is it Miss Poppy?" he asked. "She's your friend from
work."

Not knowing what Ari would or wouldn't repeat to his

father, I nodded without verbally confirming the lie. I wasn't ready to explain my relationship with Grant to my son.

Erica returned with our promised drinks and bread, and I decided to splurge and order the full chicken dinner. It came with a Greek salad large enough to be a meal on its own, and I silently thanked God for Grant's generosity in providing Ari and I with both dinner and plenty of leftovers.

I pushed away guilty thoughts of spending more of his money as I ordered myself a decadent baklava cheesecake that I'd been dying to try. Ari's eyes grew wide as he quickly abandoned his tiny bowl of ice cream that came as part of his kid's entree.

"Mommy, can I have some?"

I laughed as I could practically see the drool coming from his mouth. "Sure, buddy. How about I scoop you a bite, and then we can both try some at the same time?"

He nodded eagerly, and I hoped most of the gooey dessert would remain on the spoon rather than down the front of his shirt.

I counted to three, and we both groaned in delight as we sampled the cake. The crispy layers of phyllo combined with the crunchy nuts and smooth cheesecake had my tastebuds doing backflips. I spooned some more onto an empty bread plate so Ari could sample a few bites without dogging every mouthful I knew I was going to take.

Surprising myself, I almost finished the entire slice. My stomach finally shouted at me to stop before it burst. Boxing the rest along with our stockpile of dinner leftovers, we thanked Erica for her wonderful service, and she offered a friendly wink as we exited the restaurant. Ari fell asleep on the ride back to our apartment, and his enthusiasm for the entire evening was a balm to my soul. Those precious smiles and laughs reminded me of God's promises in *Isaiah 61* of providing joy instead of mourning. I carried Ari up the stairs and deposited him safely in bed.

After changing into an oversized t-shirt and tackling my bedtime routine, my cell phone caught my eye while charging on my nightstand. It had truly been a wonderful evening, and I felt a nudge to check in with Grant.

Figuring it was late enough that he either wouldn't see the text or wouldn't reply, I typed, *Thank you so much for dinner. We had a great time.*

A message popped back that he had "liked" what I wrote. Quick to respond, his message said, *You're welcome.*

I hesitated, not sure what else I could or should say. My phone lit up again with another message.

Do you think you'll be coming back into the office tomorrow?

Probably. Ari and I both needed this tonight. More than you know.

Grant sent back a smiling emoji. *Did you get dessert?*

Of course!

Which one did you order?

Baklava cheesecake. I've been eyeballing it for a while.

How was it?

I sent back a gif of a drooling cartoon character.

Lol. Glad you enjoyed it.

Ok, well I better let you go. I need to get to bed, and I'm sure you do too.

Thanks for texting me.

Sure.

No, I mean, I've had you on my mind for most of the day. I'm still new to all of this praying and Bible stuff, but I did pray for you. Every time you came to mind, I just took it as a sign that I should pray.

Tears pooled in my eyes. *That means a lot. Thank you.*

Good night, Lauren. Hopefully, I'll see you tomorrow.

Good night, Grant.

I sighed and closed my eyes, clutching my phone to my chest.

I slept more soundly than I could remember, perhaps knowing that there was nothing Nathan could do to me from inside of a jail cell. The usual knots in my shoulders had dissolved, and I noticed my standard aches and pains were also absent that morning.

"Hmm," I murmured, testing out my limbs in bed.

Ari was still asleep, so I took advantage of the time to brush my teeth and start putting on light makeup for work. My son arrived in the bathroom, surprising me with a dry overnight diaper that had me leaping for joy. I helped him take care of his bathroom needs while promising we would go after school to pick up the coolest big boy underwear possible.

"It's going to be a good day," Ari declared as I dropped him off at daycare.

I sank to my knees to meet his eyes. "Oh yeah? Why do you say that, buddy?"

He tapped his heart. "Because I think God told me."

"God told you?"

He nodded triumphantly. "Yep. Sometimes I see angels, and they wave at me."

The daycare worker overhearing our conversation gave a tolerant smile, but I held my son's gaze. "What do the angels look like?"

He grinned. "They're tall, Mommy. They like me. Sometimes, I hear them singing."

I ignored the disbelieving gasp from another parent eavesdropping on our conversation and hugged my son tightly. "I'm so proud of you, buddy."

"Proud of me?" his muffled response came from against my chest.

"*So* proud!" I kissed the top of his head and pulled him in for another squeeze. "You make my heart so happy, Ari Levi Fein."

He presented me with the most beautiful smile I'd ever seen, and I knew I'd have that image saved in my memories for the rest of my days. I kissed his cheeks about twenty times before the daycare worker reminded me that it was time for my son to get to class.

I shook my head in wonder as I returned to my car.

"Hey," one of the parents called to me in the parking lot.

I whirled around to see the same mom who had vocalized her skepticism in the lobby.

"Do you really believe in all that stuff?" she asked. "Kids seeing angels?"

"Why wouldn't I? I've dealt with enough demons in this life. If evil is real, then good has to be real too."

She considered my point. "I thought that kind of stuff only happened in movies."

"My son and I have been through hell. The only way we've survived has been by the grace of God, and I'm sure, countless angels protecting us too."

She held my gaze, and as I stared into sad, blue eyes, I realized she was familiar with the same demon that had been tormenting me and my son. "I'm Lauren," I said, extending my hand out to her.

She didn't take it. Instead, she wiped tears away from her cheeks. "My daughter's dad talks a lot about angels and demons. He says he's a Christian."

"Mine does too," I said, equal to the challenge. "He's also

sitting in a jail cell right now for attacking two police officers after trying to break into my home."

"Oh," she murmured. "I'm sorry, I didn't know."

I waved her off. "I grew up in a religious cult and was basically tricked into an arranged marriage with my ex—only he never bothered to tell me it was 'arranged.' He beat me and my son, looked at porn, and the entire time he did that, he lifted hands in services, prayed, and pretended he was seeking God. He got the entire congregation to turn on me and shun me for leaving him, and his mother goes around pretending her son is being persecuted by law enforcement because he believes in Jesus."

"How can you believe in God after all of that?"

I took a step toward her, hoping she wouldn't run. "If I had to base my relationship with God on the example of the people around me, I would have run a long time ago. Even my parents make excuses for why they won't leave the same place that shunned me."

"That's horrible!" she gasped.

"But I know God is real because He answers my prayers. He talks to me through the Bible, through nature, and sometimes I hear him in my heart. He's allowed me to go through so much, but He's also brought me through it."

"If God's so loving, why would he let you suffer at all? I mean, you seem like a really nice person. You didn't deserve to be treated that way."

I smiled. "No, I didn't deserve it. And trust me, I've asked God all of those questions. Why me? Why my son? I saved myself for my wedding day, and I wound up married to a monster who tortured me for fun."

"I'm so sorry," she murmured. "I shouldn't have said anything."

I reached out a hand and touched her arm. "Listen, I don't know your story or your situation, but I do know that God uses *everything* for our good. Sometimes, we go through horrible things in life to give encouragement to other people. We can offer hope on the other side of trauma. The pain is real, but it's not too big for God to heal."

"Are you going to tell me I need to forgive my ex?" she spat, pulling away from me.

I exhaled a mirthless laugh. "I would be the *last* person to preach that to anybody. I'm definitely not there yet."

"But, you seem so happy."

I smiled softly at her. "You didn't see me yesterday, crying my eyes out in front of the Movie Pub because I couldn't handle all the violence in the new *Prince of Thunder* movie."

She studied me intently. "And God really did all of that for you? It's not just denial because you grew up believing?"

I shook my head. "I have peace because I prayed, and God met me where I was at. It's still a roller coaster, but none of it is from tradition or my parents. I know because I've experienced God for myself. Last night, I had a friend bless us with dinner at my favorite restaurant. God knew exactly what my son and I needed."

"I wish I had friends like that," she murmured.

"Like I said, my name is Lauren. I don't go to any church now, but I do attend a home Bible study on Sunday nights." I handed her my Culver business card. "There are a few others who have survived the same congregation I did, and we meet together to read the Bible, pray, and support one another. They've been amazing to me, and I'm sure they'd welcome you and your daughter too."

She nodded. "Thanks."

I smiled back. "Have a wonderful day, and I'll be praying for you."

"My name is Allie," she finally said.

"Nice to meet you, Allie. Hopefully, I'll see you around since our kids are both here."

For the first time, I noticed a glimmer of hope in her cornflower blue eyes. "Thanks for talking with me. I'm sure you need to get to work." She took in my dress pants and top.

"I do, and I hope you have a great day with whatever you've got going on."

I offered one last smile before turning toward my car. Once I sat inside, I felt an overwhelming surge of peace and joy from the Holy Spirit.

"Thank you for using me," I whispered in prayer. "Thank you for giving me hope so that I could share it with Allie."

I spent a few more minutes praying for her, and as I finished, I felt the comfort of the Lord surrounding me once again. It had been so long since I'd had the strength to speak about my faith, let alone stop and truly intercede for someone other than me and my son.

"Welcome back," I whispered to the prayer warrior of old. "God's not finished with your story yet."

CHAPTER 33

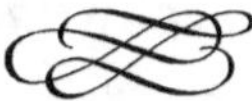

I stepped into the office on cloud nine. Poppy did a double take when she saw me.

"What in the world, or should I say *who* in the world, put that dopey grin on your face?" She eyed me over the rim of her Vincenzo's cup.

"Jesus put it there, so don't you even start with all of your copier kissing shenanigans."

She grinned back. "Glad to hear it, sweetie. I've been worried about you."

"Yesterday was just *a lot*. I spent most of the day talking to Jesus about it and processing things."

"How do you feel?"

"Lighter. Freer. I know I have a long way to go, but it actually turned out to be a pretty good day."

Poppy watched me expectantly. When I didn't elaborate, she rolled her eyes and gestured for me to keep going.

"What?" I asked.

"Girl, I *gave* him your phone number, you know I want deets."

I chuckled. "You sound like Natalie when you talk like that."

"I have to stay relevant somehow. At least I'm not 'literally' doing anything other than reading," she quipped.

"You're a whole vibe today."

"And you are like, *so* not answering the question," she said, affecting a Valley Girl accent. "Grant's going to be here any minute, and I'm sure the two of you will get right back to your smoldering, *will they/won't they?* tension that you can cut with a knife."

I blushed. "You're probably not wrong about that."

"Look, I'm going to find out one way or the other, so you might as well just tell me."

This time, I burst into a full belly laugh. "Oh my gosh, you're so crazy!"

"Been called worse." She took another sip of coffee and winked at me.

I dropped my purse into a desk drawer and shuffled through some work requests on my desk. "Things are…they're good, I think."

"They're *good*?"

"Yeah, I mean, I think we're in a good place."

"Okay, now try being even more vague when you answer this time."

I grinned at her. "Don't you want to wait for all of the 'smoldering tension' so you can watch it in real time?"

"You're enjoying this, aren't you?"

My expression was unapologetically mischievous.

Poppy stuck her tongue out at me. "Do you think there's a possibility for more than just coworkers or even friendship for the two of you? After you guys came out of the bathroom, I was practically swooning with the way Grant watched you. Then again, the way Aaron watched Grant watching you had me wondering if I was going to need to break up a fight."

"Ugh, not you too."

"What do you mean?"

"Grant also said something about Aaron watching me."

She frowned. "Your old friend looked more than just a little 'concerned,' but I hope he was just being protective of you. I thought Aaron was head over heels with the new girl he brought to Bible study."

"I hope he truly is—for both of their sakes. Ruthie deserves better than Aaron on the rebound, and my feelings for him haven't changed. You didn't see the smile he gave her when I first saw them together. Aaron's never looked at me that way."

"Were you jealous?" Poppy asked, surprised.

"No, not of their relationship, just of the freedom she has to love and be loved without all of the baggage and trauma."

"So, there's no hope for you and Grant? What did you guys talk about for so long in the bathroom?"

"I guess there's a friendship. He's not pushing me for more."

"Oh," Poppy said, her expression falling. "Been there, done that. That whole just-friends-but-we're-about-to-burst-through-our-own-skin situationship."

"No, I don't think it's like what happened with you," I said, referring to her past flirtation with Joe Trautweig, "and I won't be getting back together with Nathan the way you and Jared reconciled. Even if Nathan had a complete change of heart, I know that God set me down this path to be free from him legally, spiritually, and physically."

"Good!" she replied emphatically. "I would never suggest otherwise."

"It's hard to believe I used to be one of those people who looked down my nose at couples who got a divorce. Like they didn't love God enough and the only permissible reason was adultery."

Poppy looked stunned. "Wow…obviously, you changed your mind. What happened?"

"When Charlotte told me she was divorcing Rick, I was still in denial about Nathan. I remember telling her I didn't think I could walk with her through it, let alone when she started talking about wanting to date again. I said I wasn't sure how I felt about it."

"What did she say?"

"She called me self righteous, told me I wasn't the Holy Spirit, and that she didn't need my approval to do what was best for her and her children."

"Good for her," Poppy murmured. "How did you respond?"

"Well, I wasn't happy. I argued some Bible verses with her. Charlotte argued back and said Rick had already violated their covenant by neglecting her, verbally abusing her and her girls, looking at porn, and slandering her to others—including Nathan."

"Wait, so Charlotte's ex was friends with yours?"

I nodded. "She sent me screenshots of messages between the two of them that she'd gotten from Rick's phone. I was shocked to see how Rick talked about Charlotte and also the lies Nathan told him about me. Nathan made himself the victim of everything he did to me, all while denying he ever did those things when I would confront him about it."

"I see."

"Stupidly, I still made excuses for Nathan and for Rick. Charlotte got frustrated and finally asked if I really believed her husband needed to 'stick his appendage into someone else' in order for God to release her from the marriage. Her oldest daughter struggled badly with depression because of Rick constantly picking on her, to the point of expressing suicidal thoughts. Charlotte asked me if I believed God would be happier if her daughter killed herself just to keep a horrible marriage intact."

Poppy sucked in a breath. "Wow."

"Yeah, I didn't really have an answer for that. Looking back, I just wanted an excuse to justify why I was too scared to get my own divorce. I wasn't ready to admit just *how* bad my marriage was, and I hadn't told anyone about the physical abuse." I hesitated before tacking on, "And *other* kinds of abuse. You know what I mean."

"Oh, Lauren!" Poppy cooed, her eyes wide. "You've never mentioned any of that."

"I don't like to talk about it."

"Understandably. I'm so sorry, sweetie."

I waved her off and sniffled back tears. "Charlotte and I left the conversation pretty abruptly because Nathan caught me on the phone with her. He berated me for talking to Charlotte and regurgitated every insult I'd read in those text messages between him and Rick. He repeated Rick's accusations verbatim, and it was the wake up call I needed."

"What did you do?"

"After Nathan went to bed, I texted Charlotte a huge apology. God had shown me my own pride and fear, and I started to confess the truth about Nathan's abuse. Charlotte asked me if I believed God was more concerned about the *people* inside of a marriage or just upholding the institution. She told me I was not 'suffering for Christ' but just needlessly suffering. She asked me if I wanted Ari to grow up thinking how Nathan treated me was how all women should be treated."

Poppy took a final sip of coffee and tossed her cup into the trash. "Wow, that's heavy. It's also very true. My situation was different than yours, but I can definitely relate. I would never want Ryan to copy how Jared treated me or the kids before our separation."

"I always tell Charlotte how blessed I am that she didn't give up on me even when I almost gave up on her and our friendship. I used to think she was rough around the edges, but Charlotte just tells it like it is. She has a tough time keeping friends because they want an unfiltered diagnosis of all of the 'problem' people in their lives...until Charlotte starts to clue in that the *real* problem is the friend. I've listened to a few of her stories, and it's crazy how these women cry on her shoulder—for decades, in some cases—and then they wind up hurting Charlotte exactly how they claim they were abused or rejected themselves."

Poppy shook her head. "People really suck sometimes."

I chuckled. "Yeah, they do."

"Not all people, I hope," Grant said, poking his head in the doorway.

"Hi," I said shyly.

His eyes were bright, and I heard the smile in his voice. "Good morning."

Poppy gave a fake cough that sounded eerily like "copier" and then excused herself to the ladies' room.

"How are you doing?" He stepped inside without breaking eye contact.

I looked away and fumbled with some papers on my desk. "Better, thanks."

"Thank you for texting me last night."

I glanced up, surprised at how quickly he'd closed the

distance between us. "You're welcome, but it's not really a big deal. I had a nudge, so I did it."

Grant studied me. "You seem…different."

"Probably because you're not holding my hair back over a toilet," I deadpanned.

He rolled his eyes playfully. "Not what I meant. You just seem happier."

I smiled. "Yeah, I guess I am. Had a big come to Jesus yesterday."

"Come to Jesus?" he asked, sitting on the edge of my desk.

I smiled, recalling God's overwhelming peace and reassurance that my future didn't have to resemble my past. "I've been in survival mode for a very long time. There were some hard truths I needed to see and trauma I needed to release."

"What do you mean?"

My smile grew as I no longer felt the oppressive weight of shame. "I guess 'release' in the sense of facing the memories and seeing Nathan for who he really was. Seeing myself as the victim I was instead of blaming myself or wondering why I didn't see it sooner."

Grant returned my smile with a comforting one of his own. "That's impressive, and I'm sure it wasn't easy."

"Definitely not easy, but absolutely freeing once I stared down those evil memories. I haven't had time to really sit and revisit some of them, but I want to be free from the pain. I know I'll always carry the scars, but I don't want open wounds anymore."

I dared a glance up and beheld so much admiration in Grant's expression, I couldn't look for long. It was like staring directly at the sun.

"What?" he asked.

"You… the way you look at me. Nobody has ever looked at

me like that." I held up a hand to cut off what I knew would be his next objection. "Please, don't bring up Aaron. Trust me, I know what I'm talking about."

"Okay," Grant drawled, willing to drop the argument. "So what makes the way I look at you so different?"

I inhaled a deep breath. "Because of the way it makes *me* feel."

CHAPTER 34

His face broke into an ear splitting grin. "Is that so?"

I chuckled. "You're going to wind up with such a huge ego."

"Too late." He gave me a saucy wink, and we both laughed. I loved the way his eyes sparkled and the light atmosphere between us.

"So you were saying?" he gestured with a flourish. "I have a feeling I definitely want to hear this."

I shook my head. "You are incorrigible."

"Ooh, incorrigible? There's a word I haven't heard since 1990. Were you even alive then?"

"Actually, no!" I said, laughing. "I was born in 1991. What about you?"

"1988," he replied. "Do we need to bother doing the math?"

I winked back at him. "I mastered basic addition a while ago."

Our eyes met and held again as we smiled at one another. Almost unable to help himself, he said, "You're so beautiful."

I waved him off, but he refused to let me deflect the compliment.

"Lauren, you shine from the inside out. You're a diamond. No matter what angle you turn, there's always something new to admire."

I blushed furiously.

Grant leaned in closer. "I don't think I knew quite what it was the first few times I met you, but I know exactly what it is now."

"It's Jesus," I said quietly. "You see His light in me."

He shook his head. "No, Jesus is what I *feel* when I'm around you. Peaceful. It's the same feeling I have when I'm at the Margolins' Bible study. I don't feel that anywhere else unless I'm trying to pray, awkward as that is."

I didn't know what to do with the most heartfelt compliment I'd ever received in my life. Sharing about Jesus in the KidKare parking lot felt like a job well done. Having Grant tell me he felt God's presence just being around me filled me with awe. I remained silent, trying to process the idea that my dumpster fire divorce had been the catalyst to bring Grant closer to God.

Seemingly attuned to me once again, Grant offered a sideways smirk. "It's okay, Lauren. You can just say 'thank you.'"

I grinned back at him. "Thank you."

"Anything to put a smile on your face is a win as far as I'm concerned."

My heart puffed up two sizes larger in my chest. Desperately, I wanted to believe this was the answer to my prayers and years of languishing in marriage to Nathan. At the same time, common sense dictated I slow down the romance novel my brain wanted to write and remember that I wasn't legally free.

Calming my racing thoughts, I said, "I'm glad to hear you're praying."

"Yeah, I mean, it's still kind of weird, but I don't feel like I'm talking to the ceiling."

"Oh, you aren't!" I exclaimed, reaching my hand to cover his. "Trust me, God is real. I could never have survived what I have without Jesus. I feel His peace when I pray. I hear Him speaking to me through the Bible when I read it, and sometimes, it's just a gut feeling or a thought in my head."

He glanced at our joined hands and then turned his hand over so his palm faced mine. "I want that for me too."

I looked down at our physical connection then back into his chocolate brown eyes. "You want what exactly?"

"All of it," he said, his voice raw.

Poppy cleared her throat from the doorway. "I guess I should have taken longer to powder my nose."

I tried to slip my hand out from Grant's, but he held on an extra second before giving it a gentle squeeze.

"With a *knife*," Poppy said, smirking at me and Grant. "Might need a machete at this point."

I chuckled while Grant glanced between the two of us. "Inside joke?" he asked.

"Don't even mention the copier!" I warned, holding back a laugh.

"Like the two of you would even make it that far," she muttered. Poppy turned her head to hide the grin rapidly forming on her face. "You'll be lucky if you even get out of the office first."

Grant looked bemused. "Do I want to know?"

"I'll tell you later," I said, smiling wide. "Maybe it'll go in the memoirs."

This caught the attention of both Grant and Poppy. Grant

seemed confused while Poppy wore total shock as her eyes darted toward me.

"Seriously?" she asked, "Do you really think so?"

I took a furtive look at Grant and inhaled a deep breath. "Yeah, Poppy. I'm pretty sure."

I heard the approaching sound of squeaky loafers and jangling keys, and Poppy jumped from her position near the doorway. "So, um, I need to go ask the mighty Margolin something."

With all the subtlety of an overturned tractor trailer, Grant and I both heard her say, "Just give them a few minutes. I want to know what happens in real time before I have to wait a hundred years to read about it in her book!"

Grant shook with silent laughter still perched on the corner of my desk. "At least she's on my side," he murmured.

I leaned back against my chair and slapped my palm to my forehead. "Work will never be the same now."

"I hope not," he replied with a note of teasing.

I opened my eyes and saw light and laughter in his brown gaze. The gaping difference between Grant and Aaron, let alone Grant and Nathan stole my breath away. With Aaron, the stormy seas held anxiety and longing. The black void of Nathan Fein's eyes showed only contempt or seething rage.

"Thank you for everything," I said, knowing I would have to get back to work rather than continuing to study and stare at Grant. "For providing me and my son a night out and for being a real friend."

"It was my absolute pleasure. I'm even more happy you ordered what you really wanted. Baklava cheesecake sounds incredible."

"Oh, it was! I finished it this morning for breakfast."

Grant chuckled. "You didn't save me any?"

"I guess you'll have to just order your own."

He hesitated, and I might have guessed the unasked question sitting on his full lips. Tearing my eyes away, I didn't want to send an inadvertent invitation.

From the doorway, I heard Poppy clear her throat. "Okay, guys, I've been told the two of you need to wrap this up."

Grant winked at me as he began his retreat from the office. "Do you have plans for lunch?"

"I have some leftovers in the fridge," I replied. "A friend treated me to dinner last night, and I've been eating very well the past twelve hours."

"Glad to hear you've got such good friends. Do you think I could join you and your leftovers this afternoon?"

"I don't know about that," I said with a playful, pensive pose. "Are you sure I won't be a third wheel to you and the leftovers? I think you guys might really hit it off."

Grant chuckled. "You do have some stiff competition there, Lauren."

Poppy jumped into the fray, rolling her eyes as she brushed past Grant to sit at her desk. "Oh my gosh, you guys. Get a room that isn't *this* one and make it official already. I totally ship it, but I want to keep my job."

Grant and I both laughed, and he winked at me over his shoulder before exiting.

"Well?" Poppy asked, swiveling in her chair to face me.

"Just friends."

"Whatever. I know what a man in love looks like, and honey, that man is in L-O-V-E."

"If you say so."

"Girl, I *know* so. Everything will happen in due time, but I am so happy for you, Lauren. You absolutely deserve this."

"Trust me, I want it to be more too, but I can't get fooled

again. Yes, I'm loving every second of the banter and the swoony looks, but that's all the fun stuff."

Her expression sobered. "I get it. And I'm proud of you for being cautious. Just because you guys are into each other doesn't mean you have to get married the second you divorce Nathan."

"God forbid! The entire experience has been complete hell. I'm not opposed to being in a relationship one day, but getting married and ever going through this nightmare again is enough to make me reconsider the entire idea."

Poppy's early mischievous expression returned as she leaned in closer. "But it does feel good, doesn't it?"

I couldn't help it, and I giggled. "Oh my gosh, yes!"

She laughed along with me. "Savor every second. Just remember that right now, it's all *what if* and your imagination. It's clear you both are into each other, but take the time to make sure everything else is compatible beyond the combustible chemistry. The most important thing is Jesus, and I know you already know that."

"I do," I said. Lowering my voice, I added, "Grant said he was praying for me yesterday."

Poppy clutched her heart and feigned a swoon. "This is even better than fiction!"

"As long as there's a happy ending. This nightmare with Nathan has been so insane, sometimes it feels like fiction. As far as writing a book goes, I'm still trying to figure out what I want to keep, what I need to change to protect my son, and what needs to be exposed to protect other women and children who are stuck in the same situation I was."

Poppy's smile dimmed. "It's a blessing and a burden to know this kind of truth by experience. It's a gift to be able to write it down, and it takes courage beyond measure to share it with the world."

"You would know," I said, gesturing toward her.

"I do, and so does Rebecca, Taylor, and Carly soon enough. Are you ready to join the *Parkview Chronicles* survivor club?"

"Yeah, I think it's time. People like Nathan need to be exposed and so do their tactics."

"As do their mothers and every other enabler," she added. "Nathan's choices are still his own, but he's had plenty of help along the way to cover up his sins."

"They're also covering up their own, Poppy. It's not just about Bruce and Linda protecting Nathan's reputation. They've built their own illusion at Beth Shalom. Unfortunately, people like my parents still only see what they want to see. They refuse to confront the ugliness, but they'll gladly complain to others. If you call them on it, suddenly, there's a million excuses why they won't leave and it's not *that* bad."

"Any update on that front?"

I shook my head. "Ari said something about it on the drive to the diner last night, but I haven't heard a peep. As far as I know, my parents are still choosing comfort over confrontation."

Poppy expelled a deep breath before speaking. "Do you mind if I give you a page out of my own book?"

"Literally or figuratively?"

She stuck her tongue out at me. "Very funny. I already know you've read my book. Any advice is easier said than done, and honestly, so hard to do once your heart gets involved. I don't have much to tell you regarding your parents, but all copier jokes aside, I do want to share some wisdom courtesy of this well-earned white streak in my hair."

I flexed my fingers. "Whatcha got for me?"

"Do not make any major decisions regarding Grant based off of something Nathan has done. Let things happen the way they're supposed to, and don't let anxiety or fear drive you to force anything on your own."

Surprised by her counsel, my mouth formed an "oh."

Poppy grinned. "You thought I was going to tell you not to create a future with your imagination instead of with Grant, didn't you?"

"Yeah, basically."

"I'm pretty sure we've covered that already. There is no imagining the chemistry between the two of you. Next time, I'll make sure to bring popcorn for my front row seat."

I laughed. "You're so bad!"

"Ha! More like the tension between the two of you is so *good*. Do you think you'll have a Jewish wedding?"

I gasped while she chuckled at my expression.

"Just teasing," she amended. "Maybe."

"How about I get divorced first, work on healing all of this trauma from Nathan, and then we can talk about calling your old friend, Rabbi Peretz, to perform the ceremony some other time?"

"Deal," she said. "But I still have his phone number whenever you're ready."

CHAPTER 35

"Fancy seeing you here," Grant said, joining me in the Culver breakroom. "I thought I'd find you in tornado alley."

"No microwave outside," I quipped, digging into my roasted chicken.

He eyed my lunch. "That looks good. Might have to try it next time I go to the Diner."

"Oh, it is," I mumbled around a mouthful of food. I nudged my chin at his bag of Chick-a-Yum take out. "What did you get?"

"Spicy chicken sandwich, waffle fries, sweet tea. Nothing quite as exciting as yours. How long before one of the Culver beehive members spots us here together."

"All of CID is attending a lunch and learn," I replied with a grin, "and it's offsite. We're safe. Most of Benefits took lunch about an hour ago."

"So we're all alone?" he asked with a wink.

"Alone enough, I guess."

Grant sat in the chair across from me and plopped his lunch on the table. "Any update with the ex situation?"

"My attorney told me he posted bond and his sleazeball lawyer is suddenly asking us to send over a revised settlement proposal. We sent one back in January that they completely ignored."

"Really?" Grant's eyebrows rose high on his forehead. "I thought your ex wanted to drag things out indefinitely."

I shrugged. "I'm guessing he thinks I'll be more lenient than a judge or even what the guardian ad litem would recommend at this point, but who knows? There's always an angle with him. By the time we get a court date for the actual divorce, he'll probably have a conviction for what happened on Sunday, and obviously, any criminal proceedings are going to look terrible for him in family court. Settlement also means that I will never have my say in court or present information Nathan doesn't want to see the light of day."

"Hm," Grant replied, stroking his beard. "If you wind up settling with him, does that mean the TPO goes away so he can have visitation with your son?"

I finished another bite of my lunch. "I wouldn't think so, but considering they already let him out of jail for threatening me plus assault and attempted battery against the police, I have no idea. As far as the settlement, I know he's going to lowball me on support and splitting equity in the house. I'm not sure what he's hoping I'll do other than be desperate enough to agree to anything or too scared to face him in court. Funny enough, his attorney is actually a member of some 'Amicable Divorce Attorney Network,' and that has got to be the biggest joke ever."

"Oh, yeah?"

"The man has no shame. He's even used a bout of Covid to

pretend the lingering effects keep him from sending emails when we request information. However, he's never been too sick to make demands and expect our immediate compliance. Usually, it's pulling teeth to receive any communication from his side, so whatever the angle, it will only be to benefit Nathan."

Grant popped a waffle fry in his mouth. "I guess we'll find out soon enough. What happens in the meantime?"

"It's going to take a minute to update my financial affidavit and go over settlement terms with Sondra, so for now, just enjoy the peace and quiet of the TPO until I can figure out a long term settlement Nathan might actually consider. My attorney thinks they're going to reject it no matter what, but we can also use it in trial to show the judge that we tried to offer something reasonable. The TPO means Nathan has to leave me alone unless he wants to go right back to jail and not get out this time."

Grant paused with his wrapped sandwich still in midair. "The idea of what could happen before the police get there is what has me worried for you and your son. I mean, is this TPO all the punishment that maniac will ever get?"

I shook my head. "Short version is that Nathan will eventually stand trial or likely plea bargain on the assault and harassment charges, but there shouldn't be a custody issue anymore. He knows I won't offer primary or even joint physical custody in the settlement, and Sondra told the guardian what's going on. She's pretty confident he'll back me up on this."

"Your ex was actually fighting for that?! How did he expect to pull it off?"

I shoveled in a bite of rice. "By thinking he could fool the guardian as easily as DCFS bought his stories of being a changed man and claiming I had some vendetta against him.

His slimy behavior is obvious to *me*, but the courts and a lot of these GALs get fooled by a father acting like he wants to spend time with his kids—compared to so many who want nothing to do with them."

Grant muttered an expletive regarding his opinion of Nathan Fein. "Isn't family services supposed to actually protect children and family?"

"When Sondra talked to the GAL about the TPO, he mentioned that he'd gone over the DCFS case from two years ago. It looks like Nathan had his divorce attorney put pressure on them to close the investigation and paint me as melodramatic and manipulative. At the same time, the caseworker pushed me like crazy to move out and implied they'd go after *me* for child endangerment if they received another phone call about abuse toward Ari. I was so scared of Nathan and then even more scared the state would put him in foster care. I truly believe the only reason they substantiated the abuse had nothing to do with the bruises I'd photographed but because they have Ari on tape during his forensic interview disclosing that daddy hurt him."

"I don't get it, Lauren. Why were they threatening you instead of kicking your ex out of the house?"

"Their goal was closing the case as quickly as possible. Nathan had refused to give up the house, so the next best option was scaring me into moving out. It 'eliminated' the threat of danger on their end because we weren't under the same roof, and it also got Nathan's attorney off their back."

"So, they worked on behalf of your ex-husband that they were supposedly investigating? What the heck?!"

I exhaled a sigh of disgust and resignation. "Threatening me was more cost effective than properly punishing Nathan. They could also save themselves money while pretending they were doing their jobs. Us moving out meant that Ari was now in a safe environment. They just don't bother to include the underhanded way they got it done, and they can paint me in whatever light they want for their records. I'm not allowed to see them. Like I said, the only reason why I know about any of this is because the GAL requested them and then shared details with my attorney."

"How is that even possible? This sounds like a nightmare conspiracy movie."

"Like Nathan, DCFS has lots of power to threaten and scare people and almost zero accountability. If we had kept living together, they would have had to get family therapists involved, move our case into their long term family preservation division, schedule a new caseworker to come out for check-ins, and things like that. All of that costs money for referrals and then having man hours used on us."

"So, they took advantage of an abused mother already experiencing trauma in order to save themselves money—and all under the pretext of *protecting* you. That's despicable!"

"I don't know how anyone can work for that organization without selling their soul. I've read a few things online about how the lower level people come in with social work degrees and quickly burn out or leave when they see how corrupt the organization truly is."

After finishing his last bite and balling up the chicken sandwich wrapper, Grant tossed it into his paper bag with gusto. "Do you think this guardian will do better by you and your son? Can't he see that it's your ex with the issues, especially now with the TPO and pending charges for assault?"

"I certainly hope so. At least now I don't think we'll have to get a psychological evaluation. The GAL had suggested possibly ordering one just to put Nathan's accusations to rest, but the cost is exorbitant."

"How much?"

"Anywhere from $1,500 to $5,000 and more."

Grant whistled. "And this is on top of all these other legal bills you're already paying, right? Does your ex think you're made of money or something?"

I laughed bleakly. "Of course not! He knows that Ari and I are barely making it with the financial assistance we have, and I think that's the goal. He's cut off any access I have to marital funds, and if he bankrupts me, then I have no financial means to fight him in court. I'd either have to give away my rights to get him to agree to a settlement, or I'd represent myself in court and get blindsided by his attorney. He's not stupid, despite how often he plays clueless."

"I'm glad you have a good attorney, then."

I smiled. "Me too. I can't thank Miss Belle enough for that."

"Miss Belle?"

"That's a story for another time. Are we really going to talk about all of this divorce stuff the entire time we're having lunch?"

Grant's mouth lifted into a half smile. "Well, it is the major headline in your life right now. We can talk about something else if you want to, but I want you to know you're not alone in dealing with it."

"I really appreciate that, thank you." I reached across the table to touch his hand. "It's nice having a friend who can handle hearing the nitty gritty details. It's all so heavy."

"Happy to help share the load," he replied, holding my gaze. "You deserve so much more out of life than what you've been given." His eyes welled up with tears on my behalf, and it stole my breath away.

"Well, what do we have here?" Miss Belle crowed from the open doorway. "I came to make my afternoon tea, and I found a whole love story unfolding in the office."

The sound of squeaky loafers and jangling keys followed just behind her along with Ted Margolin's baritone voice. "And here I thought you hated the idea of office gossip being spread. Weren't you supposed to be setting up the Lunch & Learn leftovers in the kitchen?"

Miss Belle let out a tiny shriek and turned to fuss at the mighty Margolin for startling her. Grant took the opportunity to stand up from the table and throw his trash away. He offered to take my styrofoam container, but I politely declined. The turn of conversation had zapped most of my appetite, and half of my leftovers remained in the box.

"You just hate that I'm right," Ted said, his voice carrying over Miss Belle's squawking from the adjoining kitchen area.

"The jig is up," Grant mouthed to me with a playful grin.

I snickered and closed the lid to my container.

He took another furtive glance toward the doorway before standing close enough to me so he could whisper and be heard. "Thank you for everything you shared and for trusting me with it."

I wanted to brush off his comment, but calling it "no big deal" would have been an insult to the amount of faith I had in Grant Kaplan to trust him. Calling it "no big deal" ignored my own progress in trusting *any* man while still healing from the trauma Nathan had inflicted. And it certainly felt like more than "no big deal" when I considered how long I'd known Aaron Davis, but somehow Grant Kaplan seemed to see and understand me down to my soul.

All those thoughts passed through my mind as Grant studied me with a glow in his eyes and a soft smile on his lips.

Ted cleared his throat and entered the lounge area. He crossed his arms over his chest. "I got the Mama Hen out of the kitchen, but if the two of you are looking to keep this under wraps, I'd definitely take it out of the break room."

Grant chuckled as he turned his attention to our Bible study leader. "And here I was waiting for some kind of fatherly lecture."

Ted's eyes glittered in humor. "Oh, that talk's still coming, young man. I don't think Lauren is in any danger with you, but I've dealt with office gossip long enough to know that her reputation may be in trouble with whatever you have going on. Miss Belle won't share your secret, but she also isn't as discreet as she thinks she is when she's digging for information."

"Thank you, Ted," I said, standing up from the table and putting some distance between me and Grant. "I think the *Parkview Chronicles* have all documented Miss Belle's love for office romance and pretending she *doesn't* enjoy every second of it."

He barked out a laugh. "Oh, my wife can tell you all about that. She's already asked Rebecca if we're planning on having any more children."

I gasped as Grant's jaw dropped.

"How are you doing today?" Ted addressed me directly. "Any news on your psycho ex?"

"Nathan posted bond. He's out for now until he stands trial, but in the meantime, Ari and I are safe. He won't risk going back to jail, no matter how mad he is at me."

"Are you sure about that?" Grant jumped in.

Ted shook his head and ran a hand through hair sporting new shades of silver and white highlighted at his temples. "I'm having flashbacks to Rebecca dealing with her father and that old pervert, Pastor Sociopath."

"Because of the TPO?" I asked.

He shook his head with a rueful grin. "No, it's the expression on Kaplan's face. It's probably what I looked like when Rebecca said she could still stay at her old apartment after we caught her pastor lurking outside."

I glanced at Grant, wondering if he was familiar with this part of Ted and Rebecca's love story. Not faltering under the mighty Margolin's scrutiny, his brown eyes met mine and confirmed every word he'd already spoken regarding his feelings toward me.

Blushing, I said, "Well, there aren't any shotgun weddings in my future since I'm still not divorced yet, but I appreciate the sentiment, Ted."

The two men exchanged glances, and I wondered what exactly Mr. Kaplan had already confided in Culver's top, east coast producer.

Ted pressed down a knowing smile. "Okay, kids, back to work."

CHAPTER 36

It took me and Sondra about two weeks to finalize my updated DRFA, or Domestic Relations Financial Affidavit, and then sit and crunch numbers regarding how much money I would need to supplement my income from Culver. Fair or not, my overall financial needs didn't factor into the state guidelines for child support. The dollar amount would be calculated based on Nathan's income compared to mine. The only potential area for negotiation would be alimony—assuming we could agree on any sum for that.

Since Nathan earned triple my salary, I would be expected to contribute twenty-five percent of the total cost for medical and childcare bills. Money would continue to be tight even if Nathan agreed to the dollar amount we requested, but receiving my share of the equity in the house would at least help me and Ari purchase a small home of our own. Because of the gross discrepancy in what he and I had spent on our respective attorney's fees, I was certainly within my rights to ask for compensation, but it seemed unlikely Nathan would give anything voluntarily. I consoled myself that at least I would have the right of education enrollment for Ari given Nathan's limited visitation time. It was one less area he could use to control both of our lives.

As expected, we received no response to our settlement proposal. Instead, Nathan's attorney began calling the GAL and demanding the previous visitation plan be reinstated in addition to extending his time to a full weekend. I only discovered what had been done because I received a new bill from Carson Gentry. His $5,000 retainer had been depleted from his investigation into the DCFS case and time spent talking to both of our attorneys. Carson's invoice showed line items for multiple phone calls after Nathan's arrest, and I asked Sondra to follow up and get more specifics. Due to our contract with the GAL, I was responsible for fifty percent of every minute Carson spent on our case—even if it was Nathan or his attorney wasting his time.

To make matters worse, Carson didn't see the harassment situation as black and white as I assumed he would. He suggested we proceed with our scheduled mediation and try to work out visitation ourselves. He promised to give us a final recommendation once Nathan and I at least attempted to resolve the custody situation on our own. His rationale was that the two of us would have to learn to work out our differences after the divorce, but he would be at mediation to push us into some kind of a compromise. For whatever reason, Nathan's arrest didn't seem to deter the GAL from believing that he should still have unsupervised access to our son.

Sondra assured me that we still had other options, and given my precarious financial situation, she filed for an emergency hearing for temporary child support. Without legitimate support payments or a separate hearing for attorney's fees, I was not in a position to pay for Sondra's mediation costs plus splitting the hourly rate for both the mediator and the GAL. She warned me the judge would likely yell at us, but given the circumstances, she hoped he would come to see our side.

What she failed to mention was that we would spend half the day waiting for our case to be called along with everyone else scheduled to appear before the judge that day. Sondra told me to arrive at court when it opened at nine, and I assumed that meant we had a set time for our hearing. Instead, we sat and listened to several civil cases, including another divorce and two financial disputes.

When our case was finally called, Judge Sheridan did yell at both of us. He thundered about how he'd never had a case for *temporary* support come before him without mediation and how we were wasting the court's time and our own money on attorneys. I finally laid eyes on Nathan's lawyer, Trevor Wormwood, and he looked as slimy as his name suggested. He sauntered to the podium and gave his opening argument, echoing Judge Sheridan's sentiments and painting me as a greedy attention-seeker. Even though I knew his story was a complete projection, he still made a persuasive case. Panic welled up at the thought of Judge Sheridan believing the lies because so many others already had.

Sondra called me to the witness stand, and I was honest and concise in my answers. She asked me about my current financial situation, my job, and why Ari and I had moved out. She treaded carefully regarding the abuse, keeping things general rather than trying to trigger me into an emotional response. We had discussed earlier how too much emotion would be viewed as theatrical, and we were only in court to discuss the income disparity, not custody.

On cross examination, Trevor Wormwood persisted with Nathan's victim narrative. He demanded to know why I left the house when it was clear my husband loved me and wanted to reconcile. "Isn't it true that this entire proceeding is really just about how much money you can squeeze out of Mr. Fein?"

Calmly, I replied, "I don't believe *love* means putting bruises on your spouse and verbally abusing them in front of your child."

"Mrs. Fein," Trevor cut in, looking down the bridge of his hooked nose at me, "we're here to discuss why you're after Mr. Fein's money, not ancient allegations of past behavior. You need to answer the question."

Staring down the mocking gleam in his eyes, I continued as if he hadn't interrupted me. "I also don't believe *love* is degrading and humiliating your spouse by watching pornography online and then asking them to copy sex acts perpetrated against minors...of both genders."

A collective gasp went up in the courtroom, but I knew this was the time to finally share the entire truth of what I had endured. "*Love* is not insisting your spouse lie there and remain silent while you violate them for years. It certainly isn't texting your best friend, Rick Williams, and telling him that sex with your spouse feels like making love to a frigid little boy. None of those screenshots could be described as *loving*, Mr. Wormwood."

Nathan's attorney no longer wore his slimy, arrogant facade. He glanced back at Nathan who had gone deathly white. Clearly, his client had omitted how his struggles with teenage pornography lasted well beyond the police raid three years earlier.

My current laptop had been a hand-me-down gift when Nathan upgraded his own computer. Just after our initial meeting with Carson Gentry, I was clearing out files for additional memory space and stumbled upon a cache of dark web photos and videos. Sickened beyond the images themselves, I realized Nathan had explicitly detailed the acts he'd seen. He'd pressured me repeatedly into performing them. Staring at the source of Nathan's deviance felt like seeing his demon unmasked.

Without the physical evidence, I might never have believed the deeper secret Nathan was hiding. Most of his illicit collection included homosexual, transgender, and queer teens. Bitterly, I recalled how many years I'd spent feeling inadequate and unattractive to my husband. All of his shaming comments about my "boyish" figure were nothing more than a smokescreen and an accidental confession of his private desires.

Sondra and I had only planned to bring up the teenage pornography issue if Carson Gentry recommended Nathan for primary legal and physical custody of Ari. Instead, I finally released the misplaced burden of hiding the depth of his depravity. To admit what Nathan had done also meant revealing I had been abused that way. However, I was never a willing participant, and the weight of Nathan's shame belonged on his shoulders, not mine.

From behind the plaintiff's table, Sondra gave me a nod to keep going.

"I don't believe *love* is threatening to destroy your spouse because they no longer want to be abused or risk further injury to your child. So, no, I do not believe in the kind of 'love' Mr. Fein claims he has for me. That's why I took my son and left our home, Mr. Wormwood."

A pin drop could be heard in the courtroom, and Judge

Sheridan turned his attention to Nathan's attorney. "Do you have anything further?"

"No more questions," he muttered. His sullen demeanor matched Nathan's as they exchanged heated whispers. I was dismissed from the witness stand and walked back to the plaintiff's table.

Sondra then called Nathan to the stand, and I found it strange and rewarding that he would have to face a cross examination before his attorney had a chance to commence damage control.

Questioning began with asking Nathan about our marital finances. Specifically, Sondra asked him to confirm when he'd cut me off from our joint bank account and redirected his paychecks without warning. Nathan denied doing it. Sondra tried a different tack and asked him if he had ever opened his own bank account in the past three years. Nathan claimed he couldn't recall when he'd done that.

"Isn't it true that you stopped your direct deposits into the joint checking account in November of 2020 after Mrs. Fein vacated the marital residence and moved in with her parents?"

"I, uh, don't remember."

"So, you don't recall when you started making payments into a new checking account that Mrs. Fein had no access to?"

"No, I don't remember that happening."

"Mr. Fein, how did you expect Mrs. Fein to pay for things like groceries and clothing for your son?"

"I don't know."

"And were you providing any financial support to Mrs. Fein knowing that she no longer had access to the joint marital funds?"

"She got plenty from me," he clipped. "Obviously, that's not enough for Lauren, or we wouldn't be here today."

"What would you describe as 'plenty,' Mr. Fein? $100 a month? $200? Would you say that you've given Mrs. Fein $2,000 over the past two years?"

"Easily," he said, glaring at me. "If it was up to her, it would be even more."

"So, is it your testimony, Mr. Fein, that $2,000 over the course of two years for the support of your son is an adequate amount?"

I snuck a glance at Trevor Wormwood who did not look pleased.

"Perfectly adequate," Nathan said primly.

"And how much money do you earn in a month, Mr. Fein?"

Nathan pursed his lips and didn't respond.

Judge Sheridan chimed in. "Mr. Fein, you need to answer the question."

"I, uh, don't recall," he finally said.

"You don't know your salary?" Sondra asked incredulously. "We have a copy of your pay stub if you need help jogging your memory."

"I make $130,000 a year, okay? I don't know what that breaks down to a month."

"It's over $10,000 a month gross income," she responded, "and based on your own testimony, you believe that giving Mrs. Fein $200 of that $10,000 is more than adequate. Is that correct?"

"I don't know," he said again lamely.

"Is there a reason why you believe your son only requires two percent of your monthly gross income now that you and your wife are separated, but you donate roughly $1,800 a month to your synagogue? Why do you believe your congregation deserves eighteen percent of your effort, but the family you claim to love only deserves two percent?"

"Objection!" Trevor stood up. "Inflammatory."

"I'll allow it," Judge Sheridan replied. "I'm very curious to hear this answer."

"Well?" Sondra prodded. "Can you explain why you give to the synagogue in one month what has cumulatively taken you *two years* to provide your wife and son in support?"

Nathan squirmed in his seat. "I don't know."

"Mr. Fein, when weighing the decision of why you feel your wife, the primary caretaker of your son, is only entitled to $200 a month in child support, you're going to have to provide a better response than 'I don't know' to justify that decision. You do earn three times her salary."

Recovering, he puffed out his chest. "Ten percent of my income belongs to God. If you'd ever picked up a Bible, you would know that." He gave Sondra a derisive once over. "Scripture is very clear about tithing. I simply choose to go above and beyond. Unlike certain people, I'm honoring God with my money instead of trying to steal it from others with bogus court proceedings."

She raised her eyebrows and exhaled a laugh that sounded equal parts astonishment and disgust. "Is this the same Bible you're reading when you're viewing underage pornography?"

Before Trevor could get the next objection out of his mouth, Nathan bellowed, "That's a lie! The police dropped all charges against me. I didn't know they were underage, and I was only looking at *females,* no matter what crazy stories Lauren invented to make me look bad. She's the one with the psychological issues, not me!"

"Could you show me a Bible verse where the materials you downloaded onto the laptop you gave Mrs. Fein two years ago would be acceptable? Or do you only apply Biblical standards to your bank account and not your bedroom?"

Nathan's eyes widened at Sondra's revelation, then narrowed into a hateful glare I felt across the room. Grinding his teeth, he mumbled, "I don't know."

"I'll be more than happy to cite some Bible passages since you don't seem to be as familiar with those. Would that help you better answer my question?"

Ignoring his attorney's strenuous objections once again, Nathan talked over Trevor and rambled about his "ongoing issue." Sondra let him carry on as he spewed one self pitying comment after another. I recognized many of them from lies he'd told in marriage counseling to justify his addiction. With no sympathy to be found in the courtroom, Nathan's mood shifted to self righteous anger, resentfully stating how no one would let him forget his past. I glanced at Judge Sheridan, but I saw no emotion on his face.

Sondra ended her questioning, and Trevor swooped in, doing his best to save face. He tried to guide Nathan with softball questions, but even that required coaching. Nathan kept responding to Trevor's financial questions as if he was being grilled about the homosexual pornography instead. Frustrated, his attorney ended his line of questioning after Nathan made a jab about my "boyish" figure and suggested I would use the extra child support for plastic surgery.

The attorneys went up to make their closing remarks, and Sondra did a valiant job describing my situation as essentially being in a debtor's prison and never able to do better for me and my son. She highlighted the income disparity, my new job, and that there was no way to afford our apartment or childcare once the financial assistance from the state expired. She also pointed out that it wasn't the state's job to support me and my son—it was Nathan's. Ignoring the pink elephant in the room, she pointed out how Nathan clearly had the disposable income to donate his salary where he wanted, but he somehow felt a multi-million dollar charity took precedence over the wife and child he claimed to love.

When she finished, Trevor made his own closing remarks, doubling down on the narrative of me as a punitive, manipulative woman taking advantage of a troubled man. As long as the listener completely ignored Nathan's direct testimony, everything Trevor said sounded plausible. I silently prayed that our judge possessed more discernment than Rabbi Lebow.

"We've got a real problem here," Judge Sheridan began, "because clearly, we've lost the forest from the trees. The two of you have spent an obscene amount of money on this divorce, and you've clearly gotten nowhere, or you wouldn't be in my courtroom right now."

My leg shook under the table, fighting back panic at the old trigger of being blamed for Nathan's behavior.

"I know we're only here to discuss temporary child support, but if it were up to me, I would end this right now for the sake of your son. We have mediation to take a scalpel to things and divide them up, but if I could, I would take a sledgehammer to all of it."

I gulped, not sure what he meant.

"Mr. Fein, you make $130,000 a year. Your wife earns $42,000. We have a huge income disparity. None of that is up for debate. We use the law, not the Bible, to determine what each party is entitled to. Your religious sensibilities do not factor into my decision."

I held my breath, scared to believe something might finally go my way.

"I am awarding support to Mrs. Fein in the amount of $900 per month, and Mr. Fein will cover all expenses for the minor child, including childcare and medical coverage. Since Mrs. Fein has already vacated the marital residence, Mr. Fein will begin payment immediately and once a month thereafter. As I said, I can't rule on anything else, but I trust that both sides will attempt to mediate and settle the rest of this so I don't see you back in my court." Then, he pounded his gavel and dismissed us from the room.

CHAPTER 37

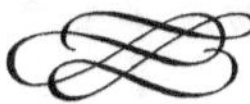

I sent out a general text to the Bible study group, followed by a more detailed version of events to Grant. His response was immediate.

Are you ok? How do you feel?

It's just all so surreal. I never told anyone other than my attorney about the kind of filth I found on that laptop. When I was on the witness stand, the words just came out.

Are you scared or triggered? Any flashbacks?

Strangely, no. It was more like this huge weight coming off of me. I'm still in shock Judge Sheridan granted me so much money. Beyond the $900 a month, having Nathan cover Ari's daycare is another $800, not including well checkups and anything else that comes up with the doctors.

There was a pause on Grant's end before he replied. *So, what happens now? Do you know when everything will finally be over?*

This would actually be easier to explain over the phone. Can you call me?

My phone rang a second later.

"Hi," I said, smiling.

"Hi," he replied. "It's good to hear your voice."

"Same."

There was a pause filled with uncommunicated emotions. Grant cleared his throat. "So, what next?"

"Sondra said we have to go to mediation since the judge yelled at us about it, but the support payments will help me cover all the lawyers. Today's hearing cost a lot of money for Sondra, so I'm not out of the woods financially, but I should be able to manage now."

"So, are you thinking maybe three more months?"

I shook my head even though I knew Grant couldn't see me. "Unfortunately, it may take that long just to get mediation scheduled. I highly doubt Nathan will settle, even though Sondra keeps telling me eighty percent of divorces end that way. She filed to make the TPO against Nathan a permanent one, and so we're waiting to find out if I have to go back to seeing him twice a month at the police station for drop off. The one good thing the GAL said was that he wasn't going to push for visitation until the court comes back with a decision on the TPO."

"What happens if mediation is a bust?"

"Sondra said we have to appear before the judge two more times."

"What?! Why?"

"In order to get a full trial, we have to submit a comprehensive summary from both sides of what we're looking to accomplish by going to court, witnesses to call, and things like that. The judge won't schedule a full trial on his calendar until he knows the scope of what he's dealing with. Since Nathan's done nothing but delay the divorce and Sondra said they're not likely to provide that information willingly, we'll need a preliminary hearing to get an Order of Schedule from Judge Sheridan. Once he signs it, it forces their side to cooperate and submit the proper paperwork based on a court ordered timeline. The added bonus is that Sondra said we can combine that hearing with a request for interim attorney's fees and ask Nathan to cover my cost for the trial."

"Can you really do that? Doesn't each side just pay their share?"

"Not exactly. Technically, we should both be able to use the 'marital assets' to pay for our lawyers. Nathan cut me off from any joint funds when he opened his new checking account and transferred everything from our savings. He's also spent almost $60,000 on his attorney."

Grant whistled. "That's insane!"

"Exactly. Even with Marianne Abbey wiping me out and Sondra's retainer and monthly fees, I still haven't spent anything close to that. The law says I'm entitled to spend just as much for my legal counsel as Nathan is, so we're going to ask for at least some of that difference. His testimony on the stand actually helped my case for that."

"Okay, so hopefully you get money for a trial, and then what? You just set a court date after you have that submission hearing?"

I sighed. "Again, not quite so simple. The judge will sign off on the scheduling order, and both sides have thirty days to get our stuff together. Then, Sondra has another thirty days to go over all the information and submit it to Judge Sheridan. Once he's got the paperwork, we wait for his clerk to tell us the next available opening he has for a full trial. Whatever we can't agree to in mediation will get decided by the judge."

Grant exhaled his own heavy breath. "That is so much. Maybe your ex will settle so he can stop hemorrhaging money to his attorney. Do you have to agree on everything at mediation in order to be done with the divorce?"

"To settle and be done, yes, we'd have to both agree. As far as mediation goes, if we can agree on *anything*, it's one less thing we have to go over in trial. I already have my car, and Nathan has his. When I moved out, I got the personal belongings I wanted, but I wasn't able to take any furniture. I wouldn't mind getting some of those from the old house or even getting some cash for the difference, but it's not make or break for me. I know Nathan won't agree to me having primary custody, any real child support, or an equitable division of the bank accounts or the house, so going to trial feels inevitable."

"After what happened today in court, do you really think he'd risk going back in front of the judge again?"

"Honestly, yes. Nathan will never let go of his need to punish me for actually going through with the divorce. He truly believes I don't deserve any money, but he's also testing to see what he can get away with."

"I can't wait for you to be free from him, Lauren. I hate that he ever made you think you deserve the way he's treated you."

I smiled at Grant's sincerity. "Seeing him on the stand today was actually therapeutic for me. At one point, he was blubbering and feeling sorry for himself. It was the same performance he always gave when he pretended to see the error of his way and wanted to change. The way he just dials up the tears and the emotions is pathological. He can flip that switch on and off in an instant. The hard part is facing how and why I ever agreed to marry him or stay married as long as I did."

"If you don't mind me asking, why did you marry him?"

I paused, wondering if I even knew the answer to that question. "I guess because I was expected to and thought I loved him. I also wanted a family, and I couldn't exactly do that being single. Dating in Messianic Judaism is extremely limited because their theology is so specific. I didn't have a lot of options, and it never occurred to me that Nathan could be anything other than what he pretended to be. He's publicly praised from the pulpit, raises his hands during worship, and volunteers like crazy. On paper, he was the ideal believer. I just assumed the weird things I noticed would resolve themselves after we got married."

"So, you settled and hoped for the best?"

"Yeah," I admitted. "At the time, I believed that God was leading me to marry Nathan, but I don't know anymore. I mean, I wouldn't have my son without him, and I know that God has a purpose for Ari. That boy is pretty incredible."

"He is," Grant said, and I could hear the smile in his voice. "It was nice to meet him this past Sunday at Bible study."

I grinned. "He really liked you too, by the way. He says you're funny."

Grant chuckled. "Yeah, I like to think I am sometimes."

"Thank you," I said, my voice turning serious.

"For what?"

"For just being there. For listening. For not judging me or trying to fix everything."

"I told you I wasn't going anywhere, Lauren."

"I know, but it's been three months since we had lunch in the breakroom, and I didn't know if you would get tired of waiting. You have to give your work requests to Poppy because Miss Belle didn't realize she had an audience when she cornered you in the hallway."

"She's still apologizing for that, you know."

I pressed my lips together. "I know. It just makes it harder working in the same office but not being able to talk to you."

"Do you miss me that much?" His voice turned soft, surprised and delighted. I could already envision the warmth in his eyes. I saw it every time he looked at me.

Blushing, I said, "Well, we text every night, you call me on the weekends when Ari is in bed, so yeah, it's hard not to want to talk to someone face to face who has become an important part of my life."

"Can I tell you that I'm actually grinning from ear to ear right now?"

I laughed. "You're sweet."

"No, *you* are," he teased, "and I love every minute that I get to spend with you—even if it's just through a phone. Bible study isn't exactly the place to talk either, not with people watching our every move."

"Also true. Oh, speaking of Bible study, I've got some important news to share."

"What's up?"

"Aaron proposed to Ruthie last weekend."

"He what?" Grant gasped. "When did you find out?"

"He texted me a couple of days ago. After you and I had our come to Jesus in the bathroom, he and Ruthie had one later that night. She called him out on his crush, and he confessed everything."

"And she still said yes?"

"Actually, she told him she would have to think about it."

"Wow, good for her."

"Yeah, probably the wake up call Aaron needed that he couldn't string her along and assume she'd just put up with him being so wishy-washy. I know he cares about Ruthie, but she told him she's not going to spend the rest of her life wondering if he settled for her."

"Smart girl," Grant murmured. "I knew I liked her when I met her, but that's definitely given me a new level of respect."

"Considering what 'settling' has cost me, I'm envious of how much more wisdom she has at twenty-three than I ever did."

"Don't beat yourself up, Lauren. You were young, inexperienced, and the snake had a convincing sob story. There was no way you could have known what he was like."

"True. If you had told me the kind of trash I'd find on his laptop, I never would have believed Nathan Fein got turned on by that."

Grant paused and then asked, "Are you coming back into the office today?"

"I don't think so. I have to pick up Ari in three hours, so it's kind of a waste."

"I'm working remotely, and I don't think I'm that far from where you are at the courthouse. Do you think we could meet up and actually have that face to face time?"

"Anywhere but Charred Cups," I said immediately. "I haven't set foot back in that place since I moved out of the house."

"Got it. Are you hungry? What about Sylvia's or Apple Thursdays? Is that on your way to the daycare?"

"Oh, I haven't been to an Apple Thursdays in forever! I used to order their Spinach Patch Pizza before they doubled the price."

"Yum! I remember those! Maybe they still have it on the menu. So, I'll see you in about thirty minutes?"

"See you there."

I arrived at Apple Thursdays and saw Grant standing by the front door and scanning the parking lot for me.

I approached and pushed a tendril behind my ear. "Hi."

His smile lit up his entire face, and he pulled me into a hug before I could overthink and refuse the gesture. I looped my arms around his waist and savored the embrace before taking a step back. His physical warmth combined with our growing emotional connection made it too easy to forget the mountains left to climb.

That wayward strand of hair fell into my eye again, and Grant tucked it behind my ear. When his gaze dipped toward my mouth, I gently moved away from his touch.

"We can't," I said quietly. "Trust me, it's not because I don't want to."

His adam's apple bobbed in his throat. "So, I'm not just imagining what's happening because I want it so badly?"

Tears stung my eyes, knowing he meant every word. "You're not alone in this, I promise. I just know that if I don't stop, I won't stop."

His chocolate brown eyes widened. "Seriously?"

I exhaled a self-deprecating chuckle. "I've got relationship trauma, but I'm still human."

He returned my laugh with one of his own. "I guess that gives me something to look forward to."

"It gives both of us something to look forward to. I've definitely thought about it more than once."

His eyes searched mine, and I allowed him a brief glimpse into the desire I normally kept hidden.

"Wow," he murmured. "You really are the most beautiful woman I have ever met."

I beamed back at him, lost in the moment, lost in his eyes, and seriously contemplating throwing caution to the wind and receiving the kiss I'd only been able to fantasize about.

From just beyond us, I heard someone call my name. I didn't immediately register the owner until I saw my mother barreling toward us.

"Who the heck is this?" she demanded, pointing at Grant. "And why aren't you at work? You have a lot of explaining to do, young lady."

CHAPTER 38

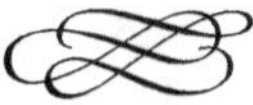

As if repeating our altercation with Rabbi Lebow, Grant wasted no time shielding me from my latest assailant.

"Listen, I don't know who you are—" he began.

"I'm her *mother*," she spat, glaring at him. "And is it true, Lauren? There are rumors flying around the synagogue that you've been cheating on Nathan this whole time."

I pressed a hand to Grant's back to keep him from attacking my mother. Coldly, I addressed her myself. "I would think you know me better than that."

"Apparently, I don't know my daughter at all. I certainly never thought I'd run into you in public cozying up to some man who isn't your husband."

"*Ex*-husband," I corrected, "and you know exactly why you haven't heard from me. Thank you for confirming why I needed a break. How could you believe a word of gossip from that place, especially about your own daughter? Haven't you learned that Beth Shalom will always do what's best for Beth Shalom?

Demonizing me is the easiest way to cover up Nathan's abuse and addiction. Trust me, they'd chew you up and spit you out just as easily."

"You still haven't answered my question, young lady."

"Lauren is a grown woman," Grant rumbled from next to me. "I'm assuming you want to be treated with respect. Your daughter deserves no less."

My mother's jaw dropped, not used to being put in her place. Nathan had never interfered during tiffs with my mother, leaving me to fend for myself. Early on, I confronted his lack of support, but he always took her side and played dumb about why I was upset. Mentally torturing me was all fun and games until I began calling Charlotte or Aaron for comfort instead. Then, it was rageful tantrums about how I didn't trust my own husband. With Nathan, all that mattered was having some way to spin me in circles for his own sick amusement.

"Grant is a friend from work," I finally said. "I just got back from court, and he agreed to meet me for moral support."

"Court?" she asked, fluttering her eyes in surprise. "You didn't tell me you were going to court. Are you officially divorced now?"

"No, we're still a ways from that, but it was a great beginning. I won't need any more money from you and Dad because the judge ordered Nathan to pay real child support. Besides, aren't you supposed to be at work right now? What are you doing here?"

"I took a late lunch," she said, her earlier anger dissipating. "I'm sorry for assuming. I didn't expect to see you, and I'm hurt that you won't talk to me or your father."

At some point, Grant's hand slipped into mine. I didn't notice until I tried to walk toward my mother and realized he and I were connected. I glanced at our joined hands and then to his eyes. He gave me a gentle squeeze before releasing me.

"Just friends?" my mother asked again.

"None of your business," I shot back.

"Lauren, please," she begged, "what is really going on with you? Did you stop talking to us because of *him*?" She shifted her focus to Grant in accusation.

"Nothing's changed, Mom. The reason I explained in your kitchen is the same reason. You and Dad chose Beth Shalom over your daughter, over your grandson, and over any integrity I thought either of you had. What does that say about you when you automatically believe the Beth Shalom rumors about me? You would rather assume the absolute worst instead of acting like you've known me my entire life. And for what? Your pride? The fact I called out your hypocrisy?"

She flattened her lips into a straight line.

"How could you be anything but proud of your daughter?" Grant demanded, taking up for me once again. "If you had a clue about the hell she's been put through by that psychopath, you would—"

"I don't even know who you are," my mother cut him off. "Mind your own business."

"Lauren *is* my business," Grant roared back. "Do you think the synagogue smut is the only time your son-in-law looked at underage porn? Have you even thought about how that garbage warps your mind? Or the kind of person you'd have to be to keep looking at it? Have you once considered what a degenerate like that could do to his wife?"

"Grant," I entreated, tugging on his sleeve, "you don't need to do this."

"What is he talking about?" my mother asked. "What did he do to you, Lauren?"

I averted my gaze.

"Lauren?" she asked again weakly. "Baby, what did he do?"

I pulled her close and whispered a small portion of his filth. Her mouth dropped in horror while sudden tears streamed down her cheeks.

She searched my face as if looking for scars. "He really did those things to you? Where would he even learn that?"

"I saw Nathan's 'inspiration' on the computer myself. He didn't clean up his laptop as well as he thought he did before he gave it to me. The entire time we were married, he told me those disgusting things were normal for husbands and wives to do."

"Well, of course it isn't!" My mother shook with self-righteous anger. Lowering her voice, she added, "Especially since it was happening to other men."

"Other *boys*," I corrected her. "I don't know how many of them in those videos were even eighteen. Nathan loved to tell me *I* looked like a boy and how he was disgusted with my body. Shaming me was his way of projecting the backlash he'd get if he admitted his real sexual desires. By humiliating me, he thought I would never tell anyone else."

"You could have told us," she whispered.

"We both know you would have chosen Beth Shalom anyway and then acted like we could just pray and fast Nathan into repentance. Didn't you already do that when you thought his addiction was for teenage girls?"

I noticed she didn't debate the point. Subdued, she asked, "Does Harvey know about any of this? I know you saw him for marriage counseling."

"He didn't get the full picture, but even he looked disturbed by what Nathan shared. It was the only time he took my side. Sort of."

She frowned. "And Harvey still kept him on the leadership team? Knowing what he was doing to you? Knowing what he was looking at online?"

"Why do you care?" I sniffled bitterly. "*You* stayed on the leadership team knowing what Nathan did to me and Ari by mentally and physically abusing us. Why wouldn't Rabbi Lebow believe Nathan's sexual appetites are no big deal when you and Dad gave him the green light to hit us too? Like it or not, supporting the synagogue means supporting Nathan."

"We never would have supported *this* kind of behavior!"

"So, gay sex is wrong, but punching me and Ari, threatening to kill me if I ever left him is okay by you?"

"I didn't say that!"

"Didn't you?" Grant asked, slipping his arm around my waist and standing next to me. "You joined that hellhole in condemning your daughter for her abuser's crimes. I've met *Harvey* face to face. I'm the one who stopped him from attacking Lauren at our office. Your beloved rabbi would have physically abused your daughter as easily as her ex-husband did. Why else would he protect someone like Nathan if he wasn't protecting his own behavior too? You think a man just wakes up one day and decides it's okay to hit women?"

"That was you?" my mother breathed. "She never told us which coworker it was."

"That was me."

"Oh, I didn't know."

Grant continued, "Your rabbi won't condemn Nathan because he's just as much of a bully. Even if he took the most misogynistic view possible on Bible verses about marriage and women, there's still no justification for the behavior he excuses in Nathan or himself. There's not a doubt in my mind that your rabbi is covering his own sins as much as he's covering

Nathan's. Based on the man I saw, I bet his wife and kids are scared to death of him."

My mother nodded, resignation on her face. Shelley Lebow barely spoke a word at synagogue, and the Lebow kids had gone to college out of state and remained there. Grant's explanation made more sense than the candy-coated version Harvey presented from the bima. I knew the second my mother fit the puzzle pieces together because her shoulders slumped in defeat. I pitied her, knowing all too well the pain of having to accept reality after willfully believing a lie for so long.

She glanced at her watch and paled. "Oh, I'm so late! I have to get back to work."

"It's okay," I said. "I'm sure Victoria will understand."

A ghost of a smile appeared on her face. "She does think the world of you, Lauren. She always asks me how you're doing."

"Well, you can tell her that I'm healing. I'm actively working to get free, and I have a bright future ahead of me." I couldn't help it and snuck a peek at Grant. He beamed at me and let his eyes do all the talking.

"I see," my mother murmured. "I hope you know what you're doing."

"I didn't when I married Nathan. I do now."

She pursed her lips but didn't push the subject. She reached out a hand to touch me, then let it fall.

"Can I call you later?" she asked. "I want to talk to your father about all of this, but we miss you. We miss Ari." Her voice broke, and I nearly cried along with her.

"Yes, I'd like that," I said.

She nodded and then quietly exited the restaurant.

Grant exhaled a long sigh and side eyed me. "You still feel up to eating?"

"Not really, but I haven't eaten anything since early this morning, and the adrenaline is wearing off."

Tucking my arm against his, Grant led me to the Apple Thursdays host stand to get a table. A slender teenage boy smiled as we approached, and his appearance reminded me of the filth my future ex-husband liked to watch. The thought that Nathan derived pleasure from harming the weak and innocent made my blood run hot and cold at the same time.

"What is it?" Grant asked as we walked toward our table. "You look upset."

I sat down across from him. "Just thinking, I guess. Processing. I never thought I would tell anybody what my ex did to me, let alone in a courtroom with a stenographer."

"Do you feel different now that you have?"

"It's all so heavy. There's some relief in knowing his secret is out, but it's embarrassing for the world to know that I allowed my husband to use me like that."

"Allowed?" he repeated skeptically.

"Well, he didn't rape me, per se."

"Didn't he?" Grant snapped. "Are you going to tell me you ever had a say in any of it? That saying 'no' was really an option?"

"I did say 'no' to him!"

"And what happened when you did, Lauren? Did he suddenly respect your wishes after ignoring them in every other area of your relationship?"

Our server interrupted before I could answer Grant's question. We placed our drink order, and Grant requested the Spinach Patch Pizza without me even asking.

"Thank you," I murmured.

"I want you to know I'm not mad at you. I'm frustrated."

"Frustrated with what?"

"Frustrated that you're minimizing how horribly you were abused. Frustrated that you're sitting there gaslighting yourself how what he did wasn't *that* bad. There isn't a single thing you've shared that hasn't shredded my heart listening to it. You don't know how much I want to punch his smug potato face for what he's done to you and Ari."

Despite myself, I giggled at his description of Nathan. "Potato face?"

The first bit of light entered Grant's eyes since our run-in with my mother. "Yep, total tater-face. Shapeless, lumpy, and the kind you just want to *mash*. With a shovel."

I burst into laughter.

Grant smiled back at me. "That's more like it. You deserve to laugh. You deserve to be happy. You deserve to be loved."

His last declaration captured my attention along with his chocolate brown eyes.

"Don't freak out," he warned. "I know there's nothing I can do under the present circumstances."

I gave a small smile in return. "I see it every time you look at me, Grant. This isn't some shocking revelation."

"Well, the last time I tried to say it, you shut me down. You told me in order to find your heart I'd have to find God's heart first."

My smile widened. "Yes, I absolutely said that."

"And I did find God," he said. "You were there the night I gave my life to Christ at Bible study. We've been talking about God and the Bible on the phone at night."

"We have," I repeated softly.

"When I tried to say it last time, I wasn't completely sure about how I felt."

"But you are now," I finished for him, melting under the heat of his gaze. It fell upon me like direct rays of sunshine.

Hesitating, he asked, "Do you think you could ever return those feelings?"

CHAPTER 39

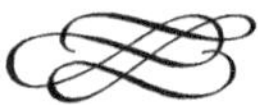

Before I could reply, our server returned with our drinks. We placed our orders, but Grant's question still lingered in the air.

"She's gone. Finally," he said, regarding our waitress, "and you still haven't given me an answer. How long do you plan to keep me in agony?"

"I thought the answer was obvious."

"Is it?" he breathed.

"Well, sure, I mean, I want to fall in love with myself too. Have you seen how amazing I am? What's not to love?"

He paused and then broke into a laugh that turned a few heads our way. Grant leaned his face toward me and lowered his voice. "That was *not* nice."

I chuckled mischievously. "Whoever told you I was nice?"

He shook his head and exhaled a heavy breath. "You're killing me over here."

"Meh, you'll live." Grinning broadly, I expected a continuation of our banter, but all humor left his face.

"Lauren," he pleaded, "no more jokes, okay?"

"Oh," I murmured.

"Call me insecure or scared that you'll run, but I need to hear you say it."

"Say what, exactly? That I love you? It's way too soon for all of that. Grant, you *know* it's too soon."

He held up a hand to calm my agitated state. "No, that's not what I meant. Of course, it's too soon. I just want to know if you think it's possible that you might one day."

"Look, anything's possible, but I have to learn to trust myself before I can trust anyone else so completely."

His hand dropped like a deadweight, and I watched the life seep out of him. Reaching across the table, I grabbed onto his wrist to keep him from retreating further. He met my eyes questioningly, and I saw confusion and despair.

"Grant, I truly mean that *anything* is possible. I'm not just saying that to spare your feelings or string you along. I like you. A lot. I love talking to you and spending time with you. We're building a friendship and the foundation for a real relationship —no matter what that ultimately looks like. I know more about you than I did about Nathan when I married him. You've been completely transparent with me, and I want to do the same for you. It's not a 'no' at all. It's an, 'I don't know, but I hope so.' Don't give up."

A hint of his smile returned. "Well, you did say you want to kiss me."

I blushed. "Yeah, that too."

"Anything worth having is worth fighting for, right? Certainly worth waiting for."

"Is that really what you think of me?"

"I've said it a hundred different ways. I hope I've shown that by my actions too."

I pushed a tendril behind my ear and looked away. "You've made your intentions very clear, and I do appreciate that. It's just hard to believe sometimes that you'll wait for me."

"I've made it this far, haven't I?" He tried for a lighter, teasing tone.

I exhaled my own sigh. "The divorce isn't over yet, and I have no idea what else I'm going to have to survive to get to the other side of it. There won't be some magical switch that gets flipped once I'm finally done with this thing."

"Lauren," he said, taking full grasp of my hand, "I know all of this already. I'm not going into anything blindly."

This time, I tried to retreat, but he wouldn't let me. I tried to slip my hand away, but Grant recaptured it.

"You can trust me," he said, staring straight into my soul. "However long it takes."

"That's the thing! I have no idea how long it's going to take. You tell me that I react to you like I'm still dealing with *him*. In my head, I know that I'm not, but the trauma is there. I can't just wish it away because I'm staring into your eyes instead of his."

"Whatever you need is what I want to give you." He rubbed his thumb back and forth across my knuckle. It was a tender gesture borne from comfort, and it was clear Grant's concern for me extended far beyond *interest*, common experiences, or even just pheromones. "I'll give you the space you need, but please don't push me away because you're afraid I'm going to reject you."

Our server deposited the Spinach Patch Pizza a few moments later, and our conversation shifted to more friendly chit-chat. I knew I needed the reprieve and a chance to fill my belly with something other than fight or flight hormones.

When it was time to leave, Grant walked me to my car.

Turning to face him, the tenderness in his expression nearly caused me to tear down my own defenses. I leaned in close to his neck and kept my arms criss crossed in front of me. Instantly, he wrapped me in an embrace with his right arm around my waist and the other cradling me close to his heart.

"I don't want to let you go," he whispered.

I sniffled back tears, wishing for so many things in that moment that weren't ready to happen.

I pushed against him gently, and he released me.

"This afternoon was exactly what I needed," I said, meeting his eyes. "Thank you."

"It sounds like you're going to be on the phone for a while with your parents, but is it okay if I text you later and check in?"

"Of course!"

He smiled back.

I inhaled a deep breath, wanting to savor every last second. "So, I'll talk to you later?"

There was a split second when I knew Grant wanted to kiss me. It was in the angle of his body toward me, the softness of his mouth, and the palpable tension drawing us together like magnets. Instead, he rocked back on his heel and exhaled. "I'll see you at work tomorrow."

"Screw it," I muttered, and pulled his face toward mine. "Grant, I want to—"

"Please," he rasped. "Stop now before I can't."

I searched his face. "Are you sure?"

He cupped my cheeks in his palms and kissed my hair, then my forehead. I pressed my hands to his to hold them in place.

"The next time I do this, I won't be kissing the top of your head. That's a promise."

I nodded.

"You need to go, Lauren, and I need to let you go. Ari is waiting for you."

The mention of my son cooled the kindling flames of desire.

"God bless you," I whispered.

"He already has," he whispered back. "It won't be like this forever."

I swallowed a bitter lump of deferred hope and forced myself to leave the parking lot. Grant didn't linger near my car, and it allowed me to refocus on the emotional evening facing me with my parents.

Ari was tired when I picked him up from daycare, and we settled on an easy dinner of scrambled eggs. Skipping bathtime, I tucked him into bed and cuddled with him until he fell asleep. I pressed tiny kisses to his cheeks and lightly brushed the curls at his temple.

My cell phone rang from the family room, and I was surprised my mother would be calling so close to Ari's bedtime. Swiping the screen to unlock it, I didn't realize I had opened myself up to someone else's mother when I answered.

"Lauren!" the shrill voice demanded.

I gasped in surprise. It had been well over two years since I'd exchanged words with the toxic former mother-in-law who despised me. "What do you want, Liora? How did you even get this number?"

Her imperious tone didn't waver. "Nevermind that. This needs to end *now*."

"What does? The divorce? Talk to your son about that. He's the one holding things up. I have nothing to say to you."

"Nathan told me about what happened in court today."

"Oh, I'm sure he did." I unleashed all the acid she so rightly deserved. "Your precious baby didn't do so great on the witness stand, but I'm sure he told you he was the victim of all of my evil lies."

She hesitated, and I knew my remark hit home. "It doesn't matter what Nathan said about it. Our attorney was irate."

My eyebrows shot up. First, at the word "our" and then at the idea Trevor Wormwood actually possessed a conscience. Smirking at my own wishful thinking, I shook my head. Trevor's ego probably couldn't stand how he'd been blindsided because of Nathan's omission of information. His slam dunk, "gotcha" moment in court had ruined his entire case.

"Liora, this sounds like a you and your attorney problem, not one that has anything to do with me. Don't call me again unless you want your name added to the TPO. I'm hanging up now, and then I'm blocking this number."

"Trevor asked me if I knew about Nathan's pornography issues," she blurted out.

"Again, what does this have to do with me? You and Harvey Lebow have been covering this up for over a decade. I guess the only real surprise was finding out that you lied about the extent of it and blamed me instead."

"Stop interrupting! I wasn't finished."

"I don't take orders from you!" I snapped. "I'm not one of your synagogue minions who falls in line with whatever *Linda* Fein commands. Your son abused me mercilessly and it still didn't stop me from speaking up, so if you think I'm going to start quivering at one of *your* tantrums—"

She cut me off. "I *know*, Lauren. I know all of it. I've always known."

I froze. "You know what exactly?"

"About the," she lowered her voice to a whisper, "gay porn."

"Excuse me?" I breathed. "I didn't even know until eight months ago. How did you know about it?"

Her voice returned to its usual haughty tone. "I discovered some items on Nathan's laptop after that cheating whore broke his heart and their engagement."

"That was nine years ago! Why didn't you say anything when you knew we were having marriage problems? Or the underage porn scandal with teenage girls? Liora, you blamed me for everything! You told the entire synagogue I have a Jezebel spirit and need deliverance."

She harrumphed. "Well, these matters aren't so simple, and frankly, there *were* areas you could have improved as a wife. Your hospitality skills still need some serious work."

"Insulting me doesn't change the truth. How do you know I'm not recording every word you're saying right now? Think about what you just admitted."

She plowed on as if I'd said nothing. "Just end this mess with Nathan. I saw what you offered in the settlement proposal. If we agree to those terms, will you promise to never go to court again?"

I shook my head, feeling as if I'd been hit by a semi-truck of confusion. "What on earth are you talking about, and why are you going through my divorce paperwork? I wasn't married to *you*. That's Bruce's unfortunate job."

"Don't you realize that everything you said in court today is public record?" she snapped.

"Of course, I realize that. It's why I didn't lie on the witness stand. Unlike you and your son who have done nothing but lie to me the entire time I've known you."

"Just stop!" she begged. "Yes, I know it was wrong to hide Nathan's *ongoing issue*, but we thought you could change him."

"Change him?" I gaped. "What are you talking about? Nathan was controlling and manipulative before we even got married. He was worse once he thought he had a prisoner for life. How on earth would I have changed anything?"

"I'm not talking about your lack of submissiveness."

"Really? Then, why don't we talk about yours? Does Bruce even get to have an opinion without asking for your permission first?"

I heard muffled arguing in the background as Liora tried to shush up a male with her. I recognized Nathan's voice, and my blood ran cold.

"Mom, I told you to butt out of it!" he roared.

"We have a reputation to maintain, Nathan Adam, and you're ruining it with your perverted sex fantasies. Anybody at synagogue could read those court records! Lauren was supposed to turn you straight. You promised us you would try! Why do you think we moved back here and pushed you to marry someone from temple? Harvey can't keep this quiet now that you've told the world about your private lifestyle. Homosexuality is a sin!" She rattled off some Bible verses that would have been equally as applicable if she looked in a mirror and said them to herself.

My skin crawled listening to her. Those precious pearls didn't belong in the mouth of a pig, certainly not while covered in the filth of her own hypocrisy.

"I'm not gay!" Nathan screamed at her.

At this point, Papa Bear entered the fray, bellowing at his golden child to 'honor' his mother. Bruce was rarely allowed a speaking role when Liora was around—unless she needed to call on some extra muscle to get whoever challenged her into line. Bruce and Linda berated Nathan like a misbehaving child, but even their rebukes had less to do with Nathan's depravity and more about how it reflected poorly on them. Things took a violent turn when I heard grunting and landed punches along with Liora's screams.

"Nathan! Leave your father alone! He's an old man!"

The returning shout from my ex-husband didn't even sound human. Uglier than anything he'd ever directed at me, Nathan called down such hideous curses and threats, I nearly felt sorry for his mother. His heavy breathing sounded like hisses, and for once, I knew Liora's tears were not just for show. Her self-pitying pleas were met with cold disregard—likely because Nathan had heard them his entire life. I was shocked to hear Liora use the exact phrases Nathan had clearly borrowed from her during our marriage.

A door slammed in the background, and I jumped. My gaze darted frantically around the room, panicked for a split second that Nathan was back outside my front door. I inhaled a deep breath and quietly repeated, "He's not here," to calm myself down.

At that point, Liora remembered she and I were still connected on the phone call.

"How much did you...?"

"All of it," I said coldly. "Don't you dare tell me that Nathan's never acted that way or that I've been lying about what he did to me and my son. It wasn't just the gay porn that you knew about, was it? You and Bruce knew about Nathan's violence too, you lying witch!"

"Let's not resort to name calling," she said in a cloying, conciliatory tone. "We all make mistakes from time to time. Bitterness is not pleasing to the Lord."

Recognizing that Nathan probably learned how to gaslight and manipulate while still nursing at the breast, I maintained my composure. "None of this was a *mistake*, Liora. You gladly sacrificed my life and my son's life to cover up the degenerate you created."

"I did not create a *gay* son."

"No, you created a monster. One made in *your* image."

"I would never look at that filth!" she said, outraged.

"No, maybe not. But you gladly accused me of every horrible deed your son committed against me. You called me abusive and mentally unstable to cover for the fact your son is. You lie every single week to the people at Beth Shalom when they ask why our marriage failed. You lie when you tell them I wasn't a good wife and that I wasn't doing my duty in the marriage bed. Would you like me to tell you what those *duties* actually included?"

"Your sex life is none of my business!"

"Of course, it's not! Yet, you had no problem slandering me and telling people I've been cheating on Nathan."

"Well, what was I supposed to do?"

"What I did today in court. Tell the truth."

"We both know that's not possible."

"So, lying about me is the *godly* solution?"

"What do you care?" she scoffed. "You left Beth Shalom."

"But my parents didn't. You called me because you don't want me telling the truth about your son, but you're perfectly fine destroying the reputation of their daughter with your lies."

She inhaled a taut breath. "Look, there's no point in bringing up the past. Your divorce needs to be over so that everyone can move on."

As much as I wanted to scream at her for the hell she'd subjected me to, I felt the Holy Spirit calming me instead. I'd had my day in court, and I won. I could allow the witch to goad me into twenty more rounds to divert her failure as a mother, but I saw the Hand of God making the impossible possible.

"If you can get Nathan to agree to the proposal we sent over, I will gladly sign it."

"Well," she hemmed, "we might need to reconsider the child support."

"Judge Sheridan awarded me even more than what we asked for in the proposal. I'd be happy to start with that amount instead since it's legally binding. We could also just go back to court. I'm sure my attorney will have me testify to everything that I didn't get to share today. Do either of those seem like better options?"

I was met with frosty silence.

"In the interest of full disclosure, I *have* been recording this conversation. How on earth do you expect Nathan to agree to anything? He's out of control!"

Through clenched teeth, she said, "I'll handle my son. You just make sure you honor your word."

CHAPTER 40

"Am I free?" I asked Sondra four weeks later. We sat in her office conference room, finalizing our signatures on all of the divorce settlement terms. Whether through miracle or manipulation, Liora got Nathan to agree to our earlier proposal. She tried to add a seven-year, non-disclosure clause regarding Nathan's porn addiction, but Sondra crossed it off and told them no dice. The Feins threatened to walk, and then Trevor Wormwood surprised us all and told the Fein's to sign the documents or find another attorney.

Apparently, the worm had grown tired of the two vipers.

"Judge Sheridan still needs to sign the document so it becomes official, but assuming he does, you will be a free woman, Lauren."

"How long do you think it will take?"

"Couple weeks, maybe a month. Just depends on his schedule. I have another client where the judge has taken over four months and still hasn't signed the final order. This was after a full trial and obvious spousal abuse."

"No," I breathed. "Please, tell me I won't be stuck waiting any longer than I already have been to be free."

"Listen, what we accomplished today was nothing short of miraculous. I was convinced we'd be in litigation for another nine months at least with mediation and then a trial. How did you think his mother got him to agree? He's basically signed away his parental rights other than the two visits a month. Not that he won't try to change it down the road, but we'll cross that bridge when we come to it."

"Nathan is terrifying when he's in a rage, but based on everything I heard, he learned from the best. Or the worst, I guess."

"Ah," she replied with a smirk, "chip off the old block?"

I sucked in a breath, remembering my phone call with Liora. "I know that he loathes me, Sondra, but the way he talked to her was even worse somehow. He legitimately *hates* her. I could physically feel it when I heard him screaming at her. He has said some truly evil things to me, but nothing like that."

Her eyes widened. "Why didn't she call the police after what he did to the father? You said she sounded scared on the phone."

"She was terrified, but it's still the same demon at work in both of them. Protecting Nathan is really just about protecting herself. If she exposes him, he'll expose *her*. It's exactly what happened in the synagogue too."

"I see."

"What I can't wrap my head around is that he despises his mother and hates how she treats him, but he clubs my son with the Bible the same way she does to him. Does he think that's just how parents are supposed to behave? And if that behavior messed you up so badly, why would you continue the cycle? It just doesn't make any sense."

Sondra looked thoughtful for a moment. "I think it's the same demon, like you said. I would just caution against blaming the mother entirely for how he's treated you. This is still a grown man who chose to abuse his wife and child in just about every way possible."

"No, I'm not blaming Liora for his choices. It's just heartbreaking to see him repeating her mistakes. Instead of breaking the cycle, he tried to break *us* instead."

"And mommy is still enabling her son to behave this way. Yes, she wants to control him, but she'll still cover for Nathan, lie for him, and go to the grave defending him."

I shook my head and sighed. "You know, I used to believe Liora had this weird, Oedipal obsession with Nathan, but it's more than that. I think the over-the-top displays were to convince Nathan how much she loves him. Unfortunately, she can't help herself from manipulating and trying to control him. Covering for his behavior is the price she pays and maybe a way to keep him on the line. He needs her to bail him out, and she'll keep doing it because it means he can't cut her off."

Sondra shook her head. "Well, whatever the reason, the settlement is signed, and this horrible season of your life is finally done."

I leaned over and gave her a hug. "Thank you for everything."

She patted my back. "You are very welcome. I hate that I couldn't get you attorney's fees, but we would have had to go to court for that. We still can if you want to."

"No, I just want to move on with my life."

"Speaking of," she said with a knowing smile, "how are things going with you and Spider Guy?"

I laughed. "We're good. Still just friends until Judge Sheridan officially releases me."

"You wouldn't be the first client of mine who fell in love while trying to get divorced. Just remember that our agreement says you can't introduce him as a significant other until six months after the divorce is finalized."

I frowned. "Well, they've already met at Bible study. I didn't even think about that. Am I in trouble?"

"Deep breath," she said, noting my panicked expression. "You aren't dating Grant, and you have only introduced him as your coworker, right?"

"Right."

"I'm not going to tell you how to live your life, but based on what I've seen over the last thirty years of being in practice, take your time before you jump into a new relationship."

"Oh, I know," I said, waving her off, "but he's not another Nathan."

"I'm not even talking about that," she replied, "although you definitely need to be on guard. I'm talking about your freedom. You will finally be able to go where you want, when you want, without worrying how your ex will twist it in court. You can pay your credit card bill without seeing my name on the statement. I've seen some pretty horrific cases of abuse, and yours ranks right up there with them. Take the time you need to rediscover yourself without the trauma before you jump into navigating someone else's needs and preferences."

I nodded. "Thank you."

"But also, go have some fun and enjoy the attention," she said with a wink. "You deserve to be happy, and if that's what Grant does for you, savor every second of it."

I leaned in to give Sondra another hug. Grinning, I walked out of her office feeling lighter than I had in three years.

My parents took me out for a celebration dinner, and my mother shocked me by ordering a bottle of champagne. We let

Ari drink lemon lime soda out of a wine glass, and we toasted to "new beginnings." He giggled as our glasses clinked together.

My mother's eyes filled with tears as she watched the two of us. "I'm so proud of you, Lauren. I know I could never do what you've done."

"But you did," I reminded her. "You finally left Beth Shalom."

"It's been hard," my dad added. "We miss the people."

"Are they going to stop being your friends just because you don't go there anymore?"

My mother frowned. "That was the impression we got. I'm sure Liora won't help in that regard. I still can't believe Harvey knew about *all* of this the entire time."

I shook my head in disgust. "You cannot convince me he isn't hiding his own demons, Mom. Not with how he threatened me or the way he's doubled down on protecting Nathan."

"I suppose the silver lining is that Nathan is at least medicated," my father said. "Of course, they're blaming all of his behavior on 'the illness' instead of calling it his *ongoing issue* anymore. Let's hope the meds work—assuming he's even taking any."

"I'll believe it when I see it," I muttered, then realized Ari was hearing our entire conversation. "Change of subject!" I said brightly.

My parents launched into a happy discussion of all the fun things they had in store for Ari's sleepover that weekend. My son laughed in delight about visiting a pumpkin patch and horse farm, and I smiled as I sipped my very sweet champagne.

Judge Sheridan signed off on our settlement agreement three weeks later, and Sondra called me at work to let me know it had been filed by the county clerk. My hand shook as I disconnected the call and laid my phone down on my desk.

"Well?" Poppy asked.

"I'm free," I whispered. "I'm finally *free*." I broke down sobbing as the grief, relief, and weight of the three-year battle slipped from my shoulders.

Poppy wrapped me in a motherly hug. "You did it," she said against my hair. "You did it, Lauren. You should be so proud of yourself."

"*God* did it." I wiped the tears from my cheeks and used a tissue to blow my nose. "I could never have survived this without Him." I whispered my broken prayers of thanksgiving while Poppy rubbed my back.

Praying beside me, she offered up her own praise and asked God to bless me with every desire of my heart.

Grant poked his head in moments later, checking on an RFP Poppy had been working on.

"What's going on?" he asked, beelining toward my desk. Poppy stepped aside as Grant knelt beside me.

I looked into those beautiful, chocolate brown eyes and gave him the most dazzling smile I had in me.

"Is it done?" he whispered.

I nodded.

Grant let out a whoop of joy and gathered me in his own embrace. I wrapped my arms around his neck and laughed. He held me tightly, and my feet didn't quite touch the ground as we clung to one another.

From just beyond us, Poppy let out a cry. Grant set me down, and we both turned to look at her.

"It's just so beautiful," she cooed. She placed a hand on each of our shoulders. "Oh, I'm just so happy for both of you!"

Grant beamed at me, and I returned his smile.

Poppy cleared her throat and laughed. "I was going to make

a joke about the copier, but how about we keep this a little more under wraps, hmm?"

I laughed. "No making out by the copy machine, I promise."

"Speak for yourself," Grant teased, pulling me closer against him.

Poppy sighed contentedly as if watching a romance novel play out in front of her. "I'm going to powder my nose and close the door behind me. Do what you need to do, but you've got about five minutes. *Kapisch*?"

I kept my arms around Grant's neck as I eyed Poppy's exit from our office. The door clicked shut, and I silently thanked God that Culver stuck the marketing department in a corner office with no windows.

Grant's hands came up to frame my face and gently push my hair out of my eyes. His gaze drifted to my lips and back up again.

"Only if you want to," he said.

"Oh, I want to."

"I love you, Lauren."

I hesitated, scared to say what my heart had known for a while. It all felt like a dream, and I didn't want to wake up.

His earlier expression of joy sobered into compassion. "You don't have to say it just because I did."

Instead of answering him, I reached up my own hand and ruffled his hair. He laughed in surprise and tried to stop me, but I mussed his perfectly coiffed curls even further. I grinned at him. "Been wanting to do that for a while."

"Speaking of," he said, tilting his face toward mine. "There's also something I've been wanting to do for a while."

Grant sealed his promise with a kiss that stole my breath away. I returned every bit of love and affection I felt with my lips. He groaned softly and held me tighter. Meanwhile, I let my hands roam freely through his hair, and Grant was gentleman enough to let me.

I didn't hear the door click open, but there was no mistaking the sound of Ted Margolin clearing his throat. "So, I guess the divorce has been finalized?"

We allowed enough space between us to part lips and face Ted. When he saw Grant's hair, he barked out a laugh and then clapped a hand over his mouth.

"Shhh!" I warned.

Chuckling, Ted replied, "Oh, there's no way anybody could look at either of you and *not* know what you've been doing. Kaplan, this is quite a look for you."

Grant grinned down at me. "Still worth every second I spent waiting for it."

EPILOGUE

SEVEN MONTHS AFTER GRANT AND I SEALED THE beginning of our happy ending with a kiss, we attended Aaron and Ruthie's wedding. He picked me up from my parents' house and eyed my black lace dress with open admiration. My parents told us to have fun, and they looked on approvingly as Grant helped me into my jacket and gave Ari a bear hug before we left. I gave my son one last kiss goodnight, and then he took off for the playroom ready to have another fun weekend with Grandma and Grandpa.

"You look beautiful," Grant said once we'd settled into his car.

"I watched some YouView videos about smokey eye makeup, so I'm glad it worked."

"Oh, it more than worked." He leaned over and nuzzled my neck. "You smell really good too."

I giggled and pushed at him gently. "It took me forever to get my hair like this. Don't mess it up!"

He leaned back to survey the intricate updo. "Did you have any help with it?"

"Charlotte walked me through it on a video call. She's the hair and makeup guru. What she can do with a curler and bobby pins is nothing short of art."

"No complaints from me," Grant said with a grin. "Is she still single and mingling?"

"Yeah, but the men she finds on these dating sites are complete trolls. She's been divorced for almost two years, and I think she's discouraged by how hard it's been to find anyone worthwhile. Her ex is already remarried."

"You told me. Honestly, wife number two sounds like another Liora Fein."

"Well, I guess somebody had to take over at Beth Shalom once the Feins left. Funny enough, Rick Williams was the one who found the court records from our hearing. I think he was trying to exonerate Nathan and then found out the truth instead."

Grant revved up the engine. "No more Beth Shalom drama, okay? Let's get out of here and watch our friends get married."

I grinned back at him. "I told Aaron last year that I wanted to dance at his wedding. I'm glad I'm not breaking my promise."

We arrived twenty minutes early at the event facility, and I greeted all of my Bible study friends with big hugs and reciprocal compliments. Rebecca and Ted Margolin looked elegant and understated in matching black. Taylor and Ian Horner both sported chic and trendy haircuts. Kyle and Abigail Goldstein only had eyes for each other as Kyle's hand remained on the small baby bump peeking through Abigail's dress. Joe and Carly Trautweig looked more relaxed than I'd seen them without the twins in their arms, and my dear friend, Charlotte, pulled out all the stops in a turquoise dress and sparkling jewelry that accentuated her pale eyes.

"You look gorgeous!" I squealed, pulling her into a hug. "Where have you been hiding this dress?"

"Special occasion with Rick that we never attended. Today, however, is a very special occasion and definitely a more worthy event."

I grinned back at her. "Jon Roseman can't take his eyes off of you, by the way."

"Ruthie's dad? Are you kidding me?" She glanced over her shoulder to find him watching both of us. "That's weird."

"Why? He's single. You're single."

"Yeah, and we're literally the only single people here over the age of forty. Plus, isn't he here to officiate the wedding?"

"You know he doesn't attend Beth Shalom anymore, don't you? He hasn't been there for a while."

She waved me off. "Let me enjoy a night out where I actually feel good about how I look without thinking about men. Dating has been nothing but one giant disappointment."

"They're not *all* bad," I said, locating Grant across the room. He caught my eye and smiled back at me.

Charlotte watched us both. "Sweetie, if I could find a man who looked at me the way that man looks at you, I don't know what I'd do with myself."

"There's one about to officiate a Jewish wedding, and he's definitely checking you out."

She rolled her eyes. "Whatever, kiddo. Let's see Blue Eyes get hitched."

A collective gasp went up when the bride entered with her sister on her arm. Ruthie Roseman was an absolute vision in gossamer white. Since Jon was officiating, he couldn't walk his daughter down the aisle. His eyes welled with tears, and I knew he missed not having Ruthie's mom there to see her get married.

Aaron looked positively spellbound as he watched Ruthie, his mouth forming an o-shape as she glided toward him. I never would have pictured Ruthie Roseman as a forest elf, but the bell sleeves of her gown, empire waist, and circlet holding her veil gave her an ethereal, sylvan appearance. Her hair fell in perfectly formed waves down her back.

When she reached Aaron at the front of the chuppah, Ruthie began the *hakafot,* or encircling of the groom as Jon explained the ancient Jewish wedding practice. The seven circles were meant as a sign of protection for her groom and the commencement of the wedding ceremony.

With an adoring smile for his daughter, Jon said, "Aaron and Ruth are here today to form a new covenant, or *b'rit hadasha* with one another. Much like the New Covenant we experience with our Lord, *Yeshua HaMashiach,* there will also be a wedding of Yeshua with His Bride, and one where all of creation will partake. We can see the symbolism in the engagement, betrothal, and wedding ceremonies that are pointed out in Scripture regarding the return of our Messiah. Tonight, we celebrate with Aaron and my beautiful Ruthie as they begin their journey together."

I snuck a glance at Charlotte who looked impressed and surprisingly emotional.

Grant's eyes shifted from me, to Charlotte, to Jon, and then back to me. "Don't get any funny ideas."

I widened my eyes in innocence. "Wouldn't dream of it." I leaned into his arm resting along the back of my chair, and he gladly drew me in tighter against his chest. I sighed and snuggled against him.

From next to me, Charlotte hissed, "Save it for your own wedding. Sheesh!"

Grant silently chuckled. I tucked my arm around his waist, but the weight of something heavy inside his coat pocket brushed against my forearm. It was hard and square, and I knew exactly what it was.

He realized I'd discovered his mystery item and ran a soothing hand up and down my back. "When you're ready, Lauren. No rush."

"But why do you have it with you *now*? We're here to see someone else get married."

He grinned and whispered close, "Because the second you tell me you're ready is the second I'm going to ask."

ACKNOWLEDGMENTS

To Rachel, for showing love and compassion when my world was coming apart and fearlessly speaking the words of healing and freedom I needed.

To Sarah, for showing the love of Christ in action and truly being a Proverbs friend who is closer than a sister.

To Phil and Carol, thank you for being so welcoming to me and my children and never ceasing to operate in kindness and humility.

To my work fam for being so awesome, understanding, and helping me laugh daily. Also, thanks for keeping my orchids alive.

Mike and Kasea, I never thought I'd have the blessing of reconnecting with both of you and your beautiful children. You two have blessed me more than I can say. All things *are* truly possible with God. I love you both!

Hannah Linder and Catherine Posey as always for the beautiful cover art and interior formatting. God bless you both!

My precious kiddos who amaze me daily, make me laugh (occasionally cry), but always make me so thankful for the privilege you gave me of being a mother. I adore you three!

My Lord and Savior who took words forged out of brokenness and despair and transformed them into a source of light and hope. You make *all* things beautiful.

COMING FALL 2025

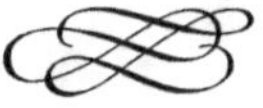

BOOK 6 IN THE BEAUTY FOR ASHES SERIES: ANI L'DODI: WITH ALL OF YOUR HEART

Following a miserable, fifteen-year marriage, Charlotte Williams slogs through the world of online dating. Her ex-husband, Rick, has poisoned her spiritual support system and now parades his hasty remarriage amongst their former friends. Despite the rejection, Charlotte refuses to dim her hilariously unfiltered honesty. She captivates the attention of Jonathan Roseman, an old friend, who sees Charlotte as the breath of fresh air missing from his life. The silver fox insists his feelings are genuine, but Charlotte struggles against the spiritual life she left behind. When new layers of betrayal threaten both Charlotte and her daughters, can Jonathan convince her they have a future together where Charlotte is protected by God and 'beloved' (*ani l'dodi*) by him?

EXCERPT FROM ANI L'DODI: WITH ALL OF YOUR HEART

I STARED AT MYSELF IN THE MIRROR, SIGHING AT THE sight of my tired eyes. No matter how "young" I looked to my daughters, there was no hiding the effects of time, trauma, or a loveless marriage followed by two years of unsuccessful dating.

Thank God, Rick Williams was no Nathan Fein, but being a petty little piglet instead of a full grown boar didn't change the damage he'd done to my self esteem. My round, pale blue eyes stared back at me in the mirror along with dark circles that no amount of carefully placed concealer could hide. I'd grown into the hooked nose I'd once despised, and I could at least thank Rick's DNA for softening up the version of it shared by both of my daughters. In general, my daughters resembled petite, more finely shaped versions of their "everything's extra with me" mother. Neither of them struggled with their weight like I did, and they each had a pretty good head on their shoulders. I'd made a vow that my girls would never suffer from the mental and emotional torment my own father used on me. It was a huge impetus for my divorce from Rick. His constant criticism of Sophie had led to drastic repercussions. Turning my mind away from that dark season for my girls, I removed the last of my makeup and washed my face.

My phone lit up with a text alert as I slathered on my overnight serum. I exited my tiny bathroom and checked my phone to find a new message from Jon.

Can I call you? I'm in the car driving.

I dialed first and then curled up on the recliner in my bedroom. "Hey," I said warmly.

"Hey," he replied with a smile in his voice. "I hope your night out was better than mine."

"Well, Lauren knows better than to preach replacement theology to me—unlike your date, apparently—so I think we're good."

He chuckled, and his tenor voice made for beautiful singing as well as a musical quality when he laughed. "I've been on a few stinkers, but this date might take the cake."

"How did you meet Susie Q anyway?"

"Sitting at Charred Cups with my daughter. Ruthie and I had a coffee date, and I saw Susie Q standing in line. Ruthie caught me watching her and told me to ask her out."

I swallowed down a lump of misplaced jealousy. Even though I'd relegated Jon to the friends only category, there was still a very female part of me that wanted him to find me attractive. Remembering exactly what his late wife looked like only reminded me of the impossible delusion that Jonathan Roseman could find me desirable by comparison. Even back in my twenties, I could never compete with Andrea Roseman's natural beauty and tender heart. Lauren kept insisting she saw interest on Jon's behalf, but I was well aware of my shortcomings. Two years of failed dating had only reinforced that.

"You still there?" he asked.

I cleared my throat. "Yeah, long night. I'm already in my pajamas."

He paused. "Do you need to go to bed? I don't want to keep you up. It is still a school night after all."

I smiled at his droll sense of humor. "All of our girls are in high school and can take the bus. It's just some new wrinkles with *Richard*."

"Ah, good ole Rick." Jon's pronunciation made it seem like he'd rather be using another word for my ex-husband. "What is the slime trying to get away with now?"

"Modified winter break for the girls."

"Is he wanting more time or less time with them this year?"

"I told him I was planning to go on vacation and asked if we could switch visitation weeks. He would have the first week of winter break over Christmas, and I would get New Year's."

"So, what's the problem? The girls can basically take care of themselves."

"He's mad that the vacation is for a singles cruise."

"Singles cruise?" he choked. "You never mentioned that before."

"Oh, it was last minute. My boss, Rosaria, is going and her friend canceled. She asked if I wanted to go with her instead, but I can't change the dates."

"Why is Rick giving you a hard time about it? I thought he'd be glad to have you go and save money on future alimony payments."

"You forget that only Rick is allowed to move on and be happy with the *real love of his life*," I said, mocking his nauseating epithet for his new wife. "I'm supposed to wallow for the rest of my days regretting the divorce and envying Stephanie."

Jon laughed. "If that woman is truly the love of his life, then

I feel sorry for him. Rick's an idiot, and you deserve so much better than how he treated you."

"Wow," I breathed.

"What? It's true, Charlotte."

"Well, you…I just…you've never said it like that before."

"Have I finally rendered you mute? I think there should be an awards ceremony for this momentous occasion. I don't even have a speech prepared."

"I guess you've got on your sassy pants tonight, Mr. Roseman. I like it."

I could hear the smile in his tone. "They are rather sassy tonight, aren't they?"

"What are they made of? Sparkles? Sequins? Satin?"

"Hardly," he deadpanned, "and I doubt they would compare to yours."

I paused, realizing this wasn't the first time it felt like our friendly banter had shifted into something more. "Jon?"

His tone changed from humor to immediate concern. "Everything okay?"

"Were you flirting just now?"

"Flirting?"

"Yeah, you know that thing that people always accuse *me* of doing, even though I'm just a ridiculously charming individual with an extensive vocabulary."

"Can I answer your question by asking *you* a question?" he replied.

I didn't realize I'd been holding my breath until my lungs burned for oxygen. I inhaled deeply and tried for a neutral tone. "I guess, yeah."

"If I *was* flirting, would you be okay with that?"

"I thought we were friends."

"Technically, you're the one who calls us *just friends* and has to mention it in every conversation we have."

"What are you saying? I mean, my girls tease me about you. Lauren teases me about you. They all act like you're interested in me, and I'm just too blind to see it."

The prolonged silence on the phone line spoke volumes, and I faltered.

He released a heavy breath. "Yes, I was flirting with you. I've *been* flirting with you for months, but you either don't see it or ignore it."

"Well, why on earth did you go on a date with Susie Q?"

"Why do you think?" He huffed out a laugh. "The woman I'd actually like to go out with says she only thinks of me as a friend, but she's the one person I want to talk to every night before I go to bed. She's the first person I want to talk to when I wake up in the morning. This wasn't the way I planned to tell you, but yes, Charlotte, I have more than friendly feelings for you, but I don't have much hope that you'll take me out of the friend zone."

"So, you've been doing what exactly? Waiting in the wings for me to catch feelings back?"

"Are you saying it's impossible?" he asked, his voice tight. "You're happy to get the emotional lift from our phone calls and texts, but that's it?"

"I never said that! And I thought we were *friends*. Friends do provide an emotional lift for one another. It's why I went out with Lauren tonight. I'm not manipulating you, Jon, and I have never given you reason to think I was stringing you along."

"Well, you're still not answering my question."

"That's because I don't know what to say."

"That's a first."

"Okay, well that was just rude. I'm hanging up now." Irritated, I swiped the phone off. It lit up with a text message a second later.

I'm sorry. That didn't come out the way I meant. I'm nervous, and I'm making a mess of all of this.

Making a mess of what exactly?

My feelings, he wrote. *I'm obviously not handling rejection very well.*

I inhaled and exhaled a deep breath knowing that my response would forever change my future. *Why are you assuming you're being rejected? And please put emphasis on the first syllable of the word 'assume.'*

Are you saying you want to be more than friends? Has something changed?

I paused, my mind traversing over multiple memories with Jonathan Roseman. When I first met him, he was an ebony haired, goateed man in love with his first wife while I was newly married to Rick Williams. I had become friends with Andrea while she was heavily pregnant with their youngest daughter, Rachel, and I had just found out I was pregnant with Sophie. My daughters had worn baby clothes passed down to us from the Roseman girls. Our lives had been intertwined for nearly two decades, just never like this.

Jon's black hair was now predominantly silver, he wore horn rimmed glasses over his perceptive, dark eyes, and I knew his daughters weren't the only females that wanted to call him "Daddy." I'd seen enough thirsty comments on his Instantpics from women of all ages.

Charlotte? he asked, *Are you still there?*

I'm here.

You didn't answer my question.

Are you sure? I finally wrote. I caught my reflection in my phone and grimaced.

I'm sure I don't want you going on a singles cruise and falling in love with somebody else. I know you like direct, so how was that?

Pretty direct.

You're still not answering.

But are you SURE?

My phone rang again, and I didn't hesitate to pick it up.

"So, I guess you're not still mad at me," he began.

"I'm not sure what I am at the moment."

"You okay?"

"Stunned is more like it."

"Why are you stunned?" His voice was calming and gentle.

Even though he couldn't see me, I gestured to my mismatched pajamas, hair pulled off my bare face, and curves that my daughters would call *thicc* and Rick called *morbidly obese*. "Jon, I mean, you could have any woman you want. I'm just…"

"You're just what?" he cut me off. "Sensational? Gorgeous? Intimidating?"

I frowned at that last word. "Yeah, I've been called that before."

"You're not intimidating because you're scary or unattractive, Charlotte. You're intimidating because I have to be at the top of my game to keep up with you. You're smart, witty, hilarious, and if I've never said this before it's because I never thought you'd let me. You're beautiful."

I scoffed.

"Let me repeat. You are *stunningly* beautiful."

"Maybe you need a thicker prescription on your glasses."

"Maybe you need to stop deflecting with sarcasm just because your ex was too much of a brain dead imbecile to appreciate the woman he trampled on for fifteen years."

I chuckled. "Okay, I won't disagree with your assessment of Rick."

"Do you think I'm lying about the rest? That it's impossible for a man to find you attractive just because *Richard* is a moron?"

"Look, I come with stretch marks and psychological damage, and contrary to your apparent high opinion of me, men my age do *not* find me all that attractive. They want a cheap hook up, someone young enough to have more kids, or a supermodel. Ironically, it doesn't matter if *they* fell out of the ugly tree and got hit in the face with every branch on the way down."

"Well, I *am* a man your age, and I'm telling you I find you a lot more than just 'attractive.' You're scared, Charlotte, and I want to know why."

"You know I can't compete with Andrea," I said with a long suffering sigh. "You loved that woman with every breath in your body. Maybe if I had never known you two as a couple it wouldn't be so hard, but I'll never be able to live up to that."

After a lengthy pause, Jon finally said, "I'm parked outside of your house. This is a conversation we need to have face to face."

OTHER WORKS BY ANA WATERS

BEAUTY FOR ASHES SERIES
Book 1: Tabula Rasa: Writing a New Story
Book 2: Ex Nihilo: Learning to Live Again
Book 3: Tikkun Olam: Restoring What Was Lost
Book 4: Lev Tahor: A Heart Redeemed